HELLHOLE

THE DUNE SERIES

BY FRANK HERBERT

Dune
Dune Messiah
Children of Dune
Heretics of Dune
Chapterhouse: Dune

BY FRANK HERBERT, BRIAN HERBERT,
AND KEVIN J. ANDERSON

The Road to Dune (includes the original short novel *Spice Planet*)

BY BRIAN HERBERT AND KEVIN J. ANDERSON

Dune: House Atreides
Due: House Harkonnen
Dune: House Corrino

Dune: The Butlerian Jihad
Dune: The Machine Crusade
Due: The Battle of Corrin

Hunters of Dune
Sandworms of Dune

Paul of Dune
The Winds of Dune
The Throne of Dune

BY BRIAN HERBERT

Dreamer of Dune
(biography of Frank Herbert)

HELLHOLE

BRIAN HERBERT
and KEVIN J. ANDERSON

TOR®

A Tom Doherty Associates Book
New York

Fic
Her

This is a work of fiction. All of the characters, organizations, and events portrayed in
this novel are either products of the authors' imaginations or are used fictitiously.

HELLHOLE

A Tor Book
Published by Tom Doherty Associates, LLC
175 Fifth Avenue
New York, NY 10010

www.tor-forge.com

Tor® is a registered trademark of Tom Doherty Associates, LLC.

Library of Congress Cataloging-in-Publication Data

Herbert, Brian.
    Hellhole / Brian Herbert and Kevin J. Anderson. — 1st U.S. ed.
        p. cm.
    "A Tom Doherty Associates book."
    ISBN 978-0-7653-2269-2
    1. Space colonies—Fiction. I. Anderson, Kevin J., 1962– II. Title.
PS3558.E617H45 2011
813'.54—dc22

                                                                    2010036113

Originally published in Great Britain by Simon & Schuster, a CBS Company

First U.S. Edition: March 2011

Printed in the United States of America

0   9   8   7   6   5   4   3   2   1

Brian: to Julie, Kimberly, and Margaux
Kevin: to Jonathan, Jessica, and Harrison
May your lives be filled with a universe of opportunities

Acknowledgements

For their help in the writing and preparation of this novel, we would like to express our gratitude to Tom Doherty at Tor Books, our editors Pat LoBrutto (Tor) and Maxine Hitchcock (Simon & Schuster UK), and our agent, John Silbersack. Kevin would like to thank Mary Thomson for her diligent transcription, and test readers Diane Jones and Louis Moesta. And, as with all our books, we owe a tremendous debt of gratitude to our wives, Janet Herbert and Rebecca Moesta Anderson, for their love and creative support.

Prologue

It was the end of the rebellion, and this day would either make or break the freedom fighters. General Tiber Maximilian Adolphus had struggled for half a decade against the corrupt government of the Constellation, taking his cause across the twenty central Crown Jewel worlds and riding a groundswell of popular support – all of which had led him to this place. A last stand where the old regime was bound to collapse.

The battle over the planet Sonjeera would decide it all.

The General's teeth ached from clenching his jaw, but he stood on the bridge of his flagship, ostensibly calm and confident. He had not intended to be a rebel leader, but the role had been forced on him, and he'd never lost sight of the goal. The ancient, incestuous system had oppressed many populations. The more powerful noble families devoured the weaker ones to steal their planetary holdings. Ultimately, even those powerful families split up and tore at one another, as if it were some kind of game. It had gone on far too long.

For five years now, the General's ever-growing forces had battled old-guard loyalists, winning victories and suffering defeats. Any reasonable person could see that the bloated system was rotten, crumbling, unfair to the majority. People across the Crown Jewels had only needed a man to serve as an example, someone to light the spark and unify their grievances. Adolphus had fallen into this role by accident, but like a piece of driftwood caught in a whitewater flood, he had been swept along to his inevitable destination.

Now his forces converged over the main prize: Sonjeera, with its glorious white stone buildings, tall towers, and ancient museums – window-dressing that made the government appear to be as marvelous as the politicians claimed it was.

Diadem Michella Duchenet, the Constellation's supreme ruler, would never admit defeat, clinging to her position of power with cadaverous claws. Rather than relinquish the Star Throne, the old woman would see the capital world laid to waste, without regard to the innocent citizens she claimed to represent and protect. And if the General allowed it to come to that, he would be no better than Diadem Michella. But he didn't see any way around it.

In the battles of the rebellion so far, Adolphus had been careful to keep civilian casualties to a minimum, but he knew the Diadem would eventually force his hand. She would draw a dark line of morality in front of him and dare him to cross it. Today might be that day ...

"Steady ahead." His flagship, the *Jacob*, was named after his father, one of the first casualties in the string of political and economic schemes that had provoked Adolphus into action. "Frigates and sweepers forward. Open the gunports and show them we mean business."

"Aye, General."

With an intense focus, he studied the screen and the planet growing larger by the minute; Sonjeera sparkled with tiny dots of ships, stations, and orbital activity. It was a sapphire laced with clouds, green continents, and city lights that sparkled across the night side. The crown jewel of all Crown Jewels.

Adolphus's eyes were dark and old beyond his years, not having seen laughter in a long time. His black hair was neatly trimmed, and his square jaw had a tendency to show beard shadow, but he had shaved carefully only a few hours before. He intended to be presentable for this engagement, no matter how it turned out. He had his obligation to history ...

His deep blue uniform was neat and impeccable, the coppery rank insignia prominent on his collar, though he sported no medals or decorations. The General had refused to let his men present him with accolades until they had actually won. He had not entered this conflict for glory or wealth, but justice.

"Tactical display, Mr Conyer. Let me see the distribution of our ships, and project the defenses that Sonjeera has mounted."

"Here they are, General." The tac officer called up a display of the 463 rebel ships – a fleet that was certainly superior to what the Army of the Constellation could muster here on short notice. Destroyers, fast harriers, frigates, sweepers, large carriers, even civilian cargo ships refitted with armor and weapons.

Above the capital planet, cargo ships and short-range in-system yachts and transports scattered, seeking shelter. A meager ring of security ships kept station near the main stringline hub, the orbiting nexus of interstellar lines that connected the Crown Jewel planets. *Not nearly enough.* The General's forces could – and would – overwhelm the security ships and seize the hub without much resistance.

"The Diadem has mounted no primary defenses that we can see yet, sir."

"She will," Adolphus said. It couldn't be that easy.

Over the codecall link, Franck Tello, the General's second-in-command and a close friend, broke in from the bridge of his own destroyer, cheery as usual. "Maybe that's the old bitch's answer. One look at our fleet, and she ran to hide in a bomb shelter. I hope she took sanitary facilities and some extra panties."

The men on the *Jacob*'s bridge chuckled, a release of tension, but Adolphus slowly shook his head. "She's not stupid, Franck. Michella knew we were coming, and she's been losing battles for years. If she was going to surrender, she would have cut a deal to save her own skin." He didn't like this.

As his fleet spread out and prepared to form a blockade, the surface-to-orbit traffic around Sonjeera increased dramatically. Passenger pods and shuttles rose into space, people evacuating the capital world in a disorderly rush.

"Maybe the bitch already fled," Tello suggested.

"That doesn't sound like her," Adolphus said, "but I'd bet a month's pay that she called for an immediate evacuation to cause chaos."

An overloaded stringline hauler accelerated away from the orbiting hub, its framework crowded with passenger pods that dangled like ripe fruit. A second hauler remained docked at the hub, but it would not be loaded in time. The last-minute evacuees would be stranded there in orbit.

"It's like a stampede. We'd better wrap this up before it turns into an even bigger mess. Four frigates, take the stringline hub," Adolphus ordered. "Minimal damage, no casualties if possible."

His first ships streaked in, broadcasting a surrender order. As they approached the hub, the second stringline hauler broke away from the dock and lurched away from the station, only half loaded. Three passenger pods disengaged and dropped free, improperly secured in the rush, and the ovoid vessels tumbled in free orbit.

"Stop that hauler! No telling who's aboard," Adolphus said into the codecall. He dispatched one of his large, slow carriers to block the vessel.

Passenger shuttles and evacuating in-system ships flurried about, retreating to the dark side of Sonjeera in panic. Adolphus clenched his jaw even harder; the Diadem had made them terrified of what he and his supposed barbarians would do ... when it was Michella they should have feared.

The second stringline hauler continued to accelerate away from the hub, even as the General's slow carrier moved to cross its path before the hauler could activate the ultrafast stringline engines.

The carrier pilot yelped over the codecall, "He's going to ram us, General!"

"Retreat and match speed, but do not deviate from the path. If the hauler pilot insists on a crash, give him a gentle one."

The rebel carrier refused to get out of the way even as the hauler moved forward. Adolphus admired the fortitude of the carrier's crew; if the fleeing hauler activated the stringline engines, they would both be a vapor cloud. The hauler closed the distance and the rebel carrier blocked it, slowed it; the two ships collided in space, but the impact was minimal.

As the four rebel frigates again demanded the surrender of the stringline hub, the ten small Constellation security ships left their stations and swept forward in a coordinated move, opening fire on the General's warships. Explosions rippled along the first frigate's hull, drawing shouts of astonishment from the crews.

"What the hell are they doing?" Franck Tello cried over the codecall. "We've got hundreds more ships than they do!"

"Return fire," Adolphus said. "Disable engines if possible ... but do what you need to do."

The frigate captains launched retaliatory fire, and three security ships exploded. Two others were damaged, but the rest circled around, undeterred. Streams of explosive projectiles flew in all directions, most of them directed at Adolphus's frigates, but countless others missed their targets and hit nearby vessels, including the evacuating in-system ships that were scrambling away from the stringline hub.

When he saw two civilian transports explode, Adolphus yelled for his fleet to close in. "No time for finesse. Eradicate those security ships!"

In a hail of return fire, the rebels blew up the vessels before they could cause further damage. The General's jaw ached. He hated useless death. "Why wouldn't they stand down? They had no chance against us."

Lieutenant Spencer, the weapons officer, cleared his throat. "Sir, if I might suggest, we can force the issue now. Threaten to blow up the whole hub if the Diadem doesn't surrender. That would cripple the Constellation's interstellar transport – the people would never stand for it."

"But that's not what *I* stand for, Lieutenant," Adolphus said. "Hostages and terrorist acts are for cowards and bullies. The people of the Constellation need to see that I'm different." The Diadem's propaganda machine had already painted him with the broad strokes of "monster" and "anarchist." If he were to sever the lines of transportation and trade among the Crown Jewels, the people would turn against him in a matter of weeks.

"General, the stringline hub is ours," said the first frigate captain. "We have the high ground. Nobody on Sonjeera is going anywhere."

Adolphus nodded, but did not let down his guard. "Harriers, round up those loose passenger pods before they burn up in orbit."

"This is making me damned nervous, General," Franck transmitted. "How can the Diadem just sit there, with almost five hundred rebel ships lining up in orbit?"

"Here it comes, sir!" broke in the weapons officer. "Constellation battleships emerging from Sonjeera's sensor shadow."

Now Adolphus understood. "The security ships were trying to stall us. All right, how many are we facing?"

Conyer ran a scan. As they stormed forward, the Diadem's ships moved in a random flurry as if to disguise their numbers. "Three hundred and twelve, sir. And that's an accurate count. Probably all the ships she's got left."

Though his rebels outgunned them by a substantial margin, he was sure Diadem Michella had given her fleet strict no-surrender orders. If the General's fleet gained the upper hand, the Constellation defenders might initiate a suicide protocol . . . though he wondered if they would follow such an order. General Tiber Adolphus engendered such loyalty among his own men, but he doubted the Diadem was capable of inspiring such dedication. However, the security ships around the stringline hub had already demonstrated their willingness to die.

"They're not slowing, General!" Lieutenant Spencer said in a crisp voice.

"Message coming in from the Constellation flagship, sir," said the communications officer.

The screen filled with the image of an older gentleman wearing a Constellation uniform studded with so many ribbons, medals, and pins that it looked like gaudy armor over the uniform shirt. The man had sad gray eyes, a lean face, and neatly groomed muttonchop sideburns. Adolphus had faced this opponent in eight previous battles, winning five of them, but only by narrow margins. "Commodore Hallholme!" Even as the Diadem's last-stand defense fleet came toward them, the General forced himself to be calm and businesslike, especially with this man. "You are clearly outgunned. My people have strongholds on numerous Crown Jewel planets, and today I intend to take Sonjeera. Only the details remain."

"But history rests on the details." The old Commodore seemed dyspeptic from the choice he faced. Percival Hallholme had been a worthy foe and an honorable man, well-trained in the rules of engagement. "The Diadem has commanded me to insist upon your surrender."

The *Jacob's* bridge crew chuckled at the absurd comment, but Adolphus silenced them. "That won't be possible at this time, Commodore." This was the last chance he would give, and he put all of his sincerity into the offer. "Please be reasonable – you know how this is going to end. If you help me secure a peaceful resolution without any further bloodshed and no damage to Sonjeera – a planet beloved by all of us – I would be willing to work out amnesty arrangements for yourself and your top-tier officers, even a suitably supervised exile for Diadem

Michella, Lord Selik Riomini, and some of the worst offenders among the nobility."

While the Constellation ships surged closer, Adolphus continued to stare at Hallholme's image, silently begging the man to see reason, to flinch, to back down in the face of harsh reality.

For a fleeting instant, Adolphus thought the old Commodore would reconsider, then Hallholme said, "Unfortunately, General, the Diadem gave me no latitude for negotiation. I am required to force your surrender at all costs, using any means necessary." He gestured to his communications officer. "Before you open fire, you should see something."

Multiple images flooded the panel screens on the *Jacob*'s bridge of forlorn-looking people, gaunt-faced, sunken-eyed, and plainly terrified. They were packed in metal-walled rooms that looked like spacecraft brig chambers or sealed crew quarters.

Adolphus recognized some of the faces.

Over the codecall channel, Franck Tello shouted, "That's my sister! She's been missing for months."

Some of Adolphus's bridge officers identified other captives, but there were thousands. The images flickered one after another.

"We're holding them aboard these ships, General," Hallholme said. He had blood on his scalp and forehead now, which he wiped with a cloth. Something had happened when the cameras went to the hostages. "*Seventeen-thousand hostages.* Members of your own families and their close associates. If you open fire upon us, you will be killing your own."

Adolphus's stomach churned with revulsion as he looked at the terrified hostages, including women, children, and the elderly. "I always thought you were a man of honor, Commodore. This loathsome act is beneath you."

"Not when the Constellation is at stake." Hallholme looked embarrassed, even disgusted with himself, but he shook it off, still holding a loth to his head. "Look at them. Have all of your rebels look at them. Once again, General, I demand your surrender."

"We've all faced tragedies, sir," said Conyer, with an audible swallow. "We should have known the Diadem would stoop to such barbaric tactics."

"We've got to take Sonjeera, General!" said the navigation officer.

On his own ship, the old Commodore barked an order, and on the transmitted images, the Diadem's guards strode into the field of view, brandishing shock prods with sizzling electric tips. The hostages tried to fight back as the guards fell upon them with the shock prods, burning skin, shedding blood. As the hostages screamed in pain, Adolphus felt the torture as if it were inflicted upon his own body.

"General, we can't let them get away with this!" said Lieutenant Spencer.

Hallholme raised his voice to a grim command. "Guards, set shock levels to lethal." His ships continued forward. "Surrender now, General. The blood will be on your hands."

The two fleets closed until they were separated by only a hair's breadth in space. All gunports were open, weapons ready to fire.

"You are an animal, Commodore." Seventeen thousand hostages. "I will not surrender. Weapons officer, prepare—"

"And we have your mother aboard, General," Hallholme interrupted, and her image flooded the screen. Adolphus had thought she was safe, sent away to a quiet village on Qiorfu under an assumed name. And yet she stared at him through the screen, her face bruised, hair bedraggled, sealed in a brig cell somewhere. But which ship?

The General froze for just an instant, a pause too short for a single breath.

For Hallholme it was enough. He barked a command, and all three-hundred Constellation warships opened fire at point-blank range.

Diadem Michella Duchenet despised the man for what he had done to her peaceful Constellation. The twenty core worlds had been unified under a stable government for centuries, with a high standard of living and a population that didn't complain too much. Tiber Adolphus had mucked everything up.

She tried not to take it personally, because a leader was supposed to be admirable, professional. But the Constellation was *hers*, and anyone who threatened it committed a personal affront against her.

She sat on the Star Throne like an angry death-angel looming over the court-martial proceedings. More than a hundred rebel warships had been destroyed before Adolphus finally declared his unconditional surrender. In desperation and under attack, some of his own men had opened fire on Hallholme's ships, but the rebel General had refused to slaughter the hostages in the heat of battle, even though it meant his defeat. Adolphus had lost thousands of men, and thousands more were prisoners of war. Now that the war was over, maybe she would have to be merciful.

The Council Hall on Sonjeera was crowded, every seat filled, and Michella had made certain that the full court-martial would be broadcast across Sonjeera, and annotated recordings would be distributed among the Crown Jewels, even out to the rugged frontier planets in the Deep Zone.

An escort of six armed guards brought Tiber Adolphus into the chamber, stripped of military rank insignia. The shackles were completely unnecessary, but the Diadem considered them an effective statement. This man had to serve as an example.

His numerous followers would also be punished; she would confiscate their holdings, put the most prominent into penal servitude, and scatter the rest to live in poverty. Adolphus was the one who mattered to her.

As he walked forward, managing to carry himself upright despite the chains, the crowd let out an angry mutter, though not nearly as loud as Michella had hoped. Somehow, the man had sparked a popular fervor across the Crown Jewels. Why, they actually viewed him as heroic! And that disturbed Michella.

The night before, while preparing for this spectacle, she had met with Lord Riomini, who came dressed in his characteristic black garments, even for a private meeting at the Diadem's palace. Selik Riomini was the most powerful of the nobles, ruler of his own planet Aeroc. He also commanded the Army of the Constellation, because his private military force comprised the bulk of the ships drawn together to fight the spreading rebellion.

"He has to be executed, of course, Selik," Michella had said, as they shared an unimaginably valuable brandy he had brought her as a gift. Riomini would likely succeed her as Diadem, and was already setting his pieces on the game board in the power plays among the nobles. Despite her age, however, Michella did not intend to retire for some time.

Riomini sipped his brandy before he answered. "That is the very

thing you must not do, Eminence. The rebellion pointed out fundamental flaws in our government and lit a spark to tinder that's been
piling up for generations. If you execute Adolphus, you make him a
martyr, and this unrest will never die. Someone else will take up his
cause. Punish him, but keep him alive."

"I refuse! That man committed treason, tried to bring down the
Constellation—"

The Black Lord set down his glass and leaned closer to her. "Please
hear me out, Eminence. If you address the grievances that formed the
basis of this rebellion, the people will calm themselves and wait to see
what you do."

Michella was ready to argue. "And what will I do?"

"Oh, you'll make a few cosmetic changes, establish numerous committees, look into the matter for the next several years, and the
momentum will die away. Soon enough, the rebellion will be forgotten.
And so will Adolphus."

Intellectually, she could see the wisdom in his words, but personally
she could not put aside her anger. "I won't let him get away with it,
Selik. I won't grant him a pardon."

Riomini just chuckled. "Oh, I would never suggest *that*, Eminence. I
have an idea that I think you'll like."

Now, the deposed Adolphus stood at attention in the center of the
polished stone floor. The noble lords in attendance listened in breathless silence as the docket of his crimes was read, one item after the
next after the next, for two hours. Adolphus denied none of the charges.
Obviously he assumed his death sentence was pre-ordained. Michella
had taken particular pleasure in informing him that his mother was
among the hostages killed during the combat operations (and she'd
issued orders to make sure that was true).

When it was all finished, the audience waited. Diadem Michella rose
slowly and grandly from her throne, taking time to summon the words
she had crafted with such care. She even fashioned the sweet, benevolent expression that had made her a beloved maternal presence
throughout the Constellation.

"Tiber Maximilian Adolphus, you have been a scourge upon our
peaceful society. Every person here knows the pain and misery you've
caused." She smiled like a disappointed schoolteacher. "But I am not a

vindictive woman. Many of your former followers, after begging me for mercy, have asked me to redress the problems that you tried to solve through violence. As Diadem, that is my duty.

"As for you, Tiber Adolphus, your crimes cannot be forgiven. Although you deserve execution, I grant you a second chance in the fervent hope that you will turn your energies toward the betterment of humankind."

She waited for the surprised buzz of conversation to rise and then subside. Finally she continued, "We therefore send you into exile on an untamed planet in the Deep Zone. Go there with as many of your followers as wish to join you. Instead of causing further destruction, I offer you a fresh start, a chance to *build* something."

She had seen images of the planet chosen for him – a wasteland, a giant scab on the hindquarters of the Galaxy. It had once been beautiful, but a massive asteroid impact had all but destroyed the world some centuries in the past. The landscape was blasted, the ecosystem in turmoil. The few surviving remnants of native flora and fauna were incompatible with human biochemistry.

As an added twist of the knife, Michella had decided to name the world *Hallholme*.

Adolphus raised his square chin and spoke. "Diadem Michella, I accept your challenge. Better to rule on the most hellish frontier planet than to serve the corrupt government on Sonjeera."

That provoked a number of boos, oaths, and hisses. Michella continued in her studiously maternal and benevolent tone. "You have your chance, Tiber Adolphus. I shall grant you the basic supplies you need to establish yourself." She paused, realizing she had run out of words to say. "I have spoken."

As the armed guards whisked Adolphus away, Michella had to hide a satisfied smile. Even his followers would admit that she was benevolent. They could not fault her. And when the deposed General failed – as assuredly he would, since she had sabotaged his equipment and tainted his supplies – the failure would be seen as his own, and no one would be the wiser.

On that horrific planet, Adolphus wouldn't last three months.

TEN YEARS LATER

1

That morning's smoke storm left a greenish haze in the air. Over the course of the day, intermittent breezes would scour the fine layer of grit from the reinforced buildings ... or maybe the weather would do something entirely different. During his decade of exile, planet Hallholme had always been unpredictable.

Tiber Maximillian Adolphus arrived at the Michella Town spaceport, several kilometers from the main settlement, ready to meet the scheduled stringline hauler with its passengers and much-needed cargo. After Lt Spencer, his driver, parked the ground vehicle in the common area, Adolphus made his way to the crowd that was already gathering.

Seeing him, his old troops offered formal salutes (the discipline was automatic for them); everyone on the colony still referred to him as "the General." Even the civilian families and penal workers greeted him with real, heartfelt respect, because they knew he had made the best of an impossible situation in this terrible place. Adolphus had single-handedly shown the colony how to survive whatever the world had to throw at them.

The landing and loading area looked like a bustling bazaar as people prepared for the scheduled downboxes from the hauler that had just docked in orbit. Underground warehouse hangars were opened, waiting for the new cargo to fall from the sky. Flatbeds were prepped to deliver perishables directly to Michella Town. The colony merchants were anxious to bid for the new materials. It would be a free-for-all.

Though the spaceport clerks had a manifest of items due to arrive from other Constellation worlds, Adolphus knew those lists were rarely accurate. He hoped the downboxes wouldn't contain another shipment of ice-world parkas or underwater breathing apparatus, which were of no use here.

The persistent mix-ups couldn't be explained by sheer incompetence. Back on Sonjeera, Diadem Michella made no secret that she would shed no tears should the banished rebel General perish on his isolated colony. And yet he and his people continued to survive.

In the first year here, Adolphus had named the initial planetary settlement Michella Town in her "honor." The Diadem knew full well it was a veiled insult, but she could not demand that he change the name without looking like a petty fool. A number of locals called the place Helltown, a name they considered more endearing than the other.

"Why the formal uniform today, Tiber?" came a familiar voice from his left. "Looks like you had it cleaned and pressed just for the occasion."

In the bustle of people anticipating the stringline hauler's arrival, he had not noticed Sophie Vence. As the colony's largest distributor of general goods, Sophie always had a strong claim on arriving shipments. And Adolphus liked her company.

He brushed the lapel of his old uniform, touched the medals on his chest, which his followers had given to him even after his defeat. "It stays clean from one occasion to the next, since I wear it so rarely." He ran his fingers along the tight collar. "Not the proper clothing for this environment."

Sophie had wavy dark brown hair, large gray eyes, and the sort of skin that looked better without makeup. She was in her early middle age, a decade younger than Adolphus, but she had been through a great deal in her life. Her generous mouth could offer a smile or issue implacable instructions to her workers. "You don't usually come to meet stringline arrivals. What's so interesting about this one? You didn't mention anything last night." She gave him an endearing smile. "Or were you too preoccupied?"

He maintained his stiff and formal appearance. "One of the Diadem's watchdogs is on that passenger pod. He's here to make certain I'm not up to any mischief."

"You're always up to mischief." He didn't argue with the comment. She continued, "Don't they realize it's not much of a surprise inspection if you already know about it?"

"The Diadem doesn't know that I know. I received a coded message packet from a secret contact on Sonjeera." Plenty of people back in the old government still wished that his rebellion had succeeded.

One of the humming flatbeds pulled up before them in a cloud of alkaline dust, and Sophie's eighteen-year-old son Devon rolled down the driver's compartment window. Strikingly good-looking, he had a muscular build and intense blue eyes. He pointed to a cleared area, but Sophie shook her head and jabbed a finger southward. "No, go over there! Our downboxes will be in the first cluster." Devon accelerated the flatbed over to the indicated area, where he grabbed a prime spot before other flatbeds could nose in.

Work administrators gathered by the colony reception area for the new batch of convicts, fifty of them from a handful of Constellation worlds. Because there was so much to be done on the rugged colony, Adolphus was grateful for the extra laborers. Even after a decade of backbreaking work and growing population, the Hallholme settlements teetered on the razor's edge of survival. He would put the convicts to work, rehabilitate them, and give them a genuine fresh start – if they wanted it.

He shaded his eyes and gazed into the greenish-brown sky, searching for the bright white lights of descending downboxes or the passenger pod. After locking onto the planet's lone terminus ring in orbit, the giant stringline hauler would release one container after another from its framework. When the big ship was empty, the pilot would prepare the hauler's skeleton to receive the carefully audited upboxes that Adolphus's colony was required to ship back to Sonjeera as tribute to the Diadem.

Tribute. The very word had jagged edges and sharp points. Among the governors of the fifty-four newly settled Deep Zone colony worlds, Adolphus was not alone in resenting the Constellation's demand for its share. Establishing a foothold on an exotic planet did not come easily. On most worlds, the native biochemistry was not compatible with

Terran systems, so all food supplies, seed stock, and fertilizers had to be delivered from elsewhere. The task was even more difficult on devastated Hallholme.

Thinking back, Adolphus sighed with ever-present regret. He had launched his rebellion for grand societal changes ... changes that most citizens knew were necessary. And he had come close to winning – very close – but under fire and faced with treachery, he had made the only choice he could live with, the only moral choice, and now he had to live with the consequences of his defeat.

Even so, Diadem Michella couldn't accept her triumph for what it was. She had never expected the colony to survive the first year, and she didn't trust Adolphus to abide by the terms of his exile. So, she was sending someone to check on him – again. But this inspector would find nothing. None of them ever did.

A signal echoed across the landing field, and people scurried to get into position. Sophie Vence smiled at him again. "I'd better get busy. The boxes are coming down." She gave him a quick kiss on the cheek, and he flushed. He hated the fact that he couldn't discipline his own embarrassment.

"Not in public," he said tersely. "You know that."

"I know that it makes you uncomfortable." She flitted away, waving at him. "Later, then."

2

As the stringline hauler arrived at the terminus ring above Hallholme, Antonia Anqui found an unoccupied viewport inside the passenger pod and looked down at the planet. The pod was a standard high-capacity model, though not nearly full; few travelers chose this particular destination. No need for crowding at the windows, which was good, since Antonia didn't want company, conversation, or any attention at all.

The young woman stared through the star-sparkled blackness to the looming globe below. Hallholme looked rugged even from space. This planet had once been lush and hospitable to life, but now it looked mortally wounded. No wonder people called it "Hellhole."

But even this was better than Aeroc, the planet she'd fled in desperation. She had ridden the stringline network through the central hub on Sonjeera and back out, taking the transport line as far away from the Crown Jewel worlds as she could go. She only hoped it was far enough to hide and make a new life for herself.

As the stringline hauler docked, loud noises shuddered through the hull of the passenger pod. The hauler itself was little more than a framework on which numerous cargo boxes or passenger pods could be hung like grapes in a cluster. Antonia waited in both anticipation and dread. Almost there, almost free.

One after another, downboxes disengaged from the framework, drifting into lower orbit where they were automatically maneuvered towards the marked expanse of the Michella Town spaceport. Each time a downbox disengaged and fell away, she flinched at the vibration and thud.

Hallholme rotated slowly beneath her, exposing patches of water, empty continents, and finally the inhabited section, not far from the concentric ripples of the impact scar itself. Antonia caught her breath when she saw the huge bull's-eye where the asteroid had struck. The shattered crater was filled with glassy shock melt, surrounded by concentric ripples. Canyon-sized cracks radiated outward in a jagged pattern. Oozing lava continued to percolate to the surface through raw scars in the ground. Five centuries meant little on a geologic timescale, and the world was still wrestling with its recovery.

Yes, Hellhole was the last place anyone would think of looking for her.

At nineteen, Antonia knew how to take care of herself better than most adults did. During her past two years on the run, she had learned many ways to elude detection. She knew how to change her identity and appearance, how to get a job that would earn enough money for her to live on without raising questions; she knew how to be afraid, and how to stand up for herself.

Two years ago – a lifetime it seemed – she had been precious and pretty, a creature of social expectations, the owner of a fashionable wardrobe with garments for all occasions and any type of weather. She had another name, Tona Quirrie, but that was best forgotten; she would never – *could* never – use it again. As a debutante on Aeroc, she had flaunted different hairstyles and cuts of clothing because her mother assured her that such things made her beautiful. These days, Antonia did everything possible to make herself less attractive: her dark brown hair hung straight down to her shoulders, and she wore only plain, serviceable clothes.

She was the daughter of the manager of a large power plant on Aeroc, one of the old civilized planets long ruled by the Riomini noble family. They had a very nice home with a large kitchen, a pool in a terrarium room, and a well-tuned piano. Her mother loved music and often played at their special parties, but the best times were when she would withdraw to the conservatory alone, playing classical pieces or evocative, intricate melodies that might have been her own compositions, and Antonia sat in the hall, just listening. She even took lessons, hoping to become as good as her mother someday. Now the music was gone from her life.

When Antonia was seventeen, a dashing young man named Jako Rullins came to work for her father in the power-plant headquarters. At twenty-one, Jako was handsome, intense, clever, and obviously moving up in the world. He quickly made himself indispensible in her father's work and often came to their home for business meetings, which turned into social occasions.

When Jako fixed his attentions on young Antonia, she had been swept away, and her parents had not objected because they liked the young man. Jako was utterly focused on Antonia whenever they were together.

Four months later, Jako asked Antonia to marry him, and her surprised parents told him to wait, explaining that she was too young, although they encouraged him to continue to court her. Despite being upset by the delay, Jako swore that he would prove his devotion to her. Antonia remembered her father smiling at the promise. "I hope you do exactly that, Mr Rullins. Just give it time."

Jako, however, seemed to feel an urgency that Antonia found bewildering. Whenever they were alone, he tried to convince her that they should just escape somewhere, get married, and live their own lives. He was so earnest and optimistic that she almost said yes, but his intensity worried her. Although she loved Jako, she saw no reason to hurry. "We'll still be together in a year, and then we can have the grand wedding I've always dreamed of."

But Jako didn't want to wait. He grew edgier and more possessive, though he still played the part of a gentleman. A month later, after the pair came home from one of their frequent dates, her world ended in blood and lies . . .

Over the next two years, Antonia learned to mistrust everyone around her. Jako taught her to be that way while the two of them were on the run. Then she escaped from him, too. With a new appearance and identity, she ran to the main Aeroc spaceport, completed an application in the colonization office, and signed aboard the next stringline ship heading for the Deep Zone planets. She didn't care which one.

The ship was bound for Hellhole.

"Anything to see out there?"

Antonia turned irritably. Next to her stood a grinning, good-humored man she'd noticed on the voyage out from the Sonjeera hub. She feared that he had somehow recognized her or tracked her down, but the man seemed cheery with everyone, blithely jabbering away, pleased with his choice to go to Hallholme.

"All the ports have the same view." She hoped he would get the hint and go away. He didn't.

"My name is Fernando – Fernando Neron. We're about to start a great adventure! And your name is?"

Though on her guard, Antonia realized that being too reticent would only raise suspicions. Besides, she'd have to get used to going by her assumed identity, so she decided to start now. "Antonia Anqui," she said. "Let's hope it's an adventure instead of an ordeal."

"Did you hear that, Vincent?" Fernando waved to another man who had been quiet during the entire trip. "She says she hopes it's an adventure instead of an ordeal!"

"I heard her." The other man nodded, more courteous than open and friendly. He had seemed preoccupied throughout the journey.

During the four-day stringline crossing, Antonia had kept to herself. Their private sleeping cabins were so tiny and claustrophobic that most passengers spent their days in the passenger pod's common room, which forced them to get to know one another.

Very few of those aboard seemed pleased with their situation. One group, an isolationist religious cult called the Children of Amadin, avoided their fellow passengers even more than Antonia did. The cult members were easily identified by square-cut hair – both men and women – and their baggy, pale blue uniforms, which did not look as though they would hold up in a dirty wilderness environment. Another oddball religious group, looking for the promised land on

Hellhole ... or at least someplace where people would leave them alone.

A group of convicts – men and women sentenced to exile on Hallholme – was kept in a separate compartment; the Constellation liked to wash its hands of such problems and let the Deep Zone administrators deal with them. Other travelers aboard the pod were commercial representatives and government officials, engrossed in their own business and hardly interested in the other passengers.

"So what brings you to a place like Hellhole, young lady? What are you – eighteen, nineteen? And very pretty, not a typical colonist." Fernando seemed genuinely friendly.

In her years on the run, Antonia had learned never to reveal too much about herself. She tried to be just open enough to sidestep further questions. "Maybe I'll tell you later. For now, I'd like to enjoy a few moments of quiet. This could be our last bit of calm before we start the hard work." She made her lips curve upward in what she hoped was a sincere-looking smile.

Fernando laughed and looked over his shoulder again. "Did you hear that, Vincent? She says we'd better enjoy the last few moments of calm."

"I agree with her." Vincent took his seat.

Without warning, the passenger pod shuddered. The clamping hooks released them, and the craft began to fall toward the planet.

3

The pod landed, and before any other passengers were allowed to disembark, local security troops came aboard to escort the prisoners off. Everything seemed very casual. When one of the convicts commented on the lax security, a guard brushed aside the concern. "If you run, where are you going to go? You've got a second chance here. The General will let you earn as much freedom as you like."

A second chance, Vincent Jenet thought. Exactly what he needed.

Waiting at the back of the passenger pod, he felt an odd flutter in his stomach as the prisoners marched away. If not for the last-minute mercy of the magistrate on planet Orsini, he could have been included among those convicts. Thankfully, Enva Tazaar's petty revenge hadn't extended that far. Being sent to Hellhole was bad enough.

Vincent's enthusiastic new friend Fernando wanted to be among the first to disembark, but Vincent was more cautious. "We'll have a long, long time to settle in here. What's your hurry?"

"I'm in a hurry to find the opportunities." Fernando flashed him a grin. "First in line, first to the prize. Aren't you anxious to begin your new life?"

During their time aboard the pod, Vincent hadn't sought the other man's companionship, but Fernando was not a man who needed someone else to hold up the other end of a conversation. Apparently, he believed Vincent needed "cheering up," which might have been true. The other man didn't pry into his situation, mainly because he spent most of the time talking about himself. Fernando's optimism was indefatigable. Fair enough, Vincent needed optimism.

"I don't look at the black clouds – I see the silver linings. I've lived on a dozen planets, made a new start over and over again. It's an old habit for me. I've made my fortune so many times, I know how to do it. Stick with me, Vincent, and before long you and I will be running Hellhole!"

"I thought General Adolphus ran Hellhole."

Fernando shifted subjects erratically. "Do you think he's really as awful as the history books paint him?"

"I have no idea. Orsini was far from the thick of the rebellion, and I was too busy at work to pay much attention to galactic politics."

Fernando lowered his voice, as if afraid of listening devices. "They say Adolphus is a ruthless monster, that he tortured the populations of entire planets, that he enslaved soldiers and forced them to fly his rebel warships – to their deaths! He would fasten their hands to dead-man switches so they couldn't leave the helm even when their ships were about to be destroyed."

Vincent frowned. "I never heard those stories." As if he didn't already have second thoughts ...

Fernando grinned again. "Well, they're probably just stories then, even if they are 'official' ones. Diadem Michella smiles a lot, but I get the impression she would be a sore loser."

"I thought she won."

"The history books say so."

Once the convicts disembarked, a haughty representative from the Diadem pushed his way to the front of the line ahead of the departing passengers, making the other businessmen and travelers wait. Next, the tight-knit religious group exited at their own pace. For all his eager jostling, Fernando didn't manage to disembark any faster than if they had simply waited their turn. Vincent glanced behind him and saw that the girl Antonia was hesitating in the back, looking lost. He knew exactly how she felt.

Emerging under the greenish-brown sky, Vincent drew a deep breath of the strange-smelling air. Fernando spread his hands wide and looked around as if he had just entered paradise. "Hellhole – the place to go, when you've got nowhere else to go! Not exactly a vacation paradise, eh, Vincent? Still, we're here and ready to make the best of it."

Back on the Crown Jewel worlds, the noble holdings were so subdivided that there was little opportunity for growth or exploration. Once the stringline transportation network was extended to the untamed Deep Zone, Diadem Michella encouraged all manner of dreamers, pioneers, and risk-takers to rush to those virgin planets and claim a place for themselves. Unlike the crowded core worlds, the DZ frontier was wide open, the landscapes new, the possibilities endless.

Of all the DZ planets opened to colonization, Hallholme was at the bottom of the list, a dumping ground for undesirables: charlatans, misfits, outcasts, and criminals. Vincent had never imagined that he would be counted among that lot. He'd led a quiet life, never bothering anyone, but even so . . .

Outside in the paved spaceport area, guards escorted the convicts in a convoy out to their camp assignment. Transport vehicles and cargo flatbeds streamed away from the landing zone towards the main town a few kilometers away. While he and Fernando waited for instructions (Vincent more patiently than his friend), the blue-garbed religious group hired a transport and hurried off to their own destination, without inviting the stragglers to join them.

As the crowd dwindled around the passenger pod, Vincent tried to figure out where he was supposed to go. His stomach was in a knot. Noticing a colony reception office on the far side of the landing field, he said, "I wonder if we need to sign in and receive supplies or a welcome kit." He looked around, hoping to find someone in authority.

"No thanks – then we'd be with all the other new arrivals, and we'll miss our chance. I know, let's go straight to town and see what we can find there." Fernando took his arm and with full (and perhaps feigned) confidence, walked to a group of supply workers unloading one of the downboxes. He talked quickly, smiled, and asked for "a quick favor." They let him and Vincent hitch a ride with a handful of businessmen from the Crown Jewel worlds.

After he reached the colony town, Vincent looked at the buildings, all of which seemed drab and squat, hunkered down against unexpected threats. He noted a lack of color, none of the verdant greens and blues of his homeworld of Orsini. Everything – even the people walking along the streets – seemed gray and brown or drab shades in between. This was going to be his new home . . .

Fernando smiled. "Ah, we're going to fit right in, my friend."

At twenty-nine, soft-spoken Vincent didn't like to call attention to himself, didn't clown around in conversations. Back on Orsini, he had lived with his retired and sickly father, Drew, tending the man's worsening medical condition. Vincent had worked in a repair shop for large machinery, eventually becoming manager; he understood cranes and lifters, construction loaders, upboxes and downboxes. He was used to crawling right inside the engines and power pods in order to fix them. A good employee, very reliable, never causing any trouble.

But when his father's condition changed from disability to terminal illness, Vincent found himself sliding into a bottomless pit of treatments, medical experts and contradictory medical specialists offering expensive and unproven options. Cheaper regimens were either ineffective or had hundreds of patients ahead of his father.

Vincent drained all the money from his savings. He refused to accept that his father was *dying*, and no treatments were going to cure him. Vincent worked overtime at the shop, trying to earn more money as a solution. While expressing sympathies, his boss, Mr Engermann, insisted that he could only afford to pay him a token bonus.

Vincent, however, knew *why* the man couldn't pay more: Engermann collected expensive glass-and-aerogel sculptures. The levitating sculptures were exquisite and innovative, but their value rested on the fact that their creator was Enva Tazaar, daughter of the planetary lord. The woman fancied herself an artist and had all the wealth and leisure time to prove it. Enva sold her sculptures as fast as she could create them, and Vincent's boss had six in his collection. Mr Engermann bought them not because he was an art lover, but to curry favor with Lord Tazaar.

But even when Vincent put in countless extra hours and turned over dozens of new work tickets, Engermann said he couldn't afford to pay any more. The situation frustrated Vincent; this wasn't how his life was supposed to be.

Upon learning of a promising experimental treatment for his father's condition, Vincent became convinced it was the cure he had been searching for. Drew Jenet didn't have much time, and Vincent had to find a way to get the money for the treatment. Though Drew begged his son to accept the inevitable, Vincent doggedly refused to surrender.

The more he thought about it, the more incensed he became that Mr Engermann wasted so much money on Tazaar sculptures, which he displayed like treasures in the headquarters office. Any one of those objects, if sold quietly on the black market, could pay for the experimental treatment. It seemed *immoral* that his boss could waste so much wealth on a frivolous thing, when another man's life could be saved.

Rationalizing his actions, Vincent broke into the repair-shop office at night and stole one of the valuable sculptures – only one – and left the remaining five untouched (a fact that baffled investigators of the crime). But he didn't need more. Selling a single sculpture yielded enough money to secure the treatment, and Vincent did so without delay or regrets. Once he solved his father's problem, he could catch his breath, slowly but surely put away a nest egg, and find a way to pay Mr Engermann back.

Though Vincent was careful, he hadn't counted on Enva Tazaar's obsessive interest in each of her sculptures. When she heard that a new buyer had made a purchase, she hired security experts to track the payment and turned the information over to authorities, who pinpointed Vincent Jenet and arrested him.

But he had already spent the money on the risky but vital treatment. Though guilty, Vincent knew he had made the right choice. He did not deny the charges; he had done what he had to do.

A week later, Drew Jenet died of complications from the procedure.

Ruined, distraught, and now on trial for theft, Vincent had nothing left to lose when the convicting magistrate offered him a choice: do prison time or relinquish all ties to his home and volunteer for relocation to the Deep Zone. Many of the untamed worlds were perfectly habitable, with pleasant climates, abundant resources, and plentiful opportunities. Though he hated uncertainty, he had to start a new life. He signed the forms with no regrets.

However, Enva Tazaar held a grudge against him for stealing one of her precious sculptures. Despite the fact that Vincent was a nonviolent prisoner, with no prior record, and a sympathetic motive for his crime, the noblewoman pulled strings to make sure he was assigned to the worst possible planet in the Deep Zone . . .

Vincent had dreaded arriving, certain that everyone would shun him for his crimes, but now that he was on Hallholme, he saw he wasn't alone. Every one of these colonists probably had some uncomfortable reason for ending up here.

Nevertheless, he expected someone to give him instructions. Surely they had some sort of standard procedures for new arrivals? He stood with Fernando in the streets of Michella Town, wondering where to go. Undaunted, his friend set off down the main street, as if he had business to accomplish. Given his obvious confidence, no one bothered to offer advice or ask them questions. Vincent muttered to his friend, "Now what do we do?"

Fernando flashed a bright smile and said, with no embarrassment whatsoever, "I haven't the slightest idea."

4

Diadem Michella's motor carriage rolled past the reflecting pools and ornamental gardens of Sonjeera's grand palace, then sped across the verdant valley toward Council City.

Previous Diadems had occupied fabulous royal residences in the heart of that sprawling metropolis, but such buildings had long since been converted to other government uses: offices, meeting chambers, festival halls, records vaults. To emphasize the importance of her supreme role, Michella separated herself from the crowds and bustle, living on an ostentatious estate out in the country.

Council City's weathered copper rooftops and ivy-covered walls gave it the aura of an intellectual center, like a university town. Seated in the rear of her state vehicle, the old woman shook her head in bitter amusement. What absurdities took place inside those structures of bureaucracy! Committees and offices were created solely to give impressive-sounding titles to nobles so they would not feel useless. Lawmakers formed childish alliances to oppose her policies – not because they objected to the policies themselves, but becasue they believed that opposing her made them appear powerful. At least it kept them busy.

Her uniformed driver steered the carriage around the perimeter of Heart Square, taking the circuitous, traditional route that was prescribed for the Diadem's arrival. According to long-established custom, the Diadem's mere passage through the city was said to bring good fortune. Silly superstition, but Michella did not dare break the routine. Tradition was the bedrock of human civilization. Anyone who tried to destroy that bedrock, as Tiber Adolphus had, needed to be dealt with. Severely.

The motor carriage came to a stop, and the polished door automatically swung open. Gathering her regal presence as naturally as she breathed, Michella stepped from the running board to the street, still spry and agile despite her advanced age. At this early hour, only a few citizens gathered in the square to watch her approach, with their hats off and heads bowed.

Wearing robes of state, members of the Constellation's parliamentary body took positions on either side of the broad steps that led up from street level to the inner chambers. She walked between them up to the entrance, and then they followed her inside as if this were a choreographed military drill. Michella smiled to herself as she heard some of them struggling to keep up with her.

The previous week, she had eavesdropped while several lords in this very chamber whispered about who might succeed her as Diadem. Due to her age, the question was on the minds of all ambitious planetary lords, but their speculation was premature. She would probably outlive them all.

Michella had only one child, her daughter, Keana, and Constellation law prohibited a son or daughter of the previous monarch from serving as supreme ruler in order to limit the power of any one noble family as well as to prevent the creation of a corrupt dynasty. Therefore, the next Diadem was not – in theory at least – Michella's concern.

The authors of such laws were so naïve.

While she had listened in annoyed silence, the whispering lords bandied about a number of names, exchanging favors and recommendations as if their machinations weren't obvious. When she could bear it no longer, Michella spoke loudly from the elevated throne. "The Council elected me Diadem for life – *for life*, and I'm not dead yet. I have ruled the Constellation for many decades, and I am still in better physical condition than most of you."

A quick, embarrassed hush had fallen, and the startled Council members issued profuse apologies. Nevertheless, she knew that most of the planetary

lords were anxious to have another leader, preferring new policies and
fresh energy. They were like carrion birds circling.

As Michella crossed the white marblene floor to her throne in the
great Council chamber, she wished she had the timely advice of
Ishop Heer. As her confidential aide, Heer was adept at picking up
inferences, hearing secret conversations, and keeping accurate lists
of everything. His surreptitious discoveries provided her with much of
the subtle, unofficial information she required to make her decisions.
However, precisely because he was so reliable, she had just dispatched
him to Hallholme to sniff out any mischief that Adolphus might be
up to. Ishop Heer might be talented, but he couldn't be in two places
at once.

No matter. Michella already knew why the nobles were agitated
today: the matter of Keana and Lord de Carre. *Again.* Somehow, she had
to find a resolution to her daughter's indiscretions. The uproar was preposterous, since affairs were common among the noble families, but
usually handled with much greater discretion. Keana's own husband
might tolerate being cuckolded, but the man's family could not ignore
the insult or the scandal.

Lifting the hem of her robe, Michella ascended to the Star Throne
adorned with constellations set in priceless jewels. She sat upon the
cushioned seat and gazed down at the U-shaped arrangement of lords
and ladies. The forty rows in the assemblage included dignitaries from
all the Crown Jewel planets, as well as political and business representatives from 183 recognized noble families. Today the seats were nearly
full; scandals tended to increase attendance.

Michella tapped her foot on a concealed panel, and a great bell
chimed in the chamber to initiate the proceedings. Tired of games, she
decided to deal forthrightly with her daughter's annoying behavior. On
her own terms. Michella spoke into her voice amplifier, "Rather than
following the agenda, today I shall supersede other scheduled topics in
order to discuss the de Carre matter." Everyone knew what she was
talking about; a murmur of approval passed through the chamber. "Lord
de Carre has been summoned – is he present?"

A titter of laughter rippled through the assemblage, but no one
voiced the obvious suspicion that he was with Keana in their not-so-
secret love nest. The nobleman was appallingly flippant about his real

duties; Louis de Carre left his son to manage the complex business and industrial matters back on his home planet of Vielinger. Such arrogant selfishness invited the ire of his fellow nobles.

"Is there no representative of the de Carre family present while this matter is up for discussion?" Michella demanded. "Did he name no proxy?"

No one spoke up.

Her annoyance was plain to everyone in the chamber. "The best interests of Vielinger must be represented, even if the planetary lord can't be bothered to attend to his duties." And, of course, she had to ensure uninterrupted production from the planet's iperion mines. She somehow doubted that de Carre's son was up to the challenge.

Lord Selik Riomini stepped onto a platform, dressed in a black robe adorned with military medals and braids. He had a rich, confident voice. "Such behavior plainly shows that the de Carres have abrogated their rights to the historic and vital holdings on Vielinger. The iperion mines are in disrepair, miners have been killed in cave-ins. It is a complete disgrace. We have to look to the future – as the deposits dwindle, we need to make sure the existing supplies of the material are managed well."

Michella suspected that many of the "accidents" had actually been caused by Riomini operatives to make the de Carre administration look incompetent. However, considering Louis de Carre's behavior, perhaps a shift in leadership was in order after all.

The Black Lord continued, "Iperion is crucial to maintaining the stringline network throughout the Crown Jewels and the Deep Zone, and those mines must be administered properly." He bowed in an awkward attempt to appear humble. "Eminence, as they served you during General Adolphus's rebellion, my private forces stand ready to take charge of Vielinger, so that we can protect the vital reserves for the good of the Constellation."

"For the good of the Riomini family, you mean." A stocky, bearded nobleman rose from his chair near the center of the front row. "Riominis will skim profits if they gain control of those strategic reserves."

Lord Riomini shook his head, marshalling calm. "Yet another of your unsupported assertions, Lord Tazaar. If Riomini, or any other family, shoulders the burden of the Vielinger operations, this worthy Council will keep a close watch on all accounts."

With a laugh, Azio Tazaar showed he was not convinced. "There are accounts, and then again there are accounts. It is not difficult to run several ledgers simultaneously ... nor is it difficult to cause tunnel collapses in the iperion mines to foment popular unrest against the de Carres."

A noblewoman in the back row spoke up, Lady Jenine Paternos, the elderly matriarch of one of the lesser families. Michella admired her for her tenacity. "Why, Lord Tazaar, you seem so indignant about Riomini ambitions, while you yourself have made no secret of your desire to take away *my* planet."

Tazaar gave an aloof chuckle but could not hide the sudden flush on his cheeks. "I merely suggested that your family would be better suited to administering one of the Deep Zone planets instead of Kappas. After all, generations of heirs have been forced to content themselves with smaller and smaller pieces of once-major holdings, and now many younger family members have no inheritance at all. It's a shame." He looked around at the seated dignitaries, most of whom faced similar crises on their own worlds. "The problem is not unique to Kappas. Without that dissatisfaction, would Tiber Adolphus ever have found support for his rebellion? Lady Paternos, you should be excited by the possibility of ruling a whole new world, a pristine planet."

Michella could barely keep up with the feuds upon feuds, most of which she found silly. The nobles behaved with very little *nobility*. In a recent committee meeting, Azio Tazaar had lost his temper and threatened to slit the throat of Lady Paternos; the Diadem had ordered the comment struck from the public record, but everyone remembered it.

Still standing, Lord Riomini looked pleased that Tazaar was being attacked from a different direction. Michella wondered if the Black Lord had in fact staged the noblewoman's outburst. "The situation on Kappas is not unlike the blatant mismanagement we have seen on Vielinger. Unrest has led to work stoppages, resulting in the delayed payment of taxes to Sonjeera, which harms the whole Constellation government. I submit to Diadem Michella" – Riomini gave her a little bow – "and all representatives here, that Vielinger would thrive with improved leadership."

Tazaar blurted, "So would Kappas. And you, Lady Paternos, could make a fresh start out in the Deep Zone."

Jenine Paternos looked ready to leap down onto the floor and begin pummeling Tazaar. "My family has held the Star Throne three times in the past, and our diadems are considered the most successful at bringing prosperity to the Constellation."

"Some of us don't have to look so far back in history to find a competent family member," Tazaar said in an acid tone. "Why don't we stop these games? How much of a bribe will it take to send you out to the frontier worlds? And good riddance."

"I will not be bribed!"

"Then you *deserve* to have your throat slit," Lord Tazaar muttered, quite intentionally reminding them of his earlier outrageous threat. "I would do it myself, but I don't want to dull a good knife on your leathery old skin."

Several people snickered, but Michella had had enough. She leaned forward on the throne. "Back to the matter at hand, before I censure you both. The question before the floor is what shall be done about Vielinger, considering Lord de Carre's mismanagement?"

"Thank you, Eminence," Riomini said to her with exaggerated patience, taking the center of attention again. "The de Carre family is in dereliction of every duty."

"Except for one!" shouted a lord from the back row of seats. "He's properly servicing the Diadem's daughter as we speak." The scoffer ducked to avoid being identified.

Though she fumed, Michella did not respond to the humiliating chuckles throughout the chamber. It was common for these meetings to become raucous and unruly; ironically, it was part of the reason the system worked. Even with the flying insults, every representative could be heard, and often the candor cut through the interminable opacity of diplomatic discussions.

Lord Riomini pressed forward. "The Constellation should commandeer Vielinger and station troops there under Riomini supervision. In good time, we can set up a cooperative arrangement among the leading families."

"I disagree in principle," Tazaar said, the instant Riomini had finished.

"I support the recommendation," Lady Paternos added just as quickly.

"Good, then we need only work out the details," Michella said with a smile. She could at last deal with the open criticism of Keana's affair, using the iperion concerns as an excuse. Louis de Carre was an embarrassment, and he needed to be removed. "This is a far more important matter than salacious gossip about romantic affairs."

Michella wished she could sweep the problem under the rug by exiling her daughter and Lord de Carre to the Deep Zone, as she had done to Adolphus and his rebels.

5

The streets of Helltown bustled with customers, vendors, and investors trying to swap items. After the contents of the down-boxes had been sorted and squabbled over, Sophie Vence obtained not only the items she'd ordered (at exorbitant cost), but also a few metric tons of useful material that her distribution network could sell at a profit.

A few hours ago, as the newcomers disembarked from the passenger pod, Sophie had watched Adolphus meet the Diadem's officious-looking watchdog (who seemed very annoyed that his surprise visit was not a surprise after all). The two men had headed off in a private vehicle to the General's headquarters residence, kilometers outside of town. She was sure he would tell her all the details later.

Constellation industrial and agricultural inspectors fanned out to copy databases, inventorying unusual items, materials, and native life forms that the Constellation might want. By carefully accounting Hellhole's productivity, the inspectors could determine the proper amount of tribute the planet owed. Sophie had offered to send a few cases of her freshly bottled Cabernet; though it was probably too coarse for Diadem Michella's palate, the wine did have some value, if only as a novelty to be sold at a good price on Sonjeera.

When the flatbeds rolled in from the spaceport, Sophie directed the routine shipments to her warehouses where line managers would unpack and sort the contents. Though she normally let employees handle the mundane work, right now she felt as excited as a kid waiting for a birthday gift. As the flatbeds were unloaded, she searched for and found the hermetically sealed, well-cushioned box she'd been anticipating. Using the utility cutter on her belt, Sophie slit the protective polymer wrap.

Devon came up flushed with excitement. "We've got a whole tank of trout fingerlings, Mother. Our fish hatcheries have been waiting for those. The algae and weed stock for the ponds should be ready. Before long, I'll be able to go fishing!"

Her heart went out to him. "Oh, Devon, I'm sorry I never took you fishing on Klief when you were a boy. It'll be a great experience for you."

Her eighteen-year-old son had studied records of their former home planet. He had only been ten when she'd taken him to the new colony in the wake of a painful divorce. She didn't regret coming here, and Tiber Adolphus was a thousand times the man her ex-husband had been – but Devon had been forced to grow up in a much more difficult place than Klief, and this planet had little to offer a growing boy. Now that he was of age, Devon was a good marriage prospect: strong, classically handsome, and good-natured ... and his mother's wealth and influence in the colony town didn't hurt. Unfortunately, Hellhole didn't have many available women in his age group.

Devon continued to chatter. "Carter also snagged us a crate that was marked 'Livestock Embryos.' I figured we could use those."

"We can always use livestock embryos. What kind of animal?"

"Goats, I think."

"The meat isn't to my liking, but goats survive here better than most other animals. At least it can be processed into sausage or jerky, and the milk and cheese is useful. Good job, Devon."

The sealed container drew her attention again, and Devon helped her remove the rest of the polymer peel to reveal dirt-encrusted masses with woody protrusions – the most beautiful thing she'd ever seen.

Devon touched one of the roots. "They survived the passage, but can they survive planting here?"

"So long as we give them tender loving care."

Sophie had been waiting six months for this rootstock to add to her vineyards. She had already been producing red grapes, but if these vines took hold – if she watered, fertilized, and protected them from the harsh weather – she might be able to add a Riesling to her catalog. Tiber would love it; not because he preferred whites to reds, but because it was another mark of much-needed civilization – of *civility* – on this planet.

"I want you to take care of this personally, Devon. Let Carter and Elbert manage the other shipments in the warehouses. Tell them to hurry, too – the weathersats show a growler coming into the area this afternoon."

Devon bolted off with more urgency than was actually necessary. She felt a glow of pride; he was a good kid.

"Excuse me, are you Sophie Vence?" came a gruff voice.

She turned to see a boulder of a man with a neatly trimmed dark beard, and a light blue pajama-like uniform identical to those of his companions, who stood together at some distance behind him. They were of mixed races, hair colors, complexions, and physical builds, but they all looked oddly the same. Sophie couldn't identify the religious sect, nor did she care. Hellhole got more than its share of fringe groups and cults, an endless string of nuts, but the General insisted that all newcomers be tolerated, provided they adhered to certain ground rules.

She proffered her formal business smile. "Yes, that's me. How can I help you?"

"I am Lujah Carey, and I represent the Children of Amadin. We require equipment and materials. I understand you are the best person to provide them."

"You weren't steered wrong, sir. What do you have in mind?"

"Everything we need for survival. We could not bring much when we left Barassa, so we liquidated all our possessions to provide money to buy the necessities."

"This isn't like a shopping mall on Sonjeera, Mr Carey. Although our manufacturing gets better every year, most of the big items still come in by stringline, and half the time we don't get what we asked *or* paid for."

"I can pay." The man showed her an account transfer card that held an extraordinarily high balance. "Amadin will provide."

"That's all well and good, Mr Carey, but Constellation credits aren't worth the same here. Our economy runs more on hard work and barter."

He looked briefly flustered, then an expression of stillness came over his face, and he continued with persistent calm. "My people will need several large overland vehicles, at least ten prefabricated shelters, along with hand tools and building materials so we can erect our own permanent structures. We have food supplies, but we will need additional agricultural resources. You may keep the entire balance on this transfer card if you help us set up a self-sustaining settlement where we can live our lives in privacy and liberty. I understand much of the planet's surface remains unclaimed?"

"Well, I could provide what you need, Mr Carey, but you have to understand how Hellhole works. No one can survive here on his own. Each person has a role. Everybody contributes. We're a tight-knit community."

The man shook his head, maintaining a determined expression. "The Children of Amadin came to escape the confinement of a secular society. We do not wish to be part of your community. We will honor Amadin in our own way."

"And that's your right – *after* one year. This should have been explained to you when you signed aboard. *All* arrivals to the planet Hallholme" – Sophie forced herself to use the planet's formal name – "are asked to put in a year of community service, to support the colony. That year benefits all of us, including new settlers. After you put in your time, we grant you a piece of land and the resources you need to establish yourselves. Think of it as a safety net: we help you settle in, get on your feet, and take care of you until you're ready to take care of yourselves."

Carey's voice became hard, suspicious of the offer. "We can take care of ourselves right now."

Sophie had seen stubborn people before. Newcomers took amenities for granted, not understanding how much Tiber Adolphus had done for this place. When he and his men had been dumped here, Hellhole was a blank slate, raw and entirely untamed. Through his management skills, the General got water pumping, shelters built, power running, fast-growing crops planted. Against all odds, he turned Hellhole into a livable, and in some ways pleasant, place.

She drew a deep breath and tried one more time. "All of the colonists for the past decade have put in a hell of a lot of backbreaking work, just so there could be a town and a spaceport and *supplies* here. We made it happen. All we ask is that newcomers do a bit of work to make this planet better for the colonists who come after."

"Colonists who came before us and those who come after us are not our concern," the religious leader said. "We came here for freedom, not to be chained to a new overlord. We will pay whatever price you ask for our equipment, then we will fend for ourselves. We'll thank you not to bother us."

Most such groups who refused to become part of the community came crawling back to the General's safety net within weeks. They simply didn't know how difficult this planet could be. Adolphus could have cracked down and imposed a year of servitude, but he refused to be a dictator (regardless of how the Constellation portrayed him). In the majority of instances, the recalcitrant groups decided that independence wasn't such a good idea after all, at least not until they had gotten on their feet.

Knowing that further argument was useless – and that someone else would sell these people the equipment if she didn't – Sophie offered him three refurbished, high-capacity overland Trakmasters and a minimal setup to give his isolated camp at least some chance of survival. The blue-garbed followers went away to pick up all the items she had designated.

Sophie called after them, "Good luck!"

Lujah Carey refused to accept even that with good grace. "We are blessed by the grace of Amadin. We don't require luck."

"We all need luck here." She had seen this too often. People didn't realize what they were getting into. Whether or not Carey and his followers wanted it, Sophie would send someone – probably Devon – out to check on them in a few weeks.

6

Though Fernando Neron didn't seem concerned about being lost in Michella Town, Vincent worried. A flurry of activity swirled around them: large family groups headed off to supply stations; loaders and flatbeds arrived at shielded warehouses where swarms of people unloaded supplies and stacked them inside; traders and shippers met their intermediaries; shops opened to display new wares; guests found temporary lodgings.

No one gave the two men a second glance.

Vincent followed him past buildings that seemed aerodynamic to provide a smooth wind profile. Towering greenhouse domes protected large-scale crops, while little waist-high domes served as flower gardens outside private dwellings – a way of defying the bleakness of Hellhole, he supposed.

They walked along a wide main street where the buildings took on a more carnival-like character, a succession of wildly different styles, some painted garish colors, others with statues or symbols sprouting from their sandy yards. The first building appeared the most welcoming, with block letters engraved in the wall, "Come join us in the truth." The second building seemed more adamant, "We have the truth," and the third said, as if it were some kind of debate conducted via proclamation, "Don't be fooled by deceivers."

Many of the churches looked like fortresses with barred windows and security fences. Hellhole seemed to be an irresistible gravitational force attracting many such fringe groups who found no place in the civilized, controlled Constellation. The media often mocked the string of ridiculous cults that came to this planet.

Fernando found it fascinating. "Look at that, Vincent – maybe we should go inside and talk to them." The next building was guarded by a two-meter-tall sculpture of a lemur. Another one had a stern-looking turtle monument out front, which seemed more threatening than welcoming. "Aren't you curious to see what all this means?"

"I'd rather take care of more important business first. Where are we going to stay, how will we get jobs?" He hurried Fernando down the street, past the main cluster of churches, toward large warehouses and busy shops.

When it became clear they weren't just going to bump into someone who would tell them how to find lodgings or work, Vincent said, "Maybe we need to go back. We shouldn't have been in such a hurry to leave the spaceport. The colony office would have been the right place to start." That was obviously the safest alternative.

Fernando made a raspberry sound. "This is our big chance, and I don't want to go backwards. We'll figure it out together, make our own way." He picked up the pace to emphasize his point.

Vincent remained concerned, despite his friend's optimism. "Michella Town doesn't look like the kind of place where somebody holds your hand."

Fernando gave a sniff and strutted along. "We don't want anybody to hold our hands. We came here to be independent and self-sufficient." He shaded his eyes and looked at the structures up and down the streets. "But it would be helpful if someone could just ... point us in the right direction."

Until now, neither man had felt a need to hurry, but Vincent realized that the colony settlement was rapidly turning into a ghost town as people scurried inside and closed doors and shutters. "Where's everybody going? I don't like the looks of this."

As the crowds dwindled, he spotted the young woman from the passenger pod. Antonia Anqui appeared forlorn and shell-shocked, as if the reality of her situation had just sunk in. She met Vincent's gaze, then pretended to be studying one of the nondescript thick-walled buildings. But the door was closed, and metal shutters sealed the windows.

Fernando waved to her. "Hi there! Looks like we're all in the same boat."

Antonia's brows drew together. "I think we've fallen through the cracks."

"At least nobody's bothering us or telling us what to do." Fernando lifted his chin. "Stick with Vincent and me, and we'll get through this."

Vincent frowned. "Not that *we* know what to do. The Constellation didn't prepare us for this."

Fernando made a raspberry sound again. "Oh, they stopped giving a damn about us as soon as they put us on the stringline ship. Sink or swim. Survival of the fittest. Fine with me – we can take care of ourselves."

Antonia gave a silent nod of agreement. Despite his friend's good cheer, Vincent suspected Fernando was hiding something from his past, and maybe Antonia was, too. Most people who came to Hellhole probably had dark marks on their records; he certainly did.

While they were discussing options, Michella Town became oddly still. Restaurants and drinking establishments, which had been wide open only minutes before, now closed their doors, drew down their awnings, and closed their shutters as tightly as blast shields. A few stragglers moved about with seeming urgency, rushing inside.

"Must be afternoon siesta." Fernando let out a nervous laugh. "Seems like they'd lose a lot of business."

Antonia looked around. "Or maybe they know something we don't."

Fernando sighed. "As soon as those shops open up again, I'm going to look for a survival guide. Do either of you have any credits I could use? I, uh, still need to open an account at one of the local financial institutions."

Before Vincent could answer, a low, warbling sound echoed through the town, a mournful siren that built in volume. "What is that?"

Antonia's dark eyes grew round. "Something bad."

"I don't like this." Vincent looked up and down the deserted streets, watched a last few people duck inside buildings and seal the doors. Several of the lower structures began to hum and actually folded themselves closer to the ground to reduce their wind profile.

The siren's tempo increased, generating a sense of real alarm. Vincent shouted, "Spread out, start pounding on doors. Somebody's got to let us in!" He ran to the nearest shuttered shop. He hammered on a door as thick as a spaceship hatch, but nobody answered. He moved to a locked-down dwelling and tried again with the same result.

Within seconds the wind picked up, blowing dust and pebbles along the street. The air's alkaline scent grew noticeably more sour. The sky overhead turned a sickly yellow-green, as if it had suddenly spoiled. A thin arc of silver lightning shot horizontally across the clouds, completing a circuit; moments later, it was followed by a rumbling growl that was uglier and more ominous than any thunder Vincent had ever experienced on Orsini.

The warning siren continued for another minute, then fell silent – which seemed even more ominous. "Looks like everybody with any common sense is off the streets by now," Antonia said.

"I hope it's just some kind of drill," Vincent said, but the knot in his stomach told him otherwise.

"If it's important, they should post signs." Fernando held out his arms with a childlike wonder, staring down at them. "Hey look – ever see anything like this? Every single hair is standing on end."

Vincent realized that his skin had a tingling, fizzing sensation, as if millions of microscopic insects were crawling over it. Antonia's long dark hair began waving and writhing, like a corona around her head.

A second burst of horizontal lightning crossed the clouds, and the deep thunder became a roar. The wind funneled between the buildings with an angry, grinding sound. The moist-metal odor of ozone permeated the air. Thin white bolts sizzled from rooftop to rooftop like a spiderweb of electricity, as if Michella Town had become a giant generator.

"We need to get into a shelter *now!*" Vincent yelled. "The static buildup will be deadly."

Antonia shouted at the silent buildings around them. "Anyone there? Hello!"

At the far end of the street, a hatch door opened on one of the large warehouses. A woman and a gangly young man looked at them with expressions of horror. "Why the hell are you still on the streets? Come on!"

Without hesitation, the three ran towards their rescuers. Ever-increasing bolts of static discharged across the buildings, and the roar overhead sounded like a hungry prehistoric beast. With each breath, Vincent felt as if he had inhaled enough ambient electricity to burn out his lungs.

The young man in the hatchway grabbed Antonia's arm and pulled her inside. Vincent and Fernando practically fell over each other as they dove for cover.

"Are you all crazy? No one stays outside during a growler!" the woman shouted. "Didn't you hear the alarm?"

"Sure, we heard the alarm, but nobody told us what it meant." Fernando seemed amused by the whole adventure. "What's a growler?"

Behind them, whip-lightning skittered along the street, etching black lines of melted dust. The bolts strafed and danced along the side of the warehouse building. Just in time, the woman sealed the hatch shut with a spray of sparks.

Vincent panted hard, and Antonia ran her hands through her wild hair. Grinning with relief, Fernando bowed like a gentleman. "Thank you very much, ma'am. Fernando Neron, at your service. These are my friends, Vincent Jenet and Antonia Anqui."

"I'm Sophie Vence, this is my son Devon – and you three are fools. Why were you just gawking out there like tourists? The weathersats announced this as one of the most powerful static storms on record."

"Good to know it isn't just an average one," Fernando quipped. "I'd hate to put up with that every day while we're here."

Sophie looked upset. "You're obviously newbies. Didn't they go over basic survival skills during your orientation briefing?"

Vincent lowered his eyes. "Sorry, ma'am, but we didn't get any orientation briefing. Once we got off the passenger pod, we've been left to fend for ourselves."

Sophie pressed a hand against her forehead. "Unbelievable! The General's going to hear about this. We don't have time to go rescuing people who have no common sense."

"We had a brochure," Fernando said helpfully, "but it mainly focused on the opportunities we would find here."

Sophie made a disgusted noise. "Typical Constellation crap. Don't believe a word of it."

Devon offered them water, first to Antonia. "Are you all right?"

The young woman drew away from his unwanted attention. "I'll be fine." Her words sounded sharper than she must have intended, and Devon looked crestfallen.

Sophie put her hands on her hips. "Well, you're safe enough in here. This building acts as a Faraday cage." Outside, the static storm continued its furious noises. "Make yourselves comfortable. It'll be a few hours before this rolls over. Do you have someplace to go after that?"

Fernando gave her a warm and enthusiastic smile. "We're open to suggestions."

7

As the car carrying General Adolphus and his unwelcome guest arrived at the headquarters estate, the static storm broke in full fury. Even with the available models and satellite predictions, Adolphus had underestimated the speed and direction of the weather. The brown, crackling mass rolled in behind them like a plague cloud spangled with lightning.

Peering through the windows of the groundcar while the driver, Lt Spencer, raced for shelter, the Diadem's watchdog studied the storm. He was perspiring heavily; beads of sweat glistened like undiscovered gems on his wax-smooth scalp, but he didn't seem panicky, just unsettled that the events were out of his control.

Good, Adolphus thought . . .

Back at the landing field, he had easily identified the Diadem's spy. They all had a certain air about them, a self-important demeanor that kept others at a distance. The large-framed man was younger than his position of importance implied, and despite his physical size, he looked slick, with hyper-alert, pale green eyes; he was solid, not fat, and entirely bald. He wore an airmask over his mouth and nose, though such measures had never been proven necessary on Hellhole; he pulled thin filmgloves onto his hands. At first glance, Adolphus thought the man was a hypochondriac, paranoid about contamination ... but then he changed his assessment. This man had an edge, a power in his confidence; he was not paranoid, but *careful*.

Wearing a full uniform and all his rebellion medals, the General had surprised the spy, smiling with brittle geniality as he introduced himself. Flustered to be spotted so quickly, the watchdog imperiously presented his credentials and put away a meticulous list he had been keeping. "I am Ishop Heer, representative of Diadem Michella Duchenet. Who informed you of this visit? How long have you known I was coming?"

Having met Heer's type before, the General deftly evaded the question. "I have told the Diadem time and again that surprise inspections are unnecessary, since I have nothing to hide. I respect and abide by the terms of my exile. I follow every letter of my promises, because I am an honorable man. Diadem Michella knows that very well by now."

"The Diadem cannot afford to make assumptions when it comes to the peace and security of the Constellation." Ishop sniffed behind his breathing mask, scrutinizing the military outfit. He tucked his list in his pocket. "None of those medals are for service to the Constellation. Odd that you'd wear a defunct uniform. To serve as a reminder that your rebellion failed, Administrator?"

Adolphus refused to be taunted. "I still have a great deal of admiration for this uniform. My intent is to be formal and respectful, as the Diadem requires of me ... but not necessarily considerate."

During the drive from the spaceport, Ishop Heer stared at the buildings and made silent notes about Michella Town as they passed through on the way to the outskirts and the General's main house. He seemed to be drinking in details, filing them away, comparing them to expectations. The man launched his first volley. "After the stringline hauler docked, I spotted a suspicious amount of orbital activity, Administrator. None of the previous inspectors made note of your advanced surface-to-orbit capability."

Adolphus cloaked his annoyance. *Because the previous inspectors were all fools who could either be fooled or bribed outright.* "Territorial Governor Goler always accepted my explanations without question." Goler, whose jurisdiction covered eleven Deep Zone planets ranging from Ridgetop to

Hallholme, actually chose to live out in the DZ rather than back on Sonjeera; the man made dutiful trips to Hallholme, Candela, and the other nine planets he administered ... but he wasn't the most observant person.

"If the Diadem accepted Governor Goler's reports without reservation, then I wouldn't be here," Ishop said. "Hallholme has installed more satellites than any other Deep Zone world seems to need."

Adolphus relaxed. "Fortunately, Mr Heer, the static storm you're about to experience will give you a dramatic demonstration of exactly why we need the sats." Above them, the sky had visibly sickened with the oncoming turmoil. "We have worse weather than any other DZ world. Our climatologists have to rewrite their models after each major storm."

"When will it hit?" Ishop looked out to the darkening sky as they left the outer buildings of the colony town behind.

The driver turned around. "I had hoped to outrun it, General, but it'll most likely catch up with us before we reach HQ."

"Increase speed, Lieutenant."

The spy gave Adolphus a dubious look, as if he were being tricked, but the skies continued to blacken, and horizontal lightning bursts appeared overhead. The General decided to make Ishop squirm just a bit more. "It's a bad storm, too – should last for hours. Our weathersats have mapped its extent. Lieutenant Spencer, it might be best if we hurry it up a bit more. Best speed."

"Yes, General." The driver accelerated the vehicle to its maximum speed for the final kilometer.

A furious rumble rolled across the sky, accompanied by a dancing strobe-display of horizontal lightning. Surface-to-sky bursts tore up the landscape, exploding little craters in the dirt. Ishop Heer looked quite satisfactorily intimidated. He adjusted his breathing mask, tugged at his filmgloves.

Still staring ahead, Adolphus said, "You see why we place so much importance on satellite launches and climate monitoring?"

The Diadem's inspector did not argue.

The General had built his home and administrative headquarters several kilometers outside of Michella Town, and now the vehicle arrived at the big estate as the weather grew worse. The large, rustic manor house had gables, a shaded porch, and numerous wide windows flanked by armored shutters. In a crude approximation of a lawn, native vegetation had been cultivated so that it spread out in a mossy, turquoise-colored swath; other sections of landscaping contained languidly swaying lumpy ferns and knotted, hardy groundcover.

His loyal men had insisted on creating a worthy residence for their revered commander, and while Adolphus did not require the extravagance or spaciousness of a mansion, he *did* want to demonstrate a tangible hope that this rugged frontier world could become civilized.

"Welcome to my estate. I've named it Elba – for obvious reasons." He smiled over at Ishop Heer, a subtle attempt to put the man in his place, to make him feel inadequate. No one in the Constellation bothered with ancient Earth military history, and the man couldn't possibly have any idea what he was talking about.

"Frankly, it might have been more appropriate if you named it St Helena," Ishop said with a sniff. He adjusted his breathing mask. "After his exile to the original Elba, the military leader Napoleon – whom you so obviously admire, Administrator – was able to escape and cause further havoc for the legitimate government. After he was defeated and sent to St Helena, though, he died a broken man."

Adolphus was surprised at the man's knowledge, even delighted. Not a single one of the previous inspectors had even recognized Napoleon's name. There was something different about this man. "You know your history, Mr Heer."

"I did my research on *you*, Administrator. Your interests are no secret to the Diadem, or to me." Behind his facemask, he was probably smiling.

Just as the storm's violent fringe cracked open around them, the driver pulled the groundcar into the underground parking bay, where they were safe from the weather. Ishop climbed out, brushed off his formal garments, and looked around as if expecting a welcoming party. He tugged his gloves to straighten them. "You are required to give me full access and accommodations until my inspection is complete, Administrator. I need to see your home, your offices, your records."

"As always, I will do precisely as Diadem Michella commands." Adolphus kept his voice stiff, giving the inspector no clue as to his state of mind.

With the big storm rolling about outside, the residence house seemed large and empty. Adolphus had live-in servants, security officers, and part-time staff, but upon receiving the weather report, he'd let them return to their families in town. For the most part, it was just him and the Diadem's spy in the big house.

Maintaining a cool smile and bland attitude, he showed his unwelcome guest through the large kitchens and past a meeting room, a series of offices used by government clerks and his household manager, a room full of filing cabinets, and a few empty offices available for use when the colony size expanded; intent only on the main records, Heer apparently found none of the rooms interesting. He noted several comments on his list, without showing them to the General. Adolphus did not offer the man refreshments, nor did Heer ask for any. Once inside the building, however, he did remove his facemask.

Ishop Heer finally perked up when they entered the General's private study, which contained his collection of old books, journals, mementoes, and trophies he had collected during the five-year-long rebellion. He stood before a framed piece of wreckage, labeled as shrapnel from one of Adolphus's fallen ships. "Do you keep so many items as a reminder of your loss, Administrator?"

"Not at all, Mr Heer. I keep them so that there remains an *accurate* record of what happened. I've seen the official histories."

The inspector's lips pursed in a sour pout, but he chose not to continue the argument.

In bright pools of light in places of honor, vitrines held six contorted, half-melted artifacts of decidedly non-human origin – rare scraps from Hallholme's original alien civilization that had been annihilated by the asteroid impact. Long fascinated by the strange detritus, Adolphus had posted a standing bounty for alien artifacts of any kind. Because the cosmic strike had created a worldwide holocaust, he doubted any functional relics would ever be found, but he held onto hope. He liked to gaze into the transparent display cases, pondering the vanished civilization.

The storm continued to whirl outside, muffled by the armored shutters sealed across the windows. Now that he was in the protection of the house, Ishop Heer focused intently on his business. "I demand to see your daily logs, Administrator, so that I may compare them with all filings since the formation of the colony. I also have the reports of previous inspectors, tribute auditors and planetary-resource assessors. I have a job to do, and you have no choice but to cooperate." His threat sounded hollow.

"By all means." Adolphus allowed the man to sit at his own desk – a moderately generous gesture – called up the databases for Ishop Heer and let him pore over the information. "So you think you can find something that all of your predecessors missed?"

The spy sounded matter-of-fact, not arrogant. He took out his list. "I'm better at the job than they were. We'll see if your nose is as clean as you'd like us to believe."

"Yes, we'll see. You have full access. Take as long as you like." Adolphus stepped away.

The documents were complete fabrications, of course – there were details he didn't dare let Michella discover – but these files should be accurate enough to satisfy Ishop Heer.

As the man read screen after screen, checking off items on his own notes and ignoring his host, Adolphus pulled one of the old volumes from a shelf and relaxed in a comfortable chair, feigning insouciance. Diadem Michella still hadn't figured out how he and his followers survived their first year here, after she had stacked the deck so heavily against him by omitting vital supplies and medicines, mislabeling food stocks, giving them defective tools and materials.

She had set them up to fail ... and yet, they hadn't.

Living on Sonjeera, surrounded by the glory of the capital city and her well-heeled advisers, the Diadem grossly underestimated how much support remained for his rebellion, even under her own nose. Among his banished soldiers were engineers, supply sergeants, biological experts, special ops crews, survivalists. Before he departed on his voyage of shame, Adolphus had sent out an invitation to the soldiers' families and friends, and – to his surprise – many accepted, choosing to forsake the rotten core of the Constellation.

Better to rule on Hellhole than to serve on Sonjeera.

While delivering the exiles, the Constellation stringline captain had smuggled Adolphus a storage crystal containing a complete database of Hallholme survey records, which helped the General and his experts make plans for their colony. That had made a great deal of difference.

After the stringline hauler departed, leaving them on the bleak planet, with no further contact expected for at least a month, Adolphus addressed those who had accompanied him into exile. "Once again, we must fight an adversary named Hallholme to survive – the planet this time, not the Commodore."

Such a bold undertaking would never have succeeded with a random group of people, but these fighters had served with him, sworn their lives to him. The General ran the fledgling colony like a military operation. He inventoried his personnel and their skills, mapped out the path to survival, kept a careful database of foodstuffs, seed stock, machinery.

Immediately laying out the grid for the main town, Adolphus dispatched scouts to explore resources – aquifers, metal deposits, native vegetation that could be processed into something useful, minerals and building stone. His teams set up greenhouse domes, foundries, bare-bones manufacturing centers, power plants. Drilling crews got the water pumping and purified; military engineers erected shelters designed to endure the harsh climate (what little was known of it). The banished workers built generators, activated energy cells, planted and harvested crops.

They survived the first year by the narrowest of margins.

Only Adolphus knew how close it was. Long before the prepackaged supplies ran out, he reviewed the accounting, did a physical inventory, met with his supply sergeants, calculated what they would need ... and the numbers didn't add up. The Diadem had intentionally reduced the promised shipments and given them too little to live on.

However, General Adolphus still had friends working behind the scenes back in the Crown Jewels. Undocumented supplies arrived in the downboxes on the next stringline delivery, additional protein to supplement the harvest from the domed greenhouses. For seven months, the colonists continued to find surreptitious stashes that appeared on no manifest.

And then the extra packages had stopped, abruptly. Adolphus suspected something bad had happened to the nameless sympathizers, but he doubted he would ever know. Regardless, those smuggled supplies had been enough to get them over the hump. Michella must have been extremely frustrated ...

Adolphus let Ishop Heer continue his work for hours. At first, the General remained in the room, making for an intentionally uncomfortable environment. The Diadem's aide always knew the General was breathing down his neck, watching him … but Ishop didn't seem to mind. He concentrated on the records with the intensity of a patient yet hungry predator.

Eventually, Adolphus went off to dinner, offering none to the other man. The act was petty, but by making his anger and annoyance plain, Adolphus showed Ishop what he expected to see (and the anger was indeed real).

Even while the General dined, Ishop did not leave his work. Hidden imagers monitored the inspector the whole time. The static-storm continued to rage at its full intensity, but Elba was shielded and safe.

When Adolphus returned to the study, Ishop had his notes stacked neatly, his screen turned to face the door. He already had the Hellhole records that were presented to the regular tribute auditors – files that the General doctored in order to minimize the apparent resources of Hellhole, thus reducing what he was required to pay to the Constellation. Adolphus also kept another set of files that he referred to as "the real records."

Ishop wore a look of triumph. "Your fascination with Napoleon is your undoing, Administrator." He leaned back in the chair, enjoying the moment. "You've been caught."

"Caught at what, Mr Heer?" A brief chill ran down his spine, but he showed none of it.

"I found your secure records containing the coded locations of additional mining operations, metal deposits, profitable industries. Secret files under a deeply hidden directory named St Helena. Did you really think I wouldn't eventually guess your password of *Josephine?*" He sounded immensely pleased with himself as he tapped the screen. "None of the previous inspectors discovered that you've got an entire secondary network of resources. Tin mines, copper mines, iron mines – fifteen in all. Two smelters and mills. None of which were recorded on your accounting sheets."

"Those are merely pilot projects," Adolphus said, knowing the answer wouldn't hold up under detailed scrutiny. "I have hundreds of test shafts and geological surveys. Not all of them are viable. Are you saying the Diadem would like me to include a shipment of raw bauxite as part of our next tribute payment?"

"It seems profitable enough," Ishop said. "These resources increase the calculations of this planet's net worth, which affects the amount of tribute you owe. The mere fact that you would conceal them from the Diadem raises questions. She has long suspected you of hiding information from her."

Adolphus clenched his jaw, looking both angry and guilty, and Ishop reveled in his reaction. For years, the Diadem's inspectors had poked around, showing their lack of imagination, frustrated because they never found anything. This man had actually followed the hidden hints that none of the others noticed.

Finally, Adolphus said, "I am impressed."

The second set of records was a red herring, however. The General had established and buried them long ago just in case he needed a bone to throw to any particularly persistent spy – a handful of mines that were no more productive or exciting than most others. Adolphus knew he would be fined, and supposedly embarrassed, but the Diadem's man rejoiced in his victory, so the hidden information had served its purpose. Let the Diadem think she had caught him.

Ishop sniffed, making a great show of checking off the last item on his list. "You remind us constantly that you are an honorable man, Administrator Adolphus. You built a tall pedestal for yourself, but your feet are made of clay just like so many others. You have cheated and lied. How is that honorable?"

Adolphus just laughed. "Perhaps you don't understand honor, Mr Heer. I made binding promises to the Diadem. I swore to pay the tribute that Sonjeera's inspectors determined to be appropriate. I did not, however, swear to tell the whole truth to my enemy. I haven't broken my word – look at the document for yourself."

"I have memorized it." Ishop hesitated, his brow furrowing as he went over the words in his mind. "You deliberately misconstrued its intent."

"No, I deliberately paid attention – very close attention – to what I agreed to do."

"And now your secret is out." The inspector turned from the data screens with a frustrated scowl. "I believe I've seen all I need to. I have factored in the additional productivity. Your required payment will henceforth increase, and I will impose penalties for your indiscretion."

"It was a risk I chose to take." Adolphus shrugged. "Otherwise, everything is in order?"

"It appears to be."

Adolphus knew what he was supposed to say, like a formal set of procedures on a checklist. "Therefore, I've cooperated with you fully, according to the terms of our agreement? Have I fulfilled my obligations to you, the duly appointed inspector from the Constellation?"

It must have seemed like a victory he didn't want to give the General, but Ishop had no choice. "Yes, you have, Administrator. I believe I am finished." He looked ready to sign a receipt, if asked.

"Good. Follow me, please." At a brisk pace, Adolphus led the Diadem's watchdog past a withdrawing room and the banquet hall, where he hosted receptions when Sophie Vence insisted. He wished she could be with him now. On a stormy night like this, it would have been good to sit by the fire, just the two of them, enjoying a fine meal and relaxing in each other's company.

Instead, he had this intruder . . .

When the two men reached the front entry that led out to the open porch, General Adolphus opened the door. With a blast of wind and a crackle of blown dust, he revealed the full force of the bombastic holocaust outside. Thanks to the storm, they couldn't even see the bright lights of Michella Town.

Taken aback by the fury of the weather, Ishop hesitated on the threshold. He fumbled for his facemask, adjusted his gloves. Adolphus tried to nudge him forward, but the man didn't budge.

Adolphus said, "You have finished your work, Mr Heer – you said so yourself. I cooperated fully during the inspection, but I am not required to have anything further to do with you. Out you go. I'm not an innkeeper, and you're no longer welcome in my home." He gave another push, harder this time, and Ishop scrambled for footing on the porch. "Good luck finding your way back to town. It's only a few kilometers."

Blinking at the wind and lightning blasts, the visitor grew pale. "You can't possibly send me out into a storm like that."

"I most certainly can. As of this moment, you are trespassing. You should leave."

The inspector gaped at him in disbelief. "I won't last more than five minutes out there!" Sweat stood out on his scalp again.

"Oh, I'd guess substantially less than five minutes, but you could surprise me. Keep your head down when you run."

"I refuse!"

"But *you* were the one who insisted on my absolute adherence to the strict exile agreement, Mr Heer. I am fully within my rights."

The Diadem's man lowered his voice to an angry growl. "If you would do this to me, then you are indeed a monster."

"Exactly as your history books portray me. Don't you read your own propaganda?"

Ishop was at a loss for words, realizing his unaccustomed powerlessness in this situation. Adolphus let the tension build in the air for a few moments longer, then, having pushed the matter far enough, he relented. He took a step back and lowered his voice. "Anyone who would abandon a person to such a hostile place is indeed a monster. Wait ... that's exactly what Diadem Michella did to me and my followers. Do you know how many we lost during the first year here, because of storms like this and countless other hazards?"

Ishop nodded nervously in spite of himself. "I ... take your point, Administrator."

"Don't believe everything you read about me, Mr Heer."

Ishop swallowed, tugged at his gloves again. "May I formally request an extension of your hospitality until such time as the weather improves?"

"If you insist. But once the storm is over, you can walk to town and find other lodgings there." He let the man back inside, and closed the door behind them. His ears rang from the sudden silence. "As soon as the next stringline hauler arrives, I expect you'll be on your way back to the Diadem with your report."

8

Sonjeera was the loveliest world in the Constellation, beneficial to the harmony of the human spirit. Princess Keana's favorite residence, commonly known as the Cottage, stood on the same expansive grounds as the Diadem's palace, but set well apart from her mother's home. More than eight centuries ago, Philippe the Whisperer, one of the most famous diadems in the old Constellation, had built the luxurious retreat on the edge of the Pond of Birds for his beautiful wife, Aria Ongenet, who met her numerous lovers there with careful discretion, so as not to embarrass the reigning sovereign.

Keana's official obligations as the Diadem's daughter were not exactly time-consuming – dedicating the occasional government building, opening orphanages, attending charity functions, cutting ribbons on new museums, making appearances at children's hospitals, or christening stringline ships. It only amounted to a few hours or days here and there, so she had plenty of time to muse about the noble bloodlines and entanglements in the Duchenet family tree. She was required to do little else.

Keana had chafed for years at the limitations and expectations placed on her. A wasted life! She had felt sorry for herself and very much alone until two years ago, when she'd found Louis de Carre. After that, her life was filled with love and excitement, colors, possibilities. She was so tired of playing by the rules!

In the whirlwind of their passion, Keana and her exuberant lover barely paid lip service to keeping their affair a secret. If her own husband didn't mind, and she had no political career anyway, why should Keana bother with the effort?

A tall, shapely woman, she was in her prime and quite pretty, with a young face, dark blue eyes, and shoulder-length auburn hair. Her handmaidens and advisers claimed she was beautiful enough not to need makeup, though her nitpicking mother (who spent more than an hour being "prepared" for each of her public appearances) disagreed. Diadem Michella had something critical to say on virtually every subject.

As the ruler's only child, Keana had grown up on the royal estate, destined to be a showpiece, not qualified for any position of political significance. When Diadem Michella retired or died, Keana would be given a stipend and an estate, and she would finish out her life in quiet ennui. By law, no Duchenet could become Diadem again for at least another generation.

As a little girl, Keana had come to the Cottage often, riding in an old carriage drawn by a team of gaxen, a species of draft animal unique to Sonjeera. At the serene pond's edge, she would listen as the carriage drivers told tales of intrigue and death. One of Aria Ongenet's lovers, a nobleman half her age, was said to have thrown himself into the churning wheel of the nearby water mill, because she refused to divorce her husband and marry him. Keana thought that a passion so profound should have overcome the hurdle of a loveless marriage. Now, with sweet Louis, she comprehended true love.

More than a decade ago, her mother's political machinations had forced Keana to marry Lord Bolton Crais, a dithering and lackluster nobleman from an influential family. She considered the man dull in the extreme, though sweet enough in his own way. Bolton had some military and administrative abilities, having served as a logistics officer in the war against General Adolphus. He hadn't particularly wanted to marry her either, or anyone else, but he did as his family asked. Bolton was never cruel to her, never unpleasant, probably not even unfaithful; in fact, he wasn't much of *anything*. And Keana didn't love him.

Louis was quite different. Though almost twenty years older than she was, the widowed Vielinger nobleman had a full head of black hair and did not look or act his actual age. A charming, witty man of extensive education, Louis always managed to surprise Keana with his kindness, his humor, his tenderness.

With Louis, at least, she felt important. During his frequent visits to Sonjeera, supposedly on business, Keana would set up an assignation at the Cottage. Their relationship gave her the excitement she craved, a taste of true passion instead of dutiful inter-family alliances. She felt alive for the first time, and Louis actually discussed things with Keana – revealing to her an entire universe beyond Sonjeera . . .

At the Cottage, a series of small pools of varying geometric shapes formed a decorative necklace around the inside courtyard and central pool. Short tunnels connected the pools, allowing swimmers to dive into one and emerge from another; one long tunnel led all the way to the Pond of Birds. According to legend, two drownings had occurred as Aria Ongenet encouraged young noblemen to swim longer and longer distances as the price of her favors. After Aria's death, the long tunnel to the pond had been sealed off for centuries, until Louis asked to have it reopened.

"You have nothing to prove – you've already won my love," Keana insisted when Louis first suggested swimming all of the pools underwater. His daring impulsiveness was precisely the opposite of the staid, conventional Bolton Crais.

"It's not for you that I must prove it," Louis said. "It is for myself."

He stood in his red-and-gold swimsuit, gazing at the pools and considering the route he had decided to swim: all of the pools at once without coming up for air, including a passage through what he dubbed the "Tunnel of Death." Keana did not find the facetious name the least bit amusing. The dashing nobleman had a muscular body, but he was no longer as young as he thought he was.

Wearing a long blue summer dress with the Duchenet crest on the collar, she raised herself on tiptoes to kiss him. With a wink, Louis said, "I'll think of a new love poem for you while I'm swimming." Then he dove smoothly into the central pool and swam underwater faster than she'd ever seen him go.

She watched him traverse each pool, never missing a stroke. With nervous steps, she hurried along the above-ground path to follow his progress, frustrated with his impetuosity.

Their relationship was not much of a secret; poor Bolton pretended not to notice that he was being cuckolded, turned a deaf ear to the whispered gossip, but he wasn't stupid. He and Keana had an "understanding," and he was willing to overlook his wife's activities.

But her mother knew that Keana and her husband kept separate bedrooms, even separate residences most of the time. The lack of children to carry on the Duchenet (and Crais) bloodlines remained a cause for friction. Diadem Michella had not borne her own daughter until quite late in her child-bearing years.

Once, in a heated argument, Michella had said, "If you can't let Bolton give you a proper heir, you'd better not get pregnant by any of your other lotharios." Incensed by the suggestion of promiscuity, Keana had stormed out of the Diadem's palace and taken up permanent residence at the Cottage. There had been no one else for her besides Louis, not even dutiful sex with her husband for the past two years. Lord de Carre already had his own son and heir, the competent and reliable Cristoph who had recently taken over management of the Vielinger iperion mines so that Louis could devote his attention to her.

Now Keana stood over the entrance to the long tunnel, looking down with concern and excitement as her lover stroked across the last small pool and then entered the dark waterway. Unable to see him anymore, she ran the length of the tunnel above ground to the outlet at the pond. Even here in the open air, she felt out of breath, and her heart was pounding.

Why didn't he surface? It was taking too long! Then she spotted movement just offshore in the murky pond, and Louis's head and arms shot out of the water. He gasped for air, struggling to breathe. Not caring about her dress, Keana jumped into the pool and stood in the waist-deep water, holding him close. She felt his heart beating against hers, and she stroked his dark, wet hair. "Now will you stop being so foolish? There's nothing you need to prove. Not to me or yourself."

Louis wiped water from his face, looked at her with a bemused expression. "Your dress and hair are soaked, my dearest."

She gave a rueful laugh, kissed him, then pushed away and swam across the pond. He caught up to her and said, "Here, let me help you with that." In the warm water, he pulled at the wet fabric. She kissed his neck as he carried her to the grass, leaving her discarded dress to float in the pond.

Afterward, as they lay naked and spent from making love, he looked up at the willows and complained about having to do actual business while here on Sonjeera. "You so easily make me lose track of time, my sweet – not just the hours, but the days as well. I've just realized I'm supposed to be at an important vote regarding Vielinger this afternoon, or maybe it was this morning."

She sighed, running a fingertip down his chest. "Politics. Do you really have to go?"

"I've probably already missed it, and I'd much rather be here with you, where I can forget all that nonsense."

She brightened. "No one will notice you're not there?"

"Oh, they'll notice all right. They'll make another attempt to weaken the de Carre family, and scheming noblemen have been trying to do that for centuries. Don't worry, they never succeed."

"Your son is managing the iperion operations," she said. "Everything is in good hands."

"The best." He smiled at her. "The nobles will argue and they'll vote, and then they'll argue again. Nothing ever changes. The Riominis keep trying to take my planet away from me, with one scheme after another. Today will be no different, whether or not I'm there. And I'd much prefer to spend the afternoon in your delightful company."

She laughed, knowing the Council of Lords would be upset by Louis's lack of seriousness. Let them huff and puff!

A troubled shadow crossed his face, though. "Of late, however, their efforts have crossed a line. Someone is sabotaging my iperion mines, making Cristoph look incompetent, though he can't possibly be to blame. Some of the citizens are even angry at me! How can that be? I have always been concerned about the welfare of my people. I think I'll make a statement in open council session one of these days, just to set the record straight."

Keana wanted to do something to help. "Would you like me to talk with my mother about it?"

Louis looked at her with a sad, endearing expression. "No offense, my darling, but your job is to grace Sonjeera's social events with your presence and be decorative, not to twist arms."

The remark stung, but Keana could not dispute the truth.

9

To the untrained eye, the cavern conditions might have appeared normal, but Cristoph de Carre knew otherwise. Tense mine operators and engineers in sealed worksuits hurried about their tasks, supervising remote-controlled machines. Extraction skimmers hovered over the blue-veined walls, peeling off raw iperion without damaging its delicate structure. The sensitive mineral was unstable before processing and had to be mined in micro-thin layers and kept very cold, otherwise it would be rendered useless for stringline purposes. The skimmers looked like fat bees with bulbous refrigerated storage compartments on their bodies to hold the harvested iperion.

"A few more veins and this part of the mine will be played out, my Lord." Lanny Oberon raised his voice to be heard above the drone of the extraction machines. He adjusted a setting below the faceplate of his sealed suit, shutting off the taslight on top of his helmet.

Cristoph did the same with his borrowed work suit. Garish work lights and various improvised fixtures gave the cavern plenty of illumination. "Then we'll just have to look harder for other veins, Lanny. Vielinger can't possibly be wrung dry." De Carre family fortunes had depended on the mines for centuries, and even the most conservative estimates suggested the supplies would last for another two decades at least. Still, it was cause for him to be concerned about his family's future, knowing that the boom days of the previous century were past.

Cristoph stood with the mining foreman on an observation platform that vibrated underfoot. On the cavern floor below, one worker rolled a portable tool cart up to a control panel that flashed a red error light. "It's still profitable to get the last harvest from the deepest tunnels, but let's try to finish our excavations without any further accidents."

Recently, there had been too many equipment malfunctions and workplace mistakes to be considered coincidence; he knew he had good people. Cristoph suspected outside involvement but couldn't prove it. He had posted additional guards at the mine facilities, processing operations, and shipping warehouses, but some said it simply made him look paranoid.

Inside his suit, Cristoph coughed several times, finally clearing the tickle in his throat. "Stuff manages to get through even state-of-the-art filter systems." The ultrafine deep-shaft dust, a byproduct of iperion extraction, was known to cause severe lung deterioration.

Oberon sympathized. "That's why we get the big paychecks, my Lord. The men know the risks and still come to work. As the iperion gets tougher to extract, the value goes up . . . and so do our shares. I can put up with a little dust."

"Of course, if someone found a new source of iperion on another Crown Jewel world, or even out in the Deep Zone, the bottom would fall out of the market," Cristoph pointed out. "And maybe we wouldn't be such a desirable target."

"They haven't found any other sources yet, my Lord. We've got to make the best of this one." Looking weary, Oberon immersed his gloved hands deep in the pockets of his dirty gray work suit. "I'm glad you've come to watch over us, sir. Haven't seen your father in some time. He's away on Sonjeera again?"

The criticism was plain in the mine supervisor's voice. Despite his annoyance at his aloof father, Cristoph felt he had to make excuses. "He spends most of his time there now. He's had to participate in a number of important votes with the Council of Lords."

The answer felt awkward because it was only partly true. Cristoph knew damned well that his father's priority was not "business." He hated how much the man had changed, turning his attentions to a hedonistic and carefree life now that the Diadem's daughter had seduced him from his responsibilities. And, with Lord de Carre abrogating his duties in favor of a sordid affair, Cristoph had to bear more and more responsibility for Vielinger.

His mother had died twenty-eight years ago of a degenerative neurological disease; she'd barely held on long enough to give birth to him. Now that his father was so frequently unavailable, Cristoph wished more than ever that she were still alive. According to the household staff, his mother had been excellent at business, helping oversee the family's commercial operations. She was sorely needed.

Louis de Carre, on the other hand, had no talent for management. He was a dandy who spent time in various expensive court activities without giving much thought to the family's commercial operations. It was up to Cristoph to fill the void and keep the de Carre holdings intact.

Raised by a succession of tutors and nannies, Cristoph had never enjoyed a close relationship with his father. Gradually, the young man's talents as a money manager and business administrator had emerged, but the noble family had problems far more serious than he could handle. Despite the profitability of the iperion operations, previous generations of de Carres had engaged in profligate spending, sinking the family into debt that could not realistically be paid off even during boom times. And already geologists had spotted plenty of telltale signs that the readily accessible veins would be gone soon.

Cristoph watched the efficient remote-controlled skimmers go about their business, stripping molecules from the walls. When their bulbous storage compartments reached capacity, the machines flew to an unloading station, where the filled units were swapped for empty ones. Mine workers handled the skimmers carefully, loading them into padded trays that rode a slow conveyor for stabilization and processing.

When Cristoph finished his inspection, he shook Oberon's hand and returned to the surface on his own. After changing out of the sealed work suit, he boarded a copter for the flight back to the family estate. On the return trip, he sat glumly by the window, staring out without seeing much of anything.

Cristoph had dug deep into the already strapped personal accounts to fund additional survey missions, core samples, satellite deep-scans in the hunt for heretofore undiscovered iperion. Thus far, they had found only two hair-thin veins in marginally accessible areas. He had instructed that the producing mine tunnels be widened and deepened to tease out additional scraps of the mineral, despite the added cost.

For the short-term, rumors of the scarcity of iperion drove up the price, but the harvesting operations were also more difficult. Even with fears that the iperion would last only another generation at most, Vielinger was a target for greedy nobles. Several rival families had already put forward motions in the Council of Lords to take the planet away from the de Carre family, citing iperion's "vital nature to the security of the Constellation." At times, Cristoph considered simply handing over the planet to the Riominis who wanted it so badly. Let them see for themselves that it was a bad investment.

For years, aware that ultimately there was a limited supply of iperion, stringline physicists had been searching for an alternate material that could serve as a quantum marker for the space lanes. Cristoph didn't doubt they would succeed sooner or later, most likely when prices grew extremely high; desperation drove innovation. As soon as one of the scientists announced an alternative, however, the iperion market would collapse, and no one would want Vielinger anymore.

In the meantime, the Riominis were trying every possible trick to drive Cristoph's family from their home. It was all a strategy game to them.

Though his father was on Sonjeera during this crisis, Louis did nothing to stand up against the power grab. Lord de Carre was completely oblivious to the true danger. The few messages Cristoph had received from his father in the past three weeks merely complimented the young man on his work and unnecessarily warned him to watch out for saboteurs.

Outsiders criticized the de Carre family, and Cristoph personally, for poor safety conditions and the purported maltreatment of miners, although he maintained a rigorous schedule of inspections and implemented stringent safety protocols. Some conspiracy rumors asserted that the de Carres were intentionally hiding substantial iperion reserves, just to drive up the price.

When representatives of other noble families came to Vielinger like vultures circling, ostensibly under orders from the Diadem herself,

Cristoph was required to offer his full cooperation. Pressure was increasing to let other noble families perform independent geological surveys and find new deposits of the dwindling resource, or for the de Carres to relinquish the iperion mines altogether.

For more than a thousand years his family had ruled Vielinger. Some of Cristoph's ancestors had been diadems, famous philosophers, humanitarians – a family legacy that now seemed to be crashing down around him.

Meanwhile, his father cavorted with the Diadem's married daughter, without a care in the world. Keana Duchenet was undoubtedly leading him on, duping him, probably as part of a plot with her mother. Cristoph didn't know why his father couldn't see it.

10

ight had fallen by the time the static storm passed. Each of Sophie Vence's warehouses was equipped with cots, a kitchen area, sanitary facilities, and emergency supplies, since her employees had no idea when they might need to ride out an unexpected weather event. While they were cooped up together, she and Devon got to know their guests.

"Can they stay here with us tonight?" he asked his mother. Raised on Hellhole, Devon would never abandon a person who needed assistance.

"They can bunk here, and tomorrow we'll find them temporary jobs." She looked at Fernando, Vincent, and Antonia. "There's plenty of cleanup to do after a big storm."

"We'd very much like to get established, ma'am," said Vincent Jenet. "I'm a good employee, and you'll find me very reliable."

"We appreciate your hospitality," Antonia said.

"You can make up for it tomorrow and earn your keep."

After dark, Sophie left Devon with the others inside the warehouse and ventured out into the dark and quiet streets. Though her line managers Carter and Elbert had transmitted reports to her, she wanted to make her own assessment of the damage done to her buildings and employees.

A bitter-tasting fog crawled through the streets like a miasma of disease. Sophie wore a thin filter over her mouth and nose, but her eyes burned. Alkaline dust coated the windows of the low rounded dwellings, so that only murky orange light seeped out from well-lit interiors.

A blanket of dust also coated her main greenhouse domes, which made the artificially lit hemispheres glow like gigantic luminescent gumdrops. Tomorrow she would sign out a few crane platforms and hoses to blast away the residue from the dust fog.

She walked along the street, greeting the hardy souls who were out and about getting a head start on the cleanup. Some townspeople used brushes to sweep away the corrosive debris or operated high-pressure blowers to clear out the cracks and crannies.

One of the men coughed heavily as he wiped off the transparent flower dome in front of his home, and Sophie clucked at him, "Put on a respirator, Rendy – are you crazy?"

"I only expected to be out here for half an hour."

"And how's that working out for you?" He tried to respond, but ended up coughing instead. Sophie gave him a stern frown; sometimes she felt like a den mother to these people. "Listen to me – it's not a weakness to be sensible about hazards. You should know that by now."

The man coughed again, his eyes irritated and red. "All right, I'll get a damn mask."

Adolphus's tough leadership kept the colonists safe, but Sophie used a lighter touch. The two made a perfect pair. Their relationship was no secret to most people in Helltown, even though the General believed he was being discreet. Thinking like an administrator and a man, he felt that gossip would be too disruptive for the status quo. To Sophie, that excuse had a whiff of bullshit. She found it ironic that all the way out here in the Deep Zone, Adolphus seemed to be as concerned about appearances as the old Diadem was.

Nevertheless, after her disastrous first marriage she was satisfied with their relationship as it was. Despite the lessons she had learned from hard experience, she still considered herself a romantic at heart.

On Klief, one of the old Crown Jewel planets, she had married a charismatic and ambitious corporate climber, five years older than she. Gregory Vence courted her with talk as convincing as any boardroom speech, and after they were married he was proud, as if it were his accomplishment alone, when she gave birth to their son Devon.

She and Gregory, though, had very different visions of her role in their future. Sophie had planned on a successful business career of her own; while she tended the baby, she continued her studies at home, learning about management, supply chains, and resource allocation. But when, on Devon's first birthday, she wanted to start searching for a suitable job, Gregory intervened, persuading her that the formative years were vital for their son.

By the time Devon was four and ready to enter early schooling, Gregory still found reasons for her to stay home; convincingly gracious on the surface, he used subtle ways to erode her confidence. When she eventually realized what he was doing, she became angry enough to take matters into her own hands.

Sophie applied for mid-level positions, only to be turned down again and again. After considerable research, she learned that Gregory had been intercepting her applications, poisoning her references, turning potential employers against her. She read confidential reports in which her own husband portrayed her as emotional and unstable; he suggested with saccharine sympathy that Sophie had been away from the real world for so long that she no longer understood it.

Sophie was furious. She filed for divorce and decided to make her own way in life, but by then Gregory Vence had become a well-connected man, and he fought her every step of the way. So much for young romance.

Though the court ordered Gregory to pay child support, he resisted, he refused, he "forgot," and so Sophie had to fight him on that as well. Never giving up, she eked out a living at low-level jobs and began to work her way up. Despite being sidelined for almost nine years, she was back on track.

Then Gregory filed court papers demanding not only that she be stripped of all rights to child and spousal support, but requesting full custody of Devon as well. That absurd legal action convinced her that as long as she stayed on Klief, she would never be free of Gregory. In spite of all she had lost, she still had her self-esteem and her son.

The Deep Zone planets had opened to new colonization only a year earlier. Hallholme seemed particularly hard and challenging, a place that needed her administrative skills. Sophie didn't want to go to a planet with an already entrenched bureaucracy. Hallholme would indeed be a challenge, but Sophie decided that it was exactly the sort of place where she could make a difference and find opportunities for herself and Devon. Best of all, Gregory would never bother to follow her to a place like that.

Before the ponderous wheels of the legal system could catch up with her, Sophie packed their possessions, cashed in her small bank accounts, and boarded a stringline hauler with Devon, leaving no forwarding address.

Even with the damned static storms and the smelly air, Hellhole wasn't so bad compared with the crap she'd left behind. Sophie had done well for herself in Helltown.

After walking the neighborhood, making note of any storm damage. Sophie made her way back to the warehouse to catch some sleep.

The next dawn, Sophie became boss instead of nurturer. She roused Vincent, Fernando, and Antonia from their bunks and told Devon to find suits for the three guests. "My son will show you how to gear up. Wear masks, eye shields, and gloves. After that storm, even long-time Hellhole residents need protection – and as newbies, you'll react badly to all the junk in the air."

"How badly?" Vincent picked up the suit Devon had handed him and tried to figure out how to don it.

"Inflammation and rashes. A cough."

Devon groaned. "The intestinal bug is the worst."

Fernando never let his optimism diminish. "I've got an iron constitution."

Sophie made several calls, reassigning work crews from regular duties to salvage her precious vineyards. The teams rendezvoused in front of the main warehouse and climbed into flatbeds that rumbled out to low hills covered with a corduroy of grapevines.

At the sight of the grayish-green powder that coated her vine stock, Sophie felt sick. She pulled the flatbed to a halt near where two crews had already arrived. "That stuff is going to kill my vines! Get out there, concentrate on the leaves and any grapes that are forming." She didn't want to think what the alkaline residue would do to the red wine's taste. All the more reason to clean off the dust as quickly as possible.

Rolling water tanks followed the suited crews up and down the vineyard rows; they used a liberal spray to rinse the hard, unripe grape clusters. Fernando Neron was thoroughly entertained by his high-power blower that scoured the dust away with bursts of air. Vincent worked alongside his friend, revisiting sloppy parts with meticulous attention to detail, and between the two of them they did a thorough job.

Devon was shy and tongue-tied around Antonia Anqui at first, but he made excuses to talk with her, offering unnecessary instructions on how to use the blower; he chatted about the varieties of grape vines they had tried, telling her how long ago they'd been planted and when his mother's vintners had bottled the first vintage; he was excited about the new Reisling rootstock that had just arrived on the stringline hauler. Sophie knew that her shy son had never met anyone on Hellhole like this girl. In her opinion, they would make an acceptable pair.

When the crews took a break for the midday meal, Devon and Antonia sat together. Deciding the two might need some encouragement, Sophie joined them. "I'm impressed with your hard work and attitude, Antonia. I can find you a position in my greenhouses, working with my son."

Antonia seemed to withdraw. Frown lines creased her brow. "That's very generous of you, but ... you don't know anything about me."

Sophie shrugged. "I know I need workers, and I've watched you work. Frankly, I don't care about your past. You're on Hellhole now – you left everything behind when you boarded that passenger pod." She gave an encouraging laugh. "Listen, if I refused to hire anyone unless I know everything about their past life, I wouldn't have any employees at all."

Sophie was a sucker for anyone who needed help. After Gregory, she had been in bad spots herself, and most Hellhole colonists had stories worse than her own. Everybody needed a second chance. Oh, some of them were rotten to the core and beyond salvation, but those sorts showed their true colors soon enough. Hellhole wasn't the sort of place that let anyone keep up pretenses for long. And if *Sophie* could make a decent life for herself, then others could, too – including Antonia.

Sophie motioned Vincent and Fernando over. "I'll make you the same offer. New arrivals are asked to perform a year of public service work, but the catalog of jobs is large. Want to work for me in the vineyards and greenhouse domes? It's not exciting, but it's stable."

Fernando piped up before his friend could contradict him. "We were hoping for something with more ... potential, ma'am. Maybe mapping the landscape, or working out in the mountains?"

"Ah, treasure seekers?" With so much of the land area completely uncharted, every starry-eyed newcomer thought he could find a bounty of diamonds or a vein of gold. "You'll have to see General Adolphus in person about that. He assigns grid mappers and topographical prospectors, if you can prove you're capable."

"We're capable!"

Vincent countered him in a hushed voice, "We don't even know what she's talking about, Fernando."

"The General's a busy man," Sophie continued, "and he usually delegates hiring, but if I send him a note, he'll see you. Convince him you're sincere." Fernando looked ready to bolt off to the main offices, but Sophie raised her hand. "I'll make that happen *tomorrow*. Right now, you need to earn your lodgings for last night."

11

The next day, as the two men approached Adolphus's Elba estate for their appointment, Fernando talked even more than usual. "I never thought we'd get a chance to meet General Adolphus in person. This could be our big break! He can't possibly be the holy terror that the official histories say he is."

Tiber Maximilian Adolphus was purported to be a ruthless traitor with the blood of millions on his hands, a man who had callously tried to ruin centuries of Constellation stability and tradition. Around the Crown Jewel worlds, children were warned that the General would leap out of their closets and eat them if they were naughty.

When he had worked in the machine shop on Orsini, Vincent had heard such things, but, from every indication in Michella Town, the locals were fiercely loyal to Adolphus for what he had done. Vincent figured he was about to see a different side of the story. Still, he was a bit nervous.

Sophie Vence had arranged their transportation out to the General's residence, and Fernando marveled at the impressive house. "Can you believe it? It's a mansion – a *mansion*, right here on Hellhole. He must have these people under his thumb." He bent over to sniff a thorny flower blooming in a large clay urn on the porch, then winced at the vinegary scent.

An aide ushered them inside. "Gentlemen. The General is expecting you. Madame Vence speaks highly of both of you."

They walked along tiled floors with carpeted runners, past a paneled banquet room and a handful of staff offices. The aide ushered them into an expansive study lined with bookshelves and glass display cases. Out of habit, Vincent brushed down his hair, straightened his shirt. He swallowed hard.

The man seated at his desk, hard at work, was immediately recognizable from numerous news stories and propaganda images. General Tiber Adolphus scanned records from his factories and scattered mining installations across the continent. He used a deskscreen to assign work teams and transmitted new instructions to offices in Michella Town, open-pit excavations, and industrial complexes that stretched for kilometers around.

Looking up from his work, Adolphus gave them a formal smile. Fernando pumped the General's hand. "Thank you for seeing us, sir. You won't be sorry you took the time."

Vincent added with a respectful nod. "We appreciate the opportunity, sir." He vividly recalled the reports of widespread unrest, battles on numerous Crown Jewel worlds, Commodore Hallholme's victorious last stand against the rebel forces, and the much-despised and vilified Adolphus facing his court-martial. Those were the things Vincent remembered about this man.

Here, though, Adolphus did not look beaten or disgraced; rather, he appeared content, strong, full of personal power. "This planet may seem to have little to offer, gentlemen, but we reap what we can. I have financed roads, shelters, factories, power plants, mines, and schools . . . though we don't have a large population of children quite yet." He leaned forward and shoved documents aside. "When Diadem Michella dispatched me here, she intended for Hallholme to be my prison, but I refuse to think of it in those terms. We've already made this into a planet that's worth something – to us if no one else – and I'm determined to make it even better."

"Hear, hear!" Fernando said. "And we'd like to help you make that happen, sir. You'll find that Vincent and I are dedicated workers."

Vincent cleared his throat nervously. "That's the truth, sir."

"No one comes to this planet expecting a vacation, and it is my practice to offer jobs to all newcomers. We have to make our settlements strong and viable. We have more work than we have colonists, which is why we ask for a year of community service, during which time you'll have food and lodging. At the end of the year, you can strike out on your own, or if you enjoy your work, you can continue to act as my employee. My aides will help you find something tailored to your talents and skills."

Fernando beamed. "We came here to make a new start."

The General regarded them with raised eyebrows. "I've reviewed your files, gentlemen, and I know exactly why you've joined us."

Vincent felt shame for what he had done, but Adolphus's words carried little sting. The General continued, "Hallholme attracts many misfits. It's a challenge to mold such fiercely independent and – let's face it – *eccentric* people into a team that works for the good of everyone. The harsh environment forces cooperation. To tame this wild world, we need education, transportation, commerce, widespread agriculture, high-end medical facilities, industry, a functional society. In short, we have to create a reason for people to come here and the infrastructure to support them when they arrive. At the moment, given a choice of all the possible planets, only people without options choose to come here."

"'The place to go when you've got nowhere else to go,'" Fernando quipped. "My friend and I were hoping you might have something special for us? Maybe a job that's not in the regular catalog?"

Vincent interrupted, "We'd appreciate your suggestions, sir."

When Adolphus regarded the two men evenly, Vincent felt as if the General were running some kind of deep scan on him. The famous exile focused more on Vincent than Fernando. "Sophie rarely recommends people to me, so I am inclined to listen. Tell me what interests you, Mr Jenet."

Vincent cleared his throat. "I'll be grateful for anything you recommend, sir, but my friend has a greater sense of adventure."

Fernando grinned. "I'd like to make the most of the wild frontier, General. I understand you occasionally commission explorers to scout the landscape?"

"Topographical prospectors." Adolphus moved several sheets of paper out of the way and called up a display on his flatscreen. "Our satellite network maps the large-scale terrain, but nothing beats actual eyes on the ground. Much of this planet is unexplored, and everywhere you go is likely to be virgin territory. Does that appeal to you? If you take grid-survey equipment and keep careful records, I'll provide you with food, supplies, an overland vehicle – everything you need. Just have a look around and tell me what you find."

"And you'd pay us for that?" Fernando asked. "How much?"

"I'll *supply* you for that. If you discover anything worthwhile, we'll discuss a finder's fee. I'd much rather have my own people discover fresh resources to be exploited, rather than an official Constellation inspector."

Fernando liked the sound of that.

Vincent had heard of inspectors trying to determine how Hellhole could be made more profitable to the Constellation, but the General cooperated very little with outsiders; he was keen to have his own.

"We'll definitely need some training, sir," Vincent said. "We wouldn't want to go out unprepared. Yesterday's static storm showed us that our briefing on the hazards around here was ... incomplete."

"We will provide full training, communications equipment, and survival gear, everything the other topographical prospectors have. The rest is up to the two of two."

"Thank you, General. We look forward to getting started."

Adolphus showed them his collection of incomprehensible objects inside display cases: nested curves, flowing silvery metal that looked not melted, but cast that way. "Please keep your eyes open while you're out there. Early settlers uncovered various artifacts of the original civilization here. I want to learn more about this planet's former inhabitants. We know almost nothing about them."

The seventy-four planets across the Constellation held many extraterrestrial lifeforms – strange plants, animals, and all sorts of organisms in between – but not a single technological civilization. The most advanced race was a herd-like group of subhumans on Tehila, docile vegetarians that built huts and lived in communities, but entirely ignored their human neighbors. The extinct civilization on Hallholme, however, had been highly advanced, judging by the few scraps the colonists had found.

Adolphus ran his fingers over a case. "Even after the asteroid impact and holocaust, there must be plenty of pieces left to be found." He looked up, eyes shining. "I will pay handsomely for anything you find."

Fernando liked that idea as well.

The discovery of alien artifacts on Hallholme had caused no furor back in the Crown Jewels, in fact, Vincent had heard little about it. "The briefing materials said that the asteroid impact was enough to kill all large lifeforms, and any artificial structure would have been obliterated. How can there be much of anything left?"

"Never underestimate a miracle of circumstance." Adolphus tapped the cover. "These few scraps give me hope." He turned away from the case. "It's just a hobby for now. I hope you can help me out. Someday, I intend to put together the pieces of the puzzle."

"If anything's out there, we'll find it, sir," Fernando promised. "You did mention a handsome reward? We'll take off as soon as we're equipped."

"And trained," Vincent reminded him pointedly.

12

The woman was tall and dark-skinned, with high cheekbones, large eyes, and lush blue-black hair. Despite her feminine curves, Tanja Hu had plenty of physical strength, which she needed daily to face the challenges as administrator of the frontier planet Candela.

Many members of Tanja's extended family were boisterous, full of laughter and bad decisions, and mystified by her lack of humor. A planetary administrator had little patience for rowdy behavior, though, and she didn't have time for jokes. The only reason they could have their parties was because she ran the planet so well. In reality, Tanja enjoyed doing her job more than she enjoyed "relaxing." It gave her a deep sense of satisfaction.

By the standards of the Crown Jewel worlds, Tanja had little political power, but the Deep Zone operated on different rules from the rest of the Constellation, and she was involved in more plans on her backwater world than any of the old-guard nobles could appreciate. That gave her more inner warmth than the moonshine her cousins brewed in the isolated mining towns she had set up for them. Even the man assigned to be her babysitter, Territorial Governor Goler on the planet Ridgetop, was oblivious to what Tanja, General Adolphus, and so many other planetary administrators were developing.

And she preferred it that way.

Tanja sat at a single canopy-covered table on the roof garden of her admin building, which floated in the placid harbor of Saporo. Candela's capitol building was eight stories tall, indistinct from other interconnected structures that floated on the harbor. The buoyant buildings in Saporo were engineered not to topple over during wind and wave action. Across the waterway, she could see a large new construction being towed into place by tugboats and aerocopters.

Over the past couple of decades, when the new frontier worlds were opened to settlement, original investors had believed that planet Candela, and the harbor city in particular, would become a booming tourist mecca with its picturesque setting of mist-capped hills ringing the clear, blue water. A semi-prosperous town had been built here by independent settlers long before the new Constellation stringline connected the Deep Zone planets with the Crown Jewels. Candela had been re-annexed into the government fold without incident twelve years earlier, and a second wave of pioneers had moved there.

As rapidly built houses began to dot the steep hills around the harbor, Elwyn Morae, the Constellation's ambitious first administrator, had even built a funicular system to carry tourists up the steep hills to reach spectacular viewpoints. The locals, including Tanja Hu, who served as his assistant and liaison with the old settlers, warned Morae he was overextending the settlement.

The first rainy season's incessant, torrential rainstorms put an end to the man's ambitious plans, causing mudslides, structural losses and loss of life. Once word about Candela's terrible weather spread around the Crown Jewels, tourists and settlers went elsewhere. The funicular was abandoned, and its two counterweighted cars left to rust in place. In the resultant uproar the disgraced and nearly bankrupt Morae quietly gathered the shreds of his fortune and returned to Sonjeera, where he recommended Tanja as his replacement (although in his state of ruin, Morae's blessing counted for little).

Tanja had the pedigree for this: she and her family were descendants of the passengers aboard the original slow ship that had set off into the Deep Zone. Because Candela was a bountiful planet, despite the worrisome rains, they lived a relatively good life, but a woman with Tanja's ambitions did not fit in with the old ways.

When she'd first accepted her position in the aftermath of Morae's debacle, she had been filled with idealism and excitement, a sense of adventure. With Constellation assistance, the possibilities for her world seemed limitless. Then reality had set in as Sonjeera's priorities became apparent. Tanja attended meetings and ceremonies on Sonjeera, but she quickly realized that she didn't want Candela to become just like the Constellation. There was a reason her ancestors had come out to the Deep Zone.

Though her own dreams did not die as dramatically as the rusted cars of the abandoned funicular, Tanja realized how much had not been explained to her. She learned the truth about Constellation politics swiftly enough. The old-guard nobles did not consider her an equal, and certainly not a force to be reckoned with. They were wrong.

Though she had to work within the framework of rules and restrictions imposed on her, Tanja made her own grand plans for her planet. And soon enough, General Adolphus would make that future possible ...

As Tanja sat under the canopy on her rooftop, she inhaled the rich moisture from a recent pattering of warm rain. Now that the clouds had blown away, the distant mountains wore a fresh mantle of white snow. During the brief but glorious season of good weather, Tanja preferred to work out in the open instead of at her desk inside the offices below. She called this her "garden office," and her staff knew to interrupt her only for the most important decisions.

She activated a flatscreen embedded in the tabletop, chose the observation systems, and kept an eye on the workers bustling about on the office floors below. Her administrative assistant, Bebe Nax, looked agitated as she spoke to someone over her implanted earadio. Tanja didn't bother to listen in. The small, feisty woman could take care of whatever it was. Tanja had few enough reliable people, whether among her employees or her extended family. Bebe was one of them, and Tanja's paternal uncle Quinn Hu was another.

She smiled at the thought of her uncle. With his wild hair and colorful clothes, Quinn looked more like an eccentric artist than a construction business manager, but he had a great head for organization and accounting. She always pictured him sitting at the controls of one of the gigantic earth-moving machines used for strip-mining the rugged hills.

Tanja glanced down at two document screens open in front of her: off-network folios containing highly confidential information. Technically, as planetary administrator of Candela, she worked for the Constellation, but Tanja felt increasingly alienated from the distant central government. Their frivolous civilized concerns had never really mattered to her, and their unrealistic expectations of Candela's contribution to the treasury were an increasingly heavy anchor dragging her people down.

One of the files on the screen had been delivered to her by courier: a revised taxation schedule specifying Candela's new tribute payments. She had been fuming about it for more than an hour.

Citing the extraordinary costs of installing and maintaining the stringline network from Sonjeera out to all of the Deep Zone planets, the Diadem demanded increased revenues, exploiting whatever goods or resources each "Deezee" world could produce. Comfortable back on the Crown Jewel planets, the powerful noble families were getting richer while the colonists struggled to keep up with the outside demands.

The fifty-four frontier colonies operated under a compact with Sonjeera that calculated tributes based upon percentages of standardized production revenues. DZ wealth came primarily from raw materials and exotic native products that were shipped via stringline to the Sonjeera hub. These new tribute levels were arbitrarily set to squeeze more money from the Deep Zone. The old Diadem simply didn't understand the hardships she was imposing. Maybe she didn't care.

In her annoyance, Tanja paced around the roof garden, wrapped up in thoughts of problems and potential solutions. In order to meet the Constellation's unrelenting demands, Tanja had been forced to set up large strip-mining operations; it was rush work, messy and short-sighted, but the only way to produce sufficient material to make the inspectors happy.

During the interminable monsoon season, the miners and machinery worked in perpetual mud, processing the slop in order to extract metals. Now, thanks to this increase, they would have to work harder still, cutting corners before the rains came again . . .

On the flatscreen, she noticed that Bebe Nax was still on the earadio, looking flustered. Presently the assistant turned a pleading face up at the videocam unit on the wall, sure her boss was watching. Tanja closed out the computer files on her desktop, then hurried down a circular stairway into the office levels.

Meeting her at the doorway, Bebe said, "Sorry, Administrator. That pest Captain Walfor insists he has an appointment with you. Why do you even deal with him? He's a black marketeer!"

Tanja smiled. "So they say. Where is he?"

"In the dock-level lobby."

Bebe's disapproval was plain, but Tanja knew exactly what sort of things Ian Walfor offered. He was good-humored, rakish, and sometimes intolerable, but he had value to her. So far from Sonjeera she liked to have alternative sources for the items she needed. "Tell him I'll be right down."

Full of bluster and good cheer, Walfor was the sort of fellow who told bawdy stories to burly men in taverns, yet still had the charm and good looks to attract the ladies. He could also be irritating and demanding. Once he arrived on Candela – after an interminable journey using old-model FTL engines that bypassed the fast Constellation-controlled stringline network – he acted as if his schedule was more important than anyone else's.

No matter. Tanja liked him personally, and she could understand why he wanted to stretch his legs after such a long, slow transit from Buktu. Any man who found ways to sidestep the Diadem's transportation monopoly earned points in her book, even if the alternative delivery system was contorted, slow, and inconvenient. Walfor was also, despite the obvious illegalities of his activities, impeccably honest, at least in his dealings with the Deep Zone planets. Authorities on Sonjeera would have a much different view if they knew what Walfor was doing, but the man and his cumbersome old-style FTL freighters had thus far escaped their attention.

Walfor had a weathered face and a shock of wavy black hair. His olive eyes were flirtatious, and whenever he smiled at Tanja she knew he was imagining her in bed with him. He was doing that now, but she ignored it.

"Been a long haul from Buktu to deliver these goods. My ship and crew are in orbit, but I wanted to see you first. I could use some RandR." He smiled. "We could anchor my jetboat out in the harbor, watch the sunset, have a candlelight dinner."

"How ... antique sounding, and clichéd. Can't you think of anything more original?"

"*I* am an original myself, one of a kind." His eyes twinkled, then grew serious as he lowered his voice. "But, knowing you, we'll end up getting down to business instead. Such a beautiful woman shouldn't be so serious."

It took an effort, but she showed no hint of a smile. "I'm a serious woman. The beauty is only a secondary characteristic."

"It's the first thing I notice." He ran a hand through his hair, gestured for her to walk ahead of him along the floating walkway towards the waiting government aerocopter she had signed out. "Someday you'll relax."

"I'll relax when we've got the cargo loaded and you're on your way to Hellhole. Do you have room for the same size shipment as before?"

"Once we offload my cargo, there'll be plenty of shielded space for the haul. Let's go take a look at what you've got." He extended his arm to escort her, and she indulged him by taking it.

Walfor insisted on flying the aerocopter himself. As he worked the controls with great confidence, Tanja thought he looked particularly handsome. Maybe one day she would give him a try in the romance department ... when she had more time. The craft rose over the calm harbor, then headed north up the coast.

"Not to detract from my lovely companion," he winked at her, "but Candela's scenery is quite beautiful."

"Compared to Buktu, anything's a paradise." He didn't disagree. Walfor's frozen outpost was too far from its sun ever to become a nice place to live, but his rugged frontiersmen had made it secretly profitable.

The aerocopter cruised over several mountain villages, then arrived at Puhau, a settlement mostly occupied by Tanja's own extended family. He gave her a teasing look. "Shall we buzz your Uncle Quinn's house? Wake him up?"

"He's awake, and he works harder than you ever will."

"Then how about some of your cousins?" He grinned impishly.

"Not today, even though they might deserve it." They probably had hangovers, she thought, although despite their frequent parties and binges, they did put in their expected work time. Unlike Tanja, when her numerous relatives left the worksite at the end of the day, they actually forgot about the job.

Upon her appointment as planetary administrator, Tanja's large family had been very proud to have someone of such importance to the whole Constellation. They asked her if she would meet the Diadem in person; whenever she returned from Sonjeera, they crowded around to see what souvenirs she had brought back for them.

After Elwyn Morae departed Candela, Tanja had reclaimed his property for her own relatives, setting them up with land, houses, and employment. She saw to it that that her clan received jobs in the lucrative mining industries, along with a number of perks.

In retrospect, she realized it had been the worst possible thing to do. Apart from Uncle Quinn and a handful of others, Tanja's uncles and cousins lived embarrassingly wild lives, certain that good times had come to their whole family. Some of them, she was sure, did things intentionally to irritate her, leaving Tanja to clean up their messes.

After one reckless episode in which a pair of unruly cousins unhooked three buoyant buildings and floated them around Saporo harbor, causing great mayhem and damage, Tanja had been forced to pay off angry businessmen and government visitors. When she had confronted the perpetrators, furious, they had laughed at her, wondering why she didn't find the whole escapade as funny as they did.

Afterward, Tanja sent her rowdiest relatives to faraway towns in the hills, where they could work in the farms and strip mines. Though she loved her cousins, and they were eventually contrite, Tanja knew their behavior wouldn't change. She had no intention of letting their antics hamstring her efforts to keep Candela running; best to give them elbow room in the hills, where they could operate without many constraints. In that region, Uncle Quinn had been able to keep them in line, so far. It was the best solution for everyone.

Now the aerocopter approached a broad, raw scar on the hillsides that marked the Puhau strip-mine Quinn managed, flanked by the crowded shanties of the worker village and his little job-shack office. Atop the hillside, huge earth movers scraped the dirt and filled immense dump trucks with soils that would yield valuable metals.

Tanja hated the look of the trampled, excavated, and denuded hills.

Someday she hoped to restore the vegetation, but the constant need to fulfill the tribute quota forced her to adopt extreme methods of production. The mining teams operated around the clock, and the upcoming rainy season would make things even more difficult.

But she hadn't brought Walfor to see the current strip mine. He flew over another scarred hilltop, where young trees were taking hold to repair the industrial scars from the previous years of mining. "It's looking better," she said. "You can't see any evidence of the deep mine at all, and the tunnels are holding nicely."

While covering up the old strip mines, Tanja had maintained a series of secret, undocumented shafts through the mountains, which linked a very special mine with the open sea, where Walfor's fleet of fast boats collected the rare cargo and loaded it aboard his spacefaring FTL freighters for transport to General Adolphus on Hellhole.

A rich vein of iperion, about which the Constellation knew nothing.

Seven years earlier, Uncle Quinn had made the unexpected discovery: a mother lode of the rare substance that marked stringline paths through space. If Tanja had announced the discovery to the Constellation, Crown Jewel industrialists and government officials would have swarmed like locusts to Candela, so she chose not to inform the Diadem.

That was when she decided on a different course for her planet and her people. Only Quinn and a few trusted people knew about the iperion excavation and processing operations. General Tiber Adolphus was her only customer, because she had bought into his grand scheme. If the wrong people ever found out about her secret plans, she and everyone involved would be charged with treason.

Ian Walfor laughed with great pleasure as he swooped around the hidden operations. Later, after they finished the inspection, he guided the aerocopter back toward Saporo harbor and the floating administration buildings. "It takes a certain type of person to succeed out here in the DZ. And you, Tanja, are definitely the right type."

"Look who's talking."

As they flew on, dark clouds began to gather over the mountains, and she knew full well what they indicated. A spattering of warm rain covered the craft's windshield. Candela's monsoons would arrive soon.

13

After his encounter with the exiled rebel General, Ishop Heer was glad to be home on Sonjeera. Ishop was accustomed to manipulating people, especially the Sonjeeran nobles who treated him with little respect, but Adolphus had smoothly bullied him in spite of the fact that Ishop had caught the man evading his proper tributes to Sonjeera.

He took a deep breath of the fresh, *clean* air. After leaving that primitive and gritty DZ planet, he still felt soiled. Ishop had showered thoroughly on the passenger pod home, several times, and had even disposed of his clothes. Yes, it felt very, very good to be back on Sonjeera.

The glorious capital made adrenaline throb through his veins as he pondered the back-room intrigues, the schemes of lawmakers and their associates, and his own role in the swirling action. He was a discreet aide, a watchdog, a shadowy "expediter of difficult tasks" for the Diadem. Though he wasn't, and would never be, one of the nobles, he glided among them, unnoticed and underestimated. In some ways, that was better.

His remarkable assistant, Laderna Nell, was skilled at digging up damaging information about the Diadem's opponents. She was as organized as he needed, managed his numerous lists and kept her own. With her keen detective skills, Laderna had even uncovered embarrassing details about Michella herself – particularly a rumor that she had murdered her own brother, Jamos, as a child, then threatened to kill her little sister, Haveeda, who had witnessed the incident. Interesting data point: for the past several decades, Haveeda had not been seen in public, and was said to be living in therapeutic mental institutions, though no one could find her. It was enough to pique Ishop's curiosity.

However, he wisely held such explosive information in extreme confidence and would use it only under the direst circumstances. Ishop was loyal and would allow no one to hurt Diadem Michella.

However, if she ever tried to hurt *him* . . .

On the day after arriving back from the DZ pustule of Hallholme, he reported early to the House of Lords, accompanied by the dutiful Laderna. In a windowless anteroom, he and his quiet assistant drank stale, murky kiafa – a popular hot beverage that was stimulating and heavily sweetened – while they reviewed the information he would provide to the Council.

Gangly and nearly his height, Laderna had red hair, a long neck and brown, almond-shaped eyes. Bookish and awkward, she was nonetheless the smartest, most dedicated researcher Ishop had ever hired. She drank two cups of kiafa for every one of his, and if he failed to finish his own cup, she invariably would. Right now, she held his half-full cup in her hands, sipping as she looked over the notes on an electronic clipboard and made marks. "Emphasis points." He had made his own lists and, astonishingly, her points matched his.

Ishop would have preferred to report first to the Diadem, but Michella had been caught up in private meetings with the quarreling Tazaar and Paternos representatives. His report to the Council about Adolphus and his secret mining activities would upstage that (not that the nobles would thank him).

Laderna looked at him with bright, earnest eyes. "You seem distracted today."

"Maybe I should have finished my own kiafa, then." He looked at the cup in her hands.

Laderna realized what she'd done and quickly passed it back to him. "Oh, sorry."

He normally would have refused to touch a vessel from which someone else had drunk, but this was Laderna. He gulped the rest of the beverage, set the cup aside, and then scanned her notes, approving the suggestions. "It's time for us to go in."

Ishop entered the great hall through a side doorway, with Laderna following close on his heels. She found a place in one of the side galleries, while he took his customary seat alone at a wooden table centered in front of the Star Throne. The lawmakers and nobles were noisy as they settled into their places in the U-shaped arrangement of seats.

Everyone rose as Diadem Michella entered. The regal, gray-haired woman looked especially stern in sharp contrast with the genial public face she usually showed. Ishop was in the habit of noting the colors the Diadem chose as an indicator of her moods. Today, Michella wore a dark robe with the swirling Constellation crest on it. Yes, she was angry about something.

The gold-uniformed Sergeant at Arms called the session to order, and everyone sat. "First, we will hear the report from Special Aide Heer, who has returned from planet Hallholme with new discoveries about the activities of General Adolphus."

During the expected grumble from the listeners, Ishop gave a respectful bow and secret smile to the Diadem, then acknowledged the assembled nobles. Some of them regarded him as if he were a lesser creature to be tolerated rather than respected; no matter how good a job Ishop did, this was the reception he always received because he wasn't one of them.

While he never allowed himself to show any reaction to their disdain, he did make mental notes of the worst offenders, and conducted some preliminary investigations in case he should ever need to defend himself. It was always advisable to have scapegoats ready at hand ...

He had washed his hands and face, dressed himself fastidiously, and now stood before them with his notes and his list in hand. "Gentlemen, Ladies, nobles all, I have recently returned from Hallholme, and would like to offer my report on the exiled Tiber Maximilian Adolphus." Disapproval whickered through the seated lawmakers.

Following Laderna's suggestions, he summarized what he had seen during his inspection of Adolphus's records. He described the planet's commercial and fledgling industrial capabilities. Gesturing with his hands for extra effect, Ishop reported that Adolphus enjoyed a lavish existence because he had been hiding some of his industries from the Constellation.

Ishop swept his gaze across the audience, letting the meaning sink in, then he referred to the list one more time before speaking. "Administrator Adolphus has hidden mines, smelters, metals processing factories. His production of steel, copper, aluminum, titanium, and tin are all at least twenty per cent higher than reported. He has been cheating us all." He said the "us" intentionally, though none of the nobles would count him among their number.

Instead of the outrage he expected to hear, however, he heard only a grumble, even a titter. Lord Azio Tazaar said, "Twenty per cent more of metals that do us no good anyway? Do you want him to send cargo boxes of brass ingots to Sonjeera? It would cost ten times more to ship than it's worth." He let out a loud snort. "If that's the worst Tiber Adolphus can do, we should leave him to his schemes."

Ishop was surprised at the reaction. The noble families had so quickly forgotten the threat posed by the General. "He is a dangerous man," he reminded them. He described how Adolphus had threatened to turn him, the Diadem's lawful representative, out into a horrific static-storm.

Lord Riomini called from the front row of seats, "I would turn you out into a storm myself, Heer!" They all laughed at him.

Ishop offered a thin smile in return, pretending to take no offense because the Black Lord was the Diadem's most powerful ally, but Ishop would not forget such comments. He waited for the laughter in the chamber (not all of which was good-natured) to subside. Much as he resented it, Ishop Heer knew his place.

Recognizing Ishop's potential early on, Michella had raised him from humble beginnings, rewarding his extraordinary talents and loyalty. As a youth, Ishop always believed he could achieve his dreams, one way or another, but he was a nobody – the only child of unremarkable family and unambitious parents – and so he ran away from home.

Intent on making something of himself, even without family connections, Ishop talked his way into a low-level position in the Diadem's palace where he worked hard, always listening, keeping his eyes open for an opportunity.

Ishop carved his own niche, discovering the intricate web of politics and schemes in the palace – even among the ranks of the servants, cooks, guards, couriers, and gardeners. Everyone, it seemed, had plans to secure the job just over their head. And Ishop was better at it than his peers.

The turning point occurred while he was working in the palace garage. When he sensed something amiss in the head chauffeur's demeanor that others had not noticed, he reported his suspicions to a guard captain, a stony-faced woman who, Ishop knew, had ambitions to climb in rank. Taking a chance on the insistent young man's observations, palace security men promptly searched the chauffeur's room and found evidence of an extensive plot to assassinate the Diadem as she made her way to a gala public event.

Seventeen men and women in the palace were trapped in the unraveling web (every person on the list he had made). Ishop was willing to share credit with the ambitious guard captain. Unfortunately the stern woman was not. And so Ishop set out to destroy her as well. Using his detailed observations of the traitorous chauffeur, Ishop fabricated evidence that linked the female guard captain to the chauffeur and the various coconspirators. They all died horribly.

It was like clearing deadwood from a forest, and Ishop soon had a wide open path before him. He learned how to do what was necessary, first for himself and then – after she took him under her wing – for Diadem Michella.

The old woman often showed Ishop her appreciation, and he was always grateful for what she had done for him. Now, Ishop performed whatever tasks the Diadem required with a discreet, sometimes extreme, touch. Over the years he had disposed of three lesser noblemen, all of whom wanted a bigger piece of the Constellation pie for themselves. Each death had been made to look like an accident, check one, check two, check three. Diadem Michella never wanted to know the grisly details; she merely informed him that she wanted it done – and quickly. She and Ishop had a smooth working relationship, and she rewarded him with a comfortable apartment in the government quarter, sexual liaisons with expensive courtesans, and generous payments into his personal accounts.

Ishop didn't need to impress these self-important noblemen. He had what he deserved, didn't he? Intelligence and talent had carried him to the top, and he had struck the ceiling of realistic possibilities. Michella occasionally created a new position or title for him, but he always felt a vague, unsatisfied hunger, as if he had attended one of the Diadem's fancy receptions and tried to make a meal of the dainty appetizers that, while delicious, were not actually filling . . .

The stocky, bearded Lord Tazaar spoke out. "I have no more love for the rebel Adolphus than any of you, but why should we complain if he's established a functional civilization on that death trap of a planet? Who cares if he digs out a few more tons of iron? We *want* him to operate the colony efficiently in order to generate profits for the Constellation. We take our tribute. The reports I've seen show an increasing flow of tax dollars from Hallholme. Why continue to harass him unnecessarily?"

"We expect that sort of efficiency from a military man, Lord Tazaar," the Diadem said. "But he is also dangerous. We must harness Administrator Adolphus like a beast of burden, making certain he plows the right fields and conceals nothing from us. That is why I instructed my aide to keep a close eye on him."

Lord Riomini's next comment was far more barbed than his previous one: "If Ishop Heer is so talented, maybe we should grant *him* control of all Tazaar assets!"

Red-faced, Azio Tazaar was about to retort when Michella cut him off with an angry word. "Enough! Finish your report, Mr Heer."

Ishop bowed toward the Star Throne, ready to take his leave. He glanced at his list again, though he didn't need to. "In summary, Eminence, Administrator Adolphus claims to be abiding by the terms of his exile agreement. He does, however, under-report his planet's resources and industrial production so as to avoid paying the appropriate level of tribute. Despite these illicit activities, he seems to be contained for the moment, though he may yet pose a further threat to the Constellation."

"And therefore we should continue to watch him," noted the Diadem, who waved a hand to dismiss him. "Thank you, Mr Heer." She drew a deep breath to face a tedious and unpleasant task. "Next on the agenda, we shall continue the debate on the Paternos matter and the disposition of planet Kappas."

No longer needed as Constellation politics swirled around and past him, Ishop departed from the chamber, and Laderna trotted up beside him. She whispered with great fervor, "Good job, Ishop!" She touched his arm affectionately, and he gave her hand a fond pat, but he was annoyed that the nobles had not seen the threat Adolphus continued to pose. His mind progressed to other schemes.

That evening, the Diadem summoned Ishop for a private debriefing, and he described his time with the General in greater detail. He didn't believe for a minute that General Adolphus was a beaten, cooperative man, but the off-books mining operations really posed no significant threat to the Constellation. It was frustrating.

Normally, Michella would have been angry to hear how she had been cheated, but she was distracted by the brewing feud involving the Tazaars and Paternos. The Diadem shook her head. "I don't know why they bother. Kappas isn't even much of a planet, and certainly not very profitable. But because the Paternos refuse to surrender it, that makes the Tazaars want it even more."

"Indeed, it doesn't seem worth fighting for, Eminence ... therefore, there must be another reason. Something personal."

Michella smiled. "Perceptive, as usual, Ishop. Yes, years ago, the Paternos cast a deciding vote against the Tazaars on some matter. I've forgotten the details ... and so have all the other members of the Council, except for Lord Tazaar, of course. Grudges last a long time."

"There are always currents flowing beneath the surface – and predatory fish swimming there."

"Yes, and you are one of my defenses against them. The trick, Ishop, is for me to keep you pointed in the right direction, so that you never turn against me."

"I would never do that, Eminence!" He was sure he sounded convincing.

"I believe you, Ishop. After all, you are like the son I never had."

The sincerity in her voice was touching, but he could not let himself forget that she had murdered her own young brother and locked away her only sister. Michella's husband had died before Keana's first birthday, though Ishop hadn't found any reasons to suspect her of involvement in that. The man's death seemed to be an accident, pure and simple.

Like the son I never had. All things considered, Ishop wondered how safe it was to be part of the Diadem's close family ...

14

It was the sixteenth anniversary of the battle of Qiorfu, the official start of his rebellion against the Constellation, and General Adolphus knew none of his surviving men would ever forget it. Back in Michella Town, drinking establishments would be crowded with old soldiers reminiscing about the lost war.

Instead of leading his men in a moment of silence for fallen comrades, Adolphus made a habit each year of spending this night alone. He wanted nothing to do with somber parades or maudlin reminiscences. Someday – when the wounds stopped hurting, when Hallholme was free and civilized and the people had their own government to be proud of – he might institute a national holiday to mark what had actually happened.

But not yet.

Always attuned to his moods, Sophie had watched his sadness increase for days. She knew what this date meant for the General, his close friends, and his failed hopes. She touched his arm, asking softly, "Are you sure you don't want me there with you?"

"Not for this. Not tonight."

Before she returned to her own residence in town, she left him a bottle of her best wine. He accepted the bottle, kissed her goodbye, and then sent his staff away. Alone in his study, Adolphus removed the cork and poured a glass of the rich Cabernet, letting it breathe as he sat back and stared into his memories.

The Adolphus family had once been important nobles on the Crown Jewel planet Qiorfu, whose prominence and wealth had declined over the generations. The Lubis Plain shipyards were the planet's largest source of income – a dumping ground where damaged or decommissioned ships from the Constellation space navy were fixed, stored, or dismantled for scrap and parts.

A century earlier, the Adolphus family had subcontracted the Lubis Plain operations to the Riomini family, which was like letting a hungry predator into a livestock pen. The ambitious Riominis had consolidated and expanded the base of operations, becoming the primary employers on Qiorfu.

Tiber Adolphus was the second son of Jacob, an old respected patriarch who liked to tend his olive groves on the grassy hills that overlooked the bustling industrial expanse of Lubis Plain. Stefano, the older son, was the natural heir, but Jacob planned to split the Adolphus holdings between his two children, as many noble families had done for generations. Their mother was a quiet woman who spent most of her time in a studio in the manor house, writing poetry thousands of lines long, which she never allowed anyone to read; she spent very little time with her boys.

Stefano, though, picked at the division of the territory, trying to mince up and draw lines around structures and plots of land that were of particular interest to him, pressuring their father to shift the boundaries in a complex gerrymandered map. Tiber became frustrated with his brother's pettiness: whenever he made concessions, Stefano found something else to object to. The quarrel degenerated until Tiber concluded that his brother would never be satisfied.

Seeing how distraught the conflict was making their old father, Tiber decided to relinquish all interest in the property. Subdividing their Qiorfu holdings would only weaken the Adolphus family, so he signed over his entire inheritance to Stefano. Tiber supplied a legal document forsaking his claim to the family wealth and signed up for service in the Constellation military. It was traditional for planetary rulers to get rid of their "extra inheritors" by enrolling them in officer training to start them on military careers.

There, Tiber found himself surrounded by numerous second, third, and fourth sons of waning noble families; he and his fellows jokingly called themselves the "second-string nobles." The ever-increasing surplus of high-level personnel had bloated the space navy. Due to special-interest lobbying, the Constellation had constructed hundreds of unnecessary FTL starships for its military and created countless irrelevant positions and an attendant bureaucracy. It became a thriving, noxious weed that no one could uproot.

Tiber scored well in the intense training at the military academy. After growing up near the Lubis Plain shipyards, he was already familiar with most ship configurations and knew many soldiers personally. An intelligent and talented man with a keen eye for tactics, he quickly began to make his mark and received numerous increases in rank.

Then he received word that Stefano had died on Qiorfu from an allergic reaction to medicine. Suddenly Tiber was the sole heir to the Adolphus family fortunes, and though he was a rising star in the military with a clear promotion path, he resigned his commission, bade farewell to his comrades, and rushed back to Qiorfu to take up his new responsibilities and comfort his devastated father. His mother had retreated even further into her poetry.

Once back home, though, he learned the insidious subtleties of Constellation law. Over the years, ambitious noble families – the Riominis, Tazaars, Craises, and Hirdans – had passed seemingly innocuous legislation that prevented a noble son from reclaiming his inheritance once he had relinquished it. Tiber was told there was nothing he could do.

But he knew his cause was just, so he fought, this time via the judicial system. Tiber pleaded his case before the Supreme Magistrate on Sonjeera, and was appalled when the court dismissed it. "The law is clear, young man. Accept it."

Using new attorneys, Adolphus appealed and lost again. He then took his case to the public, but engendered little sympathy; the other nobles brushed it aside, for his family had minimal influence, and the common people didn't care about the inflated problems of the nobility. The Riominis administered the Lubis Plain shipyards with exceptional efficiency, and the Black Lord had a very powerful propaganda machine.

Back home, old Jacob Adolphus was weary, broken by the loss not only of his eldest son, but the loss of his family wealth and prestige. His mother's hair had gone very gray, and she ate dinner with them, but rarely said a word. With no other prospects, Tiber left home again and reapplied for military service, but because of his absence and because he had shown himself to be a "troublemaker," he entered two steps below the rank he had held before.

Since the Constellation navy had so many spaceships and so little to do, many vessels were given busy-work assignments, usually involving scientific matters that would not otherwise have been funded. Tiber found himself running a small long-range FTL scoutship with a crew of seventy. Built for espionage and reconnaissance, it was now assigned to astronomy duty. They were dispatched with orders to study a well-cataloged and predictable nova that was due to flare up. Adolphus's ship would be there to observe the event.

As a student of military history and tactics, Tiber had a passing interest in astronomy and he was pleased to be in command of even a small vessel. The Constellation military gave them a precise time and location for the predicted nova, which puzzled him: if the astronomy was so well understood, why send a survey ship and crew to observe the event?

His first officer was Franck Tello, the second son of a weak noble family, who had turned to the Constellation military like so many other second-string nobles. Tello was a good-natured young man who loved his family and understood his position, missed his home planet of Cherby but accepted the fact that he would have to go wherever he was sent.

Once Tiber and his crew got to know one another better, he realized that his entire ship was filled with surplus family members from the weakest noble families; every single crewman was a second or third son of an already dissipated family – someone who cluttered the inheritance chain.

The scout ship took up its position very close to the binary star, dispatched their detectors, and prepared to wait. The two tightly orbiting stars danced around each other, the blue dwarf siphoning star gases from the red giant until enough new material built up to trigger a collapse with a resulting flash of light and radiation. The nova would happen soon.

Always curious, Tiber studied the unstable system, read reports of previous nova outbursts, and compiled the data. With actual stars in front of him, rather than theoretical descriptions from his astrophysics lessons, he ran the calculations himself, as an exercise.

And found that the Constellation scientists had provided erroneous information.

It was a basic mistake, and he rechecked his calculations. He brought in Franck, who came up with the same answer. Adolphus reread his orders, dispatched a question to military headquarters, and received confirmation that yes, his ship was supposed to be in that precise position on that particular date. He was reprimanded for questioning orders.

The only problem was, when the nova exploded, their location would be squarely in the death zone. Gathering redundant astronomical data should not be a suicide mission. Though loath to disobey a direct command, especially after receiving confirmation from his superiors, he did not intend to let his ship and crew be wiped out because some careless scientist had made a mathematical error.

A more terrifying thought occurred to him: what if this was not a mistake, after all?

Franck was the first to suggest a possible conspiracy. "Captain, many of us aboard this vessel happen to be inconvenient members of noble families, and not all have renounced their inheritances, as I did. Wouldn't some powerful lords consider it *fortuitous* if this ship and crew were accidentally lost?"

Adolphus was astounded. His instinct was to disbelieve his first officer, to argue with the very idea of something so dishonorable, but then he remembered how the Supreme Magistrate had so brusquely swept aside his inheritance claims, no doubt because the Riominis wanted all of Qiorfu, not just the shipyards. If he himself were killed in an unfortunate accident during a survey mission, he wouldn't be able to do anything to help his father hold onto the family estate.

In his heart Adolphus knew that Franck Tello was right.

He left a survey buoy with full scientific instrumentation in place and withdrew the scout ship to a safe distance. Though he was technically disobeying orders, the astronomical data would be gathered as requested.

When the star flared up exactly according to their captain's calculations and vaporized the survey buoy – where their ship should have been – the second-string nobles were convinced that they had been ordered to their deaths. The Constellation was trying to eliminate them!

Maintaining communications silence, an outraged Adolphus issued orders to his crew, and the FTL scout ship raced to nearby Cherby, Franck Tello's home planet. The voyage took two weeks, and they arrived at the planet without announcing themselves, only to discover that all of the Tello family holdings had been taken over by their arch-rivals, the Hirdans. Franck's older brother had been killed in a "hunting mishap," and his father chased out of the house, griefstricken by the erroneous news that Franck was dead as well. The new landlords already occupied the family's great house.

None of them had intended to start a civil war ... not then.

In a rage, Franck armed himself from the scout ship's weapons lockers and marched into his family home. He gunned down the treacherous Hirdans as they were moving supplies in. Unified by the knowledge that they had all been betrayed, Adolphus's second-string nobles swept away the remaining usurpers, locked them up, and reinstated the Tellos, claiming Cherby as a reconquered world.

Fearing that his own planet would face a similar takeover, Adolphus commandeered a group of larger military vessels on Cherby and flew off to Qiorfu. Arriving home, Adolphus discovered that his father had recently, and conveniently, died, and Lord Selik Riomini had already staked his claim to the holdings. His mother had been moved to a very small cottage off the estate, where she was under constant guard. A Riomini military adviser had been installed as the provisional governor, and the Black Lord himself planned to take up residence soon.

This was the last of many straws for Tiber Adolphus. He and his growing band of malcontents performed a daring raid, took over the Lubis Plain shipyards, and seized a fleet of old but still-functional warships.

Franck Tello gave a grim smile. "Second-string ships for second-string nobles."

In an impromptu ceremony, his men unanimously granted Adolphus the rank of general.

Thus began the rebellion, on Cherby and Qiorfu. Throughout the military, a large number of second-string nobles – those most likely to be sympathetic to Adolphus's cause – served as low-level communications officers. When he transmitted his shocking revelations of the Constellation's treachery, the first people to hear the message were members of at-risk families.

After rescuing and moving his mother, and setting up a new identity for her, General Adolphus broadcast a passionate and convincing declaration of independence across the Constellation, calling for all second-stringers to rise up against the corrupt system. The initial message sparked spontaneous mutinies on numerous Constellation battleships; some of the crew uprisings succeeded, some failed. But the rebellion was born, and grew.

Adolphus led a campaign with his FTL ships for five bloody years across multiple systems, engaging in impossible battles, collecting many victories and many defeats. In desperation, Diadem Michella pulled together blueblood officers under the command of Lord Selik Riomini to form the powerful Army of the Constellation. And one of the battlefield commanders was Commodore Percival Hallholme . . .

Now, on the evening of the anniversary, Adolphus sat in his chair. He picked up the glass of Cabernet, swirled it a little, and raised a silent toast to his heroic men who had died, and to those who remained in exile with him. He took a long, slow sip.

The wine tasted bitter, but he forced himself to swallow. It was not the grapes, he suspected, but the memories. He drained his glass and spent the rest of the evening alone with his thoughts.

15

Captain Escobar Hallholme considered the Adolphus manor house an unpleasant reminder of Qiorfu's former ruling family. The young officer would have preferred to raze the old mansion from the sloping hillside and build a new residence for himself. But his father insisted that the original structure be preserved for reasons he did not completely explain.

The old commodore did point out that, although it had been rebuilt, expanded, and redesigned numerous times, the manor house was the ancestral home of a respected family, long before the Constellation Charter was drawn up and signed by the original nobles. Portions of the redstone walls dated back more than two thousand years, and the olive groves carried their own weight of age. The structure held the gravitas of history – and, recently, of treason.

Escobar didn't like the place. He didn't need any reminders of all that history or the part his family had played in it.

He had just showered and shaved and stood in a thin, blue dressing robe on the second level of the manor house. A silver-service tray sat on a table near him, but he had barely touched his cup of dark, sweet kiafa. His wife had already taken their two children off to their tutors, and he would see them that evening at dinner, but for the time being he had plenty of work to do. That was one of the first lessons both his easort5

boys had learned, that their father had important responsibilities here on Qiorfu.

Fortunately his sons spent much of their time pestering their grandfather, delighted by his war stories. Escobar could not care less about the interminable reminiscences.

Throwing open a double window, he looked out on a lateral rampart with a guard station perched on it. He noted the ochre weathering of the stones in soft morning light, and in an objective moment, he did appreciate the beauty of the house in an antique sort of way.

As the ambitious son of the legendary Commodore Percival Hallholme, Escobar had his own military command, albeit a less glorious and fabled one than his father's – so far. As a Unit Captain, he was in charge of the Lubis Plain shipyards and the company of Riomini troops stationed there. He had even married one of the grand-nieces of Lord Riomini, a charming enough girl with good connections, though they had very little in common. She was a good mother to his sons, however.

Escobar's family shared the spacious house with the old man, and thankfully the residence had myriad rooms that each man could use for his own purposes. The room in which Escobar now stood had once been a master suite for the old Adolphus patriarchs. He had converted it to a sitting room where he sometimes conferred with visiting dignitaries. It was a place separate from the messy family areas where the boys were allowed to play.

Percival Hallholme had been granted the entire estate after his great victory against Adolphus. Situated on a promontory overlooking the plain, the house looked like the prow of a great ship from bygone days. Escobar had to admit that if he squinted, the bluegrass plain stretching into the distance resembled a sea, and the mothballed FTL vessels crowding the expansive yards looked like ships floating on placid water. Some of the old vessels were used for spare parts, but the Diadem insisted that the majority of the ships be maintained in a functional state as training craft and as a strategic reserve. Just in case ... though against what, he didn't know.

Each time Selik Riomini came to Qiorfu via stringline for an inspection visit, and to give his grand-niece a dutiful peck on the cheek, Escobar asked the Black Lord for more challenging duties. At the academy, Escobar had excelled at making tactical decisions in war maneuvers. He had been trained for action.

But he was over thirty now, and his career clock was ticking. With light brown hair and pale blue eyes, classical features, and a manner that looked both dashing and competent, he cut a striking military figure. Escobar wanted a chance to earn his own medals instead of riding on his father's coat-tails. Conceding, perhaps in an effort to keep his grand-niece happy, Lord Riomini had promised him a more exciting assignment. Although there were no current wars or even any local disturbances, the Black Lord had said cryptically, "Be patient. There may be something coming up on Vielinger."

Now he heard his father's distinctive hitching gait as the old man moved along the hallway outside Escobar's closed door. Even the most advanced doctors could not improve the old man's limp; Percival's tissue rejected replacement grafts, and he refused to wear complex prosthetics. His father told a lot of stories about his war years and purported battle injuries, so many tales and in such variation that it was difficult to sort fact from fiction, but Escobar knew a lot of the truth. When they saw the retired Commodore hobbling around in his military uniform, most people assumed the limp was from an injury suffered during the rebellion, but actually it was from a disease. In time, Escobar might show signs of the same degenerative condition, but doctors were already giving him preventive treatments.

His father tried the door handle. The fool thought he was being surreptitious. Escobar made a habit of activating the locks in this section of the manor house.

Knowing his father wouldn't go away, he yanked open the door to see Percival standing there, his silvery muttonchop sideburns even puffier than usual. He'd once been quite muscular, but his physique had sagged on him. Percival took one look at his son standing in his dressing robe. "You're out of uniform, soldier!" As usual, the retired Commodore wore his favorite gold-and-black uniform, threadbare in some places, its jacket wrinkled from the weight of the tarnished medals attached to it.

"I haven't left my room yet, sir. I was just about to dress and go down to the shipyards." His voice took on a hint of defensiveness. "It's not combat duty, but I still do important military work. I'm responsible for keeping all those ships ready."

The old man's large gray eyes narrowed. "Maybe one day you'll be fortunate enough to experience the glory of combat yourself."

"We can only hope, sir." Knowing what would come next, Escobar hurried into his adjacent bedroom to retrieve the black uniform that the servants had laid out. His outfit was gold and black like his father's, but with new-style braids and modern tailoring. So far, he had only one medal to affix to the lapel, an award presented to him for efficient management of the Lubis Plain shipyards.

Standing too close behind his son, Percival launched into one of his interminable stories. "Have I ever mentioned how I got this scar on my forehead?" He touched the edge of his receding hairline. The old man could have had the scar removed, but opted to keep it on display like one of his war medals.

Escobar had, in fact, heard the story numerous times. His mother, now dead for seven years, had endured even more repetition, but she'd lovingly pretended as if each telling was the first time she'd heard it. Love made a person patient, he supposed. Escobar loved and admired his father, but there were limits.

Percival droned on, "I was a career military officer, and I served in several theaters of war before the formation of the Army of the Constellation, before I ever went up against General Adolphus." He lowered his frame onto an antique divan, which made the furniture creak in protest.

Escobar pulled on his trousers, boots, shirt, and suspenders, then worked to secure his cufftabs. In his haste he dropped one, and it tumbled under the bed. He got down on his hands and knees on the soft carpet to find the ornament.

Unfazed, Percival continued talking. "I was in the Barassa campaign of '99, you know, and the Tanine assault of '02."

Escobar located the cufftab and stood up. To his recollection, the old man had been in the *Machi* campaign in '99, not Barassa, and during those engagements Percival Hallholme had made a number of command blunders that had garnered criticism from the Sonjeera high command. Escobar didn't point that out, at the risk of engaging the old man in one of their long arguments. Instead, he said, "You deserve all the medals you got, sir."

"The really big action, though, was when I faced off against General

Adolphus and his rebels in the skies over Sonjeera itself. The climactic battle of the whole rebellion – a clash that decided the future of the Constellation."

The Commodore heaved a long, wistful sigh. "It was eleven years ago, and I was on the bridge of my battle station, commanding the defense of the capital. And I could see quite clearly that we were going to lose!" He jabbed his finger toward his son, who was barely listening. "My entire fleet was out there, badly outnumbered. With no chance of driving off the rebel attack, I developed a key defense strategy – I filled those warships with seventeen thousand civilians we had taken from Crown Jewel planets, all of them members of the leading rebel families, including quite a few from right here on Qiorfu. We roughed up the civilians a little so they looked desperate, then transmitted their images – and dared Adolphus to open fire on us with his superior force."

The retired old soldier paused, as if he had lost his train of thought, then touched the scar on his forehead again. "Ah yes! Right after I delivered my ultimatum, that's when the traitor on my staff rushed from his station, pointed his sidearm at me, and actually fired! In that split second I jerked my head back and fired my own service automatic, killing him on the spot. The blackheart's bullet, though, tore off a chunk of my forehead and hair along with it – as if I could spare any! If I hadn't moved so quickly, I'd be dead myself. Blood was pouring into my eyes but I never passed out, never left my command station. With that traitor lying dead on the deck, I waved off anyone trying to attend to me – and I repeated my demands to General Adolphus."

Rather than the usual ring of triumph in his voice, though, Percival sounded somewhat sad. "The Diadem had commanded me to win at all costs, and I did. I was facing an enemy with a fleet almost twice the size of ours, but because of my strategy, General Adolphus knew that if he opened fire, he'd be killing many thousands of innocent civilians. I had gauged him well. *Know your enemy.* The rebel general blinked. And at the crucial moment, he refused to open fire. I, however, did not."

Percival sniffed. "We tore the rebel ships to ribbons. His own people howled for him to return fire on us, but we had left the codecall lines open, and our human shields pleaded for their lives. Adolphus wouldn't step over that line, but we kept firing. In the end, the General had no choice but to surrender what remained of his force."

Escobar slipped his jacket on, stood in front of a full-length mirror and secured his tie with a gold stickpin bearing the shield insignia of the Riomini family. "Morally sound on your opponent's part, but a poor tactical decision. It cost him the war."

The victory celebrations had painted Commodore Hallholme as a military genius. In that final battle, he had achieved victory for the Constellation while incurring minimal casualties on his side. That triumph had saved Percival's checkered career, erased all mention of prior mistakes, and made him out to be a bold tactician with nerves of steel, and even – ironically – as a great humanitarian.

Luck was on his side, Escobar thought. The Commodore retired immediately after the end of the rebellion and became a veritable recluse on Qiorfu.

Fully dressed now, Escobar hurried toward the hall door. He did not invite his father to join him in the inspection of the shipyards. The Commodore remained on the divan, still talking, as his son slipped out of the manor house and hurried away.

16

It was another grim duty for Cristoph, something that his father should have done. At one time, Louis de Carre had been so good at expressing compassion. He knew how to deal with his people when they were hurting. He would admit that he couldn't possibly understand their grief, yet he felt it anyway. In some ways, the lord had provided a good example for his son. In others . . .

With a knotted stomach, Cristoph drew a deep breath for strength as he entered the intensive-care ward. Doctors reviewed orders, technicians adjusted medical instrumentation. Hovering about were the serene and compassionate Mercifuls, intent nurses who belonged to a secular humanitarian group that had spread across many planets in the Constellation. Sometimes they remembered to flash encouraging smiles to their fading patients, sometimes they didn't. Each bed was covered with a filtration field, though the patients could see and hear. The contaminants were contained and inert, though it was too late to help the dying men and women.

Despite all the medical equipment, Cristoph knew this was little more than a hospice ward. These twelve poor miners didn't have a chance. The only question was how long they would linger, suffering the increasingly debilitating effects of their massive exposure to raw iperion. Another accident . . .

Cristoph could do so little for these people now. *His* people.

Lanny Oberon, the mining supervisor, was inside the hushed room, red-eyed, his face drawn. "My Lord, thank you for coming."

Cristoph bowed respectfully. Some of the bedridden men and women were alert enough to recognize him, and two even struggled into sitting positions, though the smiling, peaceful Mercifuls forced them back down. Three patients remained unconscious, or perhaps pretended to sleep so they didn't have to acknowledge his arrival.

"I'm so very sorry, all of you," Cristoph said. Those words had to be spoken first. "I don't know how this happened, but we will get to the bottom of it."

"Not gonna do us any good," said one of the miners.

"At least there's a bonus clause in the contract if we die in a work-related accident," said a drawn-faced female miner. "My husband and kids don't have to suffer."

The first man snorted. "We're doing all the suffering for them right now."

There was palpable anger in the room. Cristoph stood straight, showing his strength but not his fury. This was all so unnecessary! "I swear to every person here, I will see that you get the best possible treatment, that your families are taken care of, and that this type of accident never happens again."

"Oh, there'll be other accidents," said a gray-faced man lying on the other side of the room. He wheezed as he spoke. "That seems to be standard these days. Everything's falling apart. Nobody's blaming you, my Lord," he added quickly, "but it used to be so different on Vielinger . . ."

Cristoph knew that everyone was indeed blaming him, and it *was* his fault. Whether because of outright sabotage or mismanagement, he hadn't been able to prevent it. He had asked for the extra efforts to extract the last bits of iperion in the deep shafts, when in earlier days the miners would have abandoned those deposits much sooner. "Mr Oberon, introduce me to each one of these workers. I want to know their names and their families."

The mine supervisor led him from bed to bed, telling a little about each victim. Though it was difficult for Cristoph to look at these miners wasting away because of faulty – sabotaged? – equipment, he met their gazes and grasped their hands through the decon field. The least he could do for them was to show that he cared, and then he would follow through on his promise to fix the problem.

He spoke quietly to Oberon, knowing that some of the patients could hear him. "Any preliminary results of your investigations, Lanny? How did this happen?"

The mine supervisor shook his head. "These twelve were in the tail-end of our deepest shaft. A few decades ago we would have ignored the whole vein – not enough there to bother with – but it's worthwhile to plan ahead for tough times, scrape a little harder with what we've already found. To get at the iperion, this team had to do what we call a rough excavation, pulverizing rock so they could filter out any speck of the stuff."

"Much more dust in the air than usual, sir, but we had full-face breathers, respirator systems, gloves," one of the miners spoke up. "And we were told the precautions were sufficient." An angry, assenting mutter coursed around the room. Cristoph was sure he even heard a grumble from two of the supposedly unconscious men.

"You should have been safe." A hard edge of anger crept into his voice. "You should have been able to count on that – *on us*." He turned to Oberon for an explanation. "What went wrong?"

"All the respirators were defective, my Lord. Every single one. The filters were loose, punctured."

"That meant we inhaled the damn iperion!" cried one of the miners, then fell into a bout of heavy coughing for emphasis. "We spent days down there, breathing that toxic stuff, thinking we were safe. It's lodged inside us now, and our lungs are rotting from the inside out!" He raised his hand at the bedside, brushing against the thin decontamination covering.

Cristoph didn't understand how there could have been anything wrong with those breathers. "But I made sure there were regular safety inspections. I audited them myself after the last spate of accidents."

"Oh, the equipment was inspected, my Lord," Oberon said quietly. "Every piece passed the tests – and every one of them failed in practical use."

Cristoph clenched his jaw. Either an inspector had been paid off, or someone had secretly damaged the equipment to make the de Carres look incompetent and to turn the workers against them.

"Cease all iperion operations immediately, Lanny. Shut down every mine, planetwide. I want each breather, every single piece of equipment, inspected by two independent teams. I'll fund the cost for new equipment and lost wages out of my own account. We'll find the money somewhere."

In the two years since his father had gone off to play on Sonjeera with Keana Duchenet, the rival noble families had seen Vielinger as an easy target, and Cristoph as a man easily made into a scapegoat. The artificial catastrophes eroded his ability to effectively manage the major operations his father had left him to handle.

Cristoph loved this planet and its people; he cared for his family honor and their place in Constellation history. But with all these incidents – and his father's continued obliviousness, when the de Carre holdings needed a strong voice on Sonjeera more than ever – Cristoph felt like a single man fighting in vain against the fast-moving phantoms of treachery and propaganda. But he would not give up.

For centuries, the de Carre family had been benevolent wards, and Vielinger was a peaceful and prosperous world with no distinctive exports. Then, nearly two centuries ago, a scientist named Elwar Cori discovered a way to make a theoretical superfast stardrive viable. He found an odd quirk in a rare mineral found on Vielinger, which could mark a path through space, drawing a safe line to keep the recklessly fast starships on course. Before then, no one had paid much attention to the substance.

When the first stringline network was laid down across the Crown Jewels, the de Carres grew fabulously wealthy from selling iperion. Although prospectors combed Crown Jewel worlds and other scattered planets to find alternative sources of iperion, they discovered only a few modest veins, nothing to compete with Vielinger. The lucrative market transformed the planet into a world whose entire industry revolved around iperion processing, and the population had enough money to buy whatever else they needed from offplanet.

Cristoph's predecessors had become accustomed to the wealth, and their profligate spending was legendary, but the people of Vielinger didn't complain, because the wealth trickled down to them as well. Now, however, the wealth might be gone in another decade or two, but Cristoph's father continued his frivolous spending, starstruck with

Princess Keana and giving very little thought to his people, or to the future. That wasn't like him at all.

Everything had been fine before Keana. Vielinger was stable, and the de Carre administration was strong, leaving no vulnerabilities for the Riominis to exploit. But Louis was so fuzzy-headed with love that he'd left his holdings exposed. He was like a man throwing all cares to the wind, celebrating wildly on the eve of Doomsday. While he cavorted with that woman, the jackals had been circling, and now they had finally struck. When Cristoph needed his father most of all, he had no support whatsoever . . .

A young woman entered the ward. Her long brown hair hung loose except for a single braid in the back. She was thin, her movements frantic. She raced to one of the beds and stopped at the protective field. The man there stirred and looked up, then smiled at the woman. When the protective field prevented her from embracing the man fully, she shot a glare at Cristoph. "We trusted you! Weren't their jobs hard enough? Weren't you making enough profit to afford decent safety equipment? Why did you need to kill my husband?"

The miner reached a hand out of the field, trying to hold her wrist and calm her, but she pulled away.

Cristoph knew any words would sound like an excuse. Whenever he talked about sabotage and outside plans to weaken the de Carre family, people thought he was hiding behind a bizarre conspiracy theory to cover his own weakness and errors.

As he looked at this distraught woman and her fading husband – who was dying because *Cristoph* hadn't kept him safe – he knew that excuses and justifications didn't matter to her. These people deserved his best. "Apologies amount to nothing," he said. "I have failed you, but I will make it up to the people of Vielinger by ensuring that no such accident can happen again."

"Just words," the woman said coldly. "I'd rather have my husband than your words."

The codecall box buzzed at Lanny Oberon's hip, and when he took the message, his expression fell. "My Lord – a large fire at the Rapana iperion-processing center! There's been an explosion."

He didn't pause to wonder about the cause of the explosion or the peculiarly devastating timing. "Evacuate, the whole block – get everyone out of there. Check for wind conditions and clear anybody down-wind of the plume!" The smoke from the fires would be toxic to anyone without proper protection.

As he raced off with Oberon, everyone in the ward watched him go. Cristoph felt their unspoken accusations pierce his back like arrows.

Such an accident could not possibly be a coincidence. Arson, sabotage, even outright murder – the rival noble families were using his people as pawns to win their game. But even if someone else caused the disaster, the responsibility fell on his own shoulders. The additional security he'd hired – guards, inspectors, monitoring systems – had not been enough. Therefore, Cristoph had not been enough.

Oberon continued to receive codecall updates as they raced across the city to the Rapana processing center. Black-and-gray smoke rose like poisonous tornadoes. Trucks rolled up, and frantic emergency-response workers donned full-body suits, racing toward the raging fire.

Cristoph and Oberon had to stop two streets away because the swirling fumes had already reached dangerous levels. "Have them get to the people inside first!" Cristoph shouted. "What was the shift complement?"

Oberon remained grave. "At least sixty processors, packagers, and line supervisors. But ... my Lord, they must all be dead by now. Even with full-protective suits, it's too dangerous."

"This is a rescue operation until I know for sure. Get the people out. Afterward, we'll worry about salvaging what we can."

The flames were intense, flapping from breaches in the metal walls, spilling out of the shattered windows. "The iperion inside will all be contaminated, sir," Oberon said. "We'll have to scrap it all."

Cristoph's eyes burned as he continued to stare. No matter what he said and did now, the people would never forgive him, nor could he forgive himself. He felt it all slipping through his fingers.

Perhaps this tragedy was stark enough that his father would return, and the two of them could pool their skills and strength. Somehow, they might manage to rebuild after the disaster, to regain the respect of the people they ruled.

Or maybe this meant the end of the de Carre family.

17

While the business of the Constellation took place in the large public halls and small closed rooms of Council City, Keana and Lord de Carre spent their days in idyllic luxury at her Cottage. The private hideaway was a haven, and Keana cherished every moment with Louis, though he would have to attend a Council session soon enough, and then he needed to go check on his son.

But not today.

Languid in each other's company, they dined on a terrace that cantilevered out to grant them a view of the Pond of Birds, its lily gardens, and the noisy celano geese that lived there at this time of year. He read another passionate poem he had written for her, and she kept the paper with his handwriting. In return, she gave him a love letter she had composed the night before.

Keana took a last bite of seafood mousse, then sopped up the white sauce with her bread. Louis poured himself another glass of chardón and sat back. The waning sunlight cast shadow fragments across his ruggedly handsome face. He extended the bottle toward her. "A little more?"

She offered him her empty glass. "Every day with you is like a honeymoon." She made no mention of her husband, who was much more interested in his solitary hobbies and tedious supply work for the military. Bolton had never been much of a romantic, though he did care for her in his own way, more like a brother than a lover. She wouldn't care a whit if he had his own assignations, but she couldn't imagine him marshalling the passion for it. Romance just wasn't among his interests.

Out on the pond, something agitated the geese; they cackled and skittered across the water, lifting off and flying away. Keana glanced up, balancing her wine glass in two fingers. "Wonder what's disturbed them?"

Louis shrugged as he jammed the empty bottle into the ice bucket.

Keana heard glass breaking downstairs, then shouts followed by running boots. Louis reached for a pistol at his waist, but before he could draw it, red-uniformed soldiers burst onto the terrace, brandishing weapons.

Recognizing the insignia of her mother's elite guard force, Keana leaped to her feet. "I am the Diadem's daughter. How dare you disturb us?"

Without acknowledging her at all, one of the soldiers deftly confiscated the pistol from Louis, and a very young officer stepped forward, little more than an oversized boy. His smooth, round face looked as if it had never been shaved, and his voice was high-pitched as if he had not yet gone through puberty. "Lord Louis de Carre, we have orders from the Council of Lords to place you under arrest for gross negligence and financial malfeasance."

Keana was affronted. "This is absurd! Louis, what are they talking about?"

Two men held Lord de Carre's arms as he struggled to break free, more indignant than afraid. "I demand—"

One of the elite guards slapped an adhesive gag over his mouth so he couldn't speak. "For your own legal protection, Lord de Carre, we are enforcing your right to remain silent."

Keana was astonished. "You can't do this!"

The too-young officer looked blandly at Keana. "Charges will be filed in Council, Princess. You may appear at the appointed time to speak as a character witness in his defense."

"He has done nothing – he's been here with me the whole time!"

"That is precisely the problem, Princess. He has missed six important votes without appointing a proxy." Refusing to answer further questions, the young officer and his guards marched off with the prisoner, their boots clicking on the tiles. Through the gag on his mouth, Louis couldn't even shout a farewell to her.

Stunned, she looked at the wreckage of their meal and of her life. She couldn't believe what had just happened, and she had not been able to do a thing about it. That wasn't possible! Keana turned in circles on the terrace, waiting for someone to explain what had happened, to reveal that it was all a cruel joke.

A tall, slender man appeared in the doorway, wearing the gold-and-black uniform of a logistics officer for the Army of the Constellation; the medals on his chest were decorative only, because he had not served in any combat role. Bolton Crais appeared distraught, and even more terrified than she was. "I-I'm sorry this had to happen, Keana. Even when I couldn't stop the lords from taking action, I still tried to keep you out of it. But they wouldn't listen."

She stared in shock for a moment. "Bolton, what have you done? *You* ordered this?"

He shook his head, but his hazel eyes avoided hers. "My family demanded that the Diadem do something about … about your behavior. You know how they are – they didn't ask my permission. Please believe me, I had nothing to do with this. I heard about it, that's all."

"Then tell them to stop it!" Did she have to hit him in the face with the obvious solution? "Have your family retract their complaint. You and I had an understanding. Go ahead and have any dalliances you like – I don't care. Why would you do this to me?"

"I've never been interested in other women, Keana. You know that."

Actually, she hadn't known that for certain, hadn't paid attention. She felt briefly sorry for him. "Bolton, call the guards back. Command them to release Louis. Do you know what a scandal this will cause? There'll be an uproar."

"I can't command them." Bolton sounded miserable. "And I'm afraid you've already caused the scandal. It doesn't matter what I think – my family will parade me around as the wronged party, the cuckolded husband."

Keana collapsed into her chair, trembling. She didn't understand. "But why would anyone care? It is my own business!"

Bolton looked around, as if worried about eavesdroppers. "More than that, Keana. The Riominis want Vielinger, and you gave them the wedge they needed to force a power shift. The Riominis have documented two years of de Carre negligence, numerous industrial accidents that demonstrate incompetent management. Lord Riomini made a good case that his family must take charge of the Constellation's active iperion mines. He challenged Lord de Carre to a debate about the future of Vielinger, but de Carre never bothered to attend."

"Oh, that's ridiculous! I can't believe this." She knew Louis had shirked some of his tedious duties in order to spend more time with her, but she hadn't believed any of the meetings were particularly important. "Is he going to lose his holdings now because of me?" She looked at her husband, tears streaming down her cheeks. "*Do* something, Bolton!"

The other man obviously wanted to come forward to comfort her, put an arm around her shoulders, but he remained frozen. "I'm very sorry — really, I am. Perhaps you could speak with your mother? She can intercede, if she wants to." *If you give her a reason to.*

Keana wiped her face, but she grew cold inside. Diadem Michella had never been happy about her affair with Louis, or about her refusal to bear a legitimate heir. The Diadem's elite guard would not have come here without specific orders. Ah, now it started to make sense! Yes, by arresting Louis de Carre, the Diadem hoped to gain leverage over her own daughter.

Keana would do whatever she had to. For Louis. And because he loved her, he would understand. For a time, at least, Keana would have to be sequestered and "happily married" to Bolton, until he managed to get her pregnant. The duties and expectations heaped upon her were suffocating!

Neither she nor Bolton had any power to change the course of events. Even if they did work together, the sum of their efforts would amount to nothing. They were both trapped. She had to decide whether she would bow entirely to her mother's demands, or stand up to her.

18

Even after more than a week on Hellhole, Antonia struggled to convince herself that she was safe from Jako Rullins. Yes, she had a new life, a new name, and no one knew who she was or where she had come from. She had absolutely no reason to fear. He would never find her.

Still, she didn't dare underestimate him. Antonia could not relax and let her guard down. She didn't remember what it was like to feel normal.

Devon liked to talk as he worked close beside her in one of the greenhouse domes; he was an encyclopedia of everyday information about Hellhole. "When the General built the colony, everything had to be laid down from scratch. Base soil level, fertilizer matrix, primary nutrients. Humans can't eat any of the native Hellhole species."

Sophie's son worked a regular day like anyone else. The woman had raised him to understand company operations from the ground up, and now he'd taken Antonia under his wing. The young man hovered, obviously smitten with her, but not in Jako's obsessive way. Devon's attentions were sweet, but Antonia had forgotten how to believe a person could be warm and open without something dark lurking inside.

He was pleased to talk about a subject he knew so well. "We've made great strides, year after year. In the open fields, we're getting some crops to survive the native blights, and soon enough, we'll have agriculture on a larger scale. So far, only a handful of hardy cereal grains do well. Most crops need to be grown inside these domes under carefully controlled conditions."

The two crouched together over a bushy tomato plant suspended in a hydroponics solution; water gurgled through the pipes. Antonia inhaled the moisture-laden air, the furry pungent scent of the tomato leaves and nutrient chemicals in the recirculating water.

"It's a never-ending battle. The native species are damned pernicious, and only the toughest, nastiest ones survived the disaster." Devon extended a long needle probe in among the hairy tangled roots to shift some of the strands aside. "See, here's one. If we don't catch it in time, the parasite will penetrate the central root system and kill the plant within days."

Antonia saw the whip-like blue strand wrapped around the tomato's roots. As Devon touched it with the tip of his probe, the thread twitched and tightened.

"We've upgraded our filtration and entry systems, but these things still get in. Their spores are microscopic, and we've all breathed them, so we have to hope they don't adapt and start doing to our lungs what they do to these plants. Our botanists and biologists are studying them."

Helltown had more than its share of doctors. Some acted as general practitioners to tend the numerous cuts, burns, and broken bones that were so prevalent in a rugged frontier colony. Another group of medical professionals, though, treated this planet as a laboratory for new microorganisms and parasites (preferably useful ones). Xenobiologists rejoiced every time an unusual rash or infection appeared in the population so they could add it to the annals of Constellation biological research.

As she drew a breath, Antonia wondered if alien spores had been living inside her from the moment she'd stepped off the passenger pod. She watched the whip-like strand feeding on the tomato roots. "Is it a plant or an animal?"

"A little of both. You should see the cell structure under a microscope." He blinked, then seemed to realize he was rambling. "We don't really understand Hellhole biology – but we know how to get rid of these things." Devon guided the end of the needle probe, and dispensed a discharge of heat and chemical. "Be very careful. If you don't do it exactly right, these things excrete a toxin as they die. It would kill the tomato plant and make you go into convulsions if you touched it."

"How pleasant."

Devon handed her the needle probe. "Here, try it yourself. Shouldn't be hard to find another one of the critters."

As they scrutinized the next tomato plant, Antonia spotted the alien thread. It was much smaller than the first, which made the mitigation process more delicate. Devon was impressed. "I can't believe you noticed that! Very good eye." He seemed to be hoping for more conversation from her.

Without answering, Antonia maneuvered the needle tip, careful not to disturb the alien parasite. "You have to admire something so tough. Any native life form that could survive the total destruction of an ecosystem has to be ruthless and hardy. It's had to adapt, fight, and survive – and not everybody will like the changes that are necessary."

Antonia realized that *she* had certainly changed from the person she'd been.

She jabbed the needle, dispensed the hot poison, and watched the thread shrivel and die.

Devon said, "Good – just like a professional."

"Is this going to be my profession now?" Antonia felt some fondness for him in return, though she wasn't about to let down her emotional walls.

The young man kept talking. "My mother brought me here when I was ten. I don't remember my father, but she says he was a real bastard. I suppose she did things she's not proud of, too, to get me off planet and set up a new life here. I'm glad she did. This is my home now." Devon seemed embarrassed. "But I'd like to see Sonjeera someday, maybe even go to Klief and track down my father so I can punch him in the face." He gave a nervous laugh of bravado.

"Not a good idea. It's best not to reopen wounds."

He tried to draw her out, looking fascinated. "What's your most vivid memory of the Crown Jewel worlds? You were just there."

Antonia froze. "My most vivid memories are the ones I'd like to forget."

"Sorry I asked." He couldn't cover his hurt expression.

In her mind, though, Devon's question triggered a cascade of images and emotions. Details involving Jako were her most vivid recollections. He had set in motion an avalanche that forever changed her life; Antonia hadn't even seen what he was doing until it was too late . . .

On the night of their last date, when Jako escorted her back to their home with a cocky swagger, she had opened the door, intending to stand there and give him a goodnight kiss. Instead, she'd seen both of her parents dead in the entry hall. Murdered.

That had been the end of the girl named Tona Quirrie. As she screamed and screamed at the sight of the bodies and all the blood, Jako reacted with utter – and inappropriate – panic. Rather than calling the authorities, he grabbed her hand and fled. She was devastated, wailing, but Jako forced her to run.

After they'd found a place to hide, still breathing hard and terrified, he haltingly told her about his dark past. She was too dazed to grasp the appalling reality of what he revealed to her. "Jako Rullins isn't my actual name, nor is this my real appearance."

Hanging his head and averting his haunted eyes, he explained that he was an illegitimate son of Lord Selik Riomini, one of the most power-ful men in the Constellation. "I am an embarrassment to him. I muddy the waters of Riomini succession here on Aeroc. He's been trying to kill me for years . . . and now his hired assassins must have tracked us down. The Black Lord murdered your parents, and he would have killed you too if you'd been home. He controls this planet's law enforcement and the courts, you know. That's why we can't go to the authorities!" He clutched her arm. "I have to keep you safe."

Jako convinced her to go into hiding with him. She didn't know what else to do. He kept her moving, claimed to see assassins in shad-ows, told her stories of numerous times he had barely escaped with his life, how he thought he'd found peace and security in his new identity working for her father, just like a normal person . . . He was the only one she could be close to, the only friend, the only confidante. Jako wouldn't let her get close to anyone else.

One night, two weeks after the murders, they hid in an alley. Wet from a light pattering rain but warm as they huddled together, Jako had looked up to the cloud-muffled sky. "I know this isn't the wedding you ever imagined, but let's be married, right here out in the open, with no one to see or hear but ourselves." He flashed a smile at her. "It's our commitment that counts anyway, nothing else."

Not so long ago, she had wanted to marry him with all her heart; she had begged her parents to allow the wedding, and was devastated when they'd told her to wait. Now, she agreed out of desperation; they were already tied together by their hearts as well as circumstances. This was not a fairy-tale romance at all, yet Jako seemed to find it delightful. At first, she thought he was just being brave, making the best of their ragged situation. But he really did want it that way.

Their first lovemaking was clumsy, unsatisfying, and rushed – as it was so many times over the next two years, with Jako snatching a moment when he thought they might be safe. Antonia never shook off the sensation that she might be in the targeting scope of a hunter's weapon. Passion and edgy fear became inseparably linked in her mind.

They survived like that, constantly moving to elude detection, eking out a living from job to job to job. He taught her how to change her identity, how to dye her hair and cut it herself. Every time she tried to make friends, or became attached to a particular employer or place, Jako whisked her away, whispering urgently that Riomini hunters had found them again.

For Antonia it was a long, incredible nightmare, but Jako seemed to find the idea romantic: running away together and having her depend only on him.

One day she discovered to her horror that it was all a lie. Accidentally, while viewing some news coverage of unsolved crimes, she saw his image and learned that Jako wasn't a Riomini heir after all, and that hunters were after them, but not of the type she'd thought. Worst of all, she learned that *he* was the one who had hired killers to eliminate her parents just so he could set up this elaborate ruse. One of the contract assassins had been caught and had confessed everything.

During their time on the run, Jako had made certain she had no ties to keep her connected to home; he had stripped away all hope so that she would believe his preposterous story. Antonia also realized that if she confronted him with the knowledge, he would get violent, perhaps even kill her. Once she discovered the truth, she had to keep him from finding out that she knew.

By then, Jako had taught Antonia to be wary, never to trust anyone, and in the process he had unwittingly taught her how to spot the telltale signs of deception in himself. She came to understand how possessive he was, that his convoluted plot had built a cage designed to keep her with him and only him.

She bided her time for weeks until she saw her opportunity. She cut her hair again, dyed it a different color, and hurried to the Aeroc spaceport and colonization office. After forging the proper agreements and offering a new set of ID that she had obtained without Jako's knowledge, she boarded the next departing ship.

And now, on Hellhole, maybe she was at last safe . . .

Antonia glanced up when she heard excited chatter from other workers tending the hydroponic gardens. They were pointing to the top of the hemisphere overhead. Through the transparent crystal plates, she watched glowing blue spheres of diaphanous energy bounce from point to point on the metal support gridwork.

"A kind of St Elmo's Fire," Devon explained, trying to be nonchalant. "Happens all the time."

The blue static whorls furled and bounced. Some of them collided with a shower of sparks and vanished into the air. Other fairy lights continued dancing around the dome's apex.

She looked at Devon, thinking about his idealistic curiosity concerning the Crown Jewel planets. "What you have here may not be glamorous, Devon, but be content. There's a dark side to excitement and adventure."

19

Though it was the territorial capital of eleven Deep Zone colonies, Ridgetop was required to pay tribute to the Constellation just like any other world. Governor Carlson Goler had to encourage the production of useful items from all the planets he supervised under authority from the Diadem. It was his job, though he did not relish it.

The fledgling DZ settlements struggled to stand on their own feet, even though they still received regular supply shipments from the Crown Jewels. The colonists planted crops to feed *themselves*, established mining and fabrication industries to meet *their own* urgent needs and support *their own* people. They didn't have surplus resources or luxury items to please the Constellation's noble families.

On each of his eleven planets, Territorial Governor Goler had to act as if the Diadem's priorities were more important than the colonists'. No wonder the individual planetary administrators didn't like him. How could he sound credible when he didn't necessarily agree with the idea himself? He had done his best, trying to soften the blow from the Constellation behemoth, even though he could never deflect it. And he had to be careful so that his efforts weren't obvious, which meant the people didn't realize how hard he was trying.

Goler sighed . . . then sneezed. The pollens in Ridgetop's air often irritated him. He was a lanky, dark-skinned man with a quiet voice and a soft demeanor. Many of his fellow territorial governors considered him innocuous; others simply found him invisible.

With the next stringline hauler due to arrive in three days, Ridgetop's required tribute had to be prepped. Goler went out to the steep hillsides to watch heavy machinery clear another swath of spindly but beautiful goldenwood trees. Dirt roads had been carved onto the steep slopes, zigzagging through razed areas where overworked loggers clearcut the tall forest, leaving only stumps and trampled, weedy vegetation.

Because the goldenwood groves were so gorgeous and serene, such hillside scars offended Goler's sensibilities, but the logging was necessary; he knew of no other way to meet the tribute. Fortunately, after being severely shocked by cutting, the trees' root systems responded with an outburst of growth and would cover the hillsides again in a decade.

Goldenwood lumber shimmered in the sunlight like veins of precious metal, making it a much prized building material. Once processed, the boards were packed into reinforced upboxes and launched into orbit, where they would be retrieved by the stringline hauler, and rushed to Sonjeera for distribution.

Down in the cutting zone, humming lifters grasped smooth trunks, while trimmers sliced off feathery leaf clusters that looked like strips of metal foil. Scooping up armfuls of sheared-off leaves, male and female lumber workers packed them in crates. In a flash of inspiration, Goler had actually convinced the Constellation that goldenwood leaves were valuable and could be processed into exotic materials and coatings, and they had become moderately popular among nobles on the Crown Jewel world. By contrast, no one on Ridgetop saw much use in the leaves, but the settlers were happy to include them as part of the tribute to the Diadem. It eased their burden a little bit.

For eleven years now, Michella had been content enough with Goler's leadership. When he was first assigned to this DZ planet, she told him that his utmost priority was to see that the new colonists caused no trouble. "Ridgetop has already given me enough difficulties, Mr Goler. Let's not do that again."

Before his arrival, the Army of the Constellation had razed an old squatter colony and replaced all the unauthorized settlers with her own people. Over the years, under Goler's administration, Ridgetop had become a model frontier colony.

The numerous habitable planets in the Deep Zone had been known for centuries, peripherally mapped by probes and intrepid long-range explorers. But without any established stringline connections, those worlds were considered too distant and inconvenient to be worth a major settlement effort. The only way to reach them had been via old-style FTL transport, which required voyages that lasted months or years.

Back then, the DZ planets attracted only the hardiest and most desperate colonists. Few were willing to leave the comforts of Crown Jewel civilization to risk the long and expensive voyage, unless they had nothing to lose. Anyone who decided to colonize those enigmatic worlds knew it would be a one-way trip, since old FTL ships had insufficient fuel for the return voyage and had no spacedock or manufacturing facilities on the other end. They were pioneers going off into the unknown.

The newly extended stringline network changed all that. By dispatching her trailblazer vessels to lay down iperion paths to the frontier planets, Diadem Michella suddenly had fifty-four new worlds under her control. With her blessing, she invited ambitious people from the crowded Crown Jewels to go and make a new start.

Not surprisingly, the original squatters who had ventured out to claim virgin territory years earlier were not pleased with the sudden influx of outsiders. They had left the Constellation behind long ago and had been surviving without help or interference from the old government. When Michella annexed the entire Deep Zone and subsequently imposed tariffs and taxes, the independents resisted violently. The Diadem was forced to dispatch her military to squash several uprisings, including one on Ridgetop before she brought in Carlson Goler to clean up the mess and start afresh.

Even though he was Territorial Governor out here, the powerful noble families back in the Crown Jewels considered him little more than a trumped-up civil servant. But Goler did his work and paid attention to the way the wind was blowing. He had always been a realistic man, yet he had already achieved much more than he'd expected. Though fulfilling the Diadem's regular tribute was a persistent thorn in his side, Goler chose not to rock the boat. The people understood that.

He had been a career government worker on Sonjeera, with no hope of advancing himself, until his name came up for the Ridgegtop assignment because of his past loyal but unremarkable service. Out in the Deep Zone, though, he had his chance. He considered it an honor to be here in an important job, and he maintained his primary residence on Ridgetop.

His fellow territorial governors didn't hold the same view. They had their homes and offices on Sonjeera, working out of the Bureau of Deep Zone affairs – an opulent new building that had been under construction for four years on the edge of Council City. Even though the other governors maintained nominal offices in the Deep Zone, most were loath to leave the opulence and comforts of the Crown Jewels.

Goler actually liked living on Ridgetop. He had grown rather fond of the place, though the other governors rolled their eyes, considering him backward. They argued that it was impractical for a territorial governor to live anywhere other than Sonjeera – why bother with all that extra travel, they asked him, to ride the stringline from Ridgetop back to the Constellation's main hub, then back out to one of the other worlds under his jurisdiction?

The fact was, he didn't much like Sonjeera. Goler preferred his hillside home among the goldenwood groves.

However, the colonists here still regarded him as the Diadem's man. No matter how he tried to soften the blow, he was still required to impose obedience and collect the tribute payments.

Now, out in the lumber processing yards, he signed off on four sealed upboxes, smiled and thanked the workers. As the ground crew prepared the boxes' internal engines for ascent to orbit, one red-faced man wiped sweat from his eyes and let out a disgusted sigh. "Governor, can't you tell the Diadem that these trees are worth a hell of a lot more than she gives us credit for? Pad out the tribute a little so we have some breathing room?"

Goler shook his head, then sneezed again. "I wish I could, but her inspectors watch everything with hawk eyes. Breathe easy, though – I am confident the market price of goldenwood will continue to go up."

"Why is that?" The logger did not sound convinced.

"Because I happen to know the Diadem is building a new lake house out of goldenwood, and after the nobles see it, they'll all want to imitate it. When the demand increases even more because of that, we can charge them through the nose."

The other man grumbled. "I'd like to spend less of my day working for Her Eminence and more of it with my own family."

"You're doing a fine job." There wasn't much else Goler could say. "Let's get these shipments ready. After the stringline hauler leaves, you'll have weeks to take care of your own needs."

Finished with his inspection, Goler returned to his peaceful open-architecture home on the hillside. He had other work to do this afternoon, documents to check, regular reports from the administrators of the other planets he supervised, but he doubted there would be anything crucial. Goler's underlings considered him a bland and unremarkable leader, but he knew things the others didn't, a secret about Ridgetop that continued to gnaw at him . . .

He had designed the A-frame house with large window-walls for the spacious views. The treated goldenwood lumber that comprised the walls, floors, and rafters might be worth a fortune elsewhere, but on Ridgetop, *every* house was built of the substance.

The outside air held so much fluffy pollen that Goler's eyes and nose burned. He sneezed repeatedly after he came through the door. Seeing him back home, his old household servant, Tasmine, brought him a pitcher of iced herbal tea. "I sprinkled dried priniflower in the brew. That'll stop the inflammation and sneezing."

He sipped it gratefully, knowing it would take effect quickly. "Thank you, Tasmine. You work miracles." The aged woman knew more about Ridgetop's indigenous plants and their medicinal properties than any other person – but then, she had been here much longer than anyone else. "We should catalog and patent your herbal remedies, Tasmine."

She sniffed. "My knowledge is my own. I choose to share it with you, but anyone else from the Constellation can suffer and die for all I care."

Her comment did not surprise him. "We've got our own biologists, and the pharmaceutical hunters search for anything worthwhile they can bring back to Sonjeera. They may discover some local remedies without your help." A rare and potent drug would certainly help him pay the regular tribute.

Tasmine huffed. "They have their gadgets, but they have no common sense, nor experience. It'll take them longer than you think, Governor."

"Don't worry, I won't point them in the right direction." Though she seemed stiff and formal, Tasmine was one of his only friends, his only real sounding board on Ridgetop. The Constellation officials considered Goler a bit odd, and the Ridgetop people maintained their distance from the government man, though he tried to keep a cordial relationship. He had to walk a fine line.

It was from the old household servant that Goler had learned exactly what had happened here on Ridgetop, before he and the Diadem's fresh wave of colonists had arrived. The truth was very hard for him to keep inside, but he had no choice. Constellation history called it the "Ridgetop Recovery," but he knew that those innocuous words cloaked a wealth of bloodshed.

Fifteen years ago, when Constellation representatives informed the original squatters that Ridgetop had been officially annexed, the colonists flat-out refused to concede. They had come here by their own means and survived nearly a century without contact from the Constellation, but Diadem Michella did not accept their claims of independence, especially after she had spent a fortune in star crowns to establish the new stringline path out to Ridgetop.

The next ship arrived not with colonists or supplies, but with a military force. Operating under strict orders, soldiers swarmed over the Ridgetop settlement, swept through the goldenwood groves that the old settlers had tended for generations. They burned the local homes, hunted down and killed every colonist, buried the bodies in shallow graves, and razed the entire site.

Sweeping all the horrors under the rug, they erected prefabricated barracks and announced that Ridgetop had been "recovered in the name of the Constellation." No further details. A wave of eager new colonists came in to claim one of the most hospitable Deep Zone worlds.

When he took up residence here, pleased with his promotion, Goler was unaware of Ridgetop's dark history. The second-wave colony had flourished for several years before Tasmine appeared. She served in his household for some time, and when she finally convinced herself to trust Goler, she revealed to him in private that she was the last, the only survivor of the original colony. During the military operations, she had hidden in the trees and watched her family and friends slaughtered.

She'd given him proof, too, a secret video recording of the killings that showed black-uniformed Riomini mercenaries committing atrocities in the name of the Constellation. Tasmine even guided him out to one of the burial sites, where they found human bones that had been exposed by rains. Afraid to ask questions of Sonjeera, Goler ordered a discreet investigation of the site. Sadly, he didn't require much convincing.

The Ridgetop Recovery – the Ridgetop *Slaughter* – was a black secret that Diadem Michella believed to be safely buried. As much as Goler wanted to expose the horrific story to the public, he didn't dare. Despite Tasmine's wounded sense of justice, he could think of no possible positive outcome from doing so, but *he* knew the truth, and the old woman was satisfied with that.

Goler felt that the original Ridgetop squatters had been naïve fools to expect anything other than the bloody response they received. But that was no excuse. Those people had been innocent and free, and they hadn't known any better. *Goler* knew better, and he didn't dare stand against Michella's plans for expansion.

Looking through the wide windows of his home, he sipped the herbal tea and felt his sinuses begin to clear. The first of the four loaded upboxes roared into the sky, heading to orbit. From here, he could see whole sections of the mountainsides that had been clearcut of goldenwood trees.

Tasmine stood at his side and watched. When she spoke, her voice was rough and husky. "There's blood in those trees. We both know it."

Goler couldn't help but agree.

20

Tanja Hu climbed the steep hillside above Saporo Harbor without ropes or gear, sometimes picking her way along the abandoned funicular track, other times veering off onto the stable rocks. She wore a small pack and a floppy hat to keep the hot afternoon sun off her face. Her assistant Bebe Nax sometimes accompanied her on other trails, but on this route Tanja preferred to be alone.

Hiking was one of her favorite forms of exercise, and the latest weather report indicated that this might be her last chance for a climb before the seasonal rains came. The exertion was not hard for her, since she kept herself active and fit. Her cousins thought she was funny, laughing that she would try to avoid feminine plumpness. Even Uncle Quinn agreed that she was far too skinny, but Tanja didn't like the idea of any part of herself being soft.

Today this was about more than a hike.

She glanced up through the trees to the sky. At least she wouldn't have to climb back down the same way – if Ian Walfor kept his word.

Tanja made her way around the pair of weed-overgrown funicular cars, side by side on their parallel tracks. Activating the clock in her earadio, she heard the time: nearly noon. As she neared the top of the rock, perspiring and aching, she watched a white streak cross the sky, heard a distant sonic boom – Walfor showing off in one of his shuttles, probably fueling his engines with testosterone. Maybe he thought it would impress her. Though she did nothing to encourage him, she hoped he wouldn't stop trying.

The contrails in the atmosphere looped around as the ship descended towards the hilltop, where Tanja waited for him. She heard the roar of engines as Walfor switched to an alternative propulsion system. Fascinated by obsolete technology, he had a talent for merging the old with the new, processing his own fuels for the numerous old engines he collected on frozen Buktu. Bright afterburners blazed overhead, and the roar of engines grew so loud that she had to cover her ears.

Though the hilltop looked too small to accommodate the shuttle, Walfor masterfully brought down the tube-shaped ship on a flat ledge. When he'd first suggested the unorthodox meeting place, Tanja was skeptical, but he insisted that he could land on a proverbial pinhead and take off again without disturbing the pin. His abilities almost matched his boast. Pieces of rock flaked away beneath the precariously balanced craft and tumbled down the steep slopes. He left the engines rumbling as he waited for her to board.

Tanja hurried forward as a slingvator cage glided down the side of the hull. She slipped into the cage, and it reeled her upward into the open hatch. As she stepped through the open cargo area, she saw secured shipping containers piled deck to ceiling, bulkhead to bulkhead. This was one of the craft Walfor used to haul materials to and from his larger cargo ships, which surreptitiously made the rounds among carefully selected planets that were within reach of his engines.

A pair of Buktu men in gray onesuits worked in the hold, carrying e-boards, tapping in inventory entries. Adjusting a cargo strap, a plump, frizzy-haired man cordially gestured her forward, along a narrow aisle-way. "Captain Walfor is waiting for you."

Walfor's black marketeers operated an eclectic assortment of souped-up old FTL spacecraft and smaller shuttles that were no longer listed on any official records. He picked them up wherever he could.

In the original plan, the Constellation's trailblazers had laid down iperion paths from Sonjeera to all fifty-four DZ worlds, and once the paths were painted, stringline-capable vessels could race along at fantastic speeds. However, when the obscure Deep Zone planet Buktu proved to be an unprofitable destination, the Diadem signed an order to cease maintenance on that particular line, effectively cutting off Walfor and his people. With smiling generosity, Michella had offered to rescue and relocate the small population, but – much to everyone's surprise – they unanimously refused, saying they would remain behind and take their chances on their cold, isolated rock, as they had done for some time.

Unknown to the Diadem, Ian Walfor had an idea that made his out-of-the-way location valuable.

Long ago, when the original pioneers ventured into the DZ, their vessels had carried only enough fuel for a one-way trip. Arriving at their destinations, those ships were abandoned, cannibalized for spare parts, and supposedly scuttled. However, Walfor had collected a number of those old ships and put them into service as a slow-boat form of transportation. On Buktu, his hardy frontiersmen developed their own secret industrial facilities, manufacturing fuel for the FTL drives from local ices and gases, and they improved the antique propulsion systems to make the ships faster. In that manner they had thrived for years, completely beyond the notice of the Constellation.

As she reached the cockpit, Tanja said, "You don't make a subtle entrance, do you?" She strapped herself into a bucket seat beside him. "What happened to keeping a low profile?"

He looked completely innocent. "Why, I'm just delivering foodstuffs, building products, and machinery to needy villagers on your planet."

"And you'd better head out soon or you won't get to Hellhole in time. The General will be waiting for you."

Walfor went through the take-off sequence, then sped quietly across the landscape. "Are you that anxious to get rid of me?"

Tanja sat back and held on. "We've got a meeting scheduled there, and *you* take a lot longer to travel than the rest of us do. Besides, I need you to get your unauthorized cargo vessel away from Candela before the next stringline hauler arrives from Sonjeera."

Walfor didn't seem concerned. "Oh, I doubt the Constellation pilot will even rouse himself from his nap when he gets here – but we'll be long gone, don't you worry your pretty head. Right now, I can spend just a little more time with you."

She raised her eyebrows. "You realize you don't have a chance with me, right? But you're welcome to keep trying."

He grinned. "All right, then I'll keep trying."

Despite his attitude, she knew that Walfor always did as he promised. She liked him as a friend and business associate, and he performed his work very well. *Important work*, as she and General Adolphus knew. He had enjoyed his week of downtime here on Candela, but it was time for him to load the processed iperion aboard his vessel and head off ...

After they set down on a paved field 200 kilometers north, he switched to another antique propulsion system and taxied to a large, weathered warehouse – Walfor's hub for distribution to the most populated areas of the planet. As he and Tanja emerged, crewmen were busy unloading crates from the shuttle and loading them onto trucks for delivery to Puhau and other isolated mountain towns.

"That's the last of everything I brought with me from Boj," he said. "Special discount for my favorite planetary administrator. If you feel inclined to offer any personal bonuses ..."

"I've offered you and your crew plenty of hospitality in the past week. Time to get to work. Uncle Quinn has the iperion shipment ready to go."

Inside the warehouse they found seats in a cafeteria on the second level, and Walfor retrieved them each a bottle of local beer. Tanja downed hers and followed it with a container of cold water. She watched the cargo activities outside and mused aloud, "My accountants say your profit margins are so low that they can't believe you're making any money from the Candela run."

"Oh? You want me to raise my prices?"

"No, it's just that the practitioners of your profession are not exactly known for being honest."

"Maybe I'm giving you a special deal because I like you." He smiled at her, and she didn't believe it for a minute. He finally said, "All right, I have a higher calling, a long-range vision. The General's plan makes a lot of sense. If it works, then everyone in the Deep Zone makes a lot more profit." He seemed uncharacteristically sincere rather than cocky. "I think of it as an investment."

"We're each making a hefty investment," she said. *And taking a deadly risk.*

Using her own financing, Tanja had quietly purchased a group of off-the-books trailblazer vessels that had been decommissioned after the new Constellation network was complete. Since the Diadem had no further use for the vessels, Tanja was able to buy them at fire-sale prices, supposedly to be used for local planetary purposes. Ian Walfor's crew at Buktu had refitted and launched them, secretly delivering them to General Adolphus. With regular supplies of Candela iperion, the co-conspirators had everything they needed.

Finishing her water, she stood. "Much as I enjoy your company, Ian, I need to cut our date short and make arrangements to get to Hellhole myself. Your trip may take longer, but mine is a lot more roundabout. The General won't want either of us to be late."

"Oh, he'll soften up once I arrive with the iperion shipment. I'll be there."

"That's all I ask."

21

When they set off across Hellhole's unexplored vastness to search for wonders and mysteries, Vincent finally thought he understood the excitement that had so energized Fernando. Maybe they would discover something interesting after all.

In Michella Town, the two men had received clothing, rations, tools and an overland vehicle rugged enough to withstand the dangers the planet was likely to throw at them. Their safety briefing turned out to be a two-day-long workshop during which they were bombarded with details about seismic activity, volcanic eruptions, dust clouds, toxic gas plumes vented from underground reservoirs, poisonous vegetation, indigenous insect analogs, pernicious parasites, and fungal infections that could get a foothold on human flesh. Possible storms fell into several categories: thunderstorms, windstorms, lightning, hail, freak blizzards, and tornadoes, in addition to the exotic smoke storms and static outbursts, colloquially called growlers, such as they'd experienced on their arrival day. And those were only the *known* hazards. Part of their job as topographical prospectors was to discover what else this planet had to offer, both good and bad.

Vincent had studied the information carefully, reviewing it for hours, though Fernando didn't seem to be paying much attention. He could barely sit still as they prepared to depart in their well-provisioned Trakmaster.

Vincent offered to drive on the first shift, while his friend busied himself at the navigation screen, calling up charts of the many unmapped grid squares. Not surprisingly, the grid squares around Michella Town, along with the outlying industrial camps and mining outposts, had already been adequately surveyed, but much of the landscape beyond that remained an enigma, covered by only large-scale satellite over-flights.

Fernando scrolled the nav-screen to choose which place he wanted to explore first. "It's all wide open. I'm not used to having so many lucrative possibilities."

"We haven't found anything yet."

"We will. How could we not find anything in all that area?" Fernando increased the magnification, studied dry canyons, the sparkling smears of salty inland seas, river courses choked with odd alien vegetation. "What if we find monsters?"

"No monsters here. At least not big ones." He was sure Fernando had heard that part of the briefing. "The asteroid impact killed all large indigenous life forms. Nothing bigger than small birds or rodents survived."

"So the scientists say." Fernando pouted at him. "Don't spoil the mystery for me. This is an alien world, so there's no guarantee what we might find. The local experts are rewriting their theories every day."

While Vincent would have preferred to work their way methodically from one grid square to the next, Fernando selected a point at random, intrigued by the tortured, abandoned terrain. On reflection, one place seemed as good as another to Vincent, so they headed out to Fernando's chosen coordinates.

Away from what passed for civilization, the rugged Trakmaster crossed hills covered with fibrous grasses. Vincent drove cautiously, ignoring his friend's urging for greater speed and frequent side trips. He followed the procedure list from the exploration office. They stopped several times, and Vincent dutifully took images and botanical samples from knobby shrubs covered with plate-like lavender leaves. The heavy vehicle splashed through a stone-lined stream choked with rubbery algae.

The grid square that had intrigued Fernando was badlands terrain, ash and mud that had piled up in multicolored layers during the post-impact upheaval. Centuries of wind and rain had carved the mounds into fantastic shapes. From the vehicle's high cab, Fernando used the built-in imagers to take plenty of panoramic images, along with several unnecessary ones of Vincent at work.

By early afternoon they ground the Trakmaster to a halt beside a sheer wall of exposed rock. Vincent thought it looked interesting. "The General wants hands-on samplings. Let's see what's out there."

"Sure, I'm ready to stretch my legs." Fernando opened the hatch and emerged, wandering around the vehicle, while Vincent pitched their self-erecting tent so they could spend the night. Ready to go, they took grid maps, imagers, and tools, activated the vehicle's locator transponder, and then ventured into the widening arroyos, weaving their way through unusual hoodoos and rock formations.

Fernando turned around and smiled. "Look at that." Vincent didn't see what had captured his friend's interest, but the other man pointed at the ground. "Your footprints and mine. This is an unexplored sector. We could be the first human beings ever to walk here. That isn't something you can say anywhere in the Crown Jewels."

They explored side canyons where the vertical walls had sloughed away to expose strata studded with clumps of bones, empty exoskeletons, preserved native insects each the size of a fist, remains of animals both large and small.

"I bet the General would pay for these fossils!" Fernando exclaimed.

Vincent used tools from his pack to chip out specimens for the xenobiologists back in Michella Town. "These creatures must have been buried in the eruptions and mudslides." After recording exactly how the fossils were positioned in the rock wall, he extracted a bony lump that might have been something as delicate as a bird. Moving down the wall, he brushed away caked mud to expose a massive bone more than a meter in length, but he found no other parts of the animal. "Maybe it's a trash heap. Could be the aliens ate those big creatures."

"Or the big creatures ate them."

After they finished gathering specimens, Vincent looked up to see an unusual display of dark helical clouds, like ribbons of rain twisted in spirals high overhead. "Do you remember any pattern like that from our briefing?"

Fernando took images of the clouds, but an uneasy Vincent activated the locater that would guide them back to the Trakmaster. "Maybe we should hurry. I'd rather be close to shelter if that turns into a storm."

Geometrical-hail showers began to fall before they reached the vehicle. Sharp ice crystals pelted them, bouncing off the ground or sticking in the mud. Vincent and Fernando began running, yelling with good humor as they spotted their camp ahead. The hail picked up in intensity and size, and Fernando yelped as a particularly large shard struck him on the back of the head. They raced each other back to the tent and dove under the resilient overhang. Sputtering and gasping, they wiped their faces and hair, then sat inside the shelter, staring at the furor of the sparkling storm.

As the falling crystals drummed on the fabric, Vincent double-checked the seals; he hoped the tent would hold.

Fernando lay back, kicked up his feet, and drew a deep, satisfied breath. "Isn't this a great job, all by ourselves, seeing amazing things? Much better than plucking weeds or dusting off vineyards. I've always dreamed about doing something like this."

"That wasn't what you told me aboard the passenger pod."

"A man can have more than one dream, can't he? I've proved that again and again."

"So why did you come to Hellhole in the first place? Tell the truth this time."

A dismissive shrug. "This seemed like the perfect place to go."

"Hellhole is never 'the perfect place to go.' What's your real story?"

"Oh, come now, there's always a silver lining, even if it's tarnished. My whole life I've rolled with the punches from one interest to the next, one dream to another. If you want lightning to strike, you put out a lot of lightning rods."

"And *this* is where you came to seek your fortune? I take it Hellhole wasn't your first choice."

"Well, I started out on Vielinger, then moved to Marubi, then Sonjeera. My initial idea was to start a restaurant – everyone needs to eat, right? How could it fail?" Fernando described how he had convinced investors to help him establish the restaurant, but he didn't know much about managing a business, and the place went bankrupt within a year. "I tried my best, but things like that happen. My investors lost all their money, but I lost all that hard work. It hurt me as much as it hurt them, so I don't understand why the investors were so angry with me. That's just the way it goes."

On another planet, Fernando next decided to open a clothing store. "Everyone has to wear clothes, right? How could it fail?" He acquired a different group of investors, but he chose a poor location for the shop and carried the wrong selection for that area; though he greeted his customers with great aplomb and enthusiasm for each garment choice, he made very little profit. The store closed its doors within seven months, and Fernando had to leave quickly, fleeing from the furious investors.

Relaxing inside the tent with the hail shower continuing outside, Fernando made a disgusted sound. "I don't understand what I was supposed to do about that. Weren't we all partners? It was a team effort, and the team failed. I wasn't the only one responsible. But they didn't see it that way. They blamed *me*." He shook his head. "Blame is just a festering sore for people who can't move on."

And so Fernando had moved on – several times – and finally reached a point where he had to leave the Crown Jewels far behind, and quickly. "But I look at this new stage in my life as uncovering possibilities. The Deep Zone worlds are wild, untamed, and unexplored. They need an ambitious person like me. I'll do fine here."

"But why Hellhole?" Vincent asked. "There are more pleasant DZ worlds to choose from."

Fernando shook more glittering moisture from his wavy, brown hair. "Why should I go where all the other rainbow-chasers are? Give me a planet that's full of opportunities. And this is just the place."

"If you say so."

An hour later, the storm abated. The two men emerged to see a pounded and washed landscape. Vincent drew a deep breath of the clean scent of ozone. Around them, the caked sedimentary ground appeared to be covered with diamonds, while mist rose from the evaporating hail.

As Fernando trudged off to relieve himself, the crystals crunched under his feet. Vincent pointed a thumb back toward the Trakmaster. "Why not use the reclamation closet?"

The other man just gave him a sour look. "You don't understand the freedom of the outdoors."

Fernando went around an outcropping and descended into an arroyo, while Vincent returned to the vehicle, tallied the images that had been taken that day, and used the satellite connection to upload them to the survey office in Michella Town. Although he didn't have his friend's enthusiasm, Vincent was reasonably content. He had come here under bad circumstances, but he could tolerate this after all. He'd make a new life for himself, exactly as Fernando said . . .

Just then, his friend came running back to the campsite, yelling and waving his hands. His fly was still open. "You won't believe it! An alien creature. It was huge – the size of an ox, but it moved like a panther!"

Vincent frowned. "That's not even a good joke. There's nothing but fossils around here." He waved a hand at the barren landscape. "Look at this place. Nothing that large could live out here."

"It's not a joke! I saw it with my own eyes. A big animal, just on top of the ridge back there. Could be a predator. What weapons do we have?"

"We don't have any weapons. What would we shoot at? There *are* no indigenous predators. Nothing bigger than a rodent, remember."

"Tell that to the monster I just saw. Unbelievable! We're all alone out here in a wild environment, and the General gives us nothing to defend ourselves with? What was he thinking?"

"There's nothing to defend ourselves *against*. Come on, Fernando, you know that. You probably saw shadows in the mist from the evaporating hail."

"It was plain as day – and big!" Fernando stretched out his hands to indicate something extremely large.

"All right, then show me. Maybe it left footprints." Vincent tried to brush aside his automatic uneasiness. If the thing truly existed, he knew such information would be valuable to the scientists. But he was sure Fernando was just pulling his leg.

"I'm not going back over there unless you give me a weapon! There might be more of those things. Let's get back inside the Trakmaster."

Knowing his friend's penchant for exaggeration, Vincent was not convinced, but Fernando looked sincerely shaken.

22

The blistering, blue, giant star SVC-1185 was prominent in the skies of all twenty Crown Jewels, but its own planets were nothing more than lifeless rocks. Nevertheless, the uninhabited system was a perfect place for a substation along the stringline path to Ridgetop in the Deep Zone.

For years now, Turlo Urvancik and his wife Sunitha had run this route, monitoring the quantum lines that radiated outward from Sonjeera to the other planets in the Constellation. During their string-line-maintenance trips, they had traveled to countless waystation systems like this one.

As soon as their linerunner, *HDS Kerris*, arrived under the star's electric sapphire glare, Sunitha disengaged the vessel from the iperion-marked quantum path. She noted their position with satisfaction as the telescoping external sensor whips took readings. "Exactly on point."

"You are the master, my dear. The absolute master."

"I'd rather be a master than a mistress," she teased. "But don't get any ideas about having a mistress."

"Where would I find one out here? We're the only human beings in a parsec or two."

"More to the point, what other woman would have you? It's taken *me* decades to learn how to tolerate your eccentricities."

"Been a learning process for both of us." Turlo leaned over and kissed her on the cheek. He loved her thick black hair, her dark skin, her almond eyes; he never got tired of looking at her. "In another thirty years, maybe we'll figure it out." He got up and stretched. "Since you drove, it's my turn to suit up."

"Make sure you have the codplate properly fastened this time. I'd rather not have to rub the cream on again, like after your last exposure."

Turlo huffed; *he* had rather enjoyed the treatment. "Not as if I need the sperm anymore." He quickly regretted the extra comment – they both knew they wouldn't have children again. Even so, the photo-image of their lost son, Kerris, held a prominent place in the ship's tiny living quarters. The young man had been dead ten years now, since the rebellion, but reminders still popped up like landmines.

In the uncomfortable silence, Turlo removed the appropriate suit from the his-and-hers closet. As he donned it, the suit's multilayered protective fabric and life-support systems transformed his body into a blobby shapeless form. He always made a point of commenting on how nicely Sunitha's suit fit her curves (even though it seemed to be getting a bit snug in the past year).

The uneventful life of a stringline maintenance technician could lead to ennui and physical decrepitude. Substation maintenance became a casual routine, though Turlo and Sunitha did not allow themselves to take any shortcuts. She helped him seal and link the suit systems, ran all the greens, ran them a second time, then slapped him on the back. "Ready to go."

Listening to his own breathing echo in his helmet, Turlo cycled through the *Kerris's* airlock and emerged into the emptiness. Outside, the substation was the only mark of human presence in the entire system. Its mirrorshine panels drank the constant outpouring of heavy solar radiation, which powered the station and kept the iperion path aligned and intact.

In an external tool compartment, the *Kerris* held a selection of spare parts that Turlo rarely had to use. With conservative bursts of compressed air from his suitpack, he maneuvered himself over to the hodgepodge array of machinery. Turlo used a magnetic grip to catch the substation, clipped himself on with a retractable line and carabineer, and began his work. He muted his transmitting codecall circuit, since his habit of whistling while working annoyed Sunitha.

Turlo finished the routine inspection, considered replacing one of the collimation projectors; it was just barely below 50 per cent and not really in need of being swapped out. He did it anyway. He could always hand the unit to Territorial Governor Goler once they arrived on Ridgetop.

After unclipping himself, he jetted around the substation to complete a visual inspection for any meteoroid damage, but found only superficial scarring. Satisfied, he returned to the *Kerris* and cycled through to the pressurized interior after humming his way through a ten-minute radiation wash.

While he was gone, Sunitha had pulled up records and images of Ridgetop's tall goldenwood forests, even though they weren't due to arrive at the DZ planet for two more days. "Going stir-crazy. Time to stretch my legs and breathe air that hasn't come out of our lungs a thousand times over."

Turlo brushed aside the sharp comment. At the end of long trips, they both tended to be edgy. After so many years of marriage, they were utterly dependent upon each other. They couldn't live apart, and they knew for damn sure that neither of them could live with anyone else. At times, however, cooped up in this small vessel, they had a bit too much of each other's company.

As they monitored the stringlines from Sonjeera to the Crown Jewel worlds, and now out to the Deep Zone, the two of them had the opportunity to see the settled galaxy. They had gone to Nicles and Oshu, Setsai and Boj ... from Tehila to Hallholme to Ridgetop to Candela, all via the Sonjeera hub. In the wake of their son's death, Turlo and Sunitha had both needed to get away from people, wanting time alone to grieve, to repair their relationship, and just to have silence, both outside and within.

Turlo took a quick recycled shower, then put on his comfortable singlesuit before returning to the cockpit. In the meantime, Sunitha had piloted them away from the SVC-1185 substation and realigned their ship with the stringline path. She began to accelerate out of the system. "We're well ahead of schedule – ETA forty-three hours. Our first stop on Ridgetop is going to be a meal somebody else cooks for me."

"I usually cook for you."

"No, you usually *reheat* for me. Let's not forget what real cooking is."

Turlo came close to nuzzle her neck. "In the meantime, we should take advantage of our privacy. Want to fool around?"

"Hmm, you *are* nice and clean." Sunitha rose from the pilot's chair and turned to him.

A proximity alarm howled through the cockpit speakers, and Sunitha dove for the controls, saw radiating red lines streaming across the screen. "Vibration alert on the stringline – what the hell?"

Turlo took his own position. "There's no cargo hauler due on this line for six days."

"Too small for a cargo hauler, but it's speeding this way." Sunitha slapped the controls, and the linerunner disengaged from the quantum path with a lurch. The *Kerris* began drifting in empty space, spinning, while Sunitha worked the stabilizers. Turlo grabbed a support handle and pulled himself down into the copilot chair, running his own diagnostics. Once disengaged if they wandered too far from the hair-fine path, they might never find it again. The stringline was only a series of processed iperion molecules, and those quantum breadcrumbs were widely spaced, particularly out here between systems.

The alarm signal became a monotonous pulsing, sped up to a tooth-rattling staccato, then Dopplered down to a lower rhythm and zipped away.

"It's a mail drone – a stupid unscheduled message packet!" Sunitha was already extending their sensor whips, searching, searching until finally she caught a ping of the iperion path. "What the hell were they thinking?"

Turlo finished his analysis. "Must be a diplomatic communiqué from the Territorial Governor. Why couldn't he just wait for the next hauler?"

"The governor probably forgot to fill out a form or something, and the Diadem wanted it now." Grumbling sarcastically, Sunitha called up their schedule and swore. "We're three hours early – that's why nobody thought to warn us. We weren't supposed to be on the stringline path. According to our docs, we should still be at the substation. The mail drone thought the way was clear." She turned on Turlo. "Were you cutting corners? Why did you get done so fast?"

"Me? I thought *you* were anxious to get to Ridgetop."

"From now on, we have to adhere to the schedule – rigidly. No more of your hand waving."

"Yes, dear. You're right, I'm wrong." That was usually the incantation that quelled the demon of her temper, but he sensed that Sunitha was still spoiling for a fight, and he would have to roll with it.

Once she had the *Kerris* aligned on the stringline path again and started accelerating, she continued to enumerate his faults. Turlo would just have to let the storm wash over him and hope that in the aftermath he could at least earn some make-up sex. Otherwise, it was going to be a long stopover on Ridgetop, indeed.

23

The palace of the Diadem was one of seven residences Michella used on Sonjeera, depending on her schedule or her mood. For private meetings, she actually preferred the Royal Retreat, built on a promontory in the hills on the other side of the valley.

Though her official calendar was light, the Diadem rose early. First, she attended a breakfast meeting with Torii Pence, trade representative for the Hirdan family, and they reached agreement on tax credits for Hirdan investment in the manufacture of stringline hauler frames. The Council still needed to pass the final proposal, but Michella would see to it that the votes were there.

After Pence departed, the Diadem signed a document renewing the confinement of her sister, Haveeda, for another three years. She took no pleasure in this action – Haveeda was still just a terrified little girl in Michella's memory – but the action was necessary to protect Duchenet family secrets. If only her sister hadn't threatened to reveal what she knew about the death of their younger brother, Jamos. According to the official report, the four-year-old had fallen out of a tree and struck his head, while the horrified girls watched, helpless to intervene. The actual events had been somewhat different, and Haveeda had unfortunately seen things she shouldn't have . . .

After submitting the secret document for Haveeda's caretakers,

Michella went to her private library to read a book of her favorite poems, wanting to relax, but she found herself staring at the pages. Restless, she paced the large room.

Her other appointment of the day was problematic, though it shouldn't have been. Selik Riomini was her strongest ally, and their goals were closely aligned. He employed his private army and behind-the-scenes connections to help the Diadem maintain her position, despite calls for her resignation due to advancing age. Because Michella allowed the Black Lord to have so much influence in her administration, it was in his best interests to support her.

But sometimes he overreached . . .

Though staff informed her that Lord Riomini was waiting on the top level veranda, she decided to ignore him for half an hour. He was a punctual man who considered lateness a personal insult, but the Diadem let him stew so that he could grasp *her* displeasure over what she had learned.

The original relationship between the Duchenets and the Riominis had involved the ambitious nineteen-year old Michella and an elderly lord, Gilag Riomini. There were whispered rumors that Michella was sleeping with the old man to arrange votes, but their relationship had been purely business. The two families promoted their own interests by thwarting a coalition of the Crais and Tazaar families that would have put Lord Albo Crais on the Star Throne . . .

Now, standing by her reading desk, biding her time, Michella stared at the Constellation Charter on the wall, a copy of the ancient original that resided at the Interplanetary Museum. Touching a button at the corner of the frame, she scrolled randomly through the long document, pausing at the Rule of Succession. The article related to the transfer of power from one Diadem to the next, specifically designed to avoid the corruption and inherent weaknesses of a generational monarchy, and yet it had also shaped the politics of the Constellation, forcing ever-shifting alliances among the nobles.

Because of that clause, Michella had no reason to groom her daughter for the position, and was forced to deal with outsiders like the Riominis. But no matter how closely allied, the interests of two families could not coincide all of the time. By law, the Diadem of the Constellation *must* take into account the interest of every noble family in the Council of Lords, without favoring one to the detriment of others. Not even the Riominis . . .

Finally deciding she had made Selik wait long enough, Michella went out onto the veranda to meet him for their luncheon. Lord Riomini stood at a viewing rail with his back to her. His body language clearly revealed his agitation and tension. *Good.* She wanted him to understand her displeasure with his suggestion that his planet become a second stringline hub, much like Sonjeera.

Like a black-uniformed statue, Riomini did not even turn towards her when she calmly went to a table that had been set for two. She accepted a glass of mint tea from the young female servant, then sipped the calming, warm beverage. Just the right temperature to enhance the mint; it was one of her favorites.

Gazing past the rigid Lord Riomini, she saw her main palace twinkling like a jewel in the sunlight on the other side of the valley. Some distance away, the sprawling government buildings of Council City were abuzz with ground vehicles and aircraft. On the horizon, the spaceport launched regular shuttles to the huge stringline hub complex in orbit.

"If you don't stop pouting, Selik, I'll begin the meeting without you – and I shall play both parts, with me scolding you, and you trying unsuccessfully to fend off my verbal blows. Make no mistake, you are wrong this time. Very wrong."

Surrendering, Riomini turned and made his way to the table. Tiers of decorations adorned his black military jacket, most of which she had bestowed herself for his service during the rebellion.

He took a seat across from her, ordered a glass of red wine instead of mint tea, and drank deeply without seeming to taste the vintage. "I think you're being stubborn, Eminence. With all of Aeroc's exports, I simply want to make my operations more efficient and cost-effective. It makes perfect commercial sense. The secondary stringline hub I proposed at Aeroc would connect with the five worlds that my family now controls, nothing more. I am willing to negotiate specific tariffs to be paid back to the Constellation."

"You would not just be establishing a secondary hub, Selik – you would be establishing a *precedent*. Because the *only* hub is at Sonjeera, *all* commerce must pass through here. Sonjeera is the heart of the

Constellation. It is the only way we can impose control and respect. If I let you have a secondary hub at Aeroc, then the Tazaars will want one, and the Hirdans, and everyone else. It could spell the disintegration of the entire Constellation." She leaned across the table, met his dark-eyed gaze. "All paths lead to Sonjeera, and so it must remain."

From its large hub complex, iperion lines led to each of the nineteen other Crown Jewel worlds and to each of the fifty-four Deep Zone planets. All ships, cargo, and passengers were *required* to come first to Sonjeera, then transfer to a different outbound stringline hauler headed to a destination planet.

Riomini did not give up his schemes easily, nor did she expect him to. "Each noble family has the right to improve operations and maximize profits, Eminence. The Charter says that we are a political and economic fraternity. A monopoly on transportation is not necessarily a good thing."

"It most certainly is when you are the Diadem . . . and you may well be the next one, Selik."

He fiddled with his eating utensils, as if anxious for his meal to be served. Behind him, on a pole that angled out from the veranda, fluttered the banner of her diademacy: red and silver – the colors of the Duchenets – surrounded by a black boundary, signifying the Riomini military power that supported her. Though Riomini legions were stationed on Sonjeera, and the Black Lord commanded the Army of the Constellation, Michella had the power and authority of her office. She knew she was more than a match for him.

Michella sipped her mint tea again. "Your proposal challenges one of the guiding principles established when I set up the stringline system. Your father understood the need for this and never questioned it."

"That is history, Eminence. We must think instead of the future."

She frowned at the very idea. "I have done that for more decades than you've been alive."

Very early in her reign, while still in her twenties, Diadem Michella had launched a major public-works project to replace the slow FTL ships with direct stringline routes between the Sonjeera hub and the nearby Crown Jewel worlds. It was a paradigm shift for transportation and commerce; voyages that once took days or weeks could now be made in hours or days.

To pay for the stringline network and all the processed iperion needed to mark the routes, the Constellation charged a toll for each vessel and tariffs for cargo. Even so, transportation via stringline was vastly cheaper and swifter than using cumbersome FTL ships. Despite the expense of the massive project, the Constellation had earned back the investment. Through numerous edicts and skillful political maneuverings, the Diadem had made it impossible for other planets to connect directly to one another. Every ship had to go through Sonjeera.

Some old-style FTL vessels still made runs among the Crown Jewel worlds, but few people wanted to pay a much higher price for a much slower ship. Most of the antique craft had been decommissioned, and those that continued to fly became mere novelties and tourist attractions.

Linking the Crown Jewels with an efficient stringline network might have been enough for any ruler, but Michella had also realized the need to expand into new territory. She offered virgin worlds as a pressure-release valve for overcrowded planets and dissatisfied noble families. She had launched trailblazer ships to lay down iperion paths to the mysterious Deep Zone, eager to connect those frontier worlds to Sonjeera. Because of the vast distances involved, the trailblazer voyages took years.

In the midst of all that, General Tiber Adolphus had launched his violent rebellion before her expansion scheme had a chance to work . . .

As the food was served, Michella and the Black Lord continued to look at each other across the table, exchanging careful conversation. Lord Riomini seemed alternately defiant and intimidated. "How do you like the wine?" she asked.

He frowned down at the glass. "It tastes . . . rough."

"And so it should. It came in a recent shipment from Hallholme. One of Adolphus's colonists has set up a working vineyard."

Riomini looked as if he might choke. "Perhaps we should have it tested it for poison."

"The rebellion was the poison, but that has been neutralized." Of course she had tested the wine, and he knew that. She gave him a hard look, more serious now. "Because of that catastrophe, Selik, I am more determined than ever that all planets be utterly dependent on the Constellation – on Sonjeera. It's simple logic: if they have no options, there will never be another significant uprising. And *that* is why you cannot be allowed to have your own stringline hub at Aeroc."

Frowning, he sloshed the red liquid around in his glass and drank again. He motioned for the servant to pour more.

As the main course was served, with great fanfare from the kitchen staff, Michella's attention remained on the Black Lord, rather than the culinary presentation. Disappointed by her lack of praise, the chef led his retinue back to the kitchens.

"Why don't we talk about something much more pleasant? Something to cheer you up?" Her voice was bright, and when he gave her a blank look, she said, "The de Carre mess and the Vielinger matter. I have arranged it all in your favor."

"My favor?" He raised his eyebrows, but did not fool her for a moment. "I thought what we were doing was for the good of the Constellation."

"Of course. For the good of the Constellation."

24

When the disgraced Lord Louis de Carre was taken to Vielinger for a formal Reading of the Charges, the people did not receive him with cheers and applause.

Since learning of his father's arrest, however, Cristoph had little time to worry about the man and whatever fines or punishment the Constellation might impose. He was occupied in the aftermath of the fire at the Rapana iperion-processing center, arranging necessary medical services for the injured, including four members of the rescue team, as well as hundreds who had breathed the toxic smoke. Sixty-three had died in the poisonous blaze.

Cristoph had also attended the first funeral of the twelve miners exposed to raw iperion due to faulty breathers. The next day he attended three more funerals, and the final miner had died yesterday. Four of the families, however, had made it clear that they did not want Cristoph at the memorial services.

Shiploads of Constellation inspectors, interim security forces, mining engineers, and safety experts swarmed through the mines. They found countless supposed safety violations, but Cristoph's own inspectors had combed the same areas, studied the same equipment regularly. Everyone now considered the de Carre administrators incompetent.

Some old-guard nobles suspected it was a setup to bring down the de

Carres because that was the way they played politics. For generations, as families grew and holdings were subdivided, powerful nobles preyed upon the weaker ones – stealing property, trumping up charges, disgracing them, and shifting the balance of power. No one felt sorry for the de Carres. If the family wasn't strong enough to hold on to Vielinger, they didn't deserve to have it.

Meanwhile, the population suffered, pawns in a game that Cristoph had never considered a game . . .

When his father returned to the ancestral estate, Cristoph was reluctant to greet him, but with the de Carre legacy under fire from so many different directions, he would not be petty. Cristoph faced a more difficult task than ever, and he needed a champion in the arena of politics, someone who could face the Black Lord in the Council chambers, refute the outrageous claims, and out-debate the most silver-tongued ambassadors. Louis de Carre had once been that man, but now he dallied with a married woman and brought embarrassment to the de Carre family.

Nevertheless, he was still Cristoph's father.

Grim-faced Constellation guards escorted Louis to the front gate of the estate grounds. As he walked up the pea-gravel path and mounted the steps to the main house, Louis looked wistfully at the mossy stone arch, the topiary shrubs, and the well-tended rose garden. Cristoph waited at the open door, keeping his words to himself. Louis looked up at his son, glanced away, and took another step forward.

Before leaving them, the guard captain spoke. "Lord de Carre, by order of the Diadem, you will remain here under house arrest until the Reading of the Charges can commence in two days."

"Thank you, Captain," Louis replied. "My ancestral home will be a welcome haven for the time being." He came forward and embraced his son.

Cristoph remained stiff. "I doubt we'll have the estate much longer, Father."

"I fear you're right. I'm sorry I let you down. You and I worked well as a team when you were younger."

Cristoph could think of no suitable reply as the two walked into the great hall with its ceiling of massive timbers high over three polished wooden tables, where he, his father, and often some household servants, had spent hours playing games. But that had been back when the money flowed freely. Now the iperion production was showing signs of coming to an end; continued excavations would require more strenuous, more dangerous, and more expensive efforts.

For years, the loss of Angelique, Louis's wife and Cristoph's mother, had remained keen, and Louis had dedicated himself to running Vielinger and training his son. He had kept the image of lovely Angelique on a fireplace mantel. During his adolescence, Cristoph had encouraged his father to remarry. Louis had enough willing candidates to choose from, but seemed hesitant.

Rather, his main intent had been to find a good match for Cristoph, a loving wife and the opportunity to carry on the de Carre bloodline. The family legacy had been built over many centuries, and the people had loved and respected their noble lords, crediting them for the planet's prosperity. When Cristoph reached his mid-twenties, it had been time to consider the matter seriously, and he had noted several women who welcomed his advances. He spent hours with his father studying genealogical charts of ruling families and their holdings, discussing in a practical sense which woman might make the best match.

"Family trees don't always indicate the best romance," Louis had said. "I want you to find someone you can adore as much as I adored your mother."

And then Keana Duchenet snared his father. By seducing him, the Diadem's daughter had struck his core vulnerabilities. For two years now, Cristoph had tried to juggle the administrative responsibilities of the whole planet, including the work that Lord de Carre had simply abandoned.

Now father and son sat together in the great room and played cards out of habit, a game that interested neither of them but passed the time. Cristoph kept his feelings bottled inside, wanting to rage at his father and demand explanations. Finally, he managed only, "Why would you do it, Father? Why would you let that woman take everything away like this?" He raised his voice. "How could you be fooled?"

Instead of making excuses, Louis raised his head to show deep hurt. "Because I love her."

The Board of Magistrates set up their imposing bench out in the garden area, near the well-maintained hedge maze that formed the de Carre family crest. Squads of offworld soldiers in colorful ceremonial uniforms acted as an honor guard, but they were soldiers nevertheless. Cristoph resented them tromping through the estate grounds, but he could not object.

To face the Reading of the Charges, Louis de Carre had been provided with commoner's clothing, as if accepting a foregone conclusion. Even though his father had made no attempt at defense, Cristoph had filed appeals, hired attorneys – but to no avail.

"Why a Reading of the Charges?" he had demanded of his father. "Why not a trial? Why aren't you given a chance to explain?"

"Because there is nothing to explain. I neglected my duty. They reviewed the charges and evidence, and came to a conclusion. Reading the Charges is a mere formality, an event to amuse the nobles. I'm sorry I can't do anything for you, Cristoph. You are the last hope of the de Carre legacy now."

"*What* legacy?" Cristoph let out a bitter laugh. "I am the last one. We're going to lose everything!"

"Then start over," Louis said simply. "Find a woman. Have your family. Ah, I wish you'd been able to know your mother."

Cristoph pressed his lips together, glad his mother was not alive to see this disgraceful day. The night before, he had roamed through the manor house while everyone else slept, though his father must have lain awake, staring at the ceiling as the seconds ticked by. He looked at the portraits in the halls, faces he had seen all his life – Eduard de Carre, his great-grandfather ... Ambrose de Carre, his grandfather ... then the portrait of Louis. Someday his own portrait would have hung there, but that was unlikely now.

The triumvirate of magistrates sat at their imposing bench. The honor guard marched out and fanfares called the proceedings to order. Cristoph barely listened. This felt like a stage show, and he knew very little could be changed.

The bailiff presented a document to the three dark-robed magistrates, two men and one woman; each would read a portion of the crimes of which Louis de Carre had been accused. The list went on for pages.

Before the men could begin the Reading of the Charges, however, Louis stepped forward and interrupted the script. "Magistrates, I wish to speak on behalf of my son. I was foolish to leave him in charge of the iperion operations here on Vielinger alone. I was training him as my successor, but I'm afraid I gave him too much responsibility, too soon. He is young and well-intentioned, but not cut out for the job. He wasn't ready for the difficult decisions and for the dangers. That is my failing, not his." He avoided looking over at Cristoph, who sat on a secure trial bench at the edge of the garden.

"There have been so many tragic accidents – the basic reason we're here today. It may seem that the responsibility lies with him, but *I* am Lord de Carre. The fortunes of Vielinger rest upon my shoulders. I ask that all charges listed under his name be placed under mine. I am at fault. My son was not ready. Let me pay the price for my error in judgment."

Cristoph clenched his fists, upset with his father for painting him as an inept fool. And then he realized that was exactly his father's intent, a noble attempt to shield Cristoph from the consequences.

After the Reading of the Charges, Louis would be taken back to Sonjeera, where he would await his sentencing from the Diadem herself. Cristoph was certain they would lose the family estate.

The three magistrates conferred, glancing over at Cristoph as if he were an unusual specimen. They finally agreed. "All charges shall be listed under the de Carre name, and you are Lord de Carre." The central judge lowered her voice. "Though in the end, I'm not sure your son will appreciate this."

"Thank you, nevertheless." Just for a moment, Louis looked over at Cristoph, then turned his gaze back to the bench. The three magistrates picked up their documents and began to read.

25

For days after Louis's arrest, Keana remained frantic. No one would tell her what was happening.

"Lord de Carre is not, and never should have been, your concern," her mother said, annoyed and dismissive. "You've done quite enough already. From now on, whenever you are seen in public, you will make a point of appearing with your own husband. Bolton has already agreed to cooperate in this."

Until now, Keana's existence had been soft and comfortable, free of ambition – by design. Her few instances of petty rebellion had accomplished little; her only true success in resisting her mother's wishes had been refusing to have Bolton's children. The Diadem would never be a doting grandmother, and Keana was sure that Michella had given birth to *her* only out of duty; then, once she had a Duchenet heir, Michella's husband had conveniently died.

Now the world had fallen out from under Keana. She felt like a well-trained pet, given freedom but only within a rigidly defined set of boundaries. Suddenly, she had run to the end of her leash, and it was choking her. Ill-equipped to understand the political machinations of powerful families, she had no idea how to deal with such a crisis.

Her relationship with Louis reminded her of fanciful romantic tales, but now the romance had become a tragedy. Though already married to a perfectly respectable man, Keana had fantasized about a life with dashing Louis, being the lady of his Vielinger estate, throwing courtly balls, possibly even having children with him, just like his own fine son, Cristoph. Her daydreams had felt much more real than mere wishing; whenever Louis held her in his arms, Keana believed such things could actually come true. *That* was the life she wanted, to be his companion and lover, not just window dressing to the Diadem's plans.

She racked her brain to find something she could do to help free poor Louis. Spoiled and pampered, she was used to getting what she wanted, but Keana had never asked for anything so important. And now she was rebuffed at every turn.

She didn't quite know where to turn, but pestered anyone of importance. Keana wished she had done more to earn their loyalty, but she had always expected that, as the Diadem's daughter, she could just ask for assistance. Now they ignored her. She felt so foolish. No influential person had any reason to assist her, especially if doing so would risk incurring the Diadem's wrath.

Deeply sympathetic, her husband tried to offer his ineffective support. Typical Bolton! But she could concentrate only on the unjust ordeal Louis was facing, and how desperately she needed to see him. She just wanted to hold him. Was he here on Sonjeera, languishing in a prison cell? Had he been extradited to Vielinger? The complete lack of information terrified her.

She knew that people often disappeared when they incurred the Diadem's ire. From childhood, Keana had heard rumors about her aunt Haveeda, who had been hidden away for most of her life. As a little girl, Keana remembered seeing the gaunt and haunted woman lurking around the palace, never speaking to anyone without a watchful Michella present, then Haveeda had vanished entirely. The Diadem never referred to her. At all.

If Michella could do that to her own younger sister, she would have no qualms about ruining Lord de Carre just to force Keana back into line. But she wouldn't let her mother get away with it . . .

Keana found the Cottage an unbearable place that clamored with lone-liness and memories, so she summoned an aerocopter to take her to the Sonjeera spaceport. Someone on Vielinger could answer her questions, perhaps even Louis's son. She and Cristoph should stand together at a time like this. Michella would not expect her daughter to be persistent or resourceful; Keana had never been encouraged to develop these traits, but that was going to change.

The Council City Spaceport had a high dome and walls of glass panes framed in metal. The main building had been erected more than a century ago, during the reign of her husband's great-great-grandfather, Nok Crais II. Bolton was proud of his ancestry, though he had few of the talents of his illustrious ancestor. In fact, Bolton seemed no more than an entry on his family tree, a name that filled a space and would be quickly forgotten by later generations.

The thought was unkind, she realized. Bolton was not her enemy; he had a kind heart, but he was more like a sibling than a soul-mate. He had not wanted a change in the situation, but his own family con-trolled him like a puppet.

However, when she tried to purchase a ticket for Vielinger, the clerk behind the transport desk denied her request. "The route is restricted, unless you have special clearance."

"I am the Diadem's daughter," she said haughtily. "That should be clearance enough." She had never actually bought a ticket before, though she'd been away from Sonjeera many times. Someone else always took care of such details.

The clerk recoiled in surprise. "My Lady! I – I'm sorry." He sounded like a man being strangled. "One moment, please." The clerk sum-moned a supervisor, and Keana turned to see a uniformed female officer with perfectly straight yellow hair.

The officer recognized Keana. The woman gave a brisk bow without even stirring her hair as if she were performing in a military parade, then snapped back upright. "My Lady, I am Captain Kouvet. Considering the political turmoil on Vielinger, the House of Lords has restricted travel. Visitors are advised to stay away, and Diadem Michella issued specific security instructions to prevent your departure. I am sorry, my Lady."

Keana fumed, realizing how much her mother tried to control her movements. Michella had guessed (correctly) that her daughter wanted to rush into the situation, thereby causing further public embarrassment. "But I need to learn the whereabouts of Lord Louis de Carre."

Captain Kouvet looked flustered. "I believe he will return to Sonjeera within days. Now that the Reading of the Charges has finished on Vielinger, Lord de Carre will be brought back to the capital for formal sentencing."

"Reading of the Charges? Sentencing?" She felt dizzy.

Kouvet showed very little sympathy. "The information has only just arrived, my Lady. Maybe you should wait until the Diadem has a chance to review the matters with you."

Grasping at the promise of further information – finally – Keana pressed harder. "I would like to know now, Captain. What have you learned?"

The other woman didn't miss a beat. "This way, please."

With her heart pounding, she followed the captain to an office whose window-wall gave a view of the shuttle launchers and landing pads on the sprawling Sonjeera spaceport. Kouvet leaned over a control deck, activated a set of images. "This message arrived via mail drone. Many of the lords have already viewed it."

She adjusted controls, and the window-wall images washed away to be replaced by an aerial view of the sumptuous de Carre estate on Vielinger, with its rock-walled manor house, its famous ornamental gardens and hedge maze. On a grassy expanse where family weddings had taken place over the centuries, a number of chairs faced a wide bench where three dark-robed magistrates sat. Soldiers, all dressed in black Riomini uniforms, ringed the area.

Keana caught her breath. On the image, her beloved Louis stood before the bench in the clothing of a commoner, looking defeated. She saw a young man on the sidelines, in his mid-twenties with brown hair lighter than Louis's but similar facial features and mannerisms. She recognized Cristoph from the images Louis so often and so proudly showed her.

Keana had a sick feeling. "I demand to speak on his behalf!" With all of those Riomini soldiers present and Louis dressed as he was, she already feared the result.

Captain Kouvet spoke behind her. "I believe the events took place yesterday." She wore a grave expression. "He was found guilty of crimes against the people of Vielinger and the Constellation."

So, her mother had succeeded in blocking her efforts until it was too late. "What crimes?" Keana heard her own voice cracking.

"Something about mistreating iperion workers, my Lady, and ignoring the mines to such a degree that it put the strategic resources of the Constellation in jeopardy. Gross negligence and abrogation of noble responsibility. If you need more information, my Lady, you'll need to . . ."

She already knew the answer. "I'll have to ask my mother."

Keana left the office and crossed the terminal building. The Diadem had the power to grant Louis clemency. Perhaps if she begged and promised to bear a legitimate Duchenet heir, the old woman would surely relent. As part of the agreement, Keana would relinquish the child, leaving Louis and her free to go somewhere together and live simple lives, far from twisted politics, maybe even in the Deep Zone. A sacrifice, no matter how Keana looked at it – but it was the only solution she could see.

26

Antonia was surprised when Sophie asked her to accompany Devon out into the wilderness. For the past week, his mother had been preoccupied, even worried, as she paced outside her main warehouse. Obviously, something was troubling her.

Looking decisive, Sophie spoke abruptly as if the two had already listened to the debate going on inside her head. "Seems to me we should have heard something from the Children of Amadin by now. You two, pack up a Trakmaster with supplies and med equipment and use their vehicle beacons to locate their settlement. Make sure they're all right."

Antonia understood that Sophie was like a mother to them all, and she worried about groups of settlers even when they declined outside help. Jako would never have shown such compassion for strangers.

Devon, though, was hesitant. "They wanted to be left alone, Mom. Are you sure we shouldn't give them more time?"

"Try to be discreet, but after a month of reality here, they could be ready to change their minds. The Children of Amadin didn't look any more prepared than the last dozen or so stubborn groups we had to rescue. Cults like to show that they can face whatever tribulations their gods fling at them." She rolled her eyes and sighed. "No harm checking on them. Consider it an errand of mercy. And if they do need extra supplies, provide them at no charge. I've made enough profit from those people already." She smiled at the young woman. "Antonia, you keep my son out of trouble."

Antonia was surprised. "Just the two of us? Out there?"

"Devon knows what he's doing, and Lujah's people already know you from the outbound passage. Who better to go?"

The rationale seemed thin to Antonia. "But I barely spoke to them during the entire trip. They kept to themselves."

"At least they'll recognize you. If they don't need help, just turn around and come home." Sophie flashed a smile.

"You're not afraid to go with me, are you?" Devon teased. Antonia could see he was looking forward to spending more time with her.

Antonia liked Devon, but she felt uneasy at the thought of being alone with him. She could not risk becoming trapped, as she had with Jako. If she had to flee Hellhole, where else could she run? "It'll be fine," she forced herself to say.

After loading one of the company vehicles with supplies, they headed away from town on the last known bearing taken by Lujah Carey and his followers. Devon certainly knew plenty about the planet and its hazards. As he guided the Trakmaster around the rugged terrain, he was full of nervous conversation. He kept the vehicle uplinked to the weather satellites, always wary for hazards, but the road caused him no concern.

Antonia was content to sit in silence and look out upon the scarred world, comparing it to Aeroc. She knew that Devon wasn't overly needy, didn't require company every minute, but when they were together in the vehicle's cab, he seemed to find the silent spaces uncomfortable and tried to fill them with whatever he could think of.

"The landscape is always interesting, if you know how to look at it. Because of the impact, all the strata are scrambled. There's no telling what type of rock you'd find next to another type. We've got cassiterite for tin, bauxite for aluminum, iron ore, copper ore. Then there's slate, diorite, granite, marble – all for construction stone. Hellhole may be a mess, but it's rich in resources."

Though she had vowed to keep herself closed off, she found Devon endearing; he was trying so hard, and he was so obviously smitten with her. The young man, though knowledgeable about Hellhole, was refreshingly naïve about the ways people could hurt one another. She hoped he never found out just how harsh life really could be.

Antonia got the impression that because she came from the Crown Jewel planets, he felt she was too sophisticated for him. His nervous demeanor only heightened that impression. Maybe she could convince him – and she wanted to – that she preferred an honest man to a "sophisticated" one.

But could she trust her own judgment? Too many images were flash-burned into her mind: her murdered parents in their home, running away with Jako, believing his elaborate lies. She felt so stupid. Why had it taken her so long to notice the blood on his hands, the darkness in his heart?

But Devon Vence was not like Jako. By contrast, the young man was entirely transparent – not shallow, but open and straightforward. Too much so, perhaps.

"My mother's trying to be a matchmaker," Devon admitted, then looked away in embarrassment. "It's just that she always wants the best for me, and there aren't many colonists for me to choose from. So when you came, it just made sense to her ... she thinks that ..." Devon stumbled on his words again, then lapsed into a haven of silence and concentrated on driving. Finally, he blurted, "I don't mean there's anything wrong with you. In fact, there isn't a prettier or nicer girl on this whole planet, and that's the truth. I ... I'm glad you stayed with us." His face flushed.

"It was the best offer I had." Antonia laid a hand on his arm. "Relax, Devon. I expect to be here for a long time. But we don't know each other very well. Let's just see how it goes? Try being friends first. That's what I need most." She had made the timeless mistake of assuming that because Jako was her lover, he was also her friend.

"That would be great." Devon smiled gratefully.

Following a faint beacon from the locater IDs on the religious group's vehicles, Devon drove toward the great shatter-canyons, impact spokes, and vast central crater that Antonia had seen from orbit.

They had no way of knowing exactly which path the group had taken, but it was clear where they were going. "It's no surprise," Devon said. "At least half of the cults that come here think the impact zero-point is some kind of holy site, touched by the Hand of God. It's some of the roughest terrain on the continent. Sooner or later, we'll probably have to pave a road out there. My mother would like to make it a tollway.

No shortage of crazy people believing crazy things." Devon shrugged as he drove. "One batch after another comes here, announcing that they've got the *only* version of the truth. Then they either mock or hate everyone who believes differently, not recognizing their own tunnel vision. Then, when they try to convert you ..." He muttered something under his breath.

He guided the overland vehicle up a steep crumbling hillside then roared down into a ravine, and she knew he was trying to show off for her, testing the limits of the Trakmaster's shock absorbers.

"What if the Children of Amadin are angry when we find them?" Antonia asked.

Devon shifted the wide tracks to avoid a particularly large boulder. "I'd rather have them angry with us than find them all dying of a plague."

"Has that happened before?"

He told her about a burgeoning native mold that had grown in one independent settlement, consuming all artificial fabrics, leaving the baffled group to rush naked back to Helltown in embarrassed desperation. Then he described an infestation of small ant-like insects that crawled out of cracks in the ground two years previously, getting into everything. "Oh, they didn't cause actual harm," he added when he saw Antonia's alarmed expression. "They didn't bite or eat our food. They were just – *crawly*. It was awfully hard to get rid of them."

"Does that sort of thing happen often?" Antonia asked.

"There's always something," Devon laughed.

They descended a steep grade down one of the impact crater's ripple ridges, switchbacking down a rough rocky slope toward a basin ahead. Noting a smear on the weathersat images, Devon said, "Whoa, that came up fast! Static storm, heading our way." He looked around for shelter.

"Can we outrun it?"

"Not at this speed, not on this terrain." He scanned ahead, narrowing his gaze, no longer a shy young man struggling to make conversation with her, but intent on his work now. "There – see that dark crack in the cliff wall ahead, just to the left? That'll be a narrow box canyon. It looks big enough to fit the Trakmaster."

Without waiting for Antonia's response – what would she say? Of course she'd agree with him – Devon urged the vehicle forward over rough boulders and loose stones until he reached the opening, spun the Trakmaster around in a small clear patch, then backed in. "That'll do just fine," he said. "I'll keep you safe."

The static storm came upon them with surprising intensity. The winds whipped up and bolts of static electricity capered from boulder to boulder, then struck the Trakmaster like scorpion stings.

The air inside the vehicle felt charged and smelled like ozone; every breath crackled when Antonia inhaled. When he saw how edgy she was, Devon gave her a reassuring smile. "Don't worry, we'll be okay here. It's just a typical local storm." The winds howled, and dust scoured the hull. "Nothing out of the ordinary," he said.

Devon fixed them something to eat from the small galley. Antonia stared out through the dust-streaked window, blinking each time a flash of static crossed her field of vision. "Just a typical local storm," she whispered to herself.

She remembered sitting with her parents in their home on Aeroc, listening to the rain run down the windows and patter on the pavement outside. She had loved the rain. On quiet evenings like that, her mother had played the piano, and Antonia sat on the bench beside her, picking out harmonies.

A static flash crackled through the canyon, and a roar of wind swept pebbles down the slope ahead of them. "Nothing out of the ordinary," she reminded herself, trying to quell her fears.

27

As a war hero and savior of the Constellation, Commodore Percival Hallholme lived on a pedestal that was not of his own making. With that lofty perch came a number of problems, especially the embarrassment of the hellish planet that had been named after him. Diadem Michella had granted him an honor, but he wished the decision could be reversed. Unfortunately, that propaganda battle was already lost. Hellhole would forever be linked to the great heritage of the Hallholmes.

After his victory in the last battle of the rebellion, the Commodore was not allowed to retire without attending a naming ceremony on the planet. He had been there (presumably smug) when General Adolphus arrived in disgrace, stripped of everything.

Hallholme should have despised his enemy, the man who had single-handedly led the most destructive campaign in the history of the Constellation. But he didn't. The old man's feelings were quite complicated. After all, he knew what had really happened. Diadem Michella could say all she wanted about honor and bravery, but for Hallholme, the words did not ring true.

In the former Adolphus manor house, he awoke before dawn, as usual. Thanks to his advancing age, he slept only five hours per night, which left him with even more waking hours each day to reminisce and regret. Today, he had something special to do.

Dressed in one of his old Constellation military uniforms, with epaulets and a braided officer's cap, he rode in the back of a military staff car. As dawn brightened, the driver took him along a little-used roadway to a ridge above the Lubis Plain. The sun was just clearing the horizon beyond the shipyards.

The driver stopped the car at a gate. "Are you sure this is the place you want, sir?" Duff Adkins had served as a sergeant under the Commodore during the rebellion and had chosen to retire into the old man's service.

"Yes, I'm sure." Hallholme stepped out of the car before Adkins could hurry around to get the door for him.

Ivy, tall grass, and wild thistles choked the rusted fence and gate, and the pavement on the other side was cracked and weed-infested. The Commodore fumbled in his jacket pocket, brought out a large key, and limped forward. Aided by the driver, he cleared plants away and pushed open the gate. "Wait for me here."

"Yes, sir."

With halting steps, Hallholme made slow but steady progress along the overgrown path to the top of the hill. Looking back, he saw that the driver had followed him anyway, lagging behind at a respectful distance. He smiled to himself. Duff worried about him too much.

Now the retired officer had a view of the decaying military cemetery. Little automatons tended the gravesites, cutting weeds and grass, trying to straighten headstones, climbing the exterior walls of outbuildings to repair them.

Hallholme worked his way past the graves of the rebel soldiers who had joined the ill-fated cause of General Adolphus. He passed beneath an archway on which he noted that the engraved names of the dead were chipped and moss-filled; the brave men who had fallen in battle deserved better, even if they had fought on the opposite side. The antique gardener automatons didn't seem to be functioning properly. Even after the machines passed, weeds, tangles of vines, and tall grass remained; the headstones looked no better after being adjusted.

He shook his head in dismay. The cemetery's disrepair was but a small dishonor compared with the appalling compromises *he* had made during that last battle. No honorable soldier would have placed thousands of innocent civilian hostages on the battle lines as insurance against attack.

It was no more noble than throwing babies out of airlocks. Percival Hallholme had made Adolphus believe that all those innocents would be sacrificed if they opened fire, and the General had flinched at the crucial moment, allowing Constellation forces to slaughter them.

From history's perspective, it didn't matter. Hallholme had won the battle, saved Sonjeera, and defeated the bloodthirsty rebels, so all was forgiven. The Diadem even cheered his innovative approach, gave him a medal, named a planet after him.

Michella had ordered him to win the engagement using any and all means necessary, with no idea too extreme. But even then, Hallholme was willing to go only so far. Yes, after months of preparing for the inevitable showdown at Sonjeera, the Commodore had undertaken an extensive program to detain rebel sympathizers. Yes, he had crowded them into armored cells and had even commanded his guards to inflict pain using shock prods. General Adolphus had no doubt in his mind just how far his nemesis would go.

And the deception had worked.

Hallholme had not, in truth, placed any of the hostages aboard his warships, where they could be sliced to ribbons in a space combat. They were kept in security chambers down on Sonjeera, safe and far from the battle, with the video images relayed through the Constellation warships. The guards' shock prods had no lethal settings.

But General Adolphus and his rebels did not know that, nor would the Diadem ever make that fact public. She had been deeply skeptical about Hallholme's suggestion of restraint in the first place, certain that Adolphus's barbarians would pillage all of Sonjeera. "If the General does not believe your bluff, I'll order all the hostages executed anyway," Michella had warned Hallholme. "Defeat him by any means. That is my command."

So he had.

Behind him, Duff Adkins watched from the top of the rise. When it came to the other veteran, Hallholme didn't feel in charge any more. Adkins had a tendency toward stubbornness that the Commodore found aggravating. The man no longer followed orders . . . but then, he was no longer a soldier under Hallholme's command, so he could be forgiven. The retired non-com had repeatedly shown that he cared more about the Commodore than about himself, and Hallholme could not remain angry with Adkins for long. Such loyalty could not be purchased for any price.

One day both of them would rest in a cemetery like this, though one for Constellation veterans, not rebels. Hallholme hoped their gravestones would be tended with more care. This place was a disgrace, but he could do nothing about it. The Riomini managers of Qiorfu had blocked public access to the rebel graveyard for "security purposes," citing fears of vandalism. But Hallholme knew better. In reality, it was to show utter contempt for the defeated enemy.

The Commodore shook his head. He wished he could speak up and demand respect for the fallen soldiers who lay around him, but he couldn't cast doubt on his own loyalties. His son Escobar still had a military career ahead of him, and there were the two grandsons to think of.

Hobbling to the center of the cemetery, the retired Commodore stood at attention among the rebel gravestones, and saluted.

28

By the strict terms of his surrender, General Adolphus had been forbidden to leave the planet Hallholme, and he had accepted his exile with good grace – a fact that Diadem Michella mistrusted. He had once replied, "You have given me an entire world to roam. What more could a man want?"

Realistically, Adolphus could have slipped away at any time he chose, either through the use of bribes or by donning a disguise. But though he had the means to escape his restraints, the General would not do so. He had given his *word* and, unlike many political and military leaders, that still meant something to him.

By the same token, however, Adolphus made promises with great care. He might have agreed never to leave Hallholme, personally, but that did not prevent other Deep Zone planetary administrators from visiting *him*. Other than himself, there were fifty-three, but he wasn't sure he could trust most of them.

Over the years, through subtle overtures, Adolphus had discovered eleven like-minded administrators of nearby frontier worlds. Because the Constellation transport network required every stringline traveler to pass through the Sonjeera hub, a gathering like this required precise orchestration and complete cooperation among the participants so that the Diadem noticed nothing odd about their movements.

Adolphus was accustomed to clockwork precision. Without such skills and discipline, his rebellion would have fizzled in the first month instead of lasting five years. Employing discreet messengers who posed as businessmen traveling to Sonjeera and then back out to other DZ planets, he had spent months coordinating travel for the attendees.

The eleven sympathetic planetary administrators had created plausible excuses for their absences — a death in the family, private management retreats, long-range exploration of uninhabited areas; some even admitted going to Sonjeera. But once the conspirators arrived at the main stringline hub, each one dropped out of sight, assumed a different identity, and took passage via the colonization service aboard the next hauler for Hallholme. Pretending not to know one another, the conspirators crowded onto the passenger pod along with hopeful colonists, penal laborers, merchants, and tradesmen. They studiously ignored conversation throughout the passage, knowing they would have plenty of time to talk face-to-face at the Elba estate — and that would occur today.

Adolphus breakfasted, drank a second cup of watery coffee (so far, not even Sophie Vence's greenhouse domes had perfected a locally grown coffee crop ... and he hated kiafa), then dressed in a professional-looking suit. As a calculated move, he opted for business attire rather than his old military outfit. While the traditional uniform had made him famous to some (and infamous to others), the General preferred not to remind these planetary administrators of his past. He wanted to show his partners a different Tiber Adolphus — one with the same competence and leadership abilities, but also with the vision to create a future independent of the fossilized old Constellation.

It would be several hours before the attendees began to arrive from Michella Town. Ian Walfor would fly here in his own FTL ship from Candela, since the Constellation had stopped keeping track of his movements long ago.

The General's household staff had transformed Elba's banquet hall into a formal boardroom. The wall paneling was a richly stained wood-like veneer manufactured from fibrous native shrubbery. The grain patterns looked more like fractals than the traditional swirls of a normal tree. The central table had a covering of polished coral stone, readily available from the quarries twenty kilometers away. His kitchen workers prepared pastries, and Sophie sent fresh fruits from the greenhouses.

Despite rumors his guests might have heard about the rustic conditions on Hellhole, they would not feel deprived during the meeting.

On one wall, a flat gypsum board provided a pristine white surface as a projection area, on which Adolphus displayed the chart of Deep Zone planets. With the map's zero point aligned on *Hallholme*, the perspective was unsettling to any Constellation citizen accustomed to seeing Sonjeera as the absolute center of all the settled systems. The Crown Jewel planets did not even appear on Adolphus's chart, because he had decided they were irrelevant and outdated. He included none of the established stringline paths, but instead drew new lines that radiated from Hallholme out to Candela, Ridgetop, Tehila, Ronom, Nielad, Setsai, and Cles.

If an outsider such as Ishop Heer were to discover this chart, General Adolphus would have to kill him to protect the secret.

Sophie entered the banquet room, interrupting his reverie. "They're all here in the front room, Tiber. Even Walfor arrived in time. Would you like to make your grand entrance?"

She wore a flattering but deceptively practical dress and had taken great care with her appearance. He could not hide his admiration. "You look especially beautiful today."

"Why so surprised?" She arched her eyebrows. "I clean up pretty well when I want to. Besides, I know how important this meeting is to you."

"Not just to me – to all of us. On this planet, today, our future begins."

Sophie laughed. "Save the speeches for your guests." She brushed the front of his suit, smoothed his dark hair. "You look impressive as well. You'll do just fine."

"I want you there in the meeting," he said. "I could use your support."

"You have plenty of support. And I'd just distract you."

Adolphus gave her an intent look; it was always difficult for him to show his emotions. "I value your input. You have a pragmatic streak that some of these planetary administrators could use."

But she was insistent. "I am busy enough managing the day-to-day operations of my own businesses in Helltown. You're trying to make sweeping changes to the entire Deep Zone. Really, Tiber … this is your show. Be the General. These people are here for you."

The eleven men and women had signed on to Adolphus's ambitious plan in its early stages. Often, he knew, volunteers showed great enthusiasm at the beginning of a task, yet had no fortitude to see it through to the end. Most of these administrators, however, came from the same mold as he did and were 'second-string' nobles. Without drive and persistence one did not succeed as the leader of a fledgling colony.

Sophie flung open the wide doors of the boardroom and stepped aside so the General could place himself on the threshold. He smiled at his visitors. "Welcome, and thank you for taking such extraordinary precautions. Now we can meet for a frank discussion of our future."

Sophie took her leave, letting him concentrate on the gathered planetary administrators. At the front of the group, not surprisingly, stood Tanja Hu, Candela's beautiful and ambitious planetary administrator. Tossing back her long, blue-black hair, she replied, "It's worth the investment, and far less than we pay the Constellation each month for tribute."

"I was already on my way," Walfor said with a grin. "Brought another shipment of iperion for the next group of trailblazers, thanks to Administrator Hu."

The others responded with a mutter of satisfaction. Adolphus did a silent roll call as he ushered them into the large room: Eldora Fen from Cles, George Komun from Umber, Sia Frankov from Theser, Dom Cellan Tier from Oshu, and five more, all here for the meeting.

As the eleven chose their seats around the table, he regarded them evenly. "Years of effort and planning have nearly reached fruition. The universe is about to change beneath our very feet."

Tanja Hu lounged back in her chair and got right to the point. "The long-range trailblazers are still on schedule?"

"Precisely on schedule. And Mr Walfor's new delivery of iperion allows us to launch the final few trailblazers to the nearer systems. Within a month or so, the last of the fifty-three ships should be in flight to their destinations."

Eldora Fen whistled. "That's a hell of a lot of coordination."

"We expect and require nothing less. The Diadem won't have any idea how the whole Deep Zone suddenly slipped out of her hands." He projected the star chart on the gypsum screen and showed them the impressive scope of the scheme that had quietly been underway for six years. They all knew portions of this, but he was filling in the gaps.

Even for a man of Adolphus's background and accomplishments, this was indeed a majestic plan. An entirely new transportation network, detached and independent from Sonjeera, would eliminate DZ reliance upon the Crown Jewels. "All roads lead to Rome," he said, "and Rome is about to fall."

Bearing gifts for this meeting, the co-conspirators had brought samples and images of goods that their planets could provide in an open market. Released from paying tribute to the Diadem, the majority of DZ inhabitants would reap the benefits of their own productivity. For any frontier world that could not yet survive on its own, the new distribution network would provide a support system equivalent to what the Constellation had to offer.

"Our business today isn't so much to put our scheme into place, as to ensure its success. We've done the hard work in Phase One, and D-Day – Destination Day – should occur within the year. The trailblazers dispatched from Hallholme will reach the remaining DZ planets at approximately the same time, each having successfully laid down an iperion path along the way. That much, though, is nothing more than an engineering and logistical problem – a hard one, yes, but straightforward nevertheless." He regarded them all. "Afterwards, though, we'll face a much more difficult challenge – the political one. We can't expect the Diadem to just blow us a goodbye kiss and wish us well."

"The Constellation already cut Buktu off," Ian Walfor said. "And *we're* doing just fine."

"You're a special case, Ian," Tanja Hu said. "Nobody in the Crown Jewels cares about Buktu. They'll sure as hell care when they lose the other fifty-three DZ worlds all at once."

"What can the Diadem do about it anyway?" snorted George Komun from Umber. "By the time she finds out, the battle will already be won."

"Doesn't mean she won't try something," said Sia Frankov. "She can send the Army of the Constellation to any one of the Deep Zone destinations and hammer us."

"But she can't go to all of them at once. The Diadem would be insane to start a war on fifty-four fronts at the same time!" said Dom Cellan Tier, then he hesitated. "Wouldn't she?"

"It's not likely," the General said in a calm, commanding voice. "But she might attack here, or a few other independent planets, one by one

– and if I know Lord Selik Riomini, he'll advise that a few targets be used as horrific examples so that the other planets capitulate."

"We'll never capitulate," Komun said with loud bluster. "We've got too much at stake."

"It's easy to make promises like that before the weapons start firing," Ian Walfor said. "I say we just cut the stringlines back to the Crown Jewels as soon as we have our network in place. Then it would be years before their ships arrive." He chuckled.

"It's an option," the General said, "a desperate one I'd like to avoid, if possible. Even if we do that, the Army of the Constellation *will* come." He leaned forward. "We've got to map out all possible scenarios and agree on our response ahead of time."

Sia Frankov pointed out, "Remember, we're only a dozen Deep Zone administrators. We've still got to convince the other forty-two to join us. They may not be too happy we've painted them into a corner like this."

Adolphus nodded. "We've already got operatives and sympathizers on each of those planets, planting seeds, preparing for forceful action if necessary."

Over the past six months, hundreds of the General's old comrades had departed under assumed names to meet up with hidden loyalists in the Crown Jewel worlds; from there, they surreptitiously spread out among the Deep Zone planets. They located others who were dissatisfied with the Constellation government (not a difficult task) and put together cells that were ready to react as soon as Adolphus gave the word . . .

"I never assume that people will react according to expectations, but this is our chance – and we all know there's nothing for us back in the Crown Jewels. We have the opportunity to set up our own thriving economy far from Sonjeera. It's the best plan for the whole Deep Zone, although we may be in for some very painful birthing struggles."

Diadem Michella saw the frontier worlds as a way to open floodgates to new resources and income, but she wasn't stupid. She must know that someday the DZ would no longer tolerate such inequitable taxation. As a student of history, Adolphus had seen countless examples of self-sufficient colonies becoming strong enough to throw off the chains of their parental worlds. The tide of history favored his dreams, and he intended to attain independence sooner rather than later. In a way, this was merely the culmination of the rebellion he had begun more than fifteen years ago.

"Isn't it remarkable?" mused Dom Cellan Tier. "No one thinks much of Hellhole, but this planet is going to be a hub as powerful and influential as Sonjeera! The Deep Zone will have its own capital." Some of the others around the table grumbled at this, to the man's obvious consternation.

"Beware of recreating the problem you propose to eradicate. I didn't ask for this planet to be a new capital, or for myself to become a new Diadem." On the star chart, Adolphus summoned a secondary image to show an interconnected web of prospective stringlines that sprang from many of the colony worlds. "Hallholme will be the initial hub for our secondary network, but I intend for *all* of your planets to establish additional pathways, to link with those markets that make the most commercial sense for you. This will be a full network, not a bottleneck, as Sonjeera is. There will be no monopoly.

"So much power should not reside in the hands of one individual. Not even mine." Adolphus opened his palms. "Our task is to *share* the great resources of the Deep Zone, not to form a corrupt bureaucracy with them."

"At least we agree not to let Sonjeera bleed us dry any longer," Tanja said with a snort. "The Diadem has no idea how much we resent her out here where she's not looking."

29

Despite all the gardens and ornate architecture, some parts of Sonjeera were shadowy and rundown. Ishop Heer looked out at one such section of Council City as he glanced through the window of his tiny secondary office on the Rue de la Musique. The Street of Music – what an ironic name! If any street musicians had ever worked this area in the past, they were long gone. In the dreary neighborhood, garbage lay strewn around the shabby buildings; unsavory characters lurked in the doorways and alleys, each staking out his territory. He always felt dirty coming here, but at least Laderna kept his subsidiary offices immaculately clean.

Ishop had chosen this location with great care. For his above-board work, he had an elegant main office near government headquarters. In a nondescript place like this, however, he had the flexibility and freedom to do other sorts of work. His devoted assistant had secured this austere location according to his specific request, so they could discuss activities that must be kept private from the other noble families or even, if necessary, from Diadem Michella herself.

That morning, Laderna had contacted him by confidential, scrambled earadio, asking in a whispered voice if they could meet in the shabby secondary offices. She used their code word that meant she had vital intelligence. The very thought excited him; Laderna was not prone to exaggeration.

He was well practiced in eluding observation. In the past Michella's spies had tried to monitor him, and at first he'd been offended at her demonstration of mistrust, but the old dowager chuckled at his indignation. "My dear Ishop, even trust has its limitations." He knew she appreciated his work. For the most part, he considered himself an independent agent, without close friends. Laderna was one of the few people he genuinely trusted. But, as Michella said, even trust had its limitations.

Keeping the interior of the office spotless was the only way Ishop could concentrate on his real work, undeterred by filth and disarray. On a wall he kept several interactive lists of tasks that needed completing, investigations in progress, people to expose ... everything written in a code of his own devising, which only he and Laderna could interpret. This was his own tiny kingdom, his own miniature estate, and here Ishop could impose all the order he liked.

A month ago, Laderna had even installed a comfortable foldaway bed, in case either of them had to work late. Ishop's covert activities often involved odd hours, and Laderna avoided walking on the Rue de la Musique after dark. It had not escaped his notice that the bed was large enough for two; the dear girl would have been embarrassed to learn that her longings were painfully obvious. While Laderna's adoration was sweet, he did not want to complicate their efficient business relationship. It had the potential of becoming messy, and he did not at all like messy things.

He arrived early at the office, waiting and watching. The windows needed washing, but from the outside; inside, they were spotless. Through the streaky pane he spotted her down on the sidewalk, a gangly redhead with a large purse over her shoulder walking with brisk confidence to deter any would-be predators. Laderna knew how to handle herself; once, Ishop had seen her deliver a hard punch to a thief's nose and send him straight to the cobblestones.

When she came up the stairs, he met her at the office door and locked it behind her, then double-checked it. He noted the intensity on her face. "You're looking purposeful today."

She gave him a crafty smile. Her cheeks were flushed pink, her breathing rapid. She opened her purse, removed a sheaf of papers. "You've always said I'm good at getting information on people."

"Something profitable, I assume? Another list?"

"Another list, but not like the others." Her eyes twinkled. He found her behavior very strange.

In the past, the two had compiled confidential files on numerous nobles and wealthy merchants. Laderna's research efforts, as well as his own careful surveillance, had resulted in tangible proof of highly embarrassing activities. Rather than allowing such information to be revealed, nobles and merchants paid Ishop what he called a "record-keeping fee." It was always good to plan ahead, everything neat and tidy.

"It concerns someone we both know very well," she said.

"Who?"

"A confidential aide to the Diadem."

The information alarmed him. Another one? "How many does she have?" And how had Michella kept it a secret from him?

Laderna let out a tinkling laugh. "I mean *you*, boss."

Something roiled in his stomach. "You dug up dirt on me? Don't I pay you enough?" He had plenty of skeletons in his past, and now his thoughts raced as he tried to guess what she had uncovered about him, and what he would have to pay to keep her quiet. He tried to see what was written on the first page of the document, but with a teasing expression she yanked it out of his view.

"Not dirt, boss – I know how much you hate dirt. This is something else, and you would know best how to handle it." He grabbed for the report, but again she snatched it away with a grin. She was taunting him! "One item at a time, boss." In a coy voice Laderna said, "You're the only surviving member of your family, right?"

"My parents are gone, but they never amounted to anything. I'm not aware of anyone else, though I suppose there must be cousins or nephews or something. No one of any importance. What did you find? An inheritance from a wealthy grand-aunt I didn't know about? Am I rich?"

"Potentially rich *and* powerful – if you're willing to do certain things."

"I'm always willing to do certain things." He had never seen her like this. It bothered him.

He reached for the report again, and this time she moved closer. "A kiss for the information – otherwise, you'll have to take me by force." He couldn't believe she was being so bold.

Reluctantly, he gave her a peck on the cheek, aware that she must have some truly special information for her to be so daring. "I'm not going to sleep with you Laderna. We've already been over that."

"I asked for a kiss, nothing more." She stepped back, suddenly businesslike, although her smile seemed a bit more attractive now, and her brown eyes had a seductive glow he'd never noticed before. Finally, she handed him the file. "Item one. This is a set of genealogical reports on various families that I obtained from the oldest sections of the Constellation Archives."

He glanced down. "This is ancient information. I don't see what it has to do with me."

Laderna continued in a rush without giving him time to read the material. "Considering the Diadem's age, everyone is talking about the succession, so I thought it wise to keep files on all the nobles who qualify for consideration. I built a database of every one, whether or not they have any current standing in the Constellation."

Ishop made a dismissive noise. "They've argued for the past decade, and Michella is no closer to retirement now than she was before. Lord Selik Riomini is the obvious successor. Everything else is just talk."

"Yes, but an alliance or coalition could change at any time. I've tallied one hundred eighty-three families whose members are eligible for the diademacy – nineteen primary Crown Jewel lords plus one hundred sixty-four minor noble families."

"That many? I'm surprised, but most of them aren't relevant. They have noble names, but no power or influence." Still, he paused; a noble name was more than he could ever aspire to, no matter how excellent his service to the Diadem. "I'd like to see that list."

"I'm talking about the names, Mr Heer. The noble rolls, the upper echelon of society, whether or not they have great political influence – and I know how much it annoys you not to be included, though your service, your intelligence, and your talent warrant it."

He frowned. He had never said such a thing aloud, but it was frightening how observant this woman could be. "The best butler on

Sonjeera cannot sit in the lowliest seat at the master's table." He wondered what she was getting at.

Laderna indicated the list again. "Next item. The total includes noble families that fell into the dustbin of history for various reasons. Even without holdings, they still have the bloodline. Technically, they still qualify for consideration, though they will never even be mentioned as a possibility to become the next Diadem. Even so, it's the principle that matters. You never know what might happen. I dug deep to make sure I had compiled a comprehensive list."

"But what does this have to do—?"

"*Your* family is one of those, sir," she blurted. "It's right here on the list."

He stopped, blinked. "You're saying I have noble blood?" He chuckled because that was impossible. The nobles always treated him with little respect.

Laderna pointed at the printed genealogical reports. "Centuries ago, your family name was Osheer. The remaining members changed it after falling into disgrace, but that doesn't change your bloodline."

Ishop's mind raced. If true, such a discovery would redefine who he was, blast a hole in the ceiling that had trapped him for years. "But how can that be? I've never been ..." He fumbled for words. "My parents had no ambition at all. I ran away and made my own career in the Diadem's palace. They certainly never acted like nobles."

"How many nobles do, sir? I seriously doubt your parents had any inkling of their heritage, but the Osheers were once very powerful. Centuries ago, two of them even ruled the Constellation – you can look it up – but they fell into political disfavor, a group of nobles conspired to ruin them, and the remaining Osheers were exiled to Ogg."

"Ogg ... I was there once. A very minor, unimpressive planet, not much better than Barassa." But he did remember hearing a folktale in a beer-hall that Ogg was the home of ancient, vanquished noblemen. Some of the pieces were indeed falling into place.

And he certainly felt like a noble, acted like a noble, had the talent and intelligence of a noble ... more so than most of the real ones did. *Unless I am a real noble.*

Like an attorney presenting a compelling case, Laderna handed him another document. "As part of their banishment, the Osheer family was barred from the ranks of the nobility for seven hundred years. Hence, they were eliminated from the list of succession candidates for all those centuries, banned from holding major office. After so much time, the surviving descendants lost track, mixed in with the commoners, and they forgot who they were." Her eyes sparkled. "But now, those seven centuries have passed! No one in the Council of Lords pays attention to ancient history, and the Osheers – the *Heers* – have gone entirely unnoticed."

"Even *I* didn't notice."

She tapped the papers. "This information is only in the original signed agreements from seven hundred years ago, which I dug out of the deepest archives. I made copies for you. According to these official documents, you are entitled to reclaim your noble status whenever you like!" She gave him a quick curtsey. "My Lord."

He read the clause she had marked in red on the copy. "Interesting." Then he laughed as the pragmatic aspects became clear. "It's a nice story, but what am I supposed to do about it? Produce this evidence and demand to be considered for the Star Throne above Lord Selik Riomini, Azio Tazaar, and all the other lords? Whose holding would I take over? A nobleman without an estate or power or wealth is just a man with a fancy name."

She continued to look at him with those admiring eyes. "But the *name*, nevertheless, sir. You would have the title and the respect, and would be considered a noble. You said even the lowliest lord looked down on you in the Council chamber. And I know you very well, boss – given your ambition, you would not remain the lowliest nobleman for long. I've already started making plans. Don't you *want* this opportunity?"

His answer was automatic. "Of course I want it."

As he hungrily scanned the names of his ancestors and the enemies who had brought about their downfall, Ishop realized that he did want something more. Because generations ago a group of nobles had banded together and caused the disgrace of the Osheer family, Ishop had been left with nothing. He saw the list of their names right there in front of him. Because of those scheming families, he – and his forefathers – had been dishonored, stripped of their titles and all the advantages that came with them. Only twelve names; that wasn't so much.

His weak ancestors had accepted their defeat, and Ishop scorned them (as he did his parents) because they had rolled over and let themselves be downtrodden. But he would have scorn enough for them later. If he had started out life at a different level, he could have achieved so much more.

He felt a warmth spreading through his chest. "I *am* a nobleman! Deep inside, Laderna, I always knew that I was."

"I always knew, too, boss. Somewhere, instinctively, both of us did. But now that we have this list, what are we going to do about it?"

From this day forth, Ishop decided he would have to live up to certain standards. He had his *family honor* to uphold, and he had to start somewhere. He looked down at the list of the twelve noble families that had worked in concert to bring about the Osheer downfall. Through treachery they had changed his family history. Even though it was long in the past, they had committed an unforgiveable affront against *him*.

This was a personal matter, a *very* personal matter.

Though he hadn't known anything about the tragedy until moments ago, now it was the most important thing he could imagine. He felt soiled, damaged, wronged. "Whatever we do, Laderna, we have to be careful ... and organized. Seven centuries ago – I trust you can find me the names of their primary descendants? The twelve nobles that brought down my family? There are certain things I have to do, and I'll need your help."

She had anticipated his request, because she handed him another document, this one containing modern names. "Already compiled, boss."

He ran his gaze down the column. He saw a Yarick there, a Tazaar, a Paternos, even a Duchenet. Fascinating. "We've got a new project, Laderna – balancing the books, so to speak. To restore my family honor ... or maybe to earn it, even if nobody ever knows what we're doing."

"It's still important, boss. Tying up loose ends – I know how you think."

He paced the room, breathless with the discovery, but also amused by the series of tasks falling into place in his mind like a set of tumblers and bearings. "We can't let anyone find out what we're doing, but *I'll* know."

"And I'll know, sir. I'll help you. You can count on me."

"I would never believe otherwise." Now he matched her smile. "This puts a whole new perspective on things, Laderna. While I lay the groundwork for announcing my heritage, I suggest we work our way through the list, check off one member from each of these offending families, whoever they are."

"Best to be thorough about it, sir."

He let out a long, contented sigh. "Then I can reclaim my noble title with a light heart and a clean conscience."

"Your course of action was obvious, boss. I was already indignant on your behalf, and so I took some preemptive action." Even though she flushed with embarrassment, her eyes had a predatory gleam. "Sorry, sir, but I just couldn't wait." With a smile Laderna crossed off one of the names on the list: Lady Opra Mageros. "I've already taken care of that one for you. It was easy, and I wanted to get a head start. That leaves eleven."

He was stunned, but not displeased.

Using the foldaway bed in the secret office, he and Laderna made love for the first time. What she lacked in glamour, she more than made up for with earnestness. Afterward Laderna drifted off to sleep in his arms, but Ishop found himself unable to doze. While he listened to the low thrum of her breathing, remarkable thoughts filled his mind and he envisioned himself doing things he'd never thought possible.

A real nobleman! He could hardly believe it.

And revenge. He was going to enjoy this.

30

After a week of documenting uncharted grid squares, Vincent and Fernando reached a serene-looking valley surrounded by rough mountains. The east-facing slopes and cliffs were covered with a uniform fur of alien vegetation. On the valley floor, surrounded by dust and sand, three intriguing pools reflected the sky, like circular mirrors. Since the small crater-like lakes did not appear on the satellite images, Vincent wondered if they had only recently bubbled up from the ground.

Despite the devastated landscape, water was not scarce on Hellhole, though it needed to be filtered. These pools, however, did not look like meltwater tarns or drainage ponds. Chunks of black obsidian lay jumbled around them like distorted dark lenses. He guided the Trakmaster closer so they could inspect the area.

When the two men emerged from the vehicle, the air was silent, without a breeze. Vincent drew a cautious breath and went to the edge of the nearest pool, which appeared to be still and deep. Odd smell, but he couldn't place it. This whole planet was full of odd smells . . .

Fernando looked around. "Help me find a stick."

"You won't find a stick – there aren't any trees." Despite the moisture of the pools, the furry alien groundcover had encroached no closer than the distant hillside.

The pond appeared utterly placid, but viscous, like a pearlescent tar pit; an oily sheen swirled and reflected indistinct shapes like clouds, but when Vincent looked up, the greenish-yellow sky was clear except for a distant smoke plume from a volcanic eruption.

A loud *plop* startled him, and he jerked backward from the pool's crumbling dirt edge to see Fernando throw a second stone, which left barely a ripple. The liquid folded over the sinking rock and returned to its eerie quiescence. Grinning, the other man gave his assessment. "I'd say that's no ordinary water."

"Maybe we discovered some kind of oil," Vincent suggested. "A clear petroleum seep." He would have to take samples for the prospector office.

"You think the General would pay us a reward for this?" Fernando leaned over and squinted at his blurry reflection. "It's quite a discovery."

"It's our *job*. We're supposed to find things."

Fernando made a raspberry sound. "There should be a difference between finding *interesting* things and just more of the same old boring landscape."

Vincent sighed. "Take it up with General Adolphus when we get back to Michella Town. I'm going to check out the other pools."

Leaving his friend, he circled the first of the strange ponds and moved to the second, which was slightly larger. Seeing no runoff channel that would have filled it, he concluded that the liquid must bubble up from some underground source. Unlike other streams and lakes they'd encountered, this liquid was devoid of algae, lichens, or indigenous weeds. At the third pool, the crater lip eased down to a shore of gravel and sand. Vincent squatted on his heels. The water looked somehow *slick*.

At the far end of the first pond, Fernando picked up a large chunk of obsidian and hefted it over his head. Grinning, he walked to the edge and called out, "Hey Vincent, watch this!"

Vincent was not as interested in his friend's antics as he was in the liquid. It swirled gently with unseen currents, despite the calm air. No seismic rumbles shook the ground. Yet the water moved . . .

He heard a loud yelp, followed by a much bigger splash than he'd expected. Lurching to his feet, he saw that the edge of the pool had crumbled beneath Fernando's feet, causing him to fall into the pool. With a groan, Vincent ran around the edge of the pond towards Fernando.

Though the pool wasn't large, the other man thrashed and cried out with very real panic, choking. He clawed at the crumbly shore, finally got his elbows onto solid ground, and tried to haul himself out of the slick water.

To Vincent's shock, the gelatinous liquid *crawled* over Fernando, clinging, trying to pull him back into the pool. Fernando screamed again.

Before Vincent could reach him, his friend managed to scramble onto the dry ground and collapse in the dirt. The thick water oozed off him and trickled down his body, off his feet, and back into the pool, leaving him completely dry.

Vincent arrived, panting, dropped to his knees, shook the other man's shoulders. "Fernando!"

The man coughed, squeezing his eyelids shut, then with a sharp gasp he flung his eyes open and sat up on the ground. Vincent was amazed to see Fernando's eyes were covered with a turbulent opalescence; apparently he was blind.

Fernando reached out, waving one hand in the air. "Vincent! Vincent, are you there?"

"I'm here – what can I do? How can I help you?"

Fernando's voice had a breathy sense of wonder, tinged with madness. "The things I'm seeing! This planet, the natives . . . all the history and memories! So amazing . . ."

He collapsed onto the dirt and began convulsing.

31

In the impact basin where the Children of Amadin had gone, the hilly landscape was studded with rough, pitted boulders from a hardened lava floe. Devon and Antonia's Trakmaster descended the steep walls of the outer-crater boundary, toiling down loose slopes toward the wide basin of the central-impact scar. Simmering lava continued to blister the landscape, hefting smoke into the sky.

The locater ping from the three overland vehicles grew stronger. "That's an odd spot to establish a settlement," Devon said. "I don't see any ready water supply, native vegetation, or natural shelter."

"Not much of a promised land," Antonia agreed.

The Trakmaster rumbled across the crater floor, and ahead they finally spotted the three big vehicles and the camp the religious group had set up – the *ruins* of a camp, Antonia realized with a sinking feeling. The prefabricated shelters were battered hideously, the tents had collapsed. The abandoned Trakmasters looked as if they had been pounded by a meteor storm. She saw colorful scraps of polymer walls and tarpaulins, now covered in soot.

Approaching cautiously, Devon shone the vehicle's front lights into the smoky pall. When he ground to a halt at the edge of the empty camp, they both stared. The area was still, silent, holding its breath.

"I don't see anyone," Antonia said.

Devon drew in a deep breath and let it out slowly before saying, "We may be too late." He opened the Trakmaster's hatch and motioned for her to join him. "But I'm not going back to my mother without answers. Come with me to help keep watch. And be careful. If you see anything unusual, let me know right away. Don't investigate it yourself."

"Then we'd better stick together."

Together, they wandered through the eerie ruined camp, finding tools, shredded clothes, battered bins, broken pieces of camp equipment. "These people came here a month ago," Antonia said, "but this place looks like it's been abandoned for centuries."

Devon pressed his lips together, studying details, running possibilities through his mind. "One good storm could account for this ... but it doesn't look like it was caused by a storm. It's something else."

He crunched along and overturned a small, pitted metal box with his toe. "Sometimes these fanatical groups do strange things. A couple of years ago a guru and his cult stripped themselves naked and stood out in the middle of a growler, claiming they wanted to feel the energy of God. They felt it all right. The only survivor lasted a week in the hospital with severe burns over eighty per cent of his body. The others were just skeletons covered by slabs of cooked flesh."

The group's three off-road vehicles sat near one another in various stages of disrepair; the lead Trakmaster slumped on collapsed treads. Jumbled piles of pocked lava boulders formed dikes nearby.

Standing next to the nearest vehicle, Devon ran his fingers over the dimpled surface. Some of the impacts had cut entirely through the hull, leaving ragged holes. The sealant strips around the windows and door hatch were gone, and the cab's windows had fallen in. He opened the hatch to discover that the interior had been stripped as well. The upholstery on the passenger seats was nothing more than a few frayed remnants. "Something sure tore this up."

Behind the base of one of the seats, Antonia found a fragment of bone.

Devon's well-toned face grew grim and his eyes narrowed when she showed him. He held the ivory fragment between his fingers, while scanning the interior of the Trakmaster. "Even a high-velocity abrasive storm can't blow hard enough to scour flesh from bones *inside* a vehicle."

Antonia felt sick to her stomach and her tension heightened. She had spent years looking over her shoulder for supposed government assassins, and then she'd been fearful of Jako pursuing her. This danger seemed much less personal, but even more deadly.

"Let's take a quick look around the camp and inside the other two Trakmasters. There's got to be some kind of clue." His voice cracked, and he made a show of clearing his throat. "Stay close to me, and alert. Very alert."

The remnants of the prefab shelters contained only scraps of light blue cloth and a few more bone fragments. Antonia picked up a pipe from one of the larger tent supports. "Devon, this looks like it's been *chewed*."

Inside the lead Trakmaster, they discovered an unusual object composed of strange curves; its oily, obsidian-like surface was studded with reflective crystalline patches. The object gave off an eerie *flowing* sensation, an exotic sense of alienness. Devon picked it up, acting studiously detached in an obvious effort to hide his nervousness from her. "The General collects alien artifacts that pop up now and then, but I've never seen anything like this." He frowned at the relic.

Antonia felt skittish, looking around at the distant scarlet glow of fresh lava. Her eyes stung from the sulfurous vapors in the air. "We should take that and go back home. We're not forensic archaeologists, and I doubt we can figure out exactly what happened here."

"You're right. The General will have to send a larger team if he wants to get to the bottom of this." His voice sounded tight, though he clearly didn't want to alarm her. "And it *is* my job to keep you safe. I promised."

Antonia normally would have insisted that she could keep herself safe, but Devon knew a lot more about the real dangers of Hellhole. "All right," she said. "Let's document this, then get out of here."

After taking a series of images of the ruined camp and marking its location, they picked their way through the rubble back toward their Trakmaster, carrying the unusual alien artifact with them. They moved at a quick pace.

Antonia turned as the strange silence of the dead camp began to throb with a resonant subsonic hum that grew to a furious buzzing. Shocked, the two of them tried to locate the source of the sound. Moraines of gray-black rock from the old pyroclastic flow formed barriers on all sides, sharp and fragile rock piles that would have been a nightmare to traverse on foot.

A cloud of black insects wafted up from the shadows in the rocks, swirling like smoke. "What are those?" Antonia cried.

The swarm curved in the air and darted toward them.

"Never seen them before – but I'm not taking any chances. Come on!" Devon grabbed her hand, and they raced toward the Trakmaster. All scientific curiosity evaporated as the first of the hard-shelled insects struck them. Latching onto Antonia's arms and neck, the bugs began to slash with razor-sharp mandibles.

Although bugs landed on him as well, Devon swatted some of them off Antonia and pushed her ahead of him so she could reach the vehicle first. "Get inside!" The cab's hatch was partly open, and she slid through the gap. Devon leaped inside after her as a handful of outlier insects swirled around them. Working together, she and Devon strained to seal the hatch, but a last spurt of ravenous bugs slipped in. From outside, Antonia heard a sound like shotgun pellets peppering the hull. Swarming beetles smashed themselves against the reinforced windshield and hammered the sides of the Trakmaster.

Dozens of the hungry insects buzzed about inside the cab, and Antonia dealt with several that bit into her arms and neck. She knocked them away and smashed them against hard surfaces with the side of her fist; another landed on Devon's back, and she slapped it aside and crushed it on the dashboard.

"I'll take care of these. Just get us moving – go!" A bug flew at her face, and she swatted it out of the air. Antonia couldn't stop thinking of the other three battered vehicles, the scraps of shredded upholstery, the fragments of chewed bone.

The high-horsepower engine was already running, and Devon accelerated. The rugged tracks spat loose dirt and broken stones, grabbing for traction as the heavy vehicle lurched over bumpy terrain toward the steep crater wall. The native bugs continued to smack into the windshield with such force that they left tiny crazed divots.

Antonia heard more buzzing, watched two beetles crawl through the ventilation screens. "Devon, the air intakes!"

Without taking his eyes from the path ahead so he could keep them moving, he worked controls with his left hand. "There, sealed off the outside source." Antonia wondered how long the block would last.

In the rear imager, she saw that they were pulling away from the cloud of bugs, but thousands might still be clinging to the outer hull, chewing and scuttling. So many had already splattered on the windshield it was hard to see the path ahead, but Devon raced along, nevertheless.

Antonia moved about the vehicle's interior, methodically dispatching the straggler insects. When she was finished, panting and bleeding from numerous bites, Devon said, "Thanks. Not bad for a newbie. I hate to ask you this, but could you gather some specimens and put them in a container? Maybe someone in Helltown can ID them."

Antonia scratched at the stinging bites on her arms. "I guess we know what happened to the Children of Amadin. I thought indigenous life forms couldn't digest Terran proteins?"

"They didn't have to *digest* us." Devon looked down at his bleeding bites. "All they had to do was chew and keep chewing until there was nothing left."

32

The Diadem was no help at all. Even when Keana promised to do whatever her mother wanted, Michella refused to lift a finger on Louis's behalf. "The matter is closed." The old woman brushed the conversation aside and moved on to important things.

But Keana would not be so immediately dismissed. "Louis doesn't deserve this! Admit it, Mother. His only real crime was loving me!"

"What he has or hasn't done is irrelevant. Thanks to your scandalous actions, the Crais family is mortally offended, and you've left me a stinking mess to deal with. No one feels sorry for a man who corrupted the daughter of the Diadem. And you, Keana, are an embarrassment to your family. You have a role to play, even if it's just window dressing. Now be a dutiful princess and stop drawing unwanted attention to yourself."

It was the wrong thing to say to her. "Then put me in prison, too. Exile me along with Louis. I doubt Bolton would even care!"

Michella looked impatient. "There are bigger issues at stake than you realize – noble families jockeying for power, the trading of favors, the machinations of strong lords against waning families – and you played right into their hands. We're talking about the balance of power in the Crown Jewels, and all you can think about is silly romance?"

Though Keana left, she did not give up. She took the extraordinary step of contacting a Sonjeeran attorney on Louis's behalf. In order to pay the legal fees, in room after room she emptied her cabinets of heirloom jewelry and brought the whole pile to Buxton Trombie in Council City. The expression on the lawyer's face told her it would be enough to pay for the most extravagant defense.

An aged man with impeccably groomed gray hair, Trombie listened as Keana explained the desperate situation. "During the Reading of the Charges on Vielinger, Louis had no legal protection. The magistrates made up their minds ahead of time – it was so obvious. And now he's being brought back to Sonjeera for sentencing. He may be here already, but no one will tell me anything!"

The lawyer cleared his throat as if preparing to give an opening argument. "First off, Princess, the magistrates determined the evidence was overwhelming, and by law, he was not allowed to present a defense." He blinked his heavy-lidded eyes. "In legal matters, one must be careful with details."

Keana thought he was missing the main point. "This has nothing to do with justice – it's a conspiracy. The Riominis want to take over his holdings on Vielinger! I have it on good authority that the three magistrates judging his case are in Riomini employ."

She expected Trombie to be offended; instead, he seemed dismissive. "You are certainly correct, Princess. Lord de Carre got himself into quite an untenable situation and let his own planet slip away. If memory serves, he missed several important votes in Council and failed to properly administer the iperion facilities under his authority. His son was fortunate that the lord shouldered the burden of the charges, otherwise the magistrates would have imprisoned both of them."

Keana's instinct was to shout in indignation and claim that the charges were false, but she couldn't deny that she had distracted Louis from attending Council meetings. Caught up in love and happiness after so many years of being alone, Louis had lost his appetite for political maneuvering when he'd given his heart to her. But since the arrest, Keana had done some legal research. "The question, Mr Trombie, is what can we do about it? We have to free Louis from this trap."

"Oh, I suspect we'll have little effect, whatever we do."

"I want you to expose the corruption to the whole Constellation. There'll be a public outcry for justice."

Trombie regarded her as if she were a naïve child, which angered Keana even more. "There's simply no point to it, my Lady. Your affair with Lord de Carre is common knowledge, and the people won't sympathize with you."

Keana barely restrained herself from leaping to her feet. Did he not understand the urgency? How could she stir this man to action? "Can we file an appeal? Reverse the decision? Submit papers to request clemency?"

"I've read the decision, and it has been on the news reports. I am sorry to say, Princess, that everything seems to be in order. Lord de Carre's formal sentencing takes place here tomorrow." Trombie pushed away the jewels Keana had brought. "I have represented the Duchenet family for years, and therefore when you made your appointment with me, I was obligated to contact your mother. It seems that she has other ideas about the situation."

The door to the inner office swung open and Diadem Michella entered. From the sour frown on her face, it was obvious she had been eavesdropping on the whole conversation. With Keana too astonished to speak, the old woman swooped into a chair and took charge of the meeting. "You are misinformed, daughter. The judges who convicted Lord de Carre are not in the employ of the Riominis. They are, in fact, on *my* payroll, and they rule as *I* tell them to."

Buxton Trombie shifted uncomfortably in his chair. "Princess, I advise you to drop your attempts on behalf of Lord de Carre. Your case has no merit."

Michella placed a claw-like ring-studded hand on her daughter's arm. "You must face certain realities, dear. Political realities. I view this as an opportunity to teach you by letting you live with the consequences of your bad decisions."

Keana found her mother's touch repulsive. "I love Louis – can't you understand that? *Please.* If you grant him clemency, I will do whatever you want!" She realized she sounded like a whining child, but didn't care.

Michella frowned, as if reconsidering. "I didn't think you had it in you. I thought you would flutter away and forget about it soon enough, but now I see how determined you are." Keana responded with flashing eyes and pulled her arm free. "All right, something more lenient might be arranged for the man ... a prison term of a few years, followed by exile to the Deep Zone. Complete forfeiture of his family holdings goes without saying ... Even as Diadem, I can do nothing more."

Keana took several deep breaths. "At least let me see Louis. I'll tell him what you said. He'll be willing to go to the Deep Zone, I promise."

She clucked her tongue. "It would not be seemly for the Diadem's daughter to visit him in prison – a disgraced nobleman and a convicted criminal."

Keana fought back tears. Louis must feel so alone! Trombie gave a sober nod, tried to intercede. "It might be done discreetly, Eminence."

Michella finally showed a glimmer of compassion. Fidgeting in her chair, clearly not pleased, she nodded. "All right. I will arrange for you to visit him briefly in his cell just before his sentencing. However, I want no gawking observers, no one who can repeat gossip."

"Thank you, Mother!" It was the tiniest hint of hope, but the best news Keana had had in days.

Following her mother's instructions, Keana arrived at the east entrance of an imposing gray rock structure the following morning. Horned-gax carvings protruded from fascia and corners; according to legend, the icons warded off evil forces. A shiver ran down her back. Before today, Keana had never been to Sonjeera's highest-security prison, but she was delighted and relieved to have this opportunity to comfort poor Louis.

She wore nondescript garments to hide her identity – and who would expect the Diadem's daughter in this part of the city? After she whispered to one of the guards, he led Keana up a short stairway. She looked both ways, smelled the odd oppressive mustiness of the building, but realized with relief that at least Louis was not in one of the lower-level cells reserved for heinous criminals. Instead, the guard escorted her to a spacious wing with individual rooms for upper-class prisoners. Perhaps Louis was being treated well after all.

The gruff guard showed no sympathy for any of the detainees, nor did he seem to care who Keana was. "Lord de Carre has been left alone for the day, so that he may contemplate his sentencing without distraction.

I have orders to grant you complete privacy." The guard motioned her inside.

Not caring what the uniformed man thought, she hurried into the finely appointed detention room and heard the door shut behind her. Louis must be miserable, but she could at last offer him a little encouragement; she would do whatever she could for him. "Louis, my love – I'm here!" She ran forward but didn't see him. What if her mother had played a cruel trick on her? What if Louis wasn't here after all? The Diadem had already kept so much from her; what if her mother was simply trying to keep Keana busy chasing red herrings, while Louis was whisked away to some other place?

Her heart contracted at the memory of how forlorn he had looked during the Reading of the Charges, humiliated, broken. With her love, though, Keana could give him strength. They would go into exile together, live in quiet anonymity on some Deep Zone world.

But he did not answer her call. "Louis?" They wouldn't have much time together today, and she wanted to cherish every moment of it.

The bathroom door was closed, so she called again, knocking hard. When he still did not respond, she felt a heavy dread in her stomach and threw open the door in desperation.

Lord Louis de Carre lay sprawled on the floor in an unnatural position. He still wore his trousers, but his shirt hung on a hook beside the door. A lake of dark blood pooled all around his body.

"Louis!" she screamed. "Guard, I need a doctor!"

But the blood was cold. The body was cold.

She knelt in the red pool, grabbed Louis by the shoulders and hugged him, held him. Gaping wounds ran the length of his wrists. "Guard!" She struggled to wrap towels around both wrists to stem the flow of blood, but the bleeding had stopped some time ago. "My darling, stay with me! Don't go!"

When the disinterested guard finally appeared, he looked down at the body. Keana screamed at him, "Get a doctor, damn you! Hurry – there's still time!" But Louis had run out of time, whether or not she wanted to admit it.

An eternity later, med techs rushed into the bathroom, while a red-stained Keana scrambled aside to give them access. Her clothes, her hands, her face were so covered with Louis's blood that at first the med techs assumed *she* had been injured as well. But Keana pushed them away from her. "Help Louis!"

Dutifully, the med techs checked his wounds, removed the blood-soaked towels. "I'm sorry, Princess, but he's been gone for some time. We'll need to send in the investigators."

The gruff guard shook his head. "This isn't as unusual as you might think, especially with the noble types. After their pampered lives, they can't face the humiliation of a sentencing."

"But I was going to help him." Her throat was raw. "Louis wouldn't have killed himself!" The med techs just looked at the body, and the answers were self-evident. Keana barely kept herself from vomiting. He must have been so devoid of hope ... if only she could have seen him one last time!

Sobbing, Keana clung to the body, remembering how vital Louis had been, how alive, how he had held her not long ago, their bodies so close together. This couldn't be happening! "How did he do this? How did he get a knife?"

The guard shrugged. "They always find a way."

The second med tech picked up a piece of paper he found on the countertop, scanned the words. "Suicide note."

Keana tried to grab it from him. "Give that to me!" She thought of the love poems he had written her, the romantic letters, the cherished scraps of paper that she still kept. Now those notes were all she had left, and this one.

But the med tech held it out of her reach, and the guard confiscated the letter. "This is evidence, Princess. I need to turn this over to my superior. I'm not authorized to show it to anyone else."

"Louis didn't kill himself." Her voice sounded very small. "It's not true!"

Inwardly, though, she knew it was possible, even probable. The proud man had lost his family fortune and his honor. He had been entirely cut off from the love he shared with Keana, and the memory had not been enough to sustain him. Disgraced and in despair, he might well have chosen to end his life.

If only her mother had let her talk with him sooner! Keana could have given him strength, convinced him to endure the dark shame. If only the two of them could have fled the festering politics of the Crown

Jewels. They would have been content to live as simple people, happy together, rich in love if not in possessions. But her dreams and hopes for the future were now shattered.

Weeping, Keana slumped beside the body. "Oh, my sweet, sweet Louis!" Now it was too late.

33

On Vielinger, Cristoph felt isolated and hamstrung. He understood that his family had been set up as part of a complex plot and that his father had fallen completely into the trap. Against such powerful enemies, the de Carre family didn't have a chance. Cristoph had been a helpless pawn.

He had not spoken with his father since the Reading of the Charges. Had the man thought about anyone but himself while he dallied on Sonjeera for the past two years and ignored the needs of his holding?

During the sham proceedings on the grounds of the family estate, his father had tried to act brave and noble, and Cristoph had been forbidden to speak. It didn't matter. Cristoph knew Louis de Carre had been set up and convicted in the back rooms of Sonjeera even before his arrest. His lax attitude toward his own people and his disgraceful lifestyle had ensured that few would raise an outcry. *He got what he deserved*, they would say. How could even his son defend him?

Now Cristoph, and any children he might eventually have, would pay the price for the nobleman's folly. Though Louis had shouldered all of the blame in a belated attempt to protect his son, Cristoph had already been mired in disgrace, his administrative work distorted and misrepresented. It was all part of the ruthless, methodical destruction of his family name.

By the time this day was finished, Cristoph would have nothing. The de Carres would have nothing. The Riominis were coming to take it all.

With weak legs, the young man descended the porch steps of the manor house and walked along the red pebble pathway through the ornamental gardens. This was their age-old residence, but everything they owned was now forfeit because of his father's apathy toward an industry that was vital to the functioning of the Constellation.

Glum servants tended the plants in afternoon sunlight, trimming them in precise shapes as had been done for centuries. When the Riominis took over, the gardeners would continue to work; some of them might not even notice the change. The dirt-smudged men looked up as he passed, then turned back to their work.

Knowing what lay ahead, Cristoph had tried to drain the family accounts and hide enough wealth to survive, but the funds had already been frozen. More offworld troops had landed at the local spaceport and placed the estate operations under their control. Thuggish Riomini guards locked down the business operations and most of the family estate, barring Cristoph from seeing any but his own rooms.

Yes, they had planned this very carefully.

Cristoph stood on the grounds, gazing toward the rolling hills and forests where he and his father used to hunt, and where their ancestors had led riding parties, living out their decadent lives. His chest felt leaden with the knowledge that he represented the last de Carre generation.

As he took on more and more responsibility, he had tried to be close to his father, consulting him about family business operations, but Louis was distracted. It would have been better if Lord de Carre had found a stable and sensible woman, remarried, focused on Vielinger.

It was the fault of that Duchenet woman, who had seduced Louis. Recently, Keana had even had the temerity to contact Cristoph and offer to help with his father's legal difficulties. She sounded truly distraught, but her message had infuriated him. Maybe if she had considered the consequences long ago, this would never have happened. But Keana hadn't really cared about Louis or his future.

The drone of motors cut through his ruminations like coarse knives. In the sky, he saw a squadron of aerocopters, each marked with a black family crest. Riomini craft. They landed on the grass and in the vegetable gardens, scattering the workers. Cristoph crossed his arms over his chest as black-uniformed soldiers poured out of the aircraft and took up positions in the grounds to join their fellows who had already been stationed inside the castle.

A blond officer appeared, his cap and uniform spotless, his medals gleaming in the sun. He marched up to Cristoph. "I am Unit Captain Escobar Hallholme, representing the Riomini military services." He eyed Cristoph up and down. "You are the son?"

"I am the son of Lord Louis de Carre."

"I have been sent to inform you that your father is dead." The words were brusque. "Suicide, before sentencing could be carried out. He did not want to face the consequences of the crimes he committed."

Cristoph felt as if he'd been slammed by an artillery shell. "That's impossible!" His father had faced the Reading of the Charges with a straight back. He had admitted his error, had protected Cristoph by taking all of the accusations on his own shoulders. "He would never do that."

But his father had said, *You are the last hope of the de Carre legacy now.* Had he been planning to take his own life, even then? Tears burned in Cristoph's eyes, and he tried to tell himself they were tears of anger.

"I'm afraid the evidence is incontrovertible. Slit his wrists … rather barbaric, but effective." Escobar Hallholme seemed to take an odd satisfaction in passing along the grisly details. "The Diadem has decided that there will be no investigation into the case, so that the matter may be wrapped up as quickly and cleanly as possible. The court has made its ruling." The officer glanced at the gardens, the castle. "By order of the Diadem, the de Carre family is no longer in charge of this estate or the iperion mines. Your titles and holdings are now the property of the Riomini family. I am ordered to confiscate all de Carre assets."

Cristoph felt as if he had been dropped into the middle of an avalanche and was being pounded from every direction. "I will appeal!"

"That is not allowed." Escobar ran his gaze around the gardens, as if measuring them for something he had in mind. He handed a rolled document to Cristoph. "This writ was signed by the Diadem herself." As Cristoph opened it, the haughty commander continued, "In order to expedite the transition, your passage into the Deep Zone has been paid. A generous concession, seeing as you are now penniless."

Cristoph grappled with the crushing weight of reality. His father had killed himself! Cristoph had never imagined him to be capable of that ... and by slashing his wrists? Apparently, Louis de Carre was not the man Cristoph knew, not at all.

Cristoph forced the words out, "I intend to stay here and fight for my family's legacy."

"No, sir, you will not. I have my orders. You have one hour to gather as many personal belongings as you can carry. Afterward, I have instructions to escort you to the spaceport, where you *shall* be aboard the next stringline hauler. The colonization office at the Sonjeera hub will assist you in finding a suitable DZ world where you can make a new start."

Though Cristoph tried to dig in his heels, he realized he had no further power here, no influential friends, no alternative. With feet as heavy as stone blocks, he walked toward the fortress-like structure that had been his family home for thirty-seven generations.

From the front portico, he watched, sickened, as mercenary troops ransacked whatever they could carry – jewelry, silver settings, rare statuettes. Dead inside, Cristoph told himself that these heirlooms were just things, objects of sentimental, but minimal value – far less significant than the land and the manor house, or the people who lived here on Vielinger.

In the brief time remaining to him, he walked slowly through the corridors of his home, ignoring the unruly troops, thinking of times that would never be again, reliving them for a few fleeting moments. He erected his own walls in a fortress against pain.

Generations of love and attention had gone into this estate. There had been weddings and birthday celebrations here; children had been born in the manor house, and many de Carre patriarchs were buried in the private cemetery on a nearby knoll.

Standing at the main fireplace mantel in the gaming room, he collapsed the projected image of his mother, whom he had never known, and slipped the datadrive into his pocket. He hesitated when he saw the tall portrait of his father in the hall, alongside Eduard de Carre and Ambrose de Carre, and other forefathers. He could never take such a large painting; it would probably end up on the trash heap, but he could do nothing about that. He gathered less-formal images, some of him and his father, even one of Louis as a boy. He also found a treasured, glowing image of Keana Duchenet in his father's suite, but he left that behind.

Because Cristoph would have to fend for himself, he was pragmatic enough to retrieve a small envelope of gems his father kept behind his headboard, an emergency stash that Louis had once shown him. Cristoph also had Star Crowns hidden in his own wardrobe, which none of the ransackers had found yet. The money wouldn't last him long, but it might be enough for a few necessities.

Taking little else except memories, Cristoph de Carre walked with fatalistic stiffness away from the estate and his family's past. He wanted to say goodbye to Lanny Oberon, who had never believed that the numerous accidents were the fault of Cristoph's mismanagement or lack of care. In fact, once the iperion mines reopened – under Riomini administration – Oberon would probably want to offer Cristoph a job, try to take care of him. There was still plenty of work to do, and Cristoph was certainly qualified.

But he couldn't let that happen, and he doubted Vielinger's new overlords would allow it. They would suspect him of wanting to foment rebellion or cause sabotage. None of the other miners would want a deposed nobleman pretending to fit in. Better if he disappeared entirely. Yes, Cristoph would miss Oberon, but he couldn't let the mine supervisor take such a risk.

Instead, he would go far from here, make a clean break, turn his back on unchangeable circumstances. Maybe it would be a relief to get as far as possible from this place and these scheming nobles ...

A powerful certainty came to him: Keana Duchenet had caused this, damn her. All along, she must have been playing her part in a grand plan to bring down the de Carres and steal Vielinger. For two years, the Diadem and her daughter had conspired with the Riominis to distract Louis, weaken Cristoph, sabotage the mining operations, soften up the planet for a takeover. They had destroyed his father and defeated him, and now he was being sent into exile ...

At the spaceport's DZ colonization office, Cristoph made his choice, an unlikely selection that he realized would be a great hardship. But he had his rationale: only one man had stood up to Diadem Michella and *almost* succeeded. General Tiber Adolphus, on Hellhole.

That was reason enough for him.

34

The linerunner *HDS Kerris* streaked along the quantum path, monitoring the precise iperion demarcation. This was Turlo and Sunitha Urvancik's fifth run to the planet Barassa.

Normally, one of their colleagues, Eva McLuhan, monitored the Sonjeera–Barassa route. Eva had been an unpleasant curmudgeon who wanted little to do with human company. Whenever she reached a terminus station, she stayed just long enough to file a report and resupply her ship. But six months ago, Eva had failed to arrive at her destination; when scouts backtracked the line, they discovered Eva's small vessel parked at an isolated energy substation. All of her ship's systems were powered down, and Eva had been suited up inside the airlock with the door cycled open to space. She'd clipped herself to the bulkhead, and opened her faceplate to the vacuum.

"I guess the solitude got to her after all," Turlo said to his wife. It was a hazardous profession; working alone in the incomprehensible vastness, linerunners had to be self-reliant and able to fix any mechanical malfunctions on their own. The greatest hazard, though, was the sheer loneliness.

"That's why it's so important we've got each other." Sunitha snuggled close, wanting comfort. "I couldn't do this without you."

As the linerunner streaked along, Turlo composed a detailed map of the residual iperion on the route. "This section of the line is getting weaker, just barely within tolerance. I'm going to release another controlled dusting."

"Our records will show that the line readings weren't in the red zone."

"I'm not taking chances. Neither of us wants a lost stringline ship on our conscience."

"I just hope they don't take the extra iperion out of our paycheck."

Stringline paths decayed over time unless the iperion trail through space was regularly replenished – and that was expensive, especially with Vielinger's output on the wane.

Now, on the run to Barassa, Turlo monitored his controls, using the bare minimum of iperion needed to shore up the quantum path. Sunitha distracted him, running her fingertips through his close-cropped hair, leaning close. He tried to recall the last time he'd seen her so aroused. They were in the romantic recovery phase after their quarrel en route to Ridgetop, and Turlo felt as if it were a second honeymoon.

He called up the coordinates and pointed to their location. "In half an hour we'll be at the next substation, and we have to get off the line anyway. There's a cargo hauler due to come by within four hours."

Sunitha sighed. "Bad timing. You might lose your chance if you wait too long."

He increased the ship's acceleration. "I'll just have to keep you interested in the meantime."

He gave her a quick kiss, but she held him for a longer one. "After all the practice you've had, you should be a better kisser by now. Pay attention." She touched his lips with hers, soft and slow, breathing warm air into his mouth.

He regarded her, his eyes shining. "Once we dock at the substation, we'll have hours with nothing to do ..."

"Hours? You mean we can actually indulge in foreplay? That'll be an interesting change." In response, he swatted her playfully.

Once they anchored the linerunner to the unmanned substation, the two couldn't tear off each other's jumpsuits swiftly enough. They would perform a routine checkup of the complex later, while waiting for the large Constellation cargo hauler to hurtle past.

"It's been awhile since we did it with the gravity off," Sunitha suggested with a giggle.

Turlo flicked a switch on the wall, and they needed a minute to grow accustomed to the sinking sensation of falling but never landing. Sunitha drifted toward him, and he caught her hands, pulling her close, which accelerated them together, and they collided with enough force to make them both laugh.

Mounted on the wall stand opposite their bunk, Turlo spotted the image of their son. Proud Kerris wore his impeccable army uniform in a preserved moment of idealism and optimism, back when the young man actually believed in the Constellation's cause … before everything changed. Next to their son's image hung a shimmering medal fused to the cabin wall, which had accompanied the "personal" video message dictated by Diadem Michella herself: "It is with great personal sadness that I must inform you …"

Turlo touched the nearest wall and imparted just enough force to send them slowly spinning in the other direction, turning Sunitha away from their dead son's image, before she could notice it.

He and Sunitha rarely took such time and care with each other, enjoying the luxury of hours of forced downtime. They did not notice when automatic sensors heralded the stringline hauler that blurred past them much too swiftly for human senses to detect …

35

Tanja Hu returned to Candela from her secret meeting with General Adolphus just in time for the major rains to start.

She had been through monsoon seasons all her life, but this was different. Worse. In previous years, the people always had a day or two between major storms, a brief respite to gather themselves for the next onslaught. Now, however, it had rained every single day since she came back from Hellhole. It was a torrent, hour after hour, day after day.

She heard the rain thrumming on the metal roof of her floating home, saw the harbor's water level rising as streams and rivers overflowed their banks. The surge had caused a mechanical problem with the locks leading from Saporo harbor out to sea, and her tugboat captains and engineers were struggling in the downpour, thus far to no avail. Trees and manmade structures careened down the steep slopes as the waterlogged hillsides slipped. The harbor water was a brown, silty soup.

Her house staff took shifts manually ejecting water from the pontoons to keep her buoyant dwelling stable. Though it was well past midnight, she heard the workers pumping, felt her home continue to heel to one side, out of balance. Tanja had worked the pumps herself, and now she was miserable from warm rain and sweat.

Throughout the harbor, the floating town buildings were in similar distress. Bebe Nax maintained a detailed and ever-growing list of emergencies that needed to be taken care of. Tanja doubted that the Council of Lords back on comfortable Sonjeera had any idea about the difficulties the DZ worlds faced every day.

Through her rain-streaked window, she watched flickering emergency lights and the dark shadows of high buildings that leaned in the wind. Despite the breakwaters, locks, and other engineering stop-gaps installed to protect the harbor, more than a hundred people were confirmed dead in this evening's report. As Candela's planetary administrator, Tanja could not stop worrying about the loss of life and the high costs of repairs.

The Constellation was not likely to send aid or relief workers; in fact, they wouldn't even offer amnesty on the next tribute payment. Out in the hills, the workers were forced to continue their long shifts, despite the oppressive rain. In the open-pit excavations many kilometers to the southeast, Uncle Quinn and the rest of Tanja's relatives would be facing an even worse situation.

At noon the following day, the rain paused, as if gathering its energy for another outburst. The silence and the clearing skies were startling at first. Standing on her deck in dry clothes and a water-repellent coat, Tanja braced herself against a steady wind that made the harbor waters choppy. Above, workers hammered on her roof to secure waterproof slats. Emergency craft sped about the water with lights flashing, responding to a constant string of calls.

From the deck of her floating home, she waved as a private aero-copter taxied towards her, bouncing on the waves. With communication cut off for days, Tanja had arranged to take a rescue craft out to Puhau and the surrounding mountain villages. She would lead the expedition herself.

As Tanja climbed into the copter's passenger compartment, she saw Bebe Nax waiting for her with five volunteer nurses from the Merciful order and a doctor, all of whom wore rain gear and carried medical packs. She knew Uncle Quinn could handle an emergency and keep his mining villages secure, but he might need help. The underground tunnels of the covert iperion mines would be protected from the deluge, but the stripped hillsides and open-pit excavations would be a mess.

The pilot took off, and Tanja looked down upon her battered and drenched city. Bebe gazed out the opposite window, her brow furrowed as she mentally took notes. As the craft skimmed inland over the rugged hills, Tanja tried to see past the low-lying fog banks. Swollen creeks careened through the steep valleys; she had never imagined so many gushing waterfalls. An impractical person might have found them beautiful.

When the pilot announced that they were over Puhau, Bebe shook her head. "You must be mistaken. There's nothing down there."

Tanja peered down, but could find no words through the lump in her throat. As the craft circled, she saw scars and swaths and streaks of mud on the hillsides, entire forests sheared away from steep slopes and a water-filled open pit. But no sign of the mining village at the bottom, only a horrific brownish expanse where all the structures had been.

She put her hands against the aircraft window. "No!" Quinn had been down there, most of her relatives, all those villagers, the miners — gone!

Bebe got on the codecall and transmitted an order for emergency equipment, first-aid vehicles, mobile hospitals, and excavating machinery. When the voice on the other end of the circuit complained, the assistant snapped, "It's the order of the administrator. If you've got a problem, come out here, stand in the mud, and argue about it face to face. Once you're up to your neck in goo, you'll change your mind."

Tanja nodded a numb thanks, but couldn't tear her gaze away: all that remained of Puhau was a thick blanket of mud. What looked like the dome roof of the mine headquarters building poked through the mud at the perimeter of the flow; here and there, broken, uprooted trees stuck out of the muck.

When the pilot kept circling, Tanja demanded, "Take us down there!" Her voice cracked as she shouted the order. When she spotted a few refugees sitting on the moist ground in shock, her heart surged with hope.

"We need a stable place to set down, Administrator." The pilot altered course to the edge of the muddy lake and landed with a brown splash across the fuselage. The aircraft shifted drunkenly as its weight settled into the loose mud, but Tanja popped the door open before they came to a rest. She scrambled out with Bebe following close behind; the doctor, nurses, and pilot gathered up the supplies and emerged. They all sank up to their calves in the slurry.

The survivors stared at them. Some slogged forward. Tanja recognized one of her male cousins seated on the ground by the exposed roof of the town hall tower, and she forced her way toward him. Her boots made sucking sounds as she pulled them out of the mud. Moving only a few meters sapped her energy.

"Gavo!" she called out. He looked at her, his eyes dull; he didn't respond. She dreaded what else she might hear or see, but she had to know. "Where are the others?" The whole village ... thousands of people. And Uncle Quinn. She didn't want to hear the answer.

Gavo rose slowly to his feet. "Dead." He looked around at the heavy layer of mud that had erased the town. "Down there, buried in the damn mud." A notorious drunk, Gavo had been one of the family members who had embarrassed her with his antics in Saporo; she had sent him to live in the hills where he wouldn't cause any further embarrassment. Now he looked completely sober.

"I set up this town, Bebe," Tanja said. "I sent my cousins out here, built the village, told them to work on the stripmine so they could help me out ... and also stay out of my hair." She dashed her tears away with the back of her hand.

Bebe leaned forward to rub Tanja's cheek. "You've got mud on your face."

Tanja laughed bitterly at the absurd concern, then sloshed out into the muck to do something, anything, to look for survivors. The rescue workers fanned out, tending the handful of villagers who had escaped the disaster.

After her urgent summons, more rescue aircraft arrived, and workers established a triage zone and refugee camp on a stable rocky area. Using sophisticated detection equipment, emergency workers extracted a dozen more survivors buried under the tons of mud that had swallowed the mining operations. For the rest of the afternoon and into the early evening, aerocopters flew back and forth, ferrying distraught villagers to Saporo. Almost the entire population of Puhau had been lost.

As her grief and shock mounted, so did her anger. Bebe followed her, taking care of every detail she could think of, but Tanja was thinking of the broader picture. "These hillsides were unstable because I forced the miners to excavate so quickly. No time for planning, no proper safety embankments, or drainage control – all because of the Constellation's tribute demands."

"Your Uncle Quinn was a careful and sensible man, Administrator. I'm sure he did everything he could."

"Even a sensible man couldn't plan for this. It wasn't his fault."

"Or yours, Administrator. You know that."

Tanja did know it. The blame for all these deaths lay with Diadem Michella and her greedy pack of noble families. *Nobles?* Those vultures were anything but noble.

Tanja stayed another night in the disaster area, sleeping inside the aerocopter. Bebe brought her a blanket. Blessedly, the rain held off for a time. The muddy graveyard was pockmarked with holes where rescuers had worked.

People poured in from nearby villages to help and they worked tirelessly. In a miracle, two more residents were found in an air pocket, in the wreckage of their home, under five meters of mud. But when the monsoons resumed their onslaught with a vengeance two days later, the mudslide area became too treacherous to continue operations.

With a heavy heart, Tanja called off the search for survivors and prepared to depart for Saporo. She would never see her beloved Uncle Quinn again.

Just before leaving, she watched neighboring villagers complete a path up the mudslide area to the highest remaining slope, marking it with stones on either side, a pathway to heaven for the souls of the dead. As Tanja boarded the aerocopter to leave, she saw beautiful red and yellow flowers sprouting up from the mud, fast-growing blossoms already venturing into new territory.

36

The General imposed strict security at the Ankor industrial outpost on the other side of the continent from Michella Town, though not for the obvious reasons.

An out-of-the-way mining and fabrication complex, Ankor produced large amounts of necessary metals such as iron, copper, and tin, which helped build the scattered colony towns and support infrastructure on Hallholme. The industrial outpost produced nothing interesting enough to be included in the Diadem's required tribute, since costs prohibited shipping such mundane metals to the Crown Jewels. The site was difficult to reach, and it offered no amenities for visitors. The Diadem's officials had no desire whatsoever to visit the dirty, noisy place.

The General liked it that way.

The bulk of Ankor's labor force consisted of exiled convicts, which justified heavier security, though the workers did not, in fact, require such measures. Over the years, a handful of hard-bitten murderers and kidnappers had escaped from the compound and fled out into the wilds, but such attempts were never well planned; some escapees came crawling back and begged to be taken in, while others left only desiccating corpses on the inhospitable terrain.

Truly antisocial misfits who could never be rehabilitated were dispatched to projects that required much harder labor where they could cause little harm. The Ankor project was far too important for Adolphus to allow troublemakers.

After determining a safe window in the weather patterns, Adolphus flew a swift aircraft across the continent to the isolated site. He called ahead to inform Tel and Renny Clovis, the couple who managed the compound, and they offered to prepare the facilities for inspection, but Adolphus told them not to delay work on his account. "I don't want to disrupt your operations."

"Good, because we're right on schedule – your schedule." The voice on the codecall line was Renny's, though the two men sounded very much alike. His aircraft crossed a line of recently uplifted cliffs and flew over a sparkling salt bed that had once been an inland sea.

Colored bands of ore striped the fresh cliffs. Excavation machinery laid open the mountainside to get at the various metals, and dust and smoke wafted in circles from breezes trapped in the valley, creating a gritty, noisy work environment. While these mines and mills were necessary to the colonists on Hallholme, the operation was just a front for Ankor's true purpose.

This was General Adolphus's own spaceport launch complex.

From here, the Clovises orbited regular loads of equipment, satellites, and materials, entirely without the Constellation's knowledge. While landing his aircraft, Adolphus spotted a bullet-shaped carrier vessel riding a finger of white fire and exhaust, climbing toward the large, undocumented complex in orbit.

The General longed to go up to the orbital station, but he contented himself with second-hand reports. Even though the Diadem would never know he had left the planet's surface, *he* would know. Tiber Maximillian Adolphus would maintain his honor and his promises – at least until Destination Day, when he would jettison all ties and commitments to the Crown Jewels.

Stiff from the long flight, he climbed out of the aircraft and saw the two men coming toward him hand-in-hand. Adolphus had always disapproved of public displays of affection, even his own, believing that a casual environment affected discipline. However, a light management touch had proved effective here. Tel and Renny Clovis were adhering to the schedule, and they ran the project as a model of efficiency. Adolphus knew better than to meddle with success.

The two had fallen in love in a prison on Fleer, the original home-world of the Duchenets. Though Renny was due to be paroled in less than a year, both men had signed up for the Deep Zone colony option. Tel and Renny left Fleer together, finding themselves on Hallholme and perfectly happy about it.

First assigned to Ankor as convict workers, Tel and Renny had excelled in their work, demonstrating their leadership abilities. After completing a year of public service on Hallholme, they had chosen to stay on, and General Adolphus promoted them into management positions.

Tel – the thinner of the two – always saluted when he saw the General, while his partner came forward to shake Adolphus's hand. Either gesture of respect was acceptable. "Good to see you, gentlemen." He pointed to the still-fading vapor trail; the delivery vehicle had dwindled to a bright pinpoint of light high overhead. "What was that cargo?"

Tel shrugged. "I can't remember exactly. Renny, what was on the launch docket for today?"

"Another docking clamp for the orbital ring. Once it's installed and online, we'll be able to handle four stringline arrivals simultaneously."

Adolphus nodded at the excellent news. "Don't slow down. D-Day is in eleven months, and we have to make sure all twelve stations are ready. Our ring needs to be a genuine stringline hub, not just an amateur effort."

Ankor's busy landing field – with its warehouses, hangars, and repair/refueling facilities – reminded Adolphus of the Lubis Plain shipyards on Qiorfu. But he intended to make this much more than that.

Tel gestured. "Come with me to the office shack, General. We've got real-time images being transmitted from orbit. I have the full work record for your perusal. You can even link up and speak to the construction team if you like."

"I prefer to maintain radio silence. No matter how secure the channel is, someone could be listening in." Far too many Constellation people snooped around the General's planet. "You two are doing a fine job managing this. I won't interfere. I'll just look at the images."

Leaving Tel with the General, Renny pulled on a pair of gloves. "I'm off to run one of the clearing dozers. We're going to lay the foundation for a big new reception building. Gotta be ready when passengers begin arriving from the Deep Zone. We'll need to accommodate a much larger number of people."

"I want a fancy hotel, just like the ones on Sonjeera." Tel wore a wistful smile.

"Basic lodgings first. We can always expand." Renny gave Tel a quick peck on the cheek, then headed off to the parked construction machinery.

Adolphus knew Sophie would have considered the pair adorable, but he had never gotten used to dreamy-eyed couples. Maybe if he hadn't been thrust into a harsh reality at such an early age, he wouldn't be so jaded. The death of his brother and the loss of his inheritance ... being crushed by the Constellation's corrupt legal system ... targeted for assassination with a shipful of other second-string nobles ... all had driven him to launch his bloody rebellion. No, Tiber Adolphus had not lived a life that engendered a romantic mindset.

Neither had Sophie Vence, however, and *she* hadn't given up hope. She made no secret of the fact that she intended to soften him up. He said she was welcome to try.

Inside the headquarters shack – which had been reinforced and expanded so that it was now a far cry from a "shack" – Tel displayed images of the large orbital construction, where units were being assembled into the new stringline hub. Because Constellation haulers came only at set intervals, the General's secret work could be scheduled when there was no risk of the activities being seen. Since the next stringline ship was not due for three more days, the work above Hallholme continued at a frenetic pace.

The General's need for an extensive network of satellites to monitor the planet's tortured weather was a perfectly reasonable cover story. The satellites gave Adolphus an excuse to launch the equipment he needed to build his own stringline hub on the opposite side of the world from the Sonjeera-linked terminus. Whenever a Constellation ship was due to arrive, the Clovises shut down orbital construction operations and switched off power to the half-finished hub. If anyone bothered to scan (which they sometimes did), they would see only small blips that looked like nothing more than orbiting monitors.

Satisfied with the progress, Adolphus and Tel stepped outside to the sun-washed construction site. At the edge of the dry lakebed, Renny

Clovis operated an enormous dozer, scraping up rocks and a crumbling layer of salt. He had already cleared a foundation area for a new building far from the landing field. If the future unfolded as the General hoped, and new stringlines linked all the Deep Zone worlds, Hallholme would need extensive accommodations for the influx of travelers, including the fancy hotel Tel Clovis wanted to run.

Adolphus felt a sharp jolt beneath his feet, and the ground began to shake. Construction workers scrambled away from the swaying crane girders. The launch gantries rattled and rocked from side to side.

Tel spread his legs to brace himself. "Another aftershock, sir. We've had a bunch of quakes over the past few days."

Instead of fading after a few seconds, there were stronger jolts, and the ground bucked. Adolphus struggled to keep his balance.

Aboard his growling dozer, Renny seemed not to notice; the seismic vibrations were drowned out by the whirr and rumble of his machinery. Behind him, the dry lakebed began to collapse. A crack opened up, and broken ground poured into the sinkhole. Losing traction, his big vehicle lurched backward.

Yelling, Tel sprinted across the shaking ground with Adolphus close at his side. The crater widened, and the General saw a flash of liquid – water? – at the bottom of the collapsing crater. Some kind of silvery fluid oozed up.

Scrambling out of the cab, Renny leaped from the enormous dozer. The treads continued to move as the dozer clawed for balance on the vanishing ground. Renny dropped to the loose dirt and tried to run up the collapsing slope, but he lost his balance and slid backward.

The quake continued, and cracks opened near the launch site and landing field. Tel ran recklessly toward the widening gap just as Renny slid down with the chunks of dirt and salt cake.

The groaning dozer plunged into the exposed liquid at the bottom of the sinkhole, but the pool did not move like water. It didn't splash, but churned and pulsed. Renny plunged into the water at the bottom of the pit and tried to swim, thrashing briefly. Then something changed. He seemed stunned, paralyzed . . . and he sank without struggling.

With a scream, Tel stumbled to his knees as the ground bucked beneath him. Adolphus caught up with Tel, and they watched as the sinkhole continued to widen, earth crashing in from the sides. In less than a minute the water receded into a foaming muck, taking Renny, the dozer, and an avalanche of soil on top of it.

When the seismic event finally stopped, Tel fell face down in the dirt, sobbing and shaking.

37

With Fernando convulsing at the edge of the strange alien pool, Vincent retrieved the medkit from the Trakmaster and rushed back. He applied monitors to his friend's body and studied the garbled readings, frantic to understand what was wrong. He raced through all the standard first-aid he had been taught during the Michella Town briefing; he scanned the emergency med-manual, tried pressure-injections of stimulants and anti-allergens, but nothing had any effect. Vincent felt desperate, helpless, and alone out in the middle of nowhere.

Fernando spasmed, dropped into a coma, and lay like a dead man. Vincent half-carried, half-dragged his unconscious companion back towards the vehicle; the other man's arms and legs flopped listlessly. Strangely, though he had fallen into the pool, his clothes were not even moist.

Vincent had checked: according to the overland rig's grid maps, there were no mining camps or industrial outposts within reach, and it would take days of driving at top speed to return to Michella Town. Because Fernando had insisted on going to unknown territory in hopes of making a big discovery, they were far from any potential assistance.

Leaving his companion on the ground beside the Trakmaster, Vincent activated the self-erecting tent and pulled Fernando into its minimal shelter. His friend did not stir. Vincent tried to force water into the other man's mouth, but it dribbled out the side. "Come on, come on!" The med readings flickered and scrambled, still inconclusive. At least Fernando was alive, with stable pulse and respiration, but he remained unresponsive.

After agonizing for two hours, Vincent made up his mind to load his friend aboard the Trakmaster, strap him down, and make the best possible time to the nearest mining camp. Then, unexpectedly, Fernando awoke – making the situation even more strange.

Hunched over in the tent, Vincent called, "Are you all right? Say something!"

When Vincent looked at his friend's eyes in a certain light, the irises still had a milky sheen with an odd Fresnel effect. When Fernando spoke, the words came out ponderously, as if he were relearning how to talk. "Fernando is well ... as is Zairic."

"What happened to you?" Vincent offered him water again, and the other man drank without paying attention. "What are you talking about? Who, or what, is Zairic?"

Sitting up, Fernando looked at his hands, flexed his fingers, and then touched his forearm and elbow, as if intrigued by the bones there. He tapped a fingertip against his hard teeth, blinked his eyes, tried to focus. "I am Zairic, with all the memories of my life. Am I the first Xayan to return?" He crawled out of the tent and stood up on wavering legs to look around in amazement.

Worried that his friend was delusional and might collapse again, Vincent held onto his arm. "Here, let me help you. You're talking nonsense. There must have been chemicals or drugs in that water."

Fernando turned to him with a flash of inexpressible wonder on his face. "Not drugs, *memories*!" His expression changed again as he gazed up at the greenish sky; he seemed detached and disoriented. "How this world has changed! Fernando Neron is ... most interesting."

Vincent tried to calm his breathing. "*You're* Fernando Neron. This isn't making any sense. What did that pool do to you?"

"It is slickwater." The strangely unfocused eyes turned towards Vincent. "A liquid database that contained my life, along with most other Xayan lives. They've been preserved for a long time." He slowly surveyed the bleak hills, the barren ground, the fur of alien vegetation on the nearby slopes. "So, our planet survived the impact, although not without terrible scars." He gazed at Vincent, but seemed to be seeing only a stranger. "How long has it been?"

"Since the asteroid impact?"

"Yes, since our civilization was destroyed."

Vincent reeled as he began to understand just what Fernando was saying. "Five centuries. You know that." His friend couldn't have missed something so basic in their briefings.

"Mmmm, yes, *Fernando* knows that." He cocked his head as if checking something. "Around five hundred years . . . so the restoration of our race is occurring sooner than we thought. We were prepared to wait millennia, if necessary."

Impatient and uneasy, Vincent could not stop himself from snapping, "Start explaining yourself! What's happened to Fernando?" Maybe he was pulling Vincent's leg again, teasing him for being so serious and worried all the time. "If this is a joke, it's not funny."

His friend's expression shifted and became animated again. "It's me, Vincent – I'm back! I haven't gone anywhere, but it took Zairic longer than he expected to take care of all the details. He had so much to learn, so much to assimilate." He shook his head. "Wow, this makes my mind reel. It goes beyond my wildest dreams!"

Vincent was worried and frightened, yet curious. He knew Fernando's penchant for imagination and exaggeration, but this was different. He had *seen* Fernando fall into the slickwater and knew he could not have faked the convulsions and deep paralysis afterward. This was no scam.

"Zairic will need to fill in some of the details. Let me tell you what I know, for now. Trust me, you've never heard anything like this before. It's the best thing ever." Fernando gave a broad smile, and his eerie eyes shone with a sense of wonder. He tapped his temple. "I carry the memories, at least part of them, of the Xayans, this planet's original race that was wiped out by the asteroid impact."

Vincent was skeptical in spite of what he'd seen. "So, now you're possessed by an alien?"

"Not like that. The slickwater in those pools is an organic liquid-crystal storage reservoir, filled with energy – a nutrient-filled refuge where Xayan scientists said the people could always go if they needed to. They created it. Now it contains the preserved thoughts, the *lives*, of millions of Xayans who knew they were about to die. As the asteroid came in, they had very little warning – but enough to do this."

Vincent was still not sure how much to believe. "Like recording a final message on an emergency beacon?"

"Oh, more than just a message. They copied and stored *themselves*. The reservoirs survived the impact and the upheavals afterward, and the Xayans are still there in the pool.

"So you copied them into your own brain?"

"Not all of them – just Zairic. He's like a hitchhiker in my mind, another personality. But *I'm* still here, Vincent. He and I share. He has my life, and I have his."

His friend's expression altered again, flattened, and his face became placid as the Zairic personality came to the fore. "When Fernando fell into the pool, the slickwater recognized another intelligent life form and began to establish cellular links. This allowed Fernando to access all my information, the memories of my lost life. I sense that I am the first . . . the first of many." He reached out to Vincent. "You must help us reawaken our race. We can restore them."

His face brightened, and he spoke with a giddy exuberance that implied Fernando was back. "Yes, Vincent! See, Zairic was one of the Xayan leaders, sort of a religious philosopher. It's hard to explain – not quite a messiah, but a spiritual general who rallied his people and made them prepare for Armageddon. There were others, of course, but Zairic was the most powerful and respected." Fernando shrugged his narrow shoulders. "I'm biased, because he's the only one I have inside my head – but trust me, this guy is brilliant and peaceful. There's so much to learn about the Xayans, such amazing stuff in their culture. I wish I could describe it all for you, but I can barely grasp what I'm seeing in my head. I'm damned impressed, though. The opportunities are incredible!"

Fernando's expression faded, and the Zairic personality returned. "I am willing to share everything that the Xayans knew, if your people wish it."

"That's not my call to make. I'm just a . . ." Vincent felt entirely out of his depth. He didn't even know how to answer. He was a nobody, and so was Fernando, but now his friend carried the memories of an alien leader – assuming this wasn't some strange form of madness.

Night had fallen in the valley as they talked. Fernando-Zairic walked toward the nearest slickwater pool. "Before the asteroid hit, we ... dissolved ourselves into these reservoirs and into similar data pools around this world."

"That's why we found no evidence of Xayan bodies?" Vincent said. "We expected to see some remnants of your civilization, a few skeletons at least."

Zairic stared off into the night. "I could explain better, Vincent Jenet, if you immersed yourself. You, too, could absorb all the thoughts and memories of a Xayan life, as has Fernando Neron."

Instantly cautious, Vincent raised both hands and demurred. "I don't think so. This is too weird for me to handle." When Zairic showed no reaction at all, Vincent continued, "Now, are you saying that anyone who touches that slickwater will receive an alien personality?"

"That is how we designed the organic database, but it is only accessible to sentient creatures. Despite the destruction of our civilization, our presence remains – at least those of us who immersed ourselves into the sentient pools. From my experience with Fernando, I know that you can help the Xayans return from extinction. Your people can *become* us. We will become symbiotic partners, greater than either race."

Vincent looked at the quiescent surface of the slickwater pool. "And there's nothing left of your entire civilization? Nothing else remains?"

"Very little." Fernando-Zairic gave him a pointed look. "But enough that we can offer proof." Abruptly, he walked toward the parked vehicle. "Come, we must speak with your General Tiber Adolphus."

38

After driving at top speed over rough terrain for more than an hour, Devon finally decided he and Antonia were far enough from the wrecked camp and the cannibalistic insects. He brought the overland rig to a halt and sat breathing hard as the horrific reality caught up with him. "Sorry I put you at risk. I should have been more careful."

"You got us out of there alive. That's what counts." Antonia swallowed the lump in her throat. "Do you think we're safe now?"

She could see he was stunned as well, though he tried not to show it. "Safe from the bugs, maybe . . . but this is Hellhole. Never let down your guard." He rubbed his arms. "We'd better take care of our wounds. Those bites could be poisonous."

Now that the adrenaline rush was over, Antonia noticed that the cuts and bites on her skin had begun to swell. "I'll get the medpack." During her time on the run, Antonia had been too afraid to seek medical attention for minor cuts, infections, or illnesses; once, Jako stole antibiotics when she'd shivered through a very high fever. She had thought he was devoted to her, but he was really just protecting his own secret . . .

She located the medpack in the back compartment of the vehicle and gave it to Devon. He tore it open and rummaged through the contents. "Each kit carries six different chemicals we've found useful against

Hellhole toxins. Never seen anything like those beetles before, though." He held up a tube of ointment. "In that situation, we use this multi-salve and hope to hell we have all the bases covered."

Intent on the fixing the problem, Devon dabbed and cleaned her injuries, while Antonia took up another disinfectant pad and did the same for him. He winced when she prodded a particularly deep wound. She applied creams and bandages to his bites.

"You'll have to, um ..." Devon's voice cracked. He took a deep breath and started again. "I need you to take your shirt off."

Antonia reacted instantly, drawing away. His eyes did not meet hers, but he said, "Sorry to ask." He removed his own shirt. "We need to check each other's back and shoulders." He flushed bright red.

Antonia relaxed slightly, fighting down her instinctive reaction. Devon was not Jako. This was no time to be prudish. She shrugged out of her torn blouse and turned her back to him. Devon seemed more nervous about touching Antonia's bare skin than about the insect attack.

When he tended her bites with great care, gently applying salve to each one, she steeled herself to his touch, driving away the unpleasant memories of Jako's touch and *his* obsessive attentiveness. Antonia checked Devon's back next and put salve on the bites. He was more muscular than she had expected, but she supposed it wasn't surprising, since he had grown up on a frontier world.

"You're shivering." He touched her neck and her forehead with concern. "Do you feel feverish? That could be a symptom."

"It has nothing to do with the bites."

Antonia realized to her surprise that she was not afraid of Devon Vence, that his shyness was more endearing than ever. After Jako, she hadn't thought she'd ever be so calm around a man again. It was a small, but significant change.

"Here, give me that marker pen." He drew heavy lines around her bite welts and asked her to mark his. "We'll watch them for more swelling or reaction before we get back to Helltown." Devon poked at one of his welts. "But I don't really think we have anything to worry about. If something on Hellhole is poisonous, it's *really* poisonous, and a reaction usually sets in within the first hour. I was paying attention to the pain level all along, and since we're not writhing on the floor by now, I'm cautiously optimistic we'll be all right." He went to the Trakmaster's hatch. "I've got to make sure nothing's damaged after my reckless driving. You can stay inside and rest."

"Not a chance." She followed him, and the two slowly surveyed the vehicle's battered exterior. Aghast, Devon reached out and rubbed one of the dimples where the voracious beetles had chewed through the metal. "My mother's not going to be happy about the condition of this vehicle."

"Your mother's going to be *very* happy that you kept your wits about you and saved our lives. I'll make sure she knows."

Devon flushed at the compliment.

He took a flat scraper and went around the exterior, finding eleven more bugs, which he captured in specimen containers for the town's xenobiologists to study.

Next, he crawled beneath the undercarriage, poked around, and emerged, wiping sweat and grime from his forehead. "Not enough damage to prevent us from getting home." Then he added, so belatedly that she knew he had been mulling over the comment for some minutes, "And yes, I am very glad that I could save you."

"Next time, I'll return the favor."

There was an awkward moment as Devon fumbled unsuccessfully for a response, after which he busied himself with one more unnecessary inspection of the Trakmaster.

Antonia wrestled with her thoughts and said aloud, "Devon, you're sweet. I like you a lot, and I appreciate everything you've done – not just the lifesaving part. It's good to have a friend here." It wasn't a confession, but more of an explanation. "When I came to Hellhole, I just wanted to get *away*, because if I'd stayed on Aeroc any longer, I'd be dead now. I'm convinced of it."

Devon squeezed his fingers into fists, then released them. "I wish you'd tell me . . ."

"A man said he loved me, but he . . . he didn't get what he wanted. He arranged for my parents to be murdered, just to make sure I'd be completely dependent on him. I believed his lies. I learned my lesson, maybe too well. Now I'm not sure I'll ever trust anyone again."

The young man was shocked, then furious. He offered to hop on the next stringline passenger pod, go find her ex-boyfriend, and beat him to a pulp. "We take care of our own, Antonia. You don't need to worry about anybody here."

It was obvious that Devon believed he could defend her, but she knew that if he tried such a foolish thing, Jako would kill him without a second thought. She touched his arm gently. "There's nothing you can do about it. I just wanted to let you know why I'm a little closed off. You're so open and kind, but that's you. It's not possible for me."

Devon was heartbreakingly earnest. "It'll get better. I promise, I won't let anything happen to you here."

Not wanting to discourage him, Antonia smiled and thanked him. They clambered back into the vehicle and sealed the hatch.

As the young man drove them toward Michella Town, Antonia finally took out the black object they had found in the ruined camp. She rapped her knuckles on the strangely interlocked curves and spirals, ran her fingertips over its slick surface, the crystalline inclusions. "Have you seen anything like this in the General's collection?"

Devon glanced at it as he drove. "That one's more unusual than most . . . but they're all unusual. We'll present it to him and see what he has to say."

39

It was a matter of timing and precise execution (an ironic choice of words), allowing no margin for error.

Like another shadow, Ishop Heer moved along the upper hallway of the Paternos mansion. Despite his large form, he slid from doorway to doorway, approaching his target. His pale, bald head was covered so that the white skin would not be so visible.

He didn't need his list; he already knew what to do.

While planning this operation, Ishop had made it his business to know who slept in each bedroom. If necessary, he could kill the entire Paternos family and all the servants, a massacre that would cause an uproar throughout the Constellation ... but that was not his purpose. He would rather do his work like a surgeon removing a diseased organ. Clean and tidy.

Lady Jenine Paternos was an old woman anyway. Despite the energy she brought to Council sessions, recent rumors suggested that her health was failing, and the Council vultures were all too happy to spread such gossip. Unlike the Riomini/de Carre matter on Vielinger, which Diadem Michella considered important, she would not get involved in the petty animosity at the root of the squabble between the Tazaars and the much-weaker Paternos family. But Ishop could certainly use it for his own purposes.

Through no fault of her own, not that Ishop cared, her name was on the list.

He knew that Michella was fully satisfied with his service and wouldn't suspect a thing. Ishop had done his part to wrap up the de Carre problem, quickly and efficiently. The disgraced nobleman had been an oaf and a fop; though Louis de Carre had possessed a physically fit body, he had no fighting skills.

Just before the scheduled sentencing, and more than an hour before Keana was due to visit the man, Ishop had slipped into Louis's cell and subdued him easily; in the process he had made de Carre's death look like a suicide – in accordance with the Diadem's orders. Her insistence on having Keana find the body was a particularly cruel gesture, he thought, but he didn't want to get involved in the mother-daughter quarrel.

When Michella had quietly ordered Ishop to kill the miserable Louis, he did not allow himself to feel a bond with Lord de Carre, a man likewise humiliated and destroyed by the scheming politics of the other nobles, much as Ishop's own family had been seven centuries ago. But empathy extended only so far.

Lord de Carre's death advanced the fortunes of the Riomini family, whom he despised. Nevertheless, Ishop did as he was ordered to do; it honed his skills and kept him in the Diadem's favor. Killing de Carre had been messy, and Ishop had to scrub himself in a long, hot shower and discard the clothes he had worn before he felt clean again, but the job was done – as ordered. It was his job.

However, Michella definitely would *not* approve of the assassination of Lady Jenine Paternos. In this particular instance, Ishop wasn't working for the Diadem, but for his own family honor. He had to take care of the matter cleanly and efficiently. This was his own list, and he decided to put his needs first, for once. After all, whether or not anyone else realized it yet, he was a nobleman, not a servant.

The all-too-public squabbles between the two families provided perfect cover for what he needed to do. He was sure Lady Paternos had no knowledge that she was numbered among those who had wronged the Osheer family seven centuries ago, but her current dispute with Azio Tazaar gave Ishop just the right opportunity to dispatch two names on the list. He was pleased by how neatly the pieces fitted together, as if it was meant to be.

Ishop did not underestimate the old Paternos woman. Though he had neutralized the alarm system, he remained wary. Lady Jenine was a smart, tough crow. But Ishop was smarter.

The Paternos mansion was sturdily built and reinforced, so he froze when he felt the floor and walls move. A substantial earthquake, but he remained calm. Dust trickled down, but Ishop forced himself not to brush it away.

The tremor lasted fifteen seconds, then stopped, leaving the house to thrum and settle again. Kappas was known for its ubiquitous seismic activity of growing mountain ranges; scientists and tourists came here to study the rugged range that was being uplifted at an astonishing rate, more than a meter per year, by colliding tectonic plates. Throughout the temblor, the old house did not creak.

After the quake faded, Ishop remained motionless in an alcove, holding his breath to see if anyone might wake up and investigate the tremors. But the shaking must have been commonplace, since everyone slept through it.

Finally, he wiped the dust away and moved to the closed door of Lady Jenine's bedchamber. He pushed it open easily; the old woman liked to leave it ajar for air circulation. As he closed it again behind him, he left the same small crack. He could hear soft snores coming from the four-poster bed. The knife in his hand probed forward, pulling him like a compass needle toward its intended victim.

Drawing closer, Ishop saw the form under the blanket, a spray of gray hair across the pillow. Lifting the strands ever so carefully, he exposed the wrinkled skin of her neck. She stirred, raising her chin as if to make his work easier, and with a smooth, quick motion he drew the razor edge from one side of her throat to the other, simultaneously pressing a gloved hand over her mouth to stifle any scream. Lady Paternos squirmed, and her eyes flew open wide, but he held her down, while her neck gushed red.

Before leaving, he sliced a strip of skin from her neck, which he sealed in a small pouch and slipped into his pocket. A nice additional atrocity, and it helped with the cover story. Investigators would draw the obvious conclusion that some paid assassin had been required to bring back a cell sample to confirm the identity of the victim.

He was glad he wore gloves.

More than once in Council, Lord Azio Tazaar had boldly announced that he wanted to slit the old woman's throat. No one took the threat seriously, but they would all remember it when the body of Jenine Paternos was found. And that would take care of Lord Tazaar.

Ishop made good his escape, found a private hiding place outside, and cleaned himself, scrubbing with disinfectant rags and disposing of them. Later, passing through spaceport security under an assumed identity, he felt pleased and relieved. Though Diadem Michella treated him decently, she – and all the nobles – still regarded Ishop Heer as nothing more than a commoner. Now that Laderna had revealed the genealogical truth to him, though, he had a different view of himself. Just knowing he had noble blood changed everything for him. He deserved to exceed expectations.

On the trip back to Sonjeera, Ishop thought of the wealthy, fortunate nobles whose political machinations gained them power at the expense of families that had not been so clever, or so fortunate. Families such as his own. He'd been the Diadem's private hatchet man for a long time, but now Ishop felt *part* of the system. Soon enough, he would reveal his worth.

He'd built a career and made something of himself, surviving by any means necessary without relying on the advantages of a noble family. Ishop never had any shortage of ambition, but now he possessed new-found pride, anger . . . and a sense of justice. The twelve families on his list had to pay for the sins of their ancestors; they were loose ends that needed to be tidied up. With Laderna's help, he would make short work of the list. He was amazed to discover that she was as committed, as excited, by the project as he was.

Even now, Laderna was setting up her own part of the plan on Orsini, following Lord Tazaar. Dressed as a man, she posed as a fellow customer in the seedy pleasure districts that Azio Tazaar was known to frequent. She would have ample opportunities, but she couldn't move too soon. Everything in its time and place; she understood that.

Ishop and Laderna had studied the stringline schedules, mapping out the swiftest possible route for someone to discover Lady Jenine's body, race to the spaceport, take a stringline hauler to the Sonjeera hub, transfer out to Orsini, and assassinate Lord Tazaar. The timing had to seem *reasonable* if investigators were going to point fingers at the appropriate and obvious people.

At any time after the correct hour, Laderna would find the opportunity to apply a few drops of highly penetrating toxin to any patch of exposed skin on Lord Azio. She didn't need much, and seconds later the bearded Tazaar patriarch would be writhing and screaming in an alley. Ishop had every confidence in the dear girl's ability to slip a forged note onto his body that purported to be from a vengeful member of the Paternos family, claiming justice for the murder of Lady Jenine.

Laderna was delighted for the opportunity to make Ishop happy. Though gangly and clumsy, she had amazing skills in planning and a surprising taste for violence that he found erotic. She had noble qualities herself. After the successful assassination of Lord Azio Tazaar – added to her surprise murder of Lady Opra Mageros – Laderna was responsible for removing two names from the list of twelve, while he was responsible for only one. So far.

Ishop smiled to himself. He was going to have to catch up.

40

Loathing the system that had caused Louis's death, struggling to find something positive that she could do in her lover's memory, Keana finally obtained the necessary clearances to board a stringline ship for Vielinger. Now that Louis was gone ("out of the way" as her mother surely thought of it), Michella assumed her daughter would go back to a dutiful life with Bolton Crais. "It was a tragic mistake, dear, but I hope you've learned your lesson."

The lesson she had learned, however, was how powerful true love could be. Keana had also learned that despite her trappings of apparent wealth, she was nothing more than a pawn or another knick-knack in the Diadem's collection.

But she wasn't finished. Keana remained determined to do something . . . if only she could figure out something that would matter.

In the week following her discovery of Louis's body, she had withdrawn into mourning – a social absence that was encouraged by the Diadem. Bolton treated her with generous sympathy, giving Keana the space she needed and uttering no insipid platitudes. He had never been a jealous husband, even though she must have hurt him with her indiscretions. Swept away in her giddy romance with Louis, she hadn't given a second thought to what Bolton might be feeling. And still he forgave her.

When Keana made up her mind to go to Vielinger, to personally offer her assistance to Louis's son, she took care not to let Michella know of her plans. When she asked for his help, Bolton went out of his way to pay the bribes and arrange for her travel. He seemed anxious to convince her that ruining Louis had not been his idea. She was grateful for this small generosity.

After many sleepless nights, Keana was determined to see first-hand what the greedy Riominis were doing to her lover's estate. With the seizure of all de Carre property, Cristoph had to be suffering as much as she. From his conversation and the pictures Louis carried with him, Keana felt she already knew the younger man. Oh, how Louis had smiled when he talked about his hard-working and highly intelligent son, sure that the Vielinger family estate was in good hands. Now Cristoph had lost everything: home, fortune, and his beloved father – but the tragedy would bind them together. Keana couldn't wait to meet him.

Passing through the imposing, ornate gate of the de Carre estate, Keana was dismayed to see black Riomini banners hanging on the stone walls and flying from tall poles. It was an overcast day, as gray and bleak as her mood.

In the two years she had been in love with Louis, she had never visited the estate; he had always met her in the Cottage, where they could have privacy. But Louis had showed her images of the grounds, the main building, the manicured gardens. Feeling like a stranger, she stepped out to see a flurry of activity in the main house. Furnishings, portraits, and decorations were all being replaced.

Lord Selik Riomini did not intend to occupy the manor house himself, but would delegate it to some secondary family member, perhaps even a majordomo of his military. Riomini staff members were gutting the elegant house, erasing any sign of the previous owners, taking away the valuables to be sold at auction.

The manicured lawns had been trampled by careless booted feet; one portion had been torn up and used as a landing area for heavy aerocopters. Several of the inset windows on the luxurious balconies were broken.

Hearing a noise, Keana looked back and saw two men and an older woman gazing at her from the central garden pathway. Dressed in work clothes with the de Carre insignia on the lapels, they folded their arms across their chests in seeming disapproval. Assuming they thought she was an unwelcome Riomini, she quickly corrected the impression. "I am the daughter of Diadem Michella Duchenet. I need to speak with Cristoph de Carre. Where can I find him?"

The old woman sized her up. "Master Cristoph is no longer here." Her face was creased from age and sun exposure. "He's been run off."

One of the men was more helpful. "The soldiers gave him an hour to take what he wanted and leave. He left for the spaceport, I think."

The second man added, "That was six days ago. He's long gone by now."

Dismayed that she was once again too late to help, Keana left them and went to the manor house, peered through the windows, opened doors and poked her head inside. New staff and old staff treated each other with feigned indifference or cold looks. Anyone who glanced at Keana seemed to assume she belonged with the other side.

Sick and empty inside, needing some kind of closure, she walked the grounds by herself, a lonely figure. Under other circumstances, in another life, this might have been her house, her place with Louis. In her fantasy of what might have been, she imagined carefree times when the two of them could have strolled through the hedge maze, holding hands. On orders from the new occupants, gardeners had torn up the geometrically trimmed shrubs, leaving wide, straight thoroughfares that obliterated the de Carre family crest. Keana gingerly stepped over stumps and branches. Only a mangled shrub here and there remained of the old plantings.

She would gladly have forfeited all connection to the Diadem's wealth and power to live here, but nothing of value was left now, only the faded detritus of a once great and noble family. Even Cristoph was gone.

To the north of the manor house, she found an old voja tree with widely spread boughs that draped to the ground. Parting the branches and leaves, she found a wooden swing on a rope, where she imagined Cristoph must have played as a child. The swing looked aged and weathered; perhaps it even dated back to Louis's youth, or beyond. She sat upon it and rocked gently, her feet dragging on the ground.

Poor Cristoph must have found himself in a difficult position, aware of his father's dangerous affair. He must have wanted to meet her. It was unfair that people could be so prudish. Why should she feel ashamed? Did they not understand love? Keana had gone her own stubborn way, spending her time with Lord de Carre instead of with her own husband. She had refused to give Diadem Michella the legitimate grandchildren she wanted. And because of all that, Louis had been killed by a web of politics, which left Keana trapped and helpless as well.

As she swayed on the swing, Keana felt a weight of regret on her shoulders. If only she and Louis had been born commoners; they could have chosen their own loves and lived carefree lives. She would have been proud to watch a son like Cristoph grow up and become the fine young man that he was today. Keana's heart went out to him. Where had he gone? He must feel so lost and forlorn. She wiped tears from her cheeks.

No matter how she tried to pass the blame, though, Keana knew that at least some of what had occurred was her fault. If she had been more considerate, more *careful*, this tragedy might never have happened. Bolton would not have been publicly shamed by her blatant cuckolding. Without her to distract him, Louis would have attended important Council meetings, spent more time on Vielinger and operated the iperion mines faultlessly. His son would still be here, would still be well.

Cristoph, she thought. *Oh, Cristoph, where are you?*

The innocent young man needed her help. Feeling a new sense of purpose, Keana strode out onto the grounds. She might not have any real political power, but she did have gold and jewels. And she had ideas.

She needed to find Cristoph, if only to make certain he was safe.

41

As she stood in the Candela spaceport concourse, Tanja Hu rubbed her left temple to ease the migraine she experienced each time the Territorial Governor was due to arrive. Her babysitter, and an inept one at that.

Beside her, Bebe Nax automatically handed her a pain reliever, recognizing the signs of her boss's headache. There had been plenty of headaches since the monsoon disasters.

At the tail end of the rainiest month, a warm downpour fell outside. After the catastrophic mudslides, the citizens of Candela had begun to resume their normal lives, but this season's death toll had been horrendous. Several villages lost, along with two open-pit mines. Both in her capacity as planetary administrator and grieving relative, Tanja had attended a numbing succession of services for the dead, several at the site of buried Puhau. And Uncle Quinn . . .

In spite of her requests, though, the Constellation had not sent any relief workers or aid. But now Goler was coming to check up on Candela. He probably thought they would see him as the cavalry coming to save the day.

With his aloof but meticulous personality, Carlson Goler focused interminably on inconsequential matters. Tanja wished he would realize that everything operated just fine without his interference. Invariably, his "suggestions for improvement" caused more work for her, and she had so many more important things to do.

Nevertheless, she had to tolerate the Diadem's representative – for just a little while longer. Even though Goler pretended to be "one of them," and kept his main residence on Ridgetop instead of relaxing in a plush office in the government center on Sonjeera, she didn't believe he really belonged among the Deezees. Tanja tolerated him, but didn't trust him. She and her fellow conspirators kept Goler in the dark, which was not a difficult task.

Her left eye felt as if someone had put a spike through it, but she knew the migraine would go away as soon as Goler was gone. She took a long, deep breath, which seemed to help. *Be cheerful, competent, and subservient. Don't complain too much.* The pretending would be over soon enough ...

"I have all the records in order," Bebe said. "We can show him what he needs to see and send him on his way."

She smiled at the compact, short-haired assistant. "Thanks, Bebe."

When the passenger pod landed, Goler emerged first, dressed in a suit that did not fit him well. He was tall and lanky, with a lantern jaw and a perennially concerned expression that made him look intense. As the Constellation's official representative, he could have brought a bevy of functionaries, but Goler usually traveled alone.

Tanja stepped forward to greet the governor. "Welcome to Candela, sir." She didn't understand what he hoped to accomplish with these "keep in touch" meetings. Did he want to be *friends* with the eleven planetary administrators he oversaw? "I apologize for the sparse reception. We're still in a crisis situation around here."

Goler looked through the large concourse windows, watching the wet streaks coming down. "I'm very sorry about the recent tragedy. Those terrible mudslides ..." He straightened. "I have brought a cargo load of first-aid supplies and emergency rations. I hope it'll help."

"A little late," Tanja said before she could stop herself, and he looked stung, like a hurt little boy. She explained more carefully as she escorted him to the waiting admin car, "The injured have been taken care of, and many of the bodies are recovered. Another group of Mercifuls arrived four days ago to offer their assistance."

"I went through bureaucratic channels as quickly as I could," Goler said. "Even in emergencies, the Constellation does not react with great speed."

Though he sounded sincere, Tanja was brusque. "Governor, this didn't need to happen in the first place. No matter how often I object, the Diadem keeps imposing unreasonable requirements on us. In order to meet her tribute, we are forced to engage in reckless mining activities, and that makes the hill districts unstable. That is the direct cause of the mudslides that wiped out entire villages."

He looked deeply uncomfortable, trying to find some magic solution. "Is there anything the Constellation can do to help now?"

Again, a little late, she thought. She gave him a hard look and spoke formally to keep her anger in check. "You can convey the realities to Sonjeera, sir. See to it that Candela is excused from paying the Diadem's tribute until we can rebuild our industrial operations with the proper safety factors. Right now, as you can surely see, all of our resources have to be diverted to the recovery effort. If Diadem Michella loves her people as she claims, she will understand."

From Goler's crestfallen expression, she knew that he found the request difficult, but he swallowed hard and tried anyway. "The Diadem is most concerned for her subjects, and she will naturally be distressed over Candela's losses. I . . . I will do my best."

In other words, no. Tanja had expected little else. "Come with me, sir. My assistant has already prepared our records for your inspection."

He was still trying to make peace. "I'm sure everything is in order."

From the landing zone, they took a government boat across Saporo harbor to reach her floating admin headquarters. The rain had picked up considerably by the time the boat docked. With Bebe running ahead, she and Goler hurried across an open expanse and ducked under the shelter of overhangs. They were both drenched, but Tanja hardly gave it a thought. Her dress was locally made and would dry quickly once they were inside and in her main office.

Goler, though, looked bedraggled and miserable. He wiped his face. Bebe was attentive, as usual. "Would you like me to send for dry clothing, sir?"

"I'll get by." His attempt at a congenial grin made him look like a fool. "Let me just take a quick look at your production reports,

Administrator, and then I can be on my way and leave you to your pressing responsibilities."

Tanja sat at her desk, and the damp, hangdog governor took a chair across from her. The desk was clear glass with prismatic corners that collected spectrum strips from the available light. On a table to one side, Tanja had arranged shimmer images of her relatives who had died in the mudslide into a little shrine. She felt a surge of anger toward Goler, blaming him for his part in the Constellation's greed that had resulted in so many deaths.

On the transparent desktop, Bebe had already called up images of the few mines that were still operating. He leaned forward, plainly relieved to see Candelans working hard to meet their tribute payment to Sonjeera. Impulsively, Tanja displayed a second set of images: the village of Puhau buried in mud, then she showed the stripmines that had also collapsed in the monsoons. "These places are graveyards now. The bodies are still down there, where they will remain as a memorial."

Tanja switched off the images in a huff. She wanted to say so much more, but held her tongue. She could not afford to lose her position as planetary administrator, and the secret Candela iperion mines must not be exposed. General Adolphus depended on her supplies for his trailblazer ships.

She took a deep breath for calm. "There's your production report, Governor Goler. I know you've come here to announce an increase in the tribute, but we cannot pay it. You can see that for yourself. I'm sorry that Candela is currently unable to meet your expectations."

Goler turned gray and slumped in his chair, touched his pocket but did not remove the paper there. "This message comes directly from the Diadem, but I'm not going to give it to you. I'm going to intercede on your behalf. If Sonjeera insists on this increase, they will have my resignation letter." His courage surprised her, though Tanja wasn't sure his resignation threat would mean much to any member of the Constellation government.

Goler rose to his feet, brushed his damp and wrinkled clothes. "All right, then. I've made my necessary appearance, and I have seen what I needed to see. I can file an objective report now, so I might as well get back to Ridgetop. You have more urgent things to do than to be my hostess."

42

The General intended to have a quiet afternoon sitting on the porch with Sophie, but when the scuffed Trakmaster rattled up to the Elba estate, she rose to her feet and shaded her eyes. "That's Devon!"

The vehicle looked as if it had been chewed up in a storm, rolled down a steep hill, and then bombarded by meteors. Behind the smeared windshield he could see two people in the cab.

All calm gone, Sophie was off the porch and running across the well-trimmed native groundcover, leaving footprints in the soft vegetation. Adolphus summoned several staff members from inside in case Sophie's son needed help.

As the Trakmaster ground to a halt, Sophie met it. When Devon emerged, she was already talking, "What the hell happened – and are you all right?" Her words stopped short when she saw his face and arms covered with red marks, large welts, and healing scabs. "Did you two get in a brawl? Was it a storm?"

Devon shook his head. "Bugs – a swarm of voracious beetles, like I've never seen before."

Antonia Anqui climbed out after him, looking just as bad. "They wiped out the whole camp of the Children of Amadin. Nothing left but a few bone fragments and cloth scraps." She had a new look in her dark eyes when she glanced at Devon.

"We barely got out alive ourselves," he said, looking somewhat ashamed at the damage to the Trakmaster.

"*Devon* got us out alive," Antonia amended, and the young man blushed.

Sophie clucked over their wounds. "I don't see any infection, but I'm taking you to the Helltown medical center."

"We're healing fine, Mother."

"Not good enough. I want a full panel of tests to see if those bugs left any latent toxins."

"You can't argue with her, Devon," Antonia said. The young man sighed.

General Adolphus ran his gaze over the damage. "If it's another infestation, we'll want to know about it." He had seen several outbreaks of resurgent species in the past decade; fortunately, most infestations died back soon enough.

"We kept some specimens of the insects for the xenobiologists," Devon said. "The beetles must be breeding like crazy. Could be an increasing problem."

Adolphus nodded. "I'll review your Trakmaster's control recorder and send investigators out to the site."

"*Exterminators* might be more helpful than investigators," Antonia said.

"Flamethrowers would be an even better idea," Devon added.

"I'll put Craig Jordan on it right away – this falls under his purview as security. We don't want a cloud of those things coming into Michella Town."

Antonia ducked into the cab again and returned with a strange black object cradled in her arms. "One other thing, General. We found this artifact in the camp. It was one of the only things left intact."

"We think it's from the original alien race, sir," Devon said. "Reminds me of the artifacts in your display cases."

It was an odd oblong, half a meter long. It looked like a sealed case, or an egg, but with inverted curves and abraded, polished surfaces inset with reflective panes. Adolphus felt a thrill as he scrutinized it. "Thank you. I'll add it to my collection." If his teams kept searching, someday he might have enough pieces of the puzzle to understand this planet's original inhabitants.

Later, after Sophie had driven off to the Michella Town medical center with Devon and Antonia, the General sat in his study, pondering the new artifact on his desk. He set it aside, though, and attended to the other unpleasant but necessary matters.

The loss of the Children of Amadin had been unnecessary. The General had instituted his system for a reason, but the religious group had made their choice, a fatal one.

In the colony database, he opened an ever-growing file and added the names of each member of the Children of Amadin from the arrival records at the colonization office. Though many of the hopeful pilgrims and fortune seekers were easily forgotten, Adolphus kept track of those that had tried to make a home on Hallholme and failed.

The list was very long.

43

After leaving Vielinger forever, Cristoph de Carre got his first glimpse of life on Hellhole when he emerged from the passenger pod. Seeing the dusty, forlorn landscape, he thought he had made a mistake. Previously, the things he'd heard about the planet made it seem like a place of brave exile for the defeated rebel General, a rugged frontier full of hardship and rewards. Now he realized that no sane person with any choice would come to a planet like this.

But there was no turning back. This was his new life.

Cristoph coughed in the hot, sour-smelling air and he followed a handful of similarly dismayed colonists. Grit and dust swirled around them as they made their way to the receiving office for new arrivals.

His station in life had changed in the past few weeks. No one addressed him as "Master de Carre" or "My Lord." Only a few particularly polite people ever called him "sir." He still couldn't believe his father had committed suicide rather than face his shame, but in his gut Cristoph *knew* his father wasn't strong enough to handle a crisis that he had in large part caused. And he had left his son to live with the consequences.

At the new arrivals office, he received a cursory orientation along with the other new colonists. He glanced at the job listings for unskilled labor, but bypassed them without interest. Cristoph had no aversion to hard work, but with his management expertise and his ability to perform a variety of jobs (despite the apparent failure due to sabotage), he was determined to find something valuable to do here. He and the General had been similarly stomped by the Constellation, and Cristoph believed they shared a common bond.

On the other hand, Louis de Carre had ostensibly fought against Adolphus during the rebellion. (His father had not actually seen any combat, but he had done his duty as a noble.) Normally, Cristoph wouldn't expect the General to remember such a minor name ... but he could make no assumptions with this man.

He purchased a wide-brimmed hat from a street vendor and asked for directions to the General's headquarters. "Ah, Elba," the hat vendor said. "It's a long walk, complicated directions. You'd really trust me to tell you the way?"

"Why wouldn't I?"

The weathered man laughed. "That's your second mistake – trusting anyone."

"And what was my first?"

"Coming to Hellhole, of course."

Following the hat merchant's directions, Cristoph headed out of town along a well-traveled road over a line of scabby hills, to the General's residence. It took Cristoph almost three hours on foot, but he did not balk at the trek. If nothing else, it would prove his determination.

Knowing that Adolphus was essentially a prisoner on this planet, Cristoph was surprised to see the size of the Elba manor house, with its gables, many windows, and walls of fieldstone and pressed wood. When he gave his name to an elderly aide at the front door, the man perked up, even laughed. "A de Carre? That's a noble name. You mean from Vielinger?"

"I am the son of Lord de Carre, but it's no longer a noble name. All my holdings are gone, my family defunct. I'm in need of a new start ... and I have abilities the General might find useful."

The old man leaned forward with a darkened expression. "I fought for the General in the rebellion, and it seems to me that your family had a hand in defeating us."

"That's true, unfortunately. And now the Constellation has turned against me as well. I was hoping to speak with the General."

The aide swallowed a chuckle. "Too late to expect any sympathy from us. Go away."

"I am not looking for sympathy, but I do expect courtesy."

"A lot of newcomers want to see General Adolphus."

"Then I guess I'm just another one. I'll wait."

"Do it outside then." The veteran pointed to several benches on the long wooden porch that offered no shade from the bright afternoon sunlight.

Though he expected no favors from Tiber Adolphus, Cristoph decided to remain as long as was necessary. The bench grew harder and hotter with each passing hour. He sat perspiring, wearing the new hat he had purchased. He decided that this purposeful snub from the General must be some kind of test, and he intended to pass it.

Other visitors came and went, some sitting for awhile like Cristoph, but eventually all were invited inside the big house – except for him. At first, Cristoph assumed the others must have appointments, but when he asked them, he discovered that was not the case. All were new arrivals from a variety of Crown Jewel worlds, each person seeking his fortune. Cristoph was the only one being ignored.

Finally, at sundown, he said to the old veteran at the door, "He hasn't forgotten about me?"

"Oh, he hasn't forgotten you, or your family. Not in all these years."

Cristoph slumped back on the bench and waited. He tried to do his best to take his situation in his stride, to show a brave face. He had never imagined that he might fall from riches to rags in an eyeblink … yet here on the worst planet in the Deep Zone, what did that matter? Of all places, *this* was where he should be able to prove himself with his skills in leading projects, managing miners or other large work teams. He would start where he could, and work his way upward to the best of his abilities. He had been stripped of his possessions, but not defeated. He knew he was smart and determined. Wasn't this place supposed to be about second chances? It was not likely he could ever restore the de Carre family honor, but he could at least find his own.

The General, obviously, continued to hold a grudge. *Bitterness can last a lifetime, and beyond.*

Cristoph remained outside on the porch at sunset, with no place to sleep, and he considered giving up, but he couldn't make it back to

Michella Town before dark. He paced along the porch when he could no longer sit still.

From the front doorway, the sour veteran called, "You might as well leave. The General won't see you."

Calmly, Cristoph stretched out on the bench, as if making a bed for himself. "I'll be here in the morning. I intend to try again tomorrow."

The old man scowled. "Go away. This is not an inn."

"No, an inn would at least offer water and food to a guest."

The veteran seemed angry, but Cristoph heard a deep laugh behind him. "You're a stubborn one."

A barrel-chested man stepped past the old aide; he had close-cropped dark hair, a squarish face, and a brusque military demeanor. Cristoph levered himself off the bench and made a quick, respectful bow. "General Adolphus, I've been waiting to speak with you."

"And if I say no?" The dark eyes flashed without warmth.

Cristoph didn't want to show weakness, not in this place, not in front of this man. "Then you would be missing an opportunity."

The General folded his arms across his chest. Cristoph thought he saw a hint of a smile. "I'm listening."

In a rush, he described his responsibilities on Vielinger, which included running the iperion mines, the processing centers, managing the equipment, juggling schedules. It was an impressive list of skills, all of which he felt would be applicable here on this planet. He also explained how he had lost control of it all – the sabotaged equipment, the accidents, the arson.

"Sounds like you failed miserably."

"I failed to block another power-hungry family that wanted to take our holdings. Is that sort of thing a problem here on Hallholme?"

Adolphus narrowed his eyes. "We have enough straightforward problems on this planet. Regardless of the cause of the accidents, it sounds like you couldn't protect your workers and keep the operations running."

Cristoph's throat was dry, but he nodded. "You're right, sir. In that, I failed."

"I failed, too, during the last battle at Sonjeera," Adolphus said. "But I accepted defeat in order to save as many lives as I could."

Cristoph wasn't sure what the General wanted to hear, so he gave a blunt, honest response. "I know you must be suspicious of my intentions, sir, but the Constellation has turned against me, disgraced my father, stripped me of my inheritance."

"And you think I will save you?"

"No, sir. I intend to save myself."

"Out of all the Deep Zone planets, why would you choose Hallholme?"

With a humorless smile, Cristoph shrugged. "Isn't this the place to go when you have nowhere else to go?"

"That it is. Come inside, young man. I'll find you a work assignment." Adolphus considered for a moment. "But the work I have in mind is considered demeaning. You're going to be a dust-system maintenance technician at the spaceport. You'll get filthy crawling around inside tight spaces changing filters. Not quite the same as living on a Crown Jewel estate."

"Nothing is the same. I'll do it anyway, sir."

"Yes," Adolphus said with a firm nod. "Yes, you will."

44

I t was not a sport for old people, yet Diadem Michella played just as hard as the much younger lords and ladies. On the mown field, riders wearing their family colors were each mounted on a spirited Sonjeeran horp.

The long-necked steeds known for their racing speed and vitality looked like a cross between a horse and a giraffe, and riders sat well above the ground. Because horps could manage tremendous speeds even across the short distances of the sonic ballfield, many riders strapped themselves to the saddles with harnesses. Michella, however, believed that harnesses projected a cowardly image. She regularly selected the most spirited animal in her stable and never used a safety harness. She was a daredevil, full of life, flamboyant for the adoring public. She was the Diadem.

Keana met her mother near the stable before Michella could ride out onto the field. Since she could not publicly mourn for Louis, Keana wore a simple but elegant white outfit graced with an embroidered design influenced by the Vielinger sigil. If Michella had known of her daughter's plans to go there, she would have stopped her – it was embarrassing – but perhaps the silly girl had finally learned a valuable lesson.

Michella had thought that eliminating her lover would rein Keana in, teach her not to wander from the well-defined course of her life, but her daughter was proving more intractable than she had ever been before. It was annoying.

When Keana arrived, the Diadem was about to climb an adjustable stirrup to mount her horp, while two men held the lively gray stallion for her. After mounting, the Diadem shooed away her two helpers so she could have a moment of privacy.

Interpreting the sigil on her daughter's ensemble as a small protest, the old woman scowled deeply. "What's done is done. Move on with your life! You should be at your own husband's side. Why do you continue to push the limits of my patience?"

"Perhaps I got the trait from you, Mother. I'm not the only one in this family who pushes the limits." Keana regarded the restless animal. "That beast could easily take you on your last ride, you know. What would happen to all your schemes if you fell and broke your neck?"

Michella raised her eyebrows at the venom in her daughter's voice. "I'll decide when I'm ready to die, and it won't be at the whim of this simple-minded animal." She looked at Keana's face, saw the pain written there, and softened her tone. "I wish it had gone otherwise for you and Lord de Carre, my dear, but that relationship was doomed from the start. You were born to certain expectations, and your husband is a member of a very wealthy and powerful family. Do you know how hard I had to work to arrange your marriage with Bolton in the first place? Accept your life and start living it."

Standing beside the animal, looking up at her, Keana said, "There's something I have to do first. The Riominis have Vielinger, and Louis is dead, but there's no need to punish his son. He did nothing to embarrass you, and his father accepted all the blame. Tell me where Cristoph is – I know you gave the order to send him away after he was evicted from the estate." She fought back her emotions. "I want to make sure he's all right."

The horp jostled, anxious to be out on the playing field, but Michella savagely yanked the bit and slapped the creature into submission. Her voice was shrill. "How many times must I tell you? Stop obsessing over that family! It's none of your concern. Cristoph was turned out of his estate and stripped of his fortunes. I've no idea where he went." She no longer bothered to sound compassionate. "I'll hear no more of your stories of dewy-eyed romance and living happily ever after. Even as

Diadem, do *I* get everything I want? Hardly! I didn't want the Riominis to overrun Vielinger, but it was unavoidable, a price of doing business with them – for the good of the Constellation."

Michella gave an unregal snort. "In Council, dear, they speak openly of my successor, as if I'm not there. But I remain fit and healthy and vivacious to spite them!" She waved dismissively. "Now go watch my match. I've arranged an excellent seat for you. Time to get back to your normal life." With that, the Diadem rode the beast through a gate in a white fence, and out onto the field.

Stung, Keana made her way to the spectator stands. All her life, her concerns had been brushed aside. At every turn, she tried to *help*, but no one took her seriously. The fact that her mother refused to let her find Cristoph only made her more determined to do it. She would have to gather her own allies and do it her own way. Sometimes, it was useful to be underestimated . . .

She sat in the stands with well-dressed members of the nobility. Keana did not want to draw attention to herself; she would have preferred to disappear to a place where she could find some peace. The decay and ennui of Sonjeeran society, demonstrated in these spectacles, was painfully obvious to her now.

As the sonic ball match took place and her mother galloped like a barbarian warrior in the midst of the other horps and riders, Keana mulled over Cristoph's disappearance. She worried that something horrible had happened to him – perhaps the young man had been murdered and his body hidden. Or maybe he had just been sent far away.

She looked out on the field and watched Michella galloping high on the gray stallion, with her sonic stick extended to ground level, blasting the white game ball. Riominis, Hirdans, Craises, Tazaars and other competing nobles chased her mother with waving sticks to take the ball from her. The audience cheered for the Diadem, but Keana held her silence. She wished the animal would throw the old woman down on the field, where she could be trampled. Keana knew that her mother was responsible for what had happened to Louis, either directly or through intermediaries. The Diadem had ruined her life, squashed her dreams, and refused to help when Keana needed her the most.

Bouncing on her saddle without the safety restraint, Michella seemed in danger of flying off, but she held on nonetheless. In his characteristic black uniform, Lord Selik Riomini charged up beside her, extended his sonic stick and tried to hammer at the ball, but with a swift, expert motion, Michella fired a loud sonic rejoinder that knocked the stick out of his hands.

The old Diadem guided the ball around, then struck it high into the air. Moving in a graceful arc, it dropped straight through the basket. In celebration, a cannon shot fireworks into the air, and the crowd erupted in cheers.

But Keana merely sat in the stands, worried about Cristoph.

45

Since Fernando and his symbiotic alien presence showed no interest in driving the Trakmaster, Vincent took the controls and guided them across the rugged terrain back to Michella Town. Despite his anxiety to get back, to share what had happened to his friend, Vincent took no risks as he drove overland.

During the long trip, he observed the dramatic and irrefutable change in the other man's personality. Once frenetic and needing to talk all the time, Fernando-Zairic now seemed placid, as if he neither wanted nor needed anything. Filled with his Xayan memories and mission, he no longer looked for opportunities to make a profit. He had a certain aura of *holiness* about him, which was vastly different from the Fernando Neron that Vincent had known. There was no doubt in his mind that this was real.

Still, he worried about how to reveal the astonishing story to others – who would probably react with skepticism and even ridicule. Upon hearing such a fantastic yarn, listeners would look at Fernando's history as a scam artist and draw their own conclusions. Vincent would be painted with the same brush. Why would anyone believe them? The other man did not seem concerned, though, assuming that the truth would be sufficient.

Their best chance was to have General Adolphus listen to what Fernando (and Zairic) had to say. Vincent noted his companion's blurred eyes once more and shook his head. Just spending a few minutes with the altered Fernando should be convincing enough.

When they finally reached Michella Town, Vincent pulled the dusty Trakmaster up to the survey office, where he was required to turn over hardcopy logs of their explorations. Fernando remained in the vehicle. "I will wait here. Please arrange for us to talk to General Tiber Adolphus."

Vincent didn't know if he would ever get used to the detached voice coming out of his friend's lips. "Easier said than done." But he had come up with something that might intrigue the General.

Inside the survey office, the prune-faced manager scolded Vincent for returning early. "Given up already? Lots of ground to cover out there. Most explorers stay out *longer* than scheduled."

Vincent looked away, but did not argue. "Sorry, sir." He remembered times at the machine shop when Mr. Engermann upbraided him about a mediocre customer satisfaction response; he had always found it best to be stoic and sincere, which prevented any escalation in the lecture. He fidgeted but tried to stay calm.

It was obvious the manager liked to scowl. "And where's your companion? Did something happen to him?"

"He's in the vehicle, sir." Vincent chose not to go into further detail. "We came back early because of the magnitude of our discovery. We encountered something that will interest the General."

The man perked up. "What did you find? Show it to me."

"It's best if we speak to the General directly."

The office manager gave an officious sniff. "We do have a chain of command here." He called up a blank screen to fill out a form.

Vincent remained firm. "We made a significant find regarding the original alien race on this planet." He leaned forward, lowered his voice. "A *significant* find, sir, and it's imperative that we present it to the General in person."

The manager seemed flustered. "I'll contact him, but I make no promises."

The news enticed Adolphus, as they had hoped, and Vincent was instructed to drive immediately to Elba. An aide admitted them as soon as they arrived. "The General is expecting you."

Combing his hair and straightening his shirt, Vincent tried to make himself presentable, but Fernando-Zairic left his rumpled clothes and mussed wavy hair as they were, as if the alien part of his personality didn't know how humans were supposed to look in the first place.

General Adolphus met them in the foyer with an unexpected expression of boyish optimism on his face. "Gentlemen, I understand you found something about the original race? A significant artifact?" His voice took on a warning tone. "I am not fond of hyperbole."

Vincent cleared his throat. "Much more significant than any artifact, sir. It's the piece of the puzzle you were looking for."

"You have my attention. Show me this alien object."

Fernando stepped forward. "Sir, I am the alien object."

The General looked at Vincent guardedly. "I'm not in the mood for jokes."

"It may be hard to believe, sir, but this is not a joke. I witnessed it myself." Vincent explained what had happened to his companion at the slickwater pool. Fernando-Zairic stood too close to Adolphus, which made the other man watch him warily. Since his immersion, Fernando had a different perception of boundaries and personal space.

Zairic's voice came from Fernando's lips. "I understand your skepticism, General Tiber Adolphus. From your records, you will conclude that the man Fernando Neron is neither reliable nor believable. Therefore, I must offer proof. I can answer questions and give vivid descriptions of Xayan culture, technology, and history, but those are mere words. In order to demonstrate my sincerity, therefore, I will lead you to a knowledge reservoir of the Xayan civilization – a vault of artifacts that I believe is still intact."

Vincent was as surprised as Adolphus. He turned to his friend. "But you told me everything was obliterated in the asteroid impact."

"Not everything – or so I hope. When we knew that the asteroid would destroy our civilization and virtually all life on Xaya, we tried to preserve our race within the slickwater. However, some Xayans offered an alternative. As a secondary measure, a small group of our people created a shielded museum bunker deep in the most secure mountain range. They hoped the protected vault would survive the impact."

Though dubious, the General sounded cautiously interested. "That's an interesting claim, Mr Neron."

"I am Zairic, at the moment. And I am confident that I can locate the vault. It will require a significant excavation effort, but once you find the museum bunker, you will have all the proof you need." Fernando-Zairic perused the objects that Adolphus kept in his transparent display cases. "And a treasure trove of answers."

Adolphus wrestled with skepticism and hope. He searched Fernando's face for some kind of deceit, but the expression remained impenetrable. He turned to Vincent. "What is your opinion of all this, Mr Jenet?"

Vincent drew a deep breath, gave his honest response. "I believe something amazing happened to him, General. Beyond that ... I can't say. Will it be worth the expense and effort to dig into the heart of a mountain? That's something you'll have to decide."

46

The General had always been good at reading people, but these two were different. Unquestionably, when he arrived on this planet, Fernando Neron was a fast talker, a charmer ... but this person who claimed to be an alien messiah was not at all the man Adolphus remembered. "Zairic" was eager to show the slickwater discovery, and Vincent Jenet did not seem to have an agenda or a get-rich scheme; he appeared to want a normal life – Hellhole style, anyway.

Maybe they had stumbled onto something interesting.

Whenever the General sent topographical prospectors out on the wide-open landscape, he hoped they would make significant discoveries. It was their job. Though this report sounded more incredible than most, he was obligated to investigate.

Over the next several days, Adolphus assembled a team of geologists and xenobiologists to study the slickwater springs. And he decided to go with them.

They flew in aerocopters out to the nearest settlement – a bauxite mining complex with rounded aluminum-walled shelters – where they set down on the small landing pad, then took overland vehicles into the wilderness. Arriving in the sheltered valley after the extensive journey, the General immediately sensed the pools' eerie, otherworldly nature. In that aspect, at least, Vincent and Fernando had not exaggerated.

Adolphus walked ahead to the grainy shore of one smooth pond, which exuded a mysterious aura. The clouds gathering overhead had a resonant effect on the pearlescent water, yet the murky reflection seemed to be of a different time and a different sky. A shiver went down his spine. Despite his skepticism, he began to accept that this might be a real breakthrough about Hallholme's original inhabitants.

Three scientists trudged up behind him, carrying satchels of equipment. "Don't let the substance contact your skin," Adolphus warned. "Keep your distance. I don't want anyone else infected."

"There is nothing to fear." Fernando-Zairic made a welcoming gesture toward the slickwater. "It benefits both of our races. If *you* were to immerse yourself, General Tiber Adolphus, you might obtain the memories and experiences of a great Xayan leader. Together, you could become quite formidable."

"I'm formidable enough on my own." A frown furrowed his brow. "I'm not permanently saying no ... just exercising appropriate caution. What happened to you was an accident, Mr Neron. Before I allow anyone else to be intentionally exposed, I want more information."

If Zairic's claim was to be believed, these pools of liquid organic database had recently bubbled back to the surface, waiting to be noticed. Adolphus could not forget how he had seen Renny Clovis swallowed up by a similar liquid at the bottom of the Ankor sinkhole.

The biochemists donned gloves and used telescoping rods to scoop up samples of the viscous liquid. Geologists took careful measurements, scraped packets of the dirt from the shore, studied the obsidian chunks all around.

The setting was beautiful and serene; the hillsides around the sheltered valley were carpeted with alien vegetation. "Exquisite Xayan cities once covered this area," Fernando-Zairic said in a distant, wistful tone, as if he could still see them in his mind's eye. "Lovely, delicate structures filled with people joined together in one belief and one goal: to evolve into something better."

The General said, "None of our excavations have uncovered remnants of alien cities. Why haven't we discovered any wreckage?"

"Xayan structures are soft, living entities, designed to remain manifest only so long as they are maintained. When our people died, the dwellings died with us and faded away. Everything we are, and were, is here." Fernando-Zairic placed a palm against his own chest. He extended his hand to indicate the slickwater ponds. "And there."

While the researchers studied the pools, the General's security detail dispatched lighter all-terrain vehicles, called rollers, for a fast reconnaissance of the surrounding hills.

Several of the men served as his personal bodyguards because, even after a decade of exile, Adolphus could not shake the feeling that Diadem Michella would send assassins to eliminate him. He maintained his vigilance.

However, Michella was not blind to the widespread support his rebellion had received across the Crown Jewels, and those sentiments had not vanished during his disgrace and exile. An anonymous benefactor had even arranged deliveries of essential supplies during their initial turbulent year to keep the rebels alive. If General Adolphus were killed, the resulting uproar in the Constellation could be political suicide for the Diadem.

The sound of weapons fire on the other side of the hills astonished the General. Sharp reports cracked through the silent, dusty air, breaking the serenity like shattering glass. Adolphus activated his earadio. "What was that? Come in, Mr Jordan! Are we under attack?"

The hesitation in the response seemed interminable. "No, General, but ... it's the damndest thing you ever saw." Craig Jordan, his security chief, was a man with a loud laugh, who blustered much but never lost his calm. "It's better if we show you – we're lifting it onto the flatbed now, sir. Ugh, this thing stinks!" Adolphus heard chatter, more discussion, and loud grunts of effort.

Within minutes, the buzzing engines of the rollers filled the air again, and the three ATVs crossed the ridge, rumbling pell-mell into the valley. As they approached, Adolphus could see a large object strapped to the back of one vehicle.

The General's questions caught in his mouth at the sight of the large exotic beast slumped over the ATV's bed. It was four-legged, reminiscent of an elk, its hide covered with patches of fur and scales like scabby lichen. A cluster of gray-brown tentacles protruded from its elongated head where a true elk would have worn antlers. A black tongue lolled from its open mouth. It had three eyes.

"It was just wandering there on the hillside, so we shot it on sight. Could have been a predator," Jordan said. "We thought the xeno teams would want a specimen."

"The biologists are going to get into fistfights over who dissects this," said a second security man, red-faced with excitement. "Never seen anything this big on Hellhole. Took four of us to lift it into the cargo bed."

Through the eyes of Fernando, the alien personality of Zairic stared at the creature with calm recognition. "Long ago, this was one of the most common herd beasts on Xaya." He didn't even try to speak the creature's alien name. "Before the impact, great groups of them wandered the plains, eating the vegetation."

Vincent looked contemplative as he surveyed the carcass. "When Fernando and I were collecting animal bones, he told me he'd spotted a large creature, but I didn't believe him. What he described was nothing like this, though."

"Oh, he – I – was right to fear that creature. I know what it was now." Fernando-Zairic nodded. "Some life forms are already returning to Xaya, just as *we* hope to return."

"But our people have run extensive post-impact models." Adolphus shook his head. "*All* significant vertebrates should have perished in the asteroid strike. This creature could not have survived."

"And yet it is here, and it was alive until moments ago." Zairic looked over at the General. "Where there is one, there will be others."

Adolphus regarded the sad hulk of the slain creature. "Unless it's among the last of its kind."

Jordan shifted uncomfortably. "Maybe we shouldn't have shot it, sir, but we were all so shocked. What if it had attacked us?"

Adolphus touched the rubbery patches on the hide of the horse-sized creature. "But where did it come from? We've been studying and terraforming this world for a decade, and this thing doesn't fit with what we know."

"Humans have not been here long, and your understanding is incomplete. Who can ever hope to understand a whole world?" Fernando-Zairic smiled – an odd smile that looked as if the alien presence was consciously moving the man's features to create the expression. "Again, if you immerse yourself in the slickwater as I did, you will receive the blessing of our data and our lives, and you will understand much, much more."

Adolphus felt a chill, and a longing. "Oh, I want to understand – I just need to decide how much it's worth to me." He glanced at the slickwater pools, whose surfaces continued to dance with the patterns of ancient storms. He reached a conclusion. "Mister Neron, or *Zairic* if you prefer – give us the location of your museum bunker and guide us in our work. Let's dig down into the mountain and find out what else survived."

"That would be an excellent start." Fernando was still smiling.

47

The spy reported directly to Carlson Goler on Ridgetop, although the Territorial Governor wasn't sure he wanted to hear the news. The Constellation government dispatched many such observers to monitor activity in the Deep Zone, and the covert operatives revealed their identities only when they discovered a matter of utmost significance.

The man came to Goler's A-frame house on a hill overlooking the goldenwood groves. Dressed in the dirty clothes of a tree cutter, he had short reddish hair and a sunburned face. He kneaded a shapeless, sweat-stained hat in his hands, but the glassy edge of his stare showed that he was no meek commoner. He told Tasmine that he didn't need an appointment.

During his term on Ridgetop, the governor had spoken to this particular man three different times. In each instance, his information had indeed proved reliable and interesting, and afterward the spy had created a new identity for himself. Goler was well aware, however, that the operative worked for the Constellation, not for him.

His old household servant led the man, moving with the ponderously slow gait that she reserved for people she didn't like. "Governor, this man says he's got something to tell you." She sniffed.

"I'm sure he does." Goler gestured for the spy to take a seat facing the wide-paned windows with the panoramic view. He didn't bother to ask the man's current name, since it would be different soon enough. "Would you please bring us some food from the kitchens, Tasmine?"

The old woman made a noncommittal sound as she painstakingly hobbled out of the room. Goler wasn't fooled by her performance, since she walked without any difficulty when no one was around to see her.

The spy waited until she was out of earshot, then said in a low voice, "I'd heard rumors before, Governor, and now I'm certain. There is an entire network of independent commerce among the Deep Zone planets. A black-market trade. Undocumented ships, illegal cargo deliveries."

Goler scoffed. "That makes no sense at all. Who can ride a stringline without being detected?"

"*Off*-stringline." The man reached inside his shirt and extracted a sheaf of papers covered with handwritten notes. He hadn't wanted his observations to be copied or erased by data thieves. "Ian Walfor is running old commercial ships from Buktu to other planets using antiquated FTL propulsion. He goes to Candela, Hallholme, Nomolos, at least three other planets that I know of."

Goler laughed outright. "Those ships were scuttled or stripped down for parts as soon as they arrived in the Deep Zone decades ago."

The spy handed the sheets over to the governor. "They might have been decommissioned on paper, Governor, but once the FTL ships reached their destinations long ago, they were refurbished, not destroyed. Walfor found some way to keep them operating."

Goler spread his hands in exasperation. "Why would he do that? What possible purpose could there be? Using standard FTL to go from Buktu to Candela – let alone Hallholme or Nomolos – would take months in transit. Traveling via the Sonjeera stringline hub takes only a few days. It's a ridiculous alternative. Why would anyone bother?"

"Nevertheless, he does it." The spy was humorless and insistent.

"And just how would he fuel these FTL ships?"

"I merely report, sir. I leave it to you, and the Diadem, to investigate further."

Goler remembered that Buktu did have plenty of hydrogen ices drenched by solar radiation. Walfor might manufacture his own fuel, provided he had enough of an industrial base. He nodded slowly to himself. "Mr Walfor sounds very resourceful if he can manage all that."

The more he considered, the more plain the reasons became. For many rugged DZ individualists, bypassing Constellation tariffs and oversight would be its own reward – an alternative to the governmental stranglehold on supplies going out to the Deep Zone worlds – such a black-market network, however slow, proved the principle.

Goler ventured, "Well, the Constellation did abandon the stringline out to Buktu and effectively cut off the colony. What were those people supposed to do? She gave them no alternative. If Walfor has set up his own supply line, then the Diadem herself must bear some responsibility."

"I'm not a politician, sir," the spy said evenly, "but I'm certain that the Diadem did not intend for Administrator Walfor to *improve* his situation after being cut off."

Tasmine reentered the room bearing a tray on which she had sloppily placed cold meats and a few vegetables. "The kitchen is being cleaned right now. This is all I could find."

"That will be just fine, Tasmine. Thank you." Goler knew she could have done much more had she wanted to.

Not noticing the snub, the spy picked distractedly at one of the pieces of meat. "The Constellation government must have its portion of the trade." He pushed the handwritten papers closer to Goler. "Sonjeera needs to know."

He picked up the report. "I will inform them next time I report to Sonjeera. Thank you for such excellent work. I'll submit these papers personally."

"Perhaps it's worth an immediate mail drone, sir?" Now the spy was beginning to irritate him.

"I'll consider it. I have a number of documents that should go to Sonjeera."

The spy took a few more bites from the meats on the platter, just to be polite, then picked up his shapeless hat. "I will take my leave. I doubt you'll see me again. It's better if I take a new identity and go to a different Deep Zone planet from now on."

Goler couldn't agree more. "Yes, that would be for the best."

Tasmine waited in the hall, a hand pressed to her lower back, exaggerating her pain, and let the man find his own way out. She had eavesdropped on the whole conversation. "You should arrest that man, sir – manufacture some charges against him and isolate him in a Ridgetop prison. That would keep his mouth shut for awhile."

"Tasmine, you're ruthless."

"I've had to be." Without invitation, she ate some of the food from the tray.

Goler scrutinized the careful notes and evidence. He didn't doubt the assertions were true. "Information this big won't stay secret for long." He handed the stack of papers to Tasmine. "But for now, shred these."

She smiled. "I'd be happy to, sir."

"Then get a message to Ian Walfor. Inform him that we know what he's up to, and we want an explanation. We can always report him to Sonjeera later." So many political repercussions. He had to proceed with extreme caution.

The old woman took the papers and left, moving with a spry step now. Goler knew that his evasion was only a stopgap measure. Other covert operatives were just as likely to discover the information. Diadem Michella would find out eventually, but Goler wouldn't make it too easy for her.

48

Even though Sophie didn't need a particular reason to invite Tiber Adolphus for a nice dinner, she still tried to make each such meal a special occasion. Over the course of his career, the General had eaten enough mass-produced food in military mess halls that he viewed meals as little more than the acquisition of nourishment. Sophie took it upon herself to show him that dining could be a civilized activity with nuances in flavor and texture, pleasurable counterpoints and refreshing surprises – like a complex symphony. "If one of your goals is to make Hallholme a civilized place, then you need to lead by example," she told him.

Business concerns usually kept her too preoccupied to do it right, but she forced herself to slow down for Adolphus's benefit as well as her own. Because of their heavy responsibilities, they had to carve out time just to be together.

Now, in her living room, the General sat in a brown upholstered chair that she had come to regard as *his* chair. She had to admit he looked rather presidential in it. Tiber Adolphus had a natural air of command, reinforced by his years of military service, and if the Diadem bitch had only learned to work *with* him instead of against him, the two could have done great things for the human race.

As it was, Adolphus would just have to do great things without the Constellation.

Sophie cradled a dark green bottle in her arms as if it were a beloved child. "Presenting this year's vintage Cabernet." She showed him the plain, utilitarian label; she didn't dawdle with artistic logos, but if she ever decided to export commercial quantities of Hellhole wines, even as novelty vintages, she would have to improve the design, maybe have Devon sketch something appropriate. Or perhaps Antonia Anqui had artistic skills. Sophie decided to ask the girl.

Adolphus inspected the bottle, expressing his approval. "It'll go well with our steaks."

Though the vegetable yield from the greenhouse domes exceeded expectations, the process of raising cattle from imported embryos posed many difficulties: grazing land had to be cleared and fertilized, pasturage planted with enough grass to sustain a herd. Native weeds infiltrated the hay; some weeds sickened the livestock, while others just made the meat taste foul. Barn shelters had to be sturdy against the myriad storms, and the cattle had to remain close enough so they could get inside when the weather turned.

Given the many far more efficient ways of creating protein, raising beef as a colony food source made no economic sense. Poultry had proved a much more successful and easily managed source of protein. But it wasn't only about digestible calories, Sophie knew; one bite of a good filet proved that to anyone with taste buds.

Armand Tillman, one of the few local ranchers who had managed to keep his herd alive, occasionally slaughtered a steer and delivered the best cuts to Adolphus. The idea of accepting such an extravagant gift had made the General uncomfortable at first, and he tried to return the steaks. "I'm not the Diadem. You don't have to pay me tribute."

But Tillman insisted, and Sophie was delighted with the occasional bounty. "Don't argue too vigorously, Tiber." She had her kitchen staff prepare the steaks with such excellent care that the General did look forward to them. And, of course, to dinner with her.

The General handed the bottle back, and Sophie uncorked it (a resin composite cork, because she refused to import real corks from off-world) and poured them each a glass. The stemware was also made on Hellhole, from the ample local supply of silica and trace minerals.

She extended the wine to him. "Tell me your honest opinion."

"I'm always honest with you, but I don't have a discriminating palate." Adolphus took up his glass, swirled the wine and regarded it. "The color is rich." He inhaled deeply, then sipped and smiled. "You're improving year by year."

With a skeptical frown, she took a sip from her own glass. As always, the wine had a lingering aftertaste, some as-yet-undefined astringency imparted by chemicals in the soil. "It still has that unusual note. I'll keep working at it."

"Some might say it's distinctive, compelling."

She grimaced into her glass and swirled it again. "Some might say that, but they'd be a minority."

Adolphus sat back in his chair. "Our wine doesn't have to taste exactly like what the nobles drink on Sonjeera. We're not trying to be the Constellation."

She bent close and kissed him on the lips, tasting the wine there. She would have kissed him more deeply, but her cook sauntered in with two sizzling platters of steaks. "Later," Sophie whispered.

She lit a candle at the small dining table, and he was amused. "I keep the power running in Michella Town, and you use candles? We have better methods of lighting a room, you know."

"We probably do, but that would miss the point." As they cut into their steaks and smelled the visceral aroma of beef juices, she asked him more about the slickwater pools, about Fernando-Zairic's fantastic claims, and the strange creature that Craig Jordan had shot.

"That makes two very significant discoveries. If large animals did survive the impact centuries ago, then we'll have to completely change our models of this world." He set down his fork. "And if those slickwater pools *are* an accessible database of the original alien civilization, then this planet has just become vastly more interesting."

"So you think there's something to those pools after all?"

"I'm convinced there's a great mystery, and I'm inclined to give our friend Fernando Neron – or Zairic – the benefit of the doubt. In for a penny, in for a pound. I've already ordered large mining and excavation equipment to start digging for this supposed museum bunker deep in the mountains. It could be a treasure trove."

"Or a Pandora's Box."

"Then we'd better be careful around it." The General gave her a wry smile. "And I've decided to take another chance, too. If I divert my best mining engineers and supervisors, one of the Constellation inspectors might take notice and ask too many questions."

"Who can you send, then?"

Adolphus took a moment to reply, as if he himself wasn't sure of the decision. "Remember Cristoph de Carre? I've thoroughly investigated his situation – he was ruined by Constellation politics. If this is a trick, it goes many levels deeper than anything Michella has ever tried before. I think Cristoph is what he says he is – and he's exactly the man I need. Highly motivated, skilled, experienced in large-scale excavations. After managing the iperion mines on Vielinger, he understands tunnel operations, and he can administer large work crews. I'm going to put him in charge of the dig to find the Xayan vault."

Sophie arched her eyebrows. "He hasn't been here very long. You sure you trust him?" The man had been working low-end jobs without complaint since his arrival. Then she laughed. "Or are you sending him on a snipe hunt?"

Adolphus was amused by the reference. "This time there may actually be a snipe. Besides, choosing Cristoph de Carre has another potential benefit. Even if the excavation turns up nothing, at least I will have gauged and trained a man who could become a valuable lieutenant."

"Always thinking ahead, aren't you?"

Adolphus took another bite of his steak. "Always hopeful. And if we do find Zairic's museum chamber, all the better."

49

Each time they crossed another name off the list, Ishop Heer considered it cause for celebration. Progress! And he had to admit this was an amusing game, even though most of the loose ends had very little political relevance anymore.

Twelve names, descendants of the prominent noble families that had orchestrated the downfall of the Osheer line so many centuries ago. He had done meticulous research so that all of these people were real to him, and his resentment became *tangible*.

Since he had only recently learned of the ancient plot himself, Ishop doubted any of these scions were aware of the crimes of their forefathers; but that didn't change the basic stain of guilt in their bloodline. Ishop still blamed them. A matter of family honor. *Honor.* Ishop liked to roll the concept around in his thoughts. It made him feel noble.

And, oblivious to their danger, they were easy targets.

Laderna purred from the praise he showered on her, and she was as dedicated to the cause as he was. Erasing names was becoming a foreplay ritual for them; they made love each time they counted a new success, or moved their plans forward. Soon enough, though, this diversion would be completed and he could get down to the real business of figuring out how to make the proper return to the prominence he deserved.

Five names out of the dozen had already been scratched off, and no one had even begun to suspect a pattern. There was no reason to; after such a long time, out of 183 noble bloodlines, the families had little obvious connection to one another. But he and Laderna knew. Everything was falling into place more smoothly than he had hoped.

Laderna had preemptively taken care of the first victim, Lady Opra Mageros, by staging an engine failure in her personal aircraft. It had been ruled an accident.

Then the deaths of Lady Jenine Paternos and Lord Azio Tazaar were neatly blamed on their bloody family feud; even the surviving clan members suspected nothing and had in fact ratcheted up the mutual violence. A side effect that didn't concern him.

The next elimination was even easier. The only son of elderly Lord Hirdan, ruler of planet Jonn, was a mountaineer, and he had vanished in a whiteout at 8,000 meters. The noble heir was presumed dead. *Definitely* dead, Ishop knew, because he'd shot a grenade from an aero-copter at a snow slope above the climber, causing an avalanche that swept the victim and his two guides into a deep crevasse, where no one was likely to find them.

And then Evelyn Weilin, a charming socialite with a bright smile, expensive-looking clothes (costumes), and gaudy jewelry (fake), who had very little money remaining in her family fortune but refused to show it. She had a fondness for recreational drugs and managed to get herself invited to events where they were freely distributed to the guests. It had been easy to slip her a "special" dose of a mysterious powder that she was eager to inhale. Once it contacted the soft tissue of her nasal membranes however, the transformational acid ate swiftly through her sinuses and lungs, leaving her to writhe on the floor until her skull collapsed like a deflated balloon. No one ever found out how the drug had made its way to the party, or why no other guests had succumbed.

That left seven names on the list. He would be almost sad when this little activity was over, and he knew Laderna enjoyed it as well. Afterwards, however, he could take his rightful place among the nobles, knowing that justice had been served, even if it took 700 years.

A week had passed since the good news about poor Hirdan's death on the mountaintop, during which time Ishop accompanied Diadem

Michella to a number of Council meetings. He was a dutiful and competent aide, without whom she could not function – and that was exactly how he wanted everyone to see him. Whenever possible, he employed the phrase "for the good of the Constellation." They would accept him into their little club and he would have a noble name again, at last ... *after* he completed his personal little quest.

Unfortunately, he did foresee a difficulty ahead ... a challenge. One of the remaining names on the list was a Duchenet.

50

When he agreed to work at any job General Adolphus assigned him, Cristoph had expected to endure a year or more of humiliating labor as penance for the de Carre family's previous allegiance. He had accepted that. Nothing could be greater punishment than being forced to turn his back on his ancestral estate and walk away from everything he had known, of course, but he had steeled himself for the worst the General might throw at him.

Thus, Cristoph could not have been more surprised when, after less than a month, he was transferred from cleaning dust-scrubbers. The General summoned him and fixed the young man with an appraising gaze. "I am not a man to squander resources, Mr de Carre, and you are exactly the person for this particular job. Prove yourself – show me that I haven't made a mistake in giving you this chance."

On learning about the project, Cristoph considered the idea of an alien treasure vault buried deep inside a mountain preposterous. He wondered if this might be a setup to humiliate him, but the expense and equipment the General was dedicating to the site made that unlikely. Besides, Cristoph realized with a heavy heart, how much further could he fall? He had chosen to go to Hellhole, had waited for hours to plead his case with Adolphus. Now that he had a chance to work on something more significant than dust-scrubbers, he decided to take it at face value and do his absolute best.

He accompanied Vincent Jenet and Fernando Neron (or "Zairic") across the landscape to a line of as-yet-untouched mountains. With knowledge supposedly imparted to him from his alien memories, Fernando guided them. "It's difficult," the strange man said. "The surface topography was greatly reshaped by the asteroid impact."

For two days as the Trakmaster wandered up and down hills, into canyons and up steep slopes, Cristoph grew more and more impatient. And then Fernando told him to stop.

The three exited the vehicle and stood on a weathered, scrubby ridgetop. Fernando paced back and forth, head cocked to one side, like an old dowser using a divining rod. He wandered half a kilometer from the vehicle and paused, staring at the ground, where a gray multi-legged snake scurried away from him. The Zairic side of Fernando spoke in a peculiar, distant voice, as if disembodied and shouting across the eons. "The museum vault is down there. Dig, and you will find it."

After marking the position, they returned to Michella Town and reported to the General. Once again, Cristoph was surprised and suspicious when Adolphus accepted the strange man's assessment. "Do as he says, Mr de Carre. You shall have all necessary equipment at your disposal."

A week later, on an overcast, windy afternoon, Cristoph stood on the brushy hilltop where heavy mining machinery had blasted a deep shaft into the mountainside. On official documents, this site was an exploratory dig for possible platinum or bauxite deposits ... nothing that would draw undue attention from Constellation inspectors.

The dig went swiftly. According to Fernando-Zairic, the museum vault was originally several hundred meters down, but seismic upheavals after the asteroid impact might have altered the mountain's profile. Detectors along the ridge measured pulses from the mining blasts and created a resonance map of the deep interior. Though he should have expected it, Cristoph was still amazed when the vibration signature revealed a significant void at the heart of the mountain, exactly as predicted.

Fernando-Zairic was confident and pleased. "Yes, it is there."

For the last part of the excavation, Cristoph employed a more precise drilling tractor. If there was an ancient bunker down there, he had no intention of destroying the priceless contents by blasting his way in.

Cristoph remained with his foremen on a platform from which they remotely operated the drilling machine. According to projections, they would break through within hours. Fernando-Zairic alternated between eagerness and calm, while Vincent Jenet seemed a bit shell-shocked and out of his comfort zone. Dust blew from the excavations all around the site, and the noise of machinery outside the shaft made the air vibrate.

The dented, well-used tunneling tractor had outriggers on it and a telescoping drill bit with an attached camera, so the operators could see the strata. Tapping a key on the screen, Cristoph summoned a history of the last hour of drilling.

The female job supervisor on the drilling platform went by the nickname Nari, which supposedly meant "tough guy" in her native language. Gray hair poked from under the edges of her greasy hat; she was short and stocky, with a salty sense of humor. The woman was the most experienced member of the crew, having operated mines on two other planets, and Cristoph found he had much in common with her.

Seeing a series of blips she didn't like as she inspected the profile, Nari stopped the drilling machine and turned to Cristoph. "We're almost to the void, sir, but we've got big igneous blocks in the next few meters. The interface is clear, geometrical. Even severe shock from the asteroid impact wouldn't have created something like this. It's not natural."

"Precisely." Fernando-Zairic stepped close. "And it appears intact, as we hoped."

Nari looked at Cristoph. "So you want me to drill farther? No telling what's inside."

"That's why we're here. Break through."

Fernando-Zairic added a note of caution. "Be as gentle as you can."

More than a kilometer into the mountainside, the borer machine continued its slow progress, grinding forward to break the protective wall of the supposed museum vault. Cristoph watched the image of gray rock change to static then an abrupt black as the drilling machine shut off.

"Damn it." Nari reset the imager, to no avail. She huffed. "The rock moved. Can't tell if the machine is damaged."

"But we broke through. Look at the readings," Cristoph said.

"The vault is open." Fernando-Zairic sounded more animated than Cristoph had heard him. "We must go down there."

"Retract the drill bit. Let's go see what we've found."

After several more hours of cleanup with excavating machines, scrapers, and backhoes, Nari and her crew expanded the tunnel route and shored up the loose rock before she finally declared it safe enough for entry.

The small group crowded into a crawler that worked its way down the fresh shaft until they reached the breach in the vault wall. Throwing caution aside, Fernando-Zairic led the way, while the other men put on lighted helmets and crawled through the hole in the rock wall to enter the alien chamber.

Inside, Cristoph stared at the hall of wonders, shining his light to reveal details. Low, yellow illumination came from an unseen source inside the vault. The walls of the chamber had been assembled from thick, interlocking blocks adorned with bas-relief strips, friezes, and incomprehensible writing. Faint shapes wavered and crackled in the dusty air, ghostly squiggles of illumination that flitted about and vanished. Niches and sealed containers held ancient treasures.

Vincent whispered, "Oh, Fernando! I never should have doubted you."

"That was Zairic, not me," the man said in a bright, excited voice. "This looks exactly as he described it in my mind." Fernando peered at the hieroglyphics on the walls, nodding absently. "I can translate this writing ... but we have something more important to see."

Cristoph shone his helmet light upward, noting with concern that some of the ceiling blocks were out of alignment, having shifted after the impact and subsequent centuries of seismic rattling. Splits and sharp edges showed, and rock shards had rained down from the high ceiling to form a pile at the center of the cavern. "We might have caused some of that damage breaking in, along with the deterioration that was already occurring."

Nari was nervous. She twisted her hat around. "This place looks unstable to me. Let's back off until I can get men down here to shore up the ceiling."

"I have something more important to do first," Fernando-Zairic said. Moving with determination, he went to the opposite wall to stand before five L-shaped containers covered with more bas relief markings. The lambent glow and phantom shapes flickered around four of the containers, while the central chamber remained dark.

Following him, Cristoph peered through the translucent lid of the nearest illuminated container and realized with a start what these vessels were – sarcophagi for the original aliens. "They're coffins!"

"Hopefully not," Fernando-Zairic said. "They were designed to be preservation chambers."

Through the clear panel, Cristoph saw that the container was filled with a yellow, glutinous liquid around an immersed, fantastic body. A Xayan? The creature had a vaguely humanoid torso, head, and arms, but from the waist down the body looked more like a caterpillar or slug. In the preserving liquid, the Xayan looked gelatinous, its skin milky and translucent. The smooth, nearly featureless face had two large round eyes, but no mouth.

As Cristoph stared, the creature's blank eyes suddenly began to spiral. Vincent and Nari, standing next to the other sarcophagi, let out gasps. Then in eerie synchronization, the encased Xayans focused on their rescuers.

Fernando-Zairic sounded pleased. "Four of the five have survived."

51

Entirely focused on the preserved aliens, Fernando-Zairic worked feverishly to unseal the first lid, but couldn't move it. "We must free them. They survived the long sleep." Vincent watched in amazement and trepidation.

Behind the transparent lids, the awakening Xayans showed a collective awareness in their spiral eyes, but they could not move. Overhead, phantom squiggles of illumination crackled softly in the air, flitting about before vanishing and reappearing.

Without hesitating, Vincent helped his friend shove aside the lid. Nari and Cristoph de Carre struggled to open the second sarcophagus, then the third. As each box was opened, the strange creatures began to stir within the gelatinous liquid. In the vault's dusty air, the ghostly whispers of light took on more definition, forming spirals that disappeared like smoke in a wind.

The alien in the darkened container remained motionless.

"My companions have slept for five centuries, but now our time grows short," said Zairic. Hearing a sharp crack overhead, he looked up to see a few more pebbles split off from the ceiling and drop down in a rain of dust. The first chunks fell into the pile of debris on the cavern floor.

Nari shouted, "It's going to come down – everybody out! Move your asses."

Fernando-Zairic remained where he was. "We cannot leave yet. We must rescue them."

Vincent grabbed his friend. "I know how important this is to you, but this whole chamber is going to collapse."

The other man refused to leave the alien sarcophagi. "You don't understand, Vincent. If we finish awakening them, there won't be any need to worry. Trust me."

"What does that have to do with anything?" Cristoph looked warily upward as another shower of dust and pebbles pattered down. Spiderweb cracks extended out in jagged directions from the damaged ceiling tiles.

Fernando-Zairic thrust his arms into the goop and grabbed the submerged alien's torso. "Vincent, *trust me*. Help me lift Encix out."

Sure that the ceiling would collapse any moment, Vincent plunged his hands into the thick liquid. "You'd better be right about this." The two men lifted, helping the alien sit up in the slime-filled sarcophagus. The Xayan – Encix? – was quite heavy. Fluid dripped off the creature's head and upper body as it slowly returned to a state of awareness.

Fernando-Zairic hurried to a second container. "Quickly! Once they are conscious, they can sustain the vault with telemancy."

Flustered but hurrying, Cristoph and Nari hauled a third alien out of the liquid into the air, while Vincent and his friend rescued the fourth and last one. The four Xayan survivors moved their limbs with glacial slowness, weakly and phlegmatically.

"These others are Cippiq, Lodo, and Tryn." Fernando-Zairic glanced with sad, eerie eyes to the lone, dark sarcophagus. "Unfortunately, Allyf did not survive."

The Xayan survivor called Encix was the first to slide out of the sarcophagus and drop to the floor. Its caterpillar-like lower body moved with ripples of abdominal muscles. The other three Xayans emerged from their containers, rising tall and completely silent.

The ceiling crack widened, and more blocks shifted, loosened. Nari yelled and bolted for the tunnel opening.

Like a puppet show, the four awakened Xayans lifted their hands, revealing digits that were more like snail antennae than fingers.

Vincent heard a terrible noise overhead. He grabbed Fernando's arm. "Come on!"

Huge stones moved, and the roof of the cavern fell inward. But amazingly, the blocks and dust stopped in mid-air, frozen in place. Squiggly lights around them seemed to emanate from the four silent Xayans. The force field created a cushion that held the debris in place.

Vincent stared. Fernando just smiled. "I told you not to worry so much."

The revived Xayans continued to concentrate, and the displaced stones spun around and floated upward, where they returned to their places like puzzle pieces fitting together. The debris on the cavern floor also wafted up, like a video file being played backward. All the bits filled the crevices and finally a keystone slid perfectly into place. The ghostly light forms crackled and separated, leaving only a few dust motes in the air. The roof of the cavern was entirely intact.

Fernando-Zairic gave a satisfied nod to the alien called Encix, then regarded a stunned Nari, who had fallen to her knees in prayer. Finally he turned to Cristoph. "Your work crews will have sufficient time to reseal the ceiling. The repairs will hold for now. This vault is safe, and we can do our work."

Vincent shook his head. "You're right, I shouldn't worry so much." He still couldn't believe what had happened.

Fernando went to a niche in the stone walls, and with obvious reverence, removed a black statuette of a slug-like Xayan and carried it over to the dark sarcophagus that held the dead fifth alien. He somberly stood over the opening and immersed the statuette into the liquid around the body. "Allyf is dead. His spirit will be joined with the others who perished on this world."

With a wet whisper of movement, the four awakened Xayans slid closer, joining him and combining their silent energies. Their dark eyes spiraled slowly, hypnotically – and the limp body of the dead alien rose out of the gelatinous pool as if pulled by invisible strings. The dead form hovered in the air; the body was well preserved, but its eyes were dark, and its pale translucent skin reflected no light, in contrast to the others. The four living Xayans glided ahead to stand beside it, two on each side, using telekinetic power to hold their fallen companion aloft. Vincent thought they looked like pallbearers.

Fernando spoke aloud, in his own voice now. "Vincent, Cristoph – Zairic wants a few moments of privacy with his companions. Would all of you please return to the tunnel? It's some form of funeral ceremony, as I understand it. They've earned it, don't you think?"

Cristoph de Carre looked uneasy, but didn't argue. "They deserve that."

Fernando felt like a spectator in his own mind, watching and learning such an amazing flood of lost, alien knowledge. Zairic allowed him to observe, but Fernando wasn't sure how much he could understand, even with his alien companion's help.

Fernando had seen the fear and uncertainty on Vincent's face. His friend could not comprehend what he was witnessing, how these Originals were being awakened with their bodies and memories intact – a flash of unexpected hope after so much destruction. He wished he could communicate his own epiphany clearly. Maybe someday, if Vincent entered the slickwater pool himself, he would understand.

For now, Fernando had to remain a bystander in his own mind. He listened as the Zairic presence spoke to his newly awakened companions, exchanging mental concepts that were accompanied by dancing spirals and sparks of energy in the air.

The four Xayans expressed their grief over their companion's death. "Our dreams are smashed," said the one called Cippiq. "Allyf was with us for a reason. His ability to . . ."

Encix seemed to be the strongest, and had the most to say. Fernando realized that Encix and Tryn were both females of the species. "Allyf's specific abilities were like ours, though more refined," she said. "But all hope is not lost. We are alive, and perhaps there are still ways to resurrect our dream."

"We are alive," Lodo repeated; he seemed the most ponderous of the four. "But our abilities have been diminished by long disuse. With so few Xayan minds left, I do not know if – "

"No more of that!" Encix said. "You have not changed, Lodo. You always did complain too much."

Zairic pointed out, "The Xayan race remains, stored in the slickwater. We can awaken them, exactly as I have done here." He raised Fernando's human hands. "Our two species are compatible, and humans can learn much from our memories. The Xayans can live again, which will enable the humans to grow stronger as well. It is strange, but I believe both races will benefit greatly."

"First we must communicate with them," Encix said. "Convince them of what they – and we – must do. For *ala'ru.*"

As he witnessed and understood the conversation, Fernando knew they were referring to a remarkable evolutionary and spiritual ascension of the Xayan race – something they hoped to achieve. *Ala'ru.* He could feel his own excitement and Zairic's. The other presence inside him said, "We have the means to do so."

Together in the museum vault, the four Xayans fell silent. At the core of Fernando's mind, he felt a buzzing sensation. The lifeless body of Allyf sank back into its sarcophagus, submerged in the preservation fluid, and the clear lid closed.

"He will remain here," Encix said. "Until we need him."

The four original Xayans fell into line and followed Fernando-Zairic out of the deep chamber and up to the surface of their drastically changed world.

52

It was more than the General had dreamed of.

Preparing to receive the reawakened aliens at Elba, Adolphus felt more unsettled than he had before any battle. Over a secure channel, Cristoph de Carre had sent word about the remarkable discoveries within the mountain chamber, providing images of the shocking – revolting? – race that had originally inhabited this planet.

Even though he himself had funded the excavation project, the General hadn't allowed himself to believe entirely. Fernando Neron had been right after all.

Adolphus had been so preoccupied with the complex and converging plans for his stringline network and the possibility of independence for the entire Deep Zone, the alien relics had seemed a mere hobby ... something to dream about. But now, he expected a great many things were going to change about this planet and its place in human history.

With a last look at the strange artifacts he kept encased in vitrines in his study, the General stepped out onto the open front porch, anxious to hear the approach of the vehicle. The turquoise groundcover was in bloom, adding an unusual soapy smell to the air.

Adolphus had donned his formal military uniform – not that the Xayans would understand its meaning (unless, of course, they had learned those details from Fernando's memories). He turned to Sophie, who stood next to him, offering her silent strength. "Nothing in my career has prepared me for a first-hand meeting with aliens."

She squeezed his hand, and he was not quick to let go. "First off, stop thinking of them as 'aliens.' Hellhole is *their* world. They're the original inhabitants. We're the ones who came from outside."

A chill went up his spine. "And what if they want their planet back?"

"There are only four of them. I'm more worried about what happens when the Diadem finds out – she'll send a lot of people here to investigate."

"That's why we need to keep all this quiet until I understand it better myself. Luke Pritikin is already asking questions about the 'significant new discovery' he's heard about, and you know he's ready to report to Sonjeera."

"Pritikin was always a nosy one." She made a rude sound. Everybody in Helltown knew who worked for the Diadem. "He's a pain in the ass, but not too bright. How could he have found out already?"

"Probably bribed someone down at the survey office who had heard something, but didn't know anything worthwhile. I'm looking into the matter, but I'll keep any real information from him until I decide what to do. I've started several other absurd rumors in the meantime."

Sophie looked very concerned. "If Michella ever found out that you're hiding such important information from her official inspectors, the old bitch would – "

"I just gave him something else to chase after. He won't know the difference until it's too late."

"You distracted him? How?"

Adolphus shot her a wolfish smile, then let the anticipation build. "Our topographical prospectors have made some fascinating discoveries on their travels – red herrings that I hold in reserve for times such as these."

"Oh? Now you've got my attention."

"For instance, there's an exotic quartz forest growing out of the side of a canyon wall hundreds of kilometers northeast of here. It's spectacular-looking, but not worth anything. I let Pritikin believe *that* was the discovery he'd heard about, so he dashed off to see for himself." He leaned back, took a long breath of the fresh air. "We can't keep the slickwater pools out of the gossip web, but at least I can divert the Diadem's man, for the time being."

Sophie smiled, amused at the General's solution. Pritikin was a busy-body who took his job seriously, snooping around. There were other official and unofficial Constellation employees here on Hellhole, but Adolphus had such a tight-knit and loyal community in any position of influence, he could easily deflect anything potentially damaging. Like a shell game, he had transferred the more troublesome spies and inspectors off to remote mining operations factories, giving them just enough breadcrumbs to follow. Some of the more pliable ones turned their eyes the other way when given a worthwhile bribe. Sonjeera was far away.

"Soon enough," the General added in a low voice, "when the string-line network is done, nobody is going to be interested in a few alien ponds."

The dusty overland vehicle pulled up in front of Elba after a long, direct drive from the mountain excavations. It was late afternoon, and the lumpy ferns in the flowerbeds had started to hunker down for the evening. Adolphus stepped forward along the path, feeling anxiety mixed with anticipation.

When the Trakmaster's rear compartment opened, the four creatures that emerged were larger than he'd expected. Cristoph's transmitted images did not at all convey their eerie *strangeness*. The Xayans looked soft and pale, as if composed of cartilage and gelatin rather than bone and muscle. From the waist up, they looked humanoid, as Cristoph had said, with a torso and a pair of rubbery arms, a smooth head, large eyes, and membrane over what should have been the mouth. Below the waist, though, their vermiform bodies scuttled forward on rows of stubby caterpillar legs.

Adolphus was so engrossed by their appearance that he didn't at first acknowledge the three men climbing out of the cab. Standing like a bridge between the two races, Fernando-Zairic extended his arms. "This is a great moment for humans and Xayans. I have told my original companions about you, General Tiber Maximilian Adolphus, and they now understand a great deal ... about us." His voice modulated back and forth, occasionally allowing glimmers of Fernando's bright, fast-talking human personality.

The four original Xayans skirted the lush patch of native ground-cover and glided forward to the porch of the residence. Adolphus noted slight differences in body build or coloration among the four, spotted patterns on the gelatin that formed their skin.

The foremost creature spoke in a thrumming voice from the mouth membrane. "I am Encix, one of the leaders of Xaya. I understand that we are the only Originals to have survived the asteroid impact."

Fernando-Zairic took a step closer. "Encix was my ... equivalent during the last days of our civilization. She helmed the preservation bunker project, while I oversaw the dissolution and storage of our race into the slickwater matrix."

General Adolphus remained alert for subtleties in the conversation, but the alien emotions remained unreadable. He couldn't determine if Zairic was implying that he and Encix were partners or rivals with two competing yet desperate schemes.

Cristoph de Carre cleared his throat. "General, thank you again for your faith in selecting me for this amazing project. We've only scratched the surface of what's in the museum bunker. You might want to assign a large investigation team, and ... I'd like to volunteer my services to supervise, if I may."

Adolphus considered. "We'll discuss that after I've had time to read your full report, Mr de Carre. I don't want to send an army down there, and I hope the Xayans are willing to help us by providing explanations about their culture, science, and history – and advice?" He looked at the strange aliens.

"Our races have much to learn about each other," Encix said. "And we can only learn by sharing what we know."

When Adolphus spoke, he wondered if these creatures were accustomed to hearing speeches. "This is a landmark event, and I very much look forward to learning more about your race and the original civilization here on this planet. Would you like to come inside my home?"

The four Xayans extended their "hands" to one another, touching soft antennae-like fingertips as if to communicate. When they were finished, Encix withdrew and spoke for the four Originals. "Though this planet has been gravely wounded, it is still our home. We have been entombed for centuries. We would prefer to stay here under the open skies."

"Very well, we'll talk out here." Adolphus sat on the porch step, and Sophie joined him. He had hoped to show these strange visitors his artifacts on display, to ask them to identify and explain the objects. Some other time, he decided. He needn't worry about the artifacts when he had the actual aliens.

One of the companion Xayans – Cippiq – bowed, bending over from the waist in a fluid motion like a fern furling, before he straightened. "We offer ourselves as ambassadors from the archives of history."

From the corner of his eye, the General glimpsed curious household staff members staring through the windows at the strange Xayans. Craig Jordan had taken extensive security precautions and stationed unseen snipers in the gables in case the aliens should·prove hostile.

Lieutenant Spencer, looking nervous, emerged from the front door carrying a tray of synthesized iced tea for the humans. Sophie politely inquired of the aliens, "Are there refreshments we could offer you? We don't know your physical needs."

The four Originals moved from the walkway onto the thick, spongy ground cover. "You have provided all we need," Encix said. "Thank you."

The Xayans moved along the vegetation, their small caterpillar legs flexing and thrumming as they dragged their low bellies over the native plants. From underneath their soft abdomens, absorbent membranes crushed, processed, and absorbed the turquoise groundcover. The four aliens seemed to appreciate the feast; wet, gurgling sounds accompanied the digestion as they moved along, leaving swaths of consumed vegetation in their wake.

Adolphus found it strange and unsettling.

"It's the way they eat," Fernando-Zairic said. "But we will now nourish ourselves with a meeting of the minds, to discuss our changed situation."

The General tried to maintain a businesslike demeanor, but he felt like an excited boy. He had been fascinated by the aliens for so long. "In all of the Constellation, you are the first intelligent alien race we have encountered, and I am honored to welcome you." His voice grew husky. "When we began to colonize this world, we discovered a few remnants of your civilization, but we believed all inhabitants had been wiped out in the asteroid strike. I am, personally, relieved and delighted to see that something of your civilization has survived."

"And you've barely seen anything yet," said Fernando, smiling brightly.

Despite his excitement, Adolphus didn't know how long he could keep the Xayan presence secret from the Constellation. With only a few months until D-Day, he could not afford to let the Diadem grow too curious about Hallholme. The last thing he wanted was a flood of scientists and politicians from the Crown Jewels.

The General sipped his tart iced tea to give himself time to contemplate, then raised the issue that had been bothering him. "After a decade and a half of difficult labor, we humans have established a colony here, a home, so I hope that you don't want us to surrender the world and leave."

Acting as spokesperson, Encix said, "We do not begrudge your presence here. We four are all that remain of our race. Biologically speaking, it would take us centuries to repopulate the planet, if that were even possible – but that is not our goal. So you see, we Originals pose no threat to the continued human presence on Xaya. This planet is not important to us – our *race* is important. We will gladly relinquish it to you ... provided you help us."

Adolphus was surprised to hear this. Their race was practically wiped out, their whole planet devastated. "How can we help?"

"Not everything was lost." Fernando-Zairic drew upon the earnest emotions of his human personality. "It can return. Thanks to the slickwater, the Xayans can reawaken. Zairic's memories now live alongside Fernando Neron's. Through immersion in the pools, more people could bring back our friends, our comrades, our greatest minds. Together, humans and Xayans can be the best of both races – an incredible symbiosis. We want you to encourage your entire population to join us."

When Encix spoke, her voice throbbed with intensity. "That is what we need most, General Adolphus. With your help and with the slickwater the Xayan race is not lost after all."

53

Though he had buried the spy's report about Ian Walfor's off-grid activities, Territorial Governor Goler did not expect the information to remain secret for long. The Constellation had many eyes and ears, even in the Deep Zone.

When the Diadem's demand arrived at Ridgetop, her stern summons was intended to make Goler tuck his tail between his legs and lower his head in shame. "Governor, present yourself on Sonjeera with all due haste, so that you may personally explain these rumors of an illegal black-market transportation network. I suspect General Adolphus is behind it."

In a way, he was relieved that she had found out so quickly. Goler thought that Michella was being obtuse if she believed such things weren't going to happen so far from the central government.

He'd already sent discreet overtures to Buktu, dispatching message drones along the spotty and discontinued stringline to that isolated planet, hoping that at least one of them would get through. He had written the messages to sound like indignant demands for explanations in the name of the Diadem, but worded them carefully, leaving doors open. He had hoped Walfor could read between the lines.

Indeed, the Buktu administrator had picked up on the cues and responded with a subtle, guarded offer of a substantial bribe if the

Territorial Governor would turn a blind eye to his commercial activities. Since Goler hadn't yet responded, or even decided, he could tell the Diadem honestly that he had no arrangement with Walfor.

The next stringline ship would arrive in two days. He asked Tasmine to help him pack for a trip to the capital. "I'll need my best clothes for a meeting with the Diadem herself."

Tasmine grimaced. "Do us all a favor and spit in her face."

Sonjeera was breathtaking, bombastic, and exaggerated in all luxuries. Goler had once loved the nexus of government, but he no longer felt he belonged there. He rarely spent time at his office in the capital.

After his years on Ridgetop, he preferred the immense yet personal goldenwood groves, the elbowroom of open skies. The cultural options on Sonjeera, the performances, restaurants, and museums were simply too much, more than anyone required. Had he filtered it all out before? He did not regret maintaining his residence on Ridgetop rather than moving into government-provided apartments here.

His passenger pod landed at night, when the capital city's lights made his eyes hurt. The sky never got darker than misty gray, and he spotted only a handful of stars. No wonder people in the Crown Jewels failed to think beyond their own petty needs: their night skies formed a cataract over their eyes, and they literally couldn't see the rest of the universe.

Back on Ridgetop, the deep night was so full of stars that sometimes he felt he could just fall upward into the pitch-black emptiness . . .

Michella's escorts met him at the spaceport. "The Diadem has prepared the Luminous Garden for your meeting. You will have all the privacy you require there."

He wasn't aware that they needed privacy. "I'm honored that the Diadem would change her schedule to meet me so quickly." She wasn't even allowing him time to refresh himself or stop at his office in the Bureau of Deep Zone Affairs.

The escorts whisked him into the towering palace that, with its gardens and arboreta, covered as much total acreage as all the settled land on Ridgetop. Fountains sprayed rooster tails of mist into the air, making each breath damp and cool.

The men hurried him along curved flagstone pathways – never a straight line – around clumps of spiky foliage and flowers whose petals clacked together like laughing mouths. Two adjacent alabaster benches sat in a grove of huge drooping voja trees. The boughs were covered with phosphorescent insects, shining with thousands of tiny lights that flickered on and off.

Diadem Michella sat on one of the benches and gestured for him to take the other one. "Sit, Governor Goler. I am not pleased with your performance of late." With a flick of her hands, she sent the escorts away.

He bowed respectfully and sat. The Diadem did not bother with chitchat. She already had her speech prepared. "When I gave you responsibility for eleven planets in the Deep Zone, I expected you to be watching out for the Constellation's interests – *my* interests."

Goler maintained a quiet, cooperative tone. "I've done my best, Eminence."

"I feared as much." When she pressed her lips together, her face looked like a fruit from which all the juice had been squeezed. "We spend much of the Constellation's treasury administering the Sonjeera transportation hub. We monitor and maintain direct stringlines to every one of the Deep Zone planets – at no small expense. Even with regular tribute payments from the frontier worlds, that expanded network will not pay for itself for more than a century. Do you think I can allow a few upstart entrepreneurs to fly their own ships and bypass the whole system? Legitimate Constellation vessels are sufficient to haul all cargo that is needed."

"Majesty, I have investigated the matter, at your request. These non-stringline vessels – and there are only a few – are antique and unreliable ships that the people on Buktu repaired and refueled. As you recall, once the Constellation decommissioned their stringline, that planet lost its reliable connection to Sonjeera. Flying those ships is their only option for survival."

"Their option was to accept relocation! Before the Buktu stringline was vacated, every one of those settlers had the opportunity to go elsewhere, but they refused." She smiled with some satisfaction.

"Eminence, the Deezees do tend to be independent."

Michella's expression soured at the very word. "I offered them a solution. They should have taken it. Are you suggesting I just ignore their criminal activities?"

Overhead, several of the luminous insects flitted off, like shooting stars. He drew a deep breath, spoke calmly. "They have access to only a few old and extremely slow ships. Surely the amount of commerce they can take from the Constellation is insignificant."

"It is not the amount, it is the principle. Administrator Walfor has established a precedent. What if other people invest in independent ships? What might other planetary leaders do behind my back? My stringline network is a perfectly acceptable, efficient, and inexpensive means of commerce. Why won't they use it?"

Goler didn't point out that *bypassing* the Diadem – rubbing her face in it – was what made the idea so attractive to men like Ian Walfor. She didn't understand the Deezee mindset.

Michella leaned forward on her alabaster bench. "I called you here in person to make sure you understand how important this matter is. Stop these black-marketeers immediately. I expect you to do your job, Governor Goler. Kill them, put them in prison – I don't care what you do, just stop them. You spend all your time out there among those people. Don't let them make you look like a fool."

The stone bench felt hard and cold beneath him. When the voja trees waved languidly in a stray breeze, the motion agitated the remaining insects, making them brighten their bioluminescence. Goler looked back at Michella's expectant face. "I understand your concern, Eminence, but how am I to accomplish what you ask, given the resources I have?"

"By watching out for illegal trade, of course," she said, like an impatient mother to a foolish child.

Goler counted to three before responding, his hands spread in feigned helplessness. "Unlike other territorial governors, Eminence, I live out in the Deep Zone and watch the people as closely as I can. But how I am to monitor such a huge volume of empty space for vessels that do not travel on stringline paths? I have no ships, no police force." She didn't seem to understand how vast the Deep Zone was, compared with her tightly clustered core of Crown Jewel planets. "How am I to patrol even Ridgetop, let alone all eleven planets under my jurisdiction?"

He paused. It was time to offer her the solution before she became angrier at him. "Perhaps, Eminence, if you were to provide me with armed ships, even outdated FTL ones, I could patrol and intercept the illegal spacecraft that operate outside the bounds of the stringline network. Fight fire with fire."

The Diadem recoiled. "You want your own personal fleet?"

"I see no way to watch over such a large territory without meaningful military resources. I believe the Army of the Constellation has a surplus of FTL vessels from the war years, which are just sitting in the Lubis Plain shipyards. I could take those vessels off your hands and conscript my own crews from the Deep Zone planets. The Constellation will incur no additional expenses, nor will it need to provide personnel. Lord Riomini should be well satisfied with the plan, since it takes the burden of those vessels out of his shipyards." Goler looked up at her. "And that would allow me to find and shut down any black-market operations."

Michella considered his suggestion. "Now that you mention the rebellion, we do have all those ships we captured from General Adolphus. They've been decommissioned, but even maintaining mothballed ships isn't free. A waste of space and resources. The Black Lord often complains about it."

Goler waited, confident of the conclusion she would draw. The Diadem's lips formed a brittle, vengeful smile. "And there's a certain satisfying irony in recommissioning the General's own ships to patrol the Deep Zone and stop him from doing any further mischief. Yes, Governor, I'll have them refitted, refueled, then mounted on an expanded stringline hauler to be shipped out to Ridgetop. It shifts those expenses out of my pocket, into yours."

Goler nodded respectfully. "I am honored by your generosity, Eminence. The sooner you send them to me, the sooner I can commence patrols against the black marketeers."

"I can't work miracles, Governor, but I will dispatch a message to Qiorfu and tell Escobar Hallholme to prepare the ships for immediate dispatch." She waved a bony finger at him. "But this is your responsibility from now on. I place it squarely on your shoulders. Don't let me down."

Goler bowed again. "I am always honored to serve, Eminence."

54

Since the four Xayan Originals did not eat prepared food but grazed by rolling their caterpillar-like bodies across native vegetation, Sophie Vence's private "dinner party" was more of a cordial reception to welcome the awakened aliens – under the strictest security.

Adolphus had invited only a dozen of his most trusted associates to the function – primarily exiled veterans of the rebellion, none of whom owed any allegiance to the Crown Jewels, and he chose a late hour, when most curious observers were fast asleep. Since he did not yet want to reveal the existence of the Xayans to the Diadem, he swore the guests to absolute secrecy; these were people on whom he had earlier trusted his life. Sooner or later, Sophie knew that word would leak out, but not tonight – she hoped.

In the greenhouse, oddly geometric tables were arranged around the large conservatory with parallel spaces between them, like pieces of a puzzle in a child's game. Smiling, Sophie sat at the head of a hexagonal table next to General Adolphus. Devon and Antonia took adjacent seats; the two of them had become inseparable since their ordeal at the devastated camp of the Children of Amadin.

Acting as an intermediary, quietly answering Sophie's awkward but pragmatic questions about Xayan bodily functions, Fernando-Zairic ushered the four Xayans into her main greenhouse in Michella Town, after escorting them there in a covered vehicle. Hours after midnight, no one out in the Helltown streets noted their arrival.

Encix, Cippiq, Lodo, and Tryn entered to a rush of gasps from the twelve humans in attendance. The smallest of the Xayan guests, Tryn, said through her vibrating mouth membrane, "You seem as exotic to us as we must seem to you. Humans fascinate us, how you speak and eat, how you interact."

The four Originals and Fernando-Zairic circulated among the amazed attendees. Sophie and the General followed them, as hosts, listening to the questions and answers.

Cippiq said, "Over the course of Xayan history, we considered other civilizations abroad in the galaxy, and our observers even noted evidence from distant stars. However, rather than traveling far from our world, as you have done, our race turned its development inward, focused on our minds and souls instead of exploring unknown solar systems."

"We are fortunate that humans ventured to new worlds," Fernando-Zairic said brightly. "Otherwise, we might never have been recovered from the slickwater."

Encix sounded defensive. "We could have traveled to other planets if we had chosen to do so, but we did not need to explore outward. Our achievements were limited only by the power of our imaginations – and Xayan imagination had no limits. We could accomplish anything we could conceive. Xayan telemancers could speed across the surface of our planet and rise hundreds of meters into the air, borne by the collective power of our minds."

The General listened with great interest. "We'd all like to learn more about telemancy. It seems a very useful skill."

Fernando-Zairic seemed utterly beatific next to his four Xayan comrades. "We are happy to share our knowledge and skills with you. You have helped to awaken our lost race." He smiled. "Our demonstration at the museum vault was a necessity without artistic merit. This evening, we would like to show you our artistry."

The General raised his voice to address the human audience. "Our guests have prepared an entertainment to showcase their abilities. I assure you there is no danger."

With a smattering of applause, the audience talked excitedly.

Intrigued, Devon and Antonia glanced at each other. The four Xayans, with Fernando-Zairic among them, stood in complete silence, concentrating. Then all the tables and chairs in the conservatory floated smoothly and gently into the air, carrying observers along with their food and drink toward the top of the dome. When one startled man dropped his glass of Sophie's Cabernet, it hung in place, without spilling.

Delight and surprise passed through the people like an indrawn breath. Seated at the main table next to Sophie, unperturbed to be floating twenty meters above the floor, the General nodded with amused appreciation. Devon was laughing out loud.

Concentrating in a group below, still on the floor, the Xayans made no sound.

While the levitated chairs pulled back, the variously shaped tables spun around and the chairs rearranged the guests at different tables, slowly orbiting. It reminded Sophie of an orrery she had seen, a mechanical model of planets, moons, and stars that shifted around like cosmic clockwork.

After one complete cycle, the tables, chairs, and people returned to their starting positions and settled back down to the floor with barely a vibration. Relieved and thrilled, the audience applauded again.

Encix spoke in a flat tone. "That was a simple trick to amuse you. We can do much more with telemancy."

Adolphus cautioned, "Maybe we've seen enough for now, Encix."

Ignoring him, the Originals turned their large eyes up to the transparent greenhouse dome overhead. An uneasy flicker crossed the normally placid face of Fernando-Zairic, but he joined them nevertheless.

Suddenly the plates of glass in the segmented dome shattered into pieces that began to rain down on the audience, like glittering diamond knives. The General pushed Sophie to shelter beneath her table. People screamed. Some tried to run.

But in mid-air the transparent fragments hung and swirled, then coalesced into amazing, sharp-edged crystalline sculptures, like a blizzard of enormous snowflakes that whizzed about above each table. Breezes from outside whistled through the gaps in the dome. With only the subtlest gesture from Encix, the snowflake sculptures broke apart, separated into tiny pieces, and flew upwards to form sheets of glass again that fitted exactly into place, as if nothing had happened. Not even a crack showed.

"Telemancy has many uses," the alien said.

General Adolphus helped Sophie up, and wheels began turning in her mind. At first, she'd thought the Xayans displayed nothing more than interesting telekinetic quirks, but now she saw the true potential in their abilities. "I'll bet you wish you'd had a few telemancers during your rebellion, Tiber."

"This does pose interesting defensive possibilities," he said in a quiet voice.

Fernando-Zairic stepped forward as the uneasy audience began to recover. "Simple parlor tricks. We hope you find them entertaining."

But even now the strange aliens weren't finished with their exhibition.

"We four were chosen for preservation in the vault because of our exceptional powers," Encix said. "Many of the lives stored in the slickwater are also strong telemancers. If more humans were to resurrect Xayan memories, our potential would increase exponentially."

"One more demonstration tonight," said the one named Cippiq. "We have only just begun."

Some of the audience members tittered nervously. Shattering all the greenhouse panes had provided a terrifying thrill, but they weren't necessarily ready for more.

The original aliens touched soft fingertips to one another, as if intending to fuse their flesh. Fernando-Zairic also stood among them, eyes closed. Sophie couldn't read the expressions on the gelatinous faces of the originals. She whispered to the General, "I know they want to show off, Tiber, but they'd better not wreck my crops in the greenhouse."

"I'm not sure if I like this unexpected demonstration, either." He turned to the joined aliens, raised his voice. "I think you've shown us enough for one evening."

The Xayans ignored him.

The ground began to shake, like dry ripples in a pond beneath the dome. The tables and chairs slid. Bottles of Sophie's wine tipped over and fell to the ground. Several people were knocked off their seats.

With a great wrenching lurch that nearly threw Sophie and the

General to the floor, the large greenhouse dome and a chunk of surrounding soil ripped itself out of the ground, uprooted like a tree blown
over in a furious gale. Beside her, Adolphus braced his feet, as if he were
on the deck of his flagship in one of the battles of the rebellion.

The Xayans didn't move, didn't flinch. As the excavated greenhouse
rose even higher, the telemancers stabilized the upward movement, and
the trembling beneath the floor stopped. The dome hovered in midair,
like an island torn from the sea.

Amazed spectators got to their feet, some whispering nervously as
they rushed to the reassembled window segments. Looking down at the
scattered lights of Michella Town, the General could make out the
gaping crater that once held the greenhouse.

The anxious crowd looked to him for reassurance, and the General
stood firm and faced the Xayans. "All right, you've made your point.
We're impressed. Now please return us to the ground."

Fernando-Zairic opened his eyes. "I assure you, General – I assure you
all: we don't mean to intimidate or frighten you." His placid expression
changed to a grin, revealing a flash of the old Fernando. "You have to
admit, it's damned impressive. Don't worry, we can put the dome back,
just like we restored the shattered crystal panes."

The Zairic portion of his personality didn't seem to comprehend
the reason for such consternation, but Fernando explained, and all the
Xayans understood.

Encix bowed her supple neck. "Very well. Enough." The greenhouse
dome rotated in the sky to give everyone a perfect view of the town
lights.

Sophie squeezed the General's hand tightly and whispered with wry
disappointment, "So much for keeping this a secret."

"I'm not so sure. We've identified most, if not all, of the Diadem's
spies – I can watch them, spread around a few bribes if I need to. Who
would believe a report about this?"

"I'm more concerned about the Xayans. Do you trust them?"

Adolphus pondered a moment. "Let's see what they do."

As promised, the greenhouse dome settled back to the ground, rotating until it fit perfectly into the crater. The people let out a collective
sigh of relief, and Adolphus gave the Xayans a stiff smile. "Thank you."

The Originals released their hold upon each other, detaching their fingertips. Fernando-Zairic stepped away from them and beamed at the crowd. "Now you see why I'm so excited by the possibilities! Not only do I have all these amazing memories of an ancient civilization, I have new abilities too – and Zairic's only begun to teach me how to stretch my mental skills."

Fernando-Zairic gave a formal bow, and the four Xayans did the same, bending their soft bodies with exceptional flexibility. "We wanted to show you the powers we have, and the advantages of becoming one of us." He raised his voice. "As many of you know, I was just a human before, a regular colonist with little to show for my life. When I accidentally immersed myself in the slickwater, I became something much more significant, far beyond a simple man."

He looked around the gathered people, saw that he had their full attention. "The sentient pools wait for all of you. Countless Xayan lives are stored there, just waiting for someone to accept them. You could all have the skills we demonstrated here tonight. Imagine accepting an exciting and mysterious alien life as part of your own memories. Humans and Xayans in perfect synergy, an alliance of tremendous potential. It's a win-win situation."

"You want us to jump into those pools and . . . become aliens?" asked Devon. "Why would anyone want to do that?"

"Think about it, young man. Most of the people on this planet came here because they had nowhere else to go. This is an opportunity to be part of something wondrous. There are no drawbacks. You would remain human in appearance, like me." Fernando's voice was reverent now. "I'm still here . . . but I've got a second life, too. Another set of memories from an amazing time and place." Grinning, he turned toward Sophie. "Sophie Vence, you could establish a camp there, provide a place to stay for the curious, make the experience comforting. I promise you, people would come there."

She chuckled uncertainly. "A health spa out at Slickwater Springs?" She meant it as a joke to point out the absurdity of the idea.

But Fernando-Zairic gave an earnest nod. "An apt comparison – immersion and sharing would have amazing restorative effects for the human body. Volunteers and curiosity seekers would come and prepare to immerse themselves in the slickwater. You would provide a great service."

Considering what she had witnessed, Sophie realized that Xayan telemancy might give the General an unexpected edge against the forces of the Constellation. When the Diadem tried to crack down on his plans – and she certainly would – Michella wouldn't have any defenses against alien powers. The old bitch would certainly not expect to encounter a surprise like that.

Adolphus said finally, "This does bear further consideration. Xayan knowledge could benefit us all." Sophie could hear the ambiguity in his voice, and she understood what he was thinking. After the demonstration of such powers, he would already be calculating the advantages of an alliance with these aliens.

Sophie folded her hands together on the table in front of her, considering the pragmatic aspects. "You really think people would be willing to take on an alien . . . hitchhiker? Who would sign up for that duty?" As she said it, Sophie was sure that some of the General's loyal veterans would volunteer if he asked them to.

Antonia Anqui, though, gave a much more straightforward answer. "Anyone who doesn't like their dreary lives – in other words, most people on Hellhole."

"And to possess those telemancy powers . . ." someone else mused.

"Sounds like a scam to me," said an elderly businesswoman. Several people laughed nervously.

"I'm certainly familiar with scams – but this isn't one," Fernando said, in his own voice now. "When a few others take on Xayan memories, maybe they'll be better able to explain how wonderful it is."

Cippiq glided forward in a smooth, eerie motion. "Any person immersed in the slickwater will possess the lost memories and lives of great Xayan philosophers, leaders, dreamers. Isn't that reason enough? And some of you will become telemancers in your own right."

Encix added with an edge in her voice, "This is our world, General Tiber Adolphus. All we ask is that you give us this opportunity."

Sophie looked at Adolphus for guidance. The General seemed concerned, deep in thought. "I know there are other pools on the planet, so I can't prevent anyone from finding a reservoir. I'd rather do this right. Best if we proceed with caution, monitor and control, as the Xayans suggest. Establish an outpost by the slickwater pools, start out small." He looked at her. "We all know you're the person best suited for the job, Sophie."

She considered the idea. "I can set up the camp, and we'll see who comes." With a look at Fernando-Zairic and the four Originals, she added, "I'm certain we'll have curiosity seekers, but I can't promise you'll have any takers."

"Oh, we will have sufficient volunteers," Zairic said in his distant alien voice. "You may be surprised."

55

The nosy Constellation prospector, Luke Pritikin, remained oblivious to the fact that he had been sent off on a fool's errand. Following the (intentionally uncertain) coordinates the General had provided, Pritikin wandered the wilderness landscape for weeks until he stumbled upon the sheer-walled canyon bursting with large quartz crystals. It was a dazzling natural landmark, and the Diadem's man was quite impressed.

Back at Elba, Adolphus received a happy message from Pritikin. "I've found it, Administrator – and you are quite right. This is a remarkable area with exotic beauty, though I'm not convinced of its value to the Constellation." The inspector transmitted numerous images of tall crystals that protruded in wildly angled clusters, like fistfuls of transparent needles.

"Maybe the beauty is a value in itself," the General offered, leaning closer to the video screen.

The Constellation inspector sounded dubious. "I'll recommend it as a possible tourism opportunity, but it'll be a hard sell. People don't think of scenery when they think of Hellhole."

Adolphus smiled congenially. "I can only offer what the planet offers, Mr Pritikin. I didn't choose this place for myself." The man was innocuous, though annoying at times. At least he had been away from

Michella Town during the reception for the Original Xayans, and so far the secret had been kept.

Sophie had already departed with work crews and supplies to establish a rough camp out at the place she had named Slickwater Springs. Adolphus made her promise (without too much difficulty) that she would never enter the alien liquid herself. With a warm chuckle, Sophie had put her arms around his neck and kissed him. "Oh Tiber, my life isn't so bleak or boring that I'd want to take on another, no matter how exotic it might seem. But for a lot of people here on Hellhole, I can't say the same. Zairic's assessment may be right. We could get a lot of volunteers."

In the meantime, the General was intrigued by what the alien memories could offer him for the defense of Hellhole. The mental powers they had demonstrated were impressive, and entirely unexpected. The strange lost race was a resource the Diadem could not even imagine. A very nice surprise.

And so far, Michella's spies had no idea what was happening.

"Have a safe trip back, Mr Pritikin," Adolphus said before signing off. "Take your time."

With Sophie and Fernando-Zairic out at the pools, General Adolphus took the time to meet alone with Encix in an isolated agricultural area outside of Michella Town. The other three Originals had returned with Cristoph de Carre to their museum vault in the mountain to help excavate the lost treasures that had been sealed there for centuries. Before the female leader of the survivors also retreated to the deep redoubt, he wanted a private conversation with her, one not filtered through the perspective of Fernando-Zairic.

The Xayan civilization beckoned to the General. He had always wanted to know more about the mysterious relics, though now his proud collection seemed laughably insignificant. More importantly, considering the risky plan for his own stringline network and independence from the Constellation, the alien telemancy – and the possibility of granting the same powers to human "partners" – offered a new defensive edge he hadn't counted on.

So long as he could keep these aliens secret from Diadem Michella.

Encix joined him at the edge of a lush green wheat field, and the two of them walked a perimeter path that had been pounded down by the treads of farming machinery. Adolphus had chosen this place for its remoteness, and his security people had already swept the area to make certain no one else was around.

Encix glided alongside him on her caterpillar-like pad, her abdominal muscles rippling to propel her without disturbing the ground. Adolphus was surprised at how easily he had come to accept her intelligence and personality; the novelty of her bizarre appearance had worn off quickly.

He touched a stiff wheat stalk, feeling the plumpness of the grain as it matured. Encix extruded long fingers from the ends of her hands and imitated him, also touching the wheat. "Your vegetation survives well here," she noted.

"This species of grain has been modified for rapid growth and quick harvesting. It's necessary in this environment because so many bad things happen – storms, dust clouds, static discharges, native blights. We have to plant and harvest in a hit-and-run fashion. We load our grain silos as quickly as we can before some disaster occurs." He did not feel the need to tell her about the dozens of similar fields scattered around various settlements, nor complete details of the colony's food production. "Your planet is a hard one to settle."

Encix paused and tilted back her torso as if to absorb sunlight from the tinted sky. "This is no longer our planet, General Adolphus. Our beloved Xaya died when the asteroid struck. *This* is only a scar." She moved ahead in eerie silence. A breeze picked up like an invisible hand brushing through the wheat stalks. "We once had a thick carpet of feeding fields that we used to nourish ourselves. Xayans did not have to fight for food. Our landscape was conducive to luxurious consumption. It allowed us to develop our minds."

When Adolphus inquired about the large predator that Fernando had seen out in the badlands, Encix brushed it aside. "There were, of course, hazards on Xaya. A race grows strong through its challenges."

The General laughed without humor. "Then humans will certainly grow strong here – if given the chance."

"Zairic speaks of your race with great optimism. He says humans have tremendous potential. Once the Xayan race reawakens to full power, we can all have hope again. We will achieve what we were destined to do – what the asteroid impact thwarted during our most crucial generation."

"And what destiny is that?"

Encix hesitated. "I honor you by revealing this. Over millennia, our race developed its mental abilities. In the last years before the impact, Zairic's bold teachings brought us to the verge of a remarkable evolutionary breakthrough. He showed us that if all Xayans united their mental proficiencies, merging their minds and souls, we could initiate an extraordinary evolutionary ascension. A physical and spiritual transformation that we call *ala'ru*."

Adolphus raised his eyebrows. Some kind of alien mysticism? "What does that mean, exactly?"

"It is . . . *ala'ru*." Encix turned her soft, pale face toward him, and her features moved, mimicking an expression of sincerity as best she could. "Our bodies, our race, sheds its physical form and becomes pure thought, pure energy. Like a larva metamorphosing into an entirely different adult. Do you understand?"

"We know of creatures that transform in stages like that."

"We could have elevated our whole race to another plane, evolved and left this universe behind. We had nearly reached that point." She paused for a long moment. "But a falling asteroid ruined our hopes."

"But if you were that powerful, couldn't you use telemancy to deflect it? Weren't there enough of you?"

The alien leader thrummed in consternation, as if she had been insulted. "We had significant power, but moving the large asteroid was beyond our abilities."

Adolphus pressed his lips together. "And now only four of you remain."

"It is more than just the four of us – millions of Xayan lives are contained within the slickwater pools. If enough humans bring back those stored personalities, we can achieve a similar racial ascension, an *ala'ru*. That is how you can help us. And it would give our human partners the powers of telemancy as well."

Adolphus shook his head. "We have fewer than a hundred thousand colonists on this whole planet. The numbers won't add up, even if every person on Hallholme accepts your offer."

"But billions of your race are scattered across the star systems. Tell them our plight. Call them here to help us. Can you not help us spread the word?"

"I guarantee you that won't happen," Adolphus said frankly. "Some may be intrigued by the opportunity, but you'll never achieve the numbers you need for critical mass."

Encix did not seem discouraged. "Fortunately, Zairic tells me that when our two races join, they exhibit a kind of ..." She paused, searching through what she had learned. "Hybrid vigor. Humans and Xayans are much more powerful as partners than we are as individuals. Therefore, *ala'ru* will require far fewer proficient Xayan telemancers to achieve the level necessary."

Now Adolphus understood. "So that's why you're encouraging humans to use the slickwater. That's what you really want."

Encix moved along with her rolling caterpillar gait, circling the wheat field. "There is nothing insidious about it. We only want to be *remembered*, General Adolphus. My four companions and I were placed in the preservation bunker so that we could eventually show an outside race – your race – how to access our information. And if we can gather enough Xayan mental power to trigger *ala'ru*, our race will transform to lead an incorporeal existence, leaving your people to run the planet. That is what we want – and what you want."

Adolphus pondered, weighing the options. If the earlier demonstration at the greenhouse dome was any indication, he needed those telemancers. Once the unified DZ worlds survived the aftermath of D-Day, once he and all the newly independent colony worlds stood up to the uproar from Sonjeera, then the Original Xayans and their converts could do whatever they liked.

"I will consider it," he said. "But in the meantime, for security reasons, I would prefer that you remain out of sight. Could you possibly return to the underground vault for the time being? There are political ramifications I will need to address." He could make excuses for the camp out at the slickwater pools, and the converts like Fernando-Zairic could easily be excused as yet another oddball religious group come to Hellhole. But he couldn't explain away an actual caterpillar-like alien wandering through the streets of Michella Town.

"If that is your wish," Encix said. "My companions and I have much restoration work to do back in our preservation bunker. That is where we feel most comfortable." She paused. "Besides, we Originals were not part of Zairic's slickwater preservation plan. It does not concern us."

The General felt both relieved and troubled.

When they finished their circuit of the field, Encix stopped. "I was sincere when I told you we have no intention of reclaiming this world, General Tiber Adolphus. Xaya is of little consequence to us. It served as a storage vault for our racial memories, and now it will become our launching pad. That is all. Once we have ascended, everything that remains will be yours."

56

A long day of Council meetings wrapped up, during which time Ishop Heer hovered near the Diadem to offer his advice or to be available should she need him to discreetly attend to "unofficial" matters. At the end of the sessions, a smiling Michella handed him an envelope that contained an address and an electronic key. "Congratulations, Mr Heer. Your assistant is already supervising the transfer of your belongings."

"The transfer . . . ?"

Michella smiled to let him know he wasn't in trouble. "A little reward for your work and your loyalty to me – a more prestigious domicile."

Ishop actually liked his nondescript apartment in the government quarter for the anonymity it afforded, but he could not decline the Diadem's gift. He would rather that she recognized him as a lord of significant stature, but that would come later. "Thank you, Eminence."

Soon enough he would have a noble residence. *That* was a reward worth having. This would be just an interim step along the way, and he would be gracious to the Diadem; no need to make her ponder anything else until he had checked off the other items on his list.

When he arrived at the new address after nightfall, Ishop found a two-story traditional redstone structure set among similar buildings scattered around an expanse of manicured lawns and flower gardens. Always alert, he noted that each unit had hedges and other plants artfully set up to create privacy. *Good.* Ancient ivy, wisteria, and other plants climbed the walls. *Cozy.*

Ishop watched four men carrying his furniture and household goods into the new townhouse. All the lights were on inside and out. Laderna Nell waved to him from the second-level patio, before coming down to meet him on the lawn, carrying a file folder under one arm. All business, that one ... at least when other people could see.

She said with a conspiratorial smile, "Now you are closer to the importance and life you deserve, boss."

"Not close enough. We still have more work to do."

"One item at a time."

Laderna led him inside, and he noted immediately – with a great deal of relief – that it was immaculately clean. He suspected Laderna's hand in that. Though not technically a "royal unit" with a large serving staff and other amenities, the townhouse was still quite elegant, and located in one of the best neighborhoods in Council City.

"This place has an interesting history, in a district that *used to be* reserved for nobles," she explained, revealing how much she had already researched the address just since that afternoon. "Edwond the First, the Warrior Diadem, held his war cabinet meetings here. The plaque by the door designates this as 'Edwond House.' How marvelous to think of him making huge military decisions here, away from the prying eyes of people he didn't trust."

"How long ago?"

"Ninety-one years," Laderna said. "Time to make it a noble residence again."

"Soon enough," he whispered, reminding himself as much as her. "We mustn't get impatient."

As far as anyone knew, Laderna was merely his assistant; no one guessed the depth of their joint conspiracy, though some might whisper unkind rumors about their relationship. The nobles didn't much care what the "little people" did anyway; they had always included Ishop among them, too, although the smart ones were wary of him. As for mousy Laderna Nell, she dressed plainly in public to avoid notice. Her dowdy clothing, slumped posture, workmanlike gait, quiet voice, her entire demeanor – it was all so wonderfully misleading. She might have been an actress, Ishop decided.

Laderna clutched the folder tight against her side. "The Diadem sent her movers in without any warning. I had to retrieve this from your old apartment, where we hid it."

He had many secrets, but they were well hidden. He wasn't worried about these lumbering men discovering the wrong details. "Everything is encoded. No one could interpret the document if it fell into the wrong hands."

"Of course, boss. I have everything on private lists, but from now on perhaps we should commit it to memory." After glancing around to make sure none of the burly movers could see them, she gave Ishop a flirtatious smile. "I removed another name. Only six left now."

He grinned. He didn't know what he could possibly do without her. "Which one?"

"Lamentably, the ambitious chocolatier Randolph Suzuki had an unfortunate accident while working in his laboratory. The whole place blew up. Although he received the best medical attention, he is now, alas, a permanent vegetable."

"Confections can be so hazardous." Suzuki was one of the most unlikely names in their confidential file, a shop owner who had no high-level contacts or secret political ambitions. Nevertheless, a Suzuki lord had been instrumental in causing the Osheer downfall, centuries ago. No exceptions.

The Duchenet would be much more problematic.

In the meantime, Ishop saw no way for anyone to connect the victims in the recent spate of deaths, especially this uninfluential man. Who would ever think to look in 700-year-old archives for the victims to be linked to the forgotten Osheer family? Suzuki himself was nearly forgotten.

Only six names remained on the list, and the progress was delicious. He and Laderna had promised each other not to keep score, but of course they did. The two operated as partners with a common goal, and one day, when he became a noble under his rightful lineage, he would reward Laderna handsomely.

"You do such excellent work." Glancing sidelong at her in the shadows, Ishop didn't think she looked so gangly anymore. She beamed from the compliment, and he noticed that she had begun to carry herself with more confidence. She dressed more fashionably, showed off her figure more, stood with better posture, and moved with more grace.

"Those men certainly are slow," he said, with a wink that she could still see in the low light. "I'd like to have some privacy."

"Oh, I already took care of that. There's an extra guest bedroom in the back with a separate entrance. I had the movers set it up first."

"You think of everything," he said.

57

Even meticulous plans and precise monitoring could not allay the General's anxiety. The long wait was always the hardest part.

During the rebellion, Adolphus had known that morale faded in the extended travel times between systems from one military engagement to the next. Though his crew knew they would soon clash with Constellation loyalists, the interminable anticipation sapped their enthusiasm.

He remembered with a wistful smile that the agonizing down-time between engagements was particularly hard on Franck Tello, his second in command. Poor Franck dealt with the stress by eating: He insisted that he needed to keep up his strength for the upcoming fight, as if he were some sort of barbarian out to engage in hand-to-hand combat. Franck ate so much, and so swiftly, that he invariably made himself sick and vomited his meal, which only made him more miserable. Ah, poor Franck . . .

Now Adolphus had more waiting to do.

Though this was no military engagement, the General had been planning the operation for years: staging, watching, adjusting every schedule with as much attention to detail as he had ever given to any battle plan. Because he knew how brutally the Diadem would crack down once she learned what he was doing, Adolphus could not dabble in half measures.

Every stringline in his independent network had to be completed *at the same time*, creating a sudden and unexpected victory – a fait accompli. The new Hallholme hub and the terminus rings being delivered to the other fifty-three Deep Zone planets, near and far, must be connected simultaneously before the Diadem knew what was happening.

Destination Day.

For some time now he had been sending out refurbished, illicitly purchased trailblazer vessels filled with iperion from the secret mines on Candela. The massive deposit on her planet could have made Tanja Hu fabulously wealthy, but she had thrown her lot in with him. That decision would likely change the course of human history.

In his overall plan, Adolphus choreographed the trailblazer ships' movements in a grand dance, plotting out the lengthy travel times. The pilots flew away at normal FTL speeds, accepting the lonely long-term task, as well as the hazards of exposure to processed iperion, because they believed the General could pull off his plan. Some of the first pilots in the overall scheme had been flying for three years already to the most distant Deep Zone planets.

He had to monitor everything carefully. Progress reports arrived each week – fast message drones sent back to the Hallholme hub along the quantum path they had reeled out behind them. The trailblazers gave precise position locations, distances traveled, expected planetfall dates. Adolphus monitored each of his pilots personally so he could advise them to speed up or slow down accordingly.

Once the trailblazers dropped off the terminus rings at their destinations, the secret would be out in a matter of days – and all the surprised DZ planetary administrators would have to make a choice. In order to ensure the correct decision, Adolphus had sent out secret subversives to prepare those planets that seemed like tough nuts to crack. They were laying the groundwork for a swift and smooth transition, so that the whole enormous Deep Zone would stand unified against the expected retaliation from the Constellation. On some worlds, he would use military options to force compliance, if necessary ...

The dozen active co-conspirators were acquiring old or surplus space military ships under a variety of pretexts, refurbishing them at their planets so they could stand ready. On each stringline from Sonjeera, there were numerous vulnerable points to intercept a lumbering and overconfident Army of the Constellation should it come. He had even arranged for the defection of a few key linerunners from the old Constellation network.

Inside his Elba residence, with the doors of his private study securely locked, Adolphus reviewed the latest message from Captain Ernst Packard, who had recently departed for the DZ planet Ridgetop. The General had known Packard well, a cultured, even effete man who thrived on the finer things in life, priding himself on his clothes, appearance, taste in music, and pretentions in gourmet dining. Adolphus had been surprised when Packard moved to Hallholme, since this did not appear to be a world suited to his tastes; he was even more surprised when Packard volunteered to become one of the long-range trailblazer pilots. Neither the lonely journey, nor the cargo of hazardous iperion, seemed the sort of thing he would choose.

But Packard was persistent, and Adolphus trusted him. Four months ago, the man had flown away in a trailblazer loaded with supplies, his music library, a wealth of entertainment files, and aspirations to "get some thinking done."

Adolphus played the newest message packet, but when he saw the image of Ernst Packard, he immediately sensed that something was wrong. Because of the deleterious effects of long-term iperion exposure, the trailblazers had thick bulkheads and extensive shielding between cargo holds and living quarters. Given the long journeys, each pilot was required to wear protective gear, but Packard always dressed up to record his messages. He took off his protective suit, put on his best jacket and tie, slicked his hair back, and made himself presentable for the camera.

Now, the man was drawn and grayish, obviously ill.

"It is my occasion once more to give you an update, General. Did I mention that I've decided to write a book? By now it's expanded to at least two volumes. Having little to say is no limiting factor when one has so much excess time on one's hands! Though the remaining months stretch out before me, my time does appear to be nearly finished. However, I can last long enough to accomplish my task – you can count on me, sir. The people at Ridgetop will receive me with great cheers ... or perhaps a funeral. It's all a matter of timing.

"You see, more and more often I've neglected to wear my protective gear. The suit is so uncomfortable, and it's a shame to be uncomfortable when time is short. According to my old doctors on Ogg, before I came to Hellhole, exposure to iperion actually has a potential *positive* effect on my medical condition." Packard paused, frowned, then scratched his chin. "Did I mention my condition? It's been so long, and I've had so many imaginary conversations, I can't remember what's real and what isn't. But it is terminal, so I had nothing to lose.

"For the first couple of months, this voyage worked wonders for me. The iperion made me feel healthy again, although I couldn't take much advantage of my new joie de vivre, being cooped up alone on a ship. Now, however, I've reached the point of diminishing returns, and the adverse effects of the iperion outweigh the benefits of the treatment."

Packard smiled with good cheer. "Don't worry, though, General. Everything aboard is automated. This ship *will* reach its destination and establish a terminus at Ridgetop, whether or not I live to see it."

Packard seemed distracted for a moment, then continued. "I could start wearing the protective suit again, but what's the use? The damage is done, and I have no regrets. I hope you don't think me vain, General, but someday – if everything works out all right – I'd be honored if you'd consider naming this route the Ernst Packard Memorial Stringline." He chuckled at his own hubris. "Hmm, that sounded much less egotistical when I imagined it." He folded his hands before him and leaned closer to the imager. "Fear not, General. I'm proud of what I've done. This is Ernst Packard, your obedient servant, signing off."

Stunned, Adolphus stared at the blank screen, feeling the full weight of his heavy heart. Any difficult enterprise had its share of casualties and sacrifices. He thought of all the names on death certificates he'd signed. Then there was Franck Tello, lost in that final engagement against Commodore Percival Hallholme and the Constellation forces over Sonjeera. Franck had followed orders to the end, never doubting his General. And in those last seconds before his ship was engulfed in flames, knowing that he and his crew were doomed, Franck had saluted – a last salute . . .

Forcing himself to concentrate on his duty and on his responsibilities, Adolphus called up the stringline map and marked Packard's position en route to Ridgetop. He had faith that the ship would arrive as scheduled. He could count on Packard for that.

Someday, history would determine whether the sacrifices had been justified.

58

Though the new camp erected around the three slickwater pools appeared rugged ("rustic" was a better word, Sophie decided), the settlement would serve its purpose. The temporary buildings would offer little protection from a severe growler or volcanic eruption, but the valley was sheltered and the slickwater pools looked pristine.

If Slickwater Springs thrived, she could see about building sturdy permanent structures: a lodge house, a restaurant, sleeping quarters, isolated cabins. She told herself, only half in jest, that this could become Hellhole's first spa and resort.

Over the past week, forty people had come to see the pools – all just out of curiosity, so far.

Sophie Vence had always thought big. Arriving in the early days of Helltown, she had invested her money and sweat in two greenhouse domes. When those proved productive, she expanded the operation and took over the management of a warehousing company that had failed to meet the colony's needs. From there, the growth of her operations accelerated.

Now, hovering around the camp, Fernando-Zairic spoke to the new arrivals, filling their heads with remembered wonders of Xayan civilization. The visitors asked questions, which he eagerly answered, but sometimes he was at a loss for words. "We just don't have a mutual background of experiences for me to describe it adequately. For instance, in my head I can hear Xayan music, but I can't recreate it for you – at least not yet. Ah, if only more of you would join me."

Listening to his imaginative stories, Sophie experienced a spark of amazement that had long been gone from her life. She knew many others were tempted. Though the physical appearance of the aliens brought shudders to most people, Zairic's promises of utopia caught their attention. Anyone who volunteered to accept the slickwater memory-transference would receive all the exotic experiences of a strange life, a vicarious existence much more marvelous than their own ... not to mention the potential powers of telemancy, which interested Adolphus most of all.

Though many down-and-out Hellhole colonists found the offer appealing, no one wanted to be first.

Sophie's crews had set up stable boardwalks around the ponds' edges. With real wood scarce on Hellhole, the boards were a synthetic composite derived from native plant life and silica. She had also installed a ramp for those who wished to immerse themselves, but so far there hadn't been any takers.

The General wanted regular updates, but as yet she had nothing to tell him. Though she shared his concerns, they both realized the potential boon the reawakened Xayans could be.

She had thought Vincent Jenet would be one of the first volunteers, but he remained reluctant to immerse himself. He was worried about the risks, no matter how much his friend tried to convince him. "I saw how difficult it was for you, Fernando – you almost died. I was certain you *were* dead. How do you know the experience won't be worse for others?"

The other man's smile conveyed complete confidence. "The slickwater is now more capable of attuning to human biochemistry and cerebral morphology. Much was learned from the initial encounter with me. The next converts will have a less difficult time, I promise."

To prove his assertion, Fernando went to the edge of the boardwalk, turned to face the crowd, and allowed himself to fall backward into the slickwater pool, fully clothed. He made no splash; the mercurial liquid folded itself around him like comforting hands, and he sank under.

Vincent was anxious for his friend, but he stopped himself short of jumping in after him. Presently, Fernando emerged grinning. The slick-water dripped off his hair and face, and the pool itself buoyed him up. He laughed at the expression on Vincent's face. "I told you, it's all right now! Come on in." He stroked in the pool, closed his eyes, and spoke in a distant, alien-tinged voice. "I have told all of my waiting people the good news. They know they have a chance to live again, that we have succeeded in our desperate gamble to save our great race." He let out a contented sigh. "Who will be first among you? There must be some-one?"

The curiosity seekers watched, hesitant, skeptical, nervous. After several more days, Sophie began to wonder if anyone would take the plunge . . .

At long last, one old veteran of the General's rebellion hobbled for-ward. Former Lieutenant Peter Herald had been injured in an explosion in the battle over Sonjeera, his lungs scarred from breathing caustic vapors; he had been exiled to Hallholme like many of Adolphus's other supporters. Eking out a life there, he had worked first in the mines, then in the agricultural fields. The buildup of pulmonary scar tissue made it more and more difficult for him to breathe, especially in the dust-laden air of Hellhole, and his health deteriorated.

Loyal to his soldiers, the General insisted that Herald – like all exiled veterans – must be taken care of. However, the fact that he was depend-ent on the charity of others, no longer the man he pictured himself to be, weighed on Herald. He had been one of the first to arrive at the slickwater pools, staring at the oily swirling surface as if hypnotized. The former lieutenant's face was full of longing to experience things that his body was no longer capable of.

After days of discussion and hesitation, he stepped to the edge of the boardwalk. "All right, dammit. Somebody has to be brave." He coughed repeatedly, and his shoulders shuddered. "If this works, I hope more of you will join me. I've got nothing to lose."

From the pool, Fernando-Zairic nodded encouragement. Sophie felt tense, but she did not try to stop the veteran. She had to watch, despite her anxiety. No one knew what was going to happen. Vincent opened his mouth as if to offer a word of caution, but he pressed his lips together and held his tongue. Everyone else watched with bated breath.

Without bothering to use the ramp, Peter Herald leaned over and let himself fall into the quiet cauldron of slickwater. He shuddered and thrashed a moment, his eyes opened wide in shock – terror – then dawning amazement. He submerged. Fernando-Zairic didn't move towards him.

The people around the boardwalk drew closer to the edge. Someone wanted to throw a rope to save the man, but no one dared dive in to lend a hand.

Vincent called out, "Fernando, help him!"

"He's all right, Vincent. Trust me."

In less than a minute, Herald's head rose above the surface. Viscid fluid drained from his hair and face, and he stroked smoothly toward the ramp and climbed out of the pool. He moved with a strength and grace he had not shown just seconds earlier. The slickwater shed itself from his body, draining back into the reservoir. The veteran said nothing for a long moment.

Fernando-Zairic climbed up and stood next to the man, his hands clasped together. "Who are you? Do you know yet?"

Herald opened his eyes wide and turned to face the others. Sophie shivered when she saw that his eyes, too, now had a faint unfocused sheen that gleamed in the light. "It's true, what you said." He raised his voice. "It's all true! The wonders I have seen!" He looked around, eyes shining with an eerie pearlescence. "I don't have the words. I don't have the ... it's all true!"

Fernando-Zairic embraced him warmly. Peter Herald drew deep breaths – without coughing – and moved with a strength and vigor that Sophie found astonishing. The slickwater must have healed him.

Two other colonists needed no further encouragement. After they jumped in, Fernando and Herald helped them out to join the ranks of the converts. Other visitors pushed forward, jostling one another at the edge of the boardwalk. Sophie was sure that one man was accidentally knocked off the boardwalk and into the pool, but when he emerged, he had no complaints, only a look of awe on his face.

Sophie was amazed to see how swiftly everything – *everyone* – changed. By the end of the afternoon, ten more people chattered with great excitement, holding forth with descriptions of the Xayan lives they now carried.

Vincent's feelings seesawed. He said to Sophie, "We all came to

Hellhole because we didn't have any other options. But if what Fernando says is true, then a kind of magic has come into the lives of these people." He looked over at her. "Nonetheless, I'm happy enough with who I am. I'm not looking to become someone or something else."

"But a lot of these people are."

Sophie had never been much of a religious person, but now, as she saw the striking re-emergence of Xayan memories, she experienced an odd kind of spirituality. Fernando-Zairic seemed so very joyful as he greeted his resurrected Xayan friends.

Sophie realized she was at the beginning of something remarkable out here at Slickwater Springs. At the same time a cold fear invaded her chest, as she wondered what she had unleashed.

59

Gliding along the stringline path, the *Kerris* added a faint dusting of iperion molecules where necessary, then began to decelerate on the approach to Hallholme. This was the last trip that Turlo and Sunitha Urvancik would ever make for the Constellation.

They had already set up the details for their disappearance. Once the two linerunners reached the terminus, they would disengage the *Kerris* from its quantum path and never return to their official duties. Both of them had more important things to do: they believed in General Tiber Adolphus.

On the current run from Sonjeera, the *Kerris* had stopped at three substations along the way, as scheduled. Turlo and Sunitha had repaired and recharged each of the unmanned facilities, filed the appropriate reports, kept everything neat and tidy.

Turlo had also planted detonation devices, should they prove necessary.

"We'll be there in an hour, my dear," he said. "Any second thoughts?"

She shrugged. "How can you have any doubts? You read Kerris's final note. He'd be ashamed of us if we changed our minds now . . ."

During his service in the Army of the Constellation, their son's letters home had grown progressively less certain over the course of the rebellion. Serving aboard the flagship of Commodore Percival

Hallholme, Kerris had seen first-hand the ruthless measures the Constellation employed, particularly the appalling use of human shields, innocent civilians who were tormented (with images broadcast over narrow-band video transmissions) to intimidate the rebels.

Very shortly after Hallholme's victory at Sonjeera, which brought an end to General Adolphus and his rebellion, Turlo and Sunitha received word that their son had died bravely in the final battle. Kerris even received a posthumous medal of honor.

Only later did they learn the truth, that their son had died not in battle, but from a lethal dose of radiation because of an improperly installed fuel rod in the engine room of the flagship. A major screwup. This event occurred well after Adolphus's defeat and had less to do with glory or bravery than ineptitude.

For an idiotic victory regatta across the skies of Sonjeera, Diadem Michella insisted that Commodore Hallholme's flagship be cleaned and polished. She had rushed the matter and hired untrained personnel, who made mistakes. Radiation exposure was a slow and horrible way to die, and Kerris had plenty of time to reflect on his situation. He wrote a long, bitter farewell note to his parents, but the Constellation had not seen fit to deliver it to them. A screwup *and* a coverup.

Instead, the notice Turlo and Sunitha received had said, "*Your son died bravely in the line of duty during the final battle to defeat the traitor General Adolphus.*"

Bullshit.

Two months later, an equally disenchanted Commodore Percival Hallholme sent them a smuggled message explaining the truth, and he included Kerris's actual letter.

The retired Hallholme, it turned out, had feelings similar to their son's. He loathed the fiction that the Diadem had created around him and his victory. After Adolphus's disgrace and exile, Hallholme himself had secretly sent aid to his defeated enemy during the first year on that hellish planet.

Back then, Turlo and Sunitha were running stringline cargo haulers, and they helped the Commodore to doctor manifests, reroute supplies, and smuggle much-needed food, equipment, and medicines to the vanquished rebels. Even General Adolphus didn't know the identity of his secret benefactor, and Turlo and Sunitha had promised to keep that knowledge to themselves – which they had done to this day.

Though the two men had been enemies on the battlefield, Hallholme and Adolphus shared a similar code of honor. After defeating the rebels, the Commodore had retired and taken up residence on the old Adolphus estate on Qiorfu, apparently to revel in his triumph (as the propagandists portrayed it); Turlo knew, however, that the retired old man simply had no stomach for politics anymore. The Urvanciks hadn't had contact with him for years.

Due in part to Kerris's service during the war, Turlo and Sunitha had been cleared as linerunners by the Constellation, but they never forgot what their son had suffered because of a government that wasn't really noble at all . . .

Upon reaching Hellhole, the *HDS Kerris* docked at the Constellation's orbiting terminus ring; the General had already made arrangements to erase all record of their arrival from the station.

Turlo swept his arm before the viewscreen. "The vacation spot of the galaxy! Ready for some rest and recreation, my dear?"

"I never want to set foot on Sonjeera again. I feel like spitting every time I go there."

"Then it's time for a new career. Same job, different boss."

"An honorable boss – that makes all the difference."

Sunitha was so furious at the corrupt Constellation government that she wanted to transmit a defiant message to Sonjeera, finally speaking the words she'd held inside for years. But Turlo stopped her. Better that the *Kerris* simply vanished from the grid. They would be presumed lost in transit, like Eva McLuhan . . . succumbing to cabin fever, loneliness, and tedium, another linerunner suicide on the books. Their ship would never be found, and the Constellation would write them off.

Leaving the *Kerris* docked to the terminus ring, they shuttled down to Michella Town. They would have three days to detach the linerunner and cruise around to the other side of the planet before the next cargo hauler arrived. There, they would link up to the large secret hub being constructed over Ankor . . . and start a whole new life.

Much to their surprise, General Adolphus came to meet them in person in the colony town. Turlo bowed, though he thought he might be expected to salute. "I am honored, sir."

"Not as honored as I am." Adolphus shook Turlo's hand, then Sunitha's. "You're giving up a great deal to join my enterprise."

"We've already lost everything that matters." Sunitha's voice cracked a little.

The General's expression became somber. "I'm very sorry about what happened to your son."

"The rebellion caused plenty of pain for all of us, sir," Turlo said.

Sunitha added, "But not to the people who deserved it."

The General looked up into the greenish sky. "A new revolt is at hand, one that won't fail. In a little more than a month it'll be Destination Day. I need your help to check our new lines." He gestured them toward his private ground vehicle. "But you can spend a few days here in Michella Town. I've arranged lodgings for you, and I'll pay for anything you want – food, drink, pampering, whatever minimal luxuries we have to offer. Go ahead and enjoy yourselves. The RandR is your signing bonus."

Turlo caught his breath. "That's awfully trusting of you, sir."

"Nonsense. I know what sort of people you are. I don't take anyone into my confidence unless I trust them." General Adolphus moved toward the car, and his driver opened the door for them. "Besides, there aren't many luxuries and amenities available here. You couldn't get too extravagant even if you wanted to."

60

Fernando-Zairic remained at the alien pools, acting as an ambassa-dor to welcome the new Xayan converts like himself, helping them adjust to their dramatically changed lives.

Vincent had no intention of leaving him. As an excuse, he said he couldn't do the long mapping expeditions by himself, so he asked Sophie Vence to reassign him to Slickwater Springs, and she was happy to have a reliable extra hand. She knew Vincent was a good employee, and she had more than enough work establishing, expanding, and main-taining this fledgling settlement, especially as more and more people came to see what all the fuss was about.

Despite the growing interest in the slickwater, Sophie was relieved that the four Original Xayans had not emerged from their mountain bunker to observe the pools. Cristoph de Carre and a small team worked inside the vault under tight security. The General had asked Encix and her companions to remain isolated and out of sight, but it was unclear what would happen if the aliens decided to press the issue. Fortunately, for whatever reason, the four living Xayans seemed oddly reticent about the data-pool of restored lives, as if they had no interest in it at all.

The weeks passed, and as more and more Hellhole colonists reawakened ancient Xayan personalities, Vincent felt increasingly distant from his friend. Those who emerged from the pools with exotic secondary personalities seemed to have much more in common with Fernando, and the converts tended to keep to themselves.

Though the "shadow-Xayans," as they had begun to call themselves, still looked human, their eyes and mannerisms were distinctly different. Vincent could tell at a glance who had been baptized and who remained the same. Since human physiology was not adequate for the communication methods used by the original Xayans, the converts still spoke the common Constellation language. Even so, their conversations left him out as they discussed shared memories and histories, of which Vincent knew nothing.

He saw little of the real Fernando anymore, since the Zairic personality had become dominant, engrossed in his important business. Fernando did appear now and then, but he laughed when Vincent expressed his worries. He even made his familiar raspberry sound. "Oh, Vincent – Zairic's not forcing me to do anything against my will! Trust me, this is perfect ... just perfect. I couldn't be happier." They stood together watching two more people plunge into the eerie pool. "One of these days, you'll change your mind."

When entering the slickwater, volunteers could not choose which personality would come out of the database of Xayan memories. He might emerge from the pool as an alien leader, architect, philosopher, scientist, or common laborer. They all wanted to live again, but the alien race had their own selection process; the first ones to emerge were slanted toward the most powerful and influential leaders of the lost race.

Some presences were stronger than others and dominated the volunteer human personalities, while others were more egalitarian and shared in a beneficial common bond. A few of the reawakened telemancers exhibited mental powers like those the Originals had demonstrated during the reception back in Michella Town. Those new converts could levitate themselves off the ground, their faces awash with delight as their human personalities marveled at their new abilities. Most, though, exhibited no powers at all.

Vincent was reassured to note that not a single one of the shadow-Xayans complained about their new situation; instead, they were exuberant with a sense of wonder that had been missing from their lives ever since they'd come to Hallholme.

At the burgeoning camp, Sophie Vence had a relatively large structure for her private residence and administrative office, and Vincent lived in one of the smaller adjacent cabins erected for the support workers. After their conversion, the shadow-Xayans established a cluster of small prefab huts on the opposite side of one of the three pools, and spent most of their time together, excited about their new future.

As dusk settled over the valley, a sharp frosty wind blew in with such a dramatic temperature drop that everyone scurried inside their tents or communal cabins. Vincent could see condensed steam rising from the slickwater pools. The shadow-Xayans retreated together to their huts, and after watching his friend join the group of converts, Vincent returned to his small cabin for a quiet night alone. Outside, he heard the crackle of ice, a skittering of crystals across the ground, and a brisk wind that jabbed at loose seals in the temporary shelter.

However, once Fernando-Zairic saw that his fellows were safe, he came back to Vincent's cabin and joined him for conversation, just like old times. Vincent was surprised to have the company, "So, are you Fernando tonight, or Zairic?"

"Whichever you prefer. We share our time inside my head." The calm voice was definitely the alien one. "We're partners."

"*Fernando* is my friend. Zairic keeps trying to talk me into immersing myself, but the real Fernando would accept my decision."

The other man's voice changed. "Oh, I can't tell you how much I'd like to have you join us, Vincent, but I'm not going to pressure you. I don't understand why you're so afraid, but then, you always did worry about everything."

"I like my personality as it is." Vincent paused, recalling his dead father, his job in the machine shop, and how he had been forced to steal for an ultimately pointless medical treatment. Some people might have said he had nothing to lose. "I just don't want to be dominated by someone else in my own mind."

The raspberry sound again. "Oh, I'm not dominated. I *let* myself drop into the background, because Zairic has important work to do. Can't you see?"

"I still want my real friend Fernando back."

Fernando seemed genuinely perplexed. "But why? Zairic is clearly a superior person to the man I used to be – even I can recognize that. And I sure gave you plenty of headaches." He lowered his voice to a conspiratorial whisper. "I have my faults, you know."

"All human beings have faults. It's what makes us who we are. I liked you, warts and all, no matter what sort of nonsense you tried to make me believe. You helped me when I needed it, and I helped you when you were in trouble."

Fernando gave a wan smile. "I appreciate you saying that, but I'm doing something *important* with my life right now. At last I can be a real somebody – not somebody I just made up."

Sophie Vence began putting up permanent structures and expanding Slickwater Springs into an actual village. She strung wire fences as flimsy barriers around the boardwalks, so people wouldn't fall in accidentally, although the fence would not deter anyone intent on getting to the pools.

As word spread about Peter Herald's new vigor and how the slickwater had supposedly healed his ailments, other sick and dying colonists came to take a chance. They also emerged stronger, healthier. And often with unusual powers of telemancy.

The crowds increased, and General Adolphus received Sophie's reports with great interest, and promised to visit her soon.

Within four weeks, the first tourists arrived from the Crown Jewels.

61

While her mother pretended the de Carre matter had been settled and swept aside, Keana did not stop grieving for poor Louis, nor did she give up on her search for Cristoph. But she bided her time, kept her eyes open, and pretended to go about the life her mother expected of her.

Diadem Michella assigned her the same inane duties that had always been her daily routine: presenting meaningless civic awards, appearing at sports tournaments to hand out trophies, riding in parades. Previously, knowing that Louis was there for her had kept Keana happy enough to make it through her public appearances, but that was no longer possible.

Now, she hated every moment.

Today she was supposed to dedicate a new government building for the Bureau of Deep Zone Affairs, an enormous structure that had been under construction for years. Now, when she thought about the frontier worlds, Keana knew Cristoph was out there, stripped of everything.

Until she could find out what had happened to him, she had to keep up appearances on Sonjeera. Keana would not give the Diadem the opportunity or satisfaction of thwarting her again. She didn't know why, other than spite, Michella would try to stop her from helping

Louis's son, but Keana had already made the fatal mistake of underestimating her mother's wrath; it wouldn't happen again.

For today's ceremony, the Diadem insisted that Keana be primped and tended by a team of royal stylists. She endured hours of coiffing and the application of makeup, and after the stylists finally deemed her to be lovely and perfect, she slipped away to alter her appearance more to her liking. Keana didn't like how the eye shadow clashed with her light skin tone and blue eyes. She sat at her dressing table, using her own makeup applicators, touching up the colors. Her hands moved with jerky, tense strokes.

Shy around her, Bolton entered the room, painfully attentive. He had become a true friend after the tragedy. If only the other nobles had understood that about them, if they had accepted how much she needed Louis ...

More out of concern for her welfare than to maintain appearances, Bolton had moved into her royal apartment for the past week, although he slept in one of the guest bedrooms. (Her mother didn't need to know that, however.) Knowing her pain, he stayed out of her way, but he was there for her when she needed him – a prince in every sense of the word.

Now she rose to her feet, wearing a long dress with classic materials in a pretentious style, made by one of the Diadem's top designers. Bolton helped her by draping a red sash over one shoulder and across the front of her dress. His voice was soothing. "Under other circumstances we might have been a perfect couple, my dear, if so many people had not interfered in our lives." He sighed. "They drive me mad with their demands."

As he attached a clasp to hold the gaudy sash in place, she noted that his eyes were sad. On impulse, she gave him a quick kiss on the cheek, then withdrew. Bolton blushed and smiled.

The Bureau of Deep Zone Affairs headquarters was large, even by the standards of Sonjeeran bureaucracy. The lavish structure contained departments and agencies for all the frontier worlds with local offices for each of the eleven territorial governors. On the roof, fifty-four globes affixed to a gigantic transparent disk spun like a carousel. As she and Bolton stepped out of the limousine in front of the grandstand, the whirling globes caught her eye. Cristoph was on one of those DZ planets, but she had no idea where . . .

A crowd had already formed in the plaza, and as Keana approached the reserved area in front of the grandstand, she noted three ornate chairs. She had expected one for herself and another for her husband; the third was presumably for some bureau official. To her surprise, however, Diadem Michella arrived with a flurry of ceremony and a fanfare of horn blasts. The old woman left her carriage, followed by the ubiquitous Ishop Heer. The crowd cheered her arrival.

Annoyed, Keana turned her back and walked up to take her place. As Bolton seated himself beside her, she muttered, "If my mother wanted to do the ribbon cutting herself, why did she insist that I come here?"

When the Diadem climbed the stairs to join them, Keana and Bolton rose, bowed, and the old woman took the remaining seat of honor. Ishop Heer stood behind Michella. Other nobles and Bureau officials settled into seats behind them on the grandstand. Keana didn't acknowledge her mother.

Workmen brought a long red-and-gold ribbon around the front, along with an absurdly large, ceremonial pair of scissors, which they extended with great formality, but the Diadem directed the shears to her daughter. "Gentlemen, this is Princess Keana's event. I am merely here to observe and grant my support." Her intrusive arrival made the self-deprecating words laughable.

As Keana took the scissors, she noted that they were inscribed with the Bureau's new multi-globe seal. The Diadem gave her sweetest smile. "I know you didn't expect me this morning, my dear, but I've heard you're not feeling well. I wanted to show my support."

You could have shown support in so many more important ways. Keana barely kept the acid from her voice. "Your concern is noted, Mother."

As the ceremony began, the Diadem attempted to engage her in light conversation as if nothing had strained their relationship, but Keana was not interested in cordiality. She responded as little as she could.

Pretending not to notice her daughter's sour mood, the Diadem motioned to Ishop, who leaned forward to listen over the crowd noises. Keana heard everything her mother said. "Ishop, recent reports from Hallholme trouble me. Sounds like yet another religious cult has taken root there, possibly dangerous, and it's spreading rapidly. I haven't seen any evidence of violence, but one never knows. Every cult is dangerous in its own way."

"Yes, Eminence. I have a complete list of cults that have gone to planet Hallholme, and I've studied the reports of this one. The converts claim to have access to alien memories. That buffoon Luke Pritikin didn't notice anything."

"He's not much of a spy," Michella agreed. "None of them are. I need better intelligence on that planet."

"There have also been reports of miraculous healings, Eminence."

"Miraculous healings? It never ceases to amaze me the silly things people will believe. Maybe we should send all of the Constellation's infirm and terminally ill to planet Hallholme, give them to General Adolphus so they'll no longer be a drain on our own treasury!" She chuckled.

Ishop remained serious. "That seems to be what's happening, Eminence. The outbound passenger pods are full of the sick, and so far none of them have come back to the Crown Jewels."

"Good riddance to them, then. Why do so many weak-minded fools flock to such nonsense? What is missing in their lives that they would surrender everything to what is obviously a scam?"

Keana thought she understood, but she made no comment.

Michella pouted, still troubled. "But why would the General allow such a thing ... unless it was his idea. Ishop, go find out what's happening there, make sure he isn't up to something. I suspect Adolphus is behind this."

"To Hallholme again, Eminence?" Ishop looked uncomfortable, wiped his hands on his clean trousers. He reacted with distaste to the very mention of the frontier planet.

"I believe that's where you'll find him, Ishop." Her voice carried a sharp edge. "Maybe the General's gotten religious all of a sudden. Wouldn't that be ironic?" The Diadem gave a dismissive gesture, pretending not to care. "Just do the job right, Ishop. And relieve Pritikin of his duties. He's useless."

As the bureau chief concluded his dull presentation, thanking the Diadem for her support, music began down at crowd level. When the time came, Keana extended the ridiculous scissors and delivered a stock speech, trying not to make it sound too lackluster. Then she cut the ribbon, inaugurating the new Bureau of Deep Zone Affairs and waved numbly to the crowd as they cheered.

The people of Sonjeera were so easily fooled by appearances.

62

The Slickwater Springs camp grew as more visitors arrived, and the increasing numbers of shadow-Xayans remained there after their conversion. Sophie was forced to bring in other people to take on responsibilities. At her son's insistence, she had given Antonia Anqui a small cabin of her own, and Sophie was pleased to see how well Devon and the girl worked together managing the influx of visitors.

Sophie found his devotion to Antonia charming. The young woman turned out to be more than just a sweet, wilting flower, as had been Sophie's first impression when she'd seen the girl in Helltown. Indeed, Antonia had a hard wariness about her, scars from past pain ... but that edge softened visibly around her son. In fact, Antonia reminded Sophie of herself when she had brought Devon here to make a new life.

As she watched the new converts with all of their excitement and passion, Sophie could see that their sense of wonder was genuine, but she was not tempted to immerse herself. Watching the visitors day after day, she kept her opinions private. She ran the camp, provided access to the slickwater pools, and didn't try to talk anyone out of immersing themselves – which would breach the agreement the General had made with the Xayans.

For a while, she worried that Devon might be susceptible to

Fernando-Zairic's fervor, but fortunately, the young man was so smitten with Antonia that he wasn't likely to sacrifice his chances with her.

Nevertheless, there were risks. The process didn't always work. For unknown reasons, three eager volunteers were so severely shocked by slickwater immersion that they never awakened from their comas. They were taken to the Helltown medical center, where their condition remained unchanged.

When she demanded explanations from Fernando-Zairic, he was as dismayed as she was. "It is not intentional. I am sorry I can do nothing to bring those people back. But life – especially here on this planet – is fraught with uncertainty, danger, and tragedy. Recall that we have also saved a significant number of human lives."

"I don't think of human beings as numbers on a ledger sheet." Nevertheless, Sophie knew he was right. Many of the sick and infirm volunteers would have died from their ailments, but the Xayan symbiosis had restored them to health.

In addition to the ailing, dying, downtrodden, or hopeless, many wonder-struck people arrived, in search of something that was missing in their lives. They hoped the slickwater would give it to them.

Every three days, Vincent Jenet signed out the camp's Trakmaster and scouted the area around Slickwater Springs in ever-widening circles, working on his original survey. Alone in the control cab, he rolled the armored vehicle out of the valley, up and over the line of low hills where the General's guards had shot the native herd beast. On his numerous scouting trips, however, he had not seen another one of the elk-like creatures.

Now, off in the distance, he saw a thin cyclone stirring up dust and sucking it into the sky as it danced drunkenly across a bleak and sterile landscape. The whirlwind dissipated as he watched.

Vincent missed the days of traveling with Fernando. Though he was generally a quiet person and a loner, he had liked the other man's easy company, a non-judgmental friendship. He was not prone to taking risks, and Fernando was reckless by comparison, but during their time together his friend had pushed him out of his comfort zone, making

Vincent strive harder instead of just letting events push him around. Now their paths had greatly diverged.

Still, Vincent wanted to complete the job he and Fernando had started when they set out to map this grid square. They had rushed back to Michella Town after the slickwater discovery, and Vincent hated to leave a task unfinished.

The Trakmaster topped a low rise, and he looked down upon a burst of lush color – a shallow bowl filled with writhing scarlet vegetation of a shade so intense it hurt the eyes. He had never seen such verdant foliage in the wilderness on Hellhole.

Fascinated, he drove to the edge of the alien weed forest. The strange vegetation rose and drooped in long fleshy stalks, wagging like tongues in the air. Nothing like this had ever been documented, as far as Vincent knew, and he made careful notations and took images. The foliage was beautiful, majestic, and very eerie. He didn't want to get too close.

Knowing it was his duty as an explorer to inspect his discovery first-hand, Vincent donned a long-sleeved shirt, hat, breathing mask, gloves. No telling what sort of pollens or fumes that weed might give off.

He opened the cab's hatch and emerged into air filled with a moist rustling sound as the red fronds rippled and stirred. The plants rose taller than his head, fronds unfurling. He realized that the crackling, creaking sound was from the rapid growth of the alien plants. Large bulbous buds turned their tips to the sky and spread open to release bushels of feathery spores that flapped away like insects. The flying pollen seized up and died within seconds, dropping onto unclaimed patches of ground.

General Adolphus could dispatch a team of xenobotanists to take samples. Although not edible, native plants could provide building materials, polymers, industrial chemicals, even pharmaceuticals. Considering their furious growth rate, these plants could truly be a boon.

Gingerly, he touched one of the fronds with a gloved hand. He jerked back when the plant recoiled. By now he had learned not to underestimate anything that Hellhole might throw at him. Such explosive, intimidating growth was … disturbing. He decided to head back to Slickwater Springs and let Sophie Vence know about this strange forest.

Maybe Fernando-Zairic could draw from his alien memories and explain it to him . . .

From inside the Trakmaster's cab, a weathersat alarm chimed, and Vincent climbed inside to see the urgent meteorological alert. A large static storm was sweeping toward him.

Grinding the gears on the Trakmaster as he raced overland, Vincent watched the growler roll in, his pulse pounding. He monitored the storm's progress on his way back to Slickwater Springs and was astonished when the weather system altered its course unexpectedly.

Vincent was perhaps an hour ahead of it now. He would have to help the settlement prepare. At Slickwater Springs, Sophie Vence had her own monitoring stations, and she knew how capricious Hellhole's weather could be, so Vincent wasn't surprised when he rolled back into camp to find a lockdown already under way. Sophie, Devon, and Antonia herded all the visitors out of their tents and cabins into underground storm shelters. The population of Slickwater Springs had grown dramatically since the small bunkers were dug, and the protective vaults were going to be crowded. People would have to stand shoulder-to-shoulder and hope the onslaught didn't last long.

When she saw the Trakmaster drive up, Sophie looked relieved, waving both hands. "Vincent, open the hatch! It's the best protection we can give right now. You can fit twenty-five people in there!"

The vehicle was designed to hold eight, perhaps twelve. "Twenty-five?"

"They'd rather be crowded than corpses. Go, everybody – move!"

Vincent opened the side doors. "There's plenty of room," he lied. "Come on – inside!" People ran toward him carrying bundles of whatever valuables they had brought to Hellhole, but he shook his head. "Leave it – there's no room for your possessions, only people!"

A red-faced man blinked at him, not comprehending. "But it's all I have left. I can't—"

Other people streamed around him, dropping their own bundles on the ground and trying to secure a place in the sheltered vehicle. They pushed the red-faced man into the cargo area.

The sky had turned spoiled-green and bruised like a miasma spreading over the line of hills that enclosed the slickwater valley. Angry flashes of lightning whipped across the hilltops. Vincent saw Fernando and nearly forty shadow-Xayans sitting at the far end of the northernmost pool, where they had made their camp. The converts hadn't made any move to evacuate, entirely unconcerned.

Vincent's heart lurched. He couldn't let Fernando and all these people simply ignore the threat. He ran toward them, shouting into the rising wind. "You can't stay here! Get to shelter!" The crackling sound grew louder in the air. Even if he got Fernando to move all of his followers, there might not be room for them in the storm shelters or the Trakmaster.

Fernando just gazed up at him with a bright smile. "Look at this, Vincent! We can finally show you some of the things I've been describing."

The shadow-Xayans sat on the ground, each one holding a handful of sand. Displaying their telepathic abilities, they manipulated the dust and powder to create tiny exotic sculptures – intricate models of ancient Xayan cities.

At any other time, Vincent would have found it beautiful, but now he was frantic. As Fernando extended his cupped hands, Vincent swatted away the delicately balanced sand. "Fernando, *listen* to me! It's a static storm – you *know* what that is! There's no shelter out here. Tell your people to follow me. There's not much time." He added a pleading tone to his voice to cover the exasperation. "You can show me everything about the Xayan cities later. You can make all the sculptures you want. Just do this for me now, please!"

Fernando's face had the smooth mannequin appearance of Zairic. With his eerie eyes, he regarded the oncoming growler as if he had not noticed it before. "I understand your fear, but a storm is nothing to worry about. There are dozens of us now, and many are telemancers."

Sophie was yelling for him, "Vincent, you can't save people who don't want to be saved. Get to shelter yourself!"

But there was something in Fernando's confidence that tempted Vincent to place his own safety there, though it made no logical sense. "Wait just a minute!"

Fernando-Zairic stood up, and the shadow-Xayans followed suit, opening their fingers to let the sand fall back to the ground. They stood side by side, turned their faces toward the oncoming storm, and closed their eyes. Vincent sensed an altogether different crackle in the air – benevolent and protective.

Sophie called several more times as the storm grew louder. Static lightning crackled all around the slickwater pools now. She made a disgusted and sad sound. "I can only leave it unlocked for a few more minutes." She ducked down into the storm shelter and pulled the door closed over her head. The Trakmaster, crammed full of frantic people, sealed shut as they gave up on him.

Fernando's demeanor was utterly convincing. In unison, the shadow-Xayans smiled, let out a sigh ... and the growler passed overhead.

In the small valley, the storm lifted as if it had struck a glass dome, and slid higher into the air. Static lightning spread out in a diffuse pattern, no longer touching the ground. Vincent peered upwards in awe, seeing the underbelly of the growler as the churning brown clouds rumbled above them.

The shadow-Xayans had used their power to deflect the catastrophe from Slickwater Springs and the alien pools. When it passed over the valley and tumbled away beyond the far line of hills, it unleashed its outburst with renewed fury, as if frustrated.

The shadow-Xayans relaxed. A grinning Fernando rushed over to embrace Vincent, bubbling with excitement. "Did you see that? I told you we could take care of it."

Vincent's knees shook. "A little forewarning would have been nice."

"That would have spoiled the surprise." Fernando squatted down and scooped up some dust in his hands once more. "Now, let us show you our sand-sculptures again."

Though he still understood little of Zairic's alien, sermon-like recollections, Vincent sat with his friend every evening as he addressed his gathered converts. The ever-growing group of shadow-Xayans remained at the slickwater pools, where they sat around sharing recalled experiences. Although the converts always welcomed Vincent, he felt increasingly separated from them as the weeks passed. They did not mean to slight him, but he didn't share their set of second-hand experiences.

Though Fernando had not asked again, Vincent continued to feel the subtle pressure to accept a reawakened Xayan memory of his own. But the more he observed their fraternity and listened to their exotic reminiscences, the more reluctant he was to join them.

Vincent realized that it might be time for him to find some other job, ask Sophie or the General to reassign him.

As the shadow-Xayans gathered under the dark, open skies at the fringe of the settlement lights, Fernando-Zairic sat crosslegged and awkwardly bent over, as if he expected his body and bones to be more flexible than they actually were. Looking up with faintly opalescent eyes, Zairic watched the frequent sprays of shooting stars across the starry sky – bright orange bolides caused by disintegrating debris hitting the atmosphere.

"Our race was so close to achieving *ala'ru* before the asteroid came – within one generation of reaching the ... quorum, the critical mass, necessary to transform our entire race and fundamentally change the universe." He spread his hands. "Now, we must try again ... if we find enough people to join us."

Many of the shadow-Xayans flexed their fingers and arms as if fascinated by the rigid structure of their human bodies. "But we're so far from the critical point," one pointed out.

"Far ... but not hopelessly distant," Zairic replied. "You can feel it yourselves. Combined with human minds, we are much stronger. Hybrid vigor. Fewer of us will be required to initiate the evolutionary shift. Recall your other lives. You all trusted me when you surrendered your bodies and minds to the slickwater. With the asteroid coming, we knew what we had to do."

The shadow-Xayans nodded, muttering amongst themselves. Some wept with remembered fear.

Fernando-Zairic turned toward Vincent. "It was a horrific time for us, my friend. Once we realized that even our telemancers could not prevent the annihilation, slickwater was our only hope of preserving who we were. We entered the pools, one after another, by the hundreds, then thousands, then millions, all across the planet. We dissolved ourselves into the storage liquid, hoping that some spark of our *selves* would survive the celestial bombardment."

Vincent tried to picture so many Xayans simply dissolving to store their lives in the liquid-crystal medium. But was the memory record actually *them*, or merely a copy of who they once were? What about their souls? It was a question he wasn't sure how to ask.

Zairic's voice built in power as he addressed the converts. "I promised you that we could survive, and we have survived. Now trust me again. We will awaken, and we *will* achieve *ala'ru*."

Vincent spoke up. "But the four Originals survived intact, too. Wouldn't it have been better to save more actual Xayans? That vault could have held more, and you could have created more vaults. This ... slickwater plan was awfully risky. How did you know any outside race would ever come to this planet? And that our bodies and minds would be compatible with Xayans?"

"Both plans were risky, Vincent." Fernando smiled, and spoke in his own voice, excited. "What other choice did they have? When the world is going to end, why not gamble?"

Vincent couldn't believe an entire race would bet their existence on the idea that someday an unknown race might stumble upon their damaged planet and accidentally figure out how to resurrect them from the slickwater. The Xayans must have had some other reason to hope they would be found and restored. "I would have chosen something with a little higher chance of success," he said. "The odds against it seem incredible. It makes me shudder to think how unlikely it was."

"And yet it came true. Can't argue with results." Fernando kept smiling, then his expression became bland again as Zairic spoke. "Encix and her people wanted to save the civilization, but we did not have the time or resources to preserve more than a handful of Xayans in museum bunkers. My group wanted to use slickwater to save as many individual lives and memories as possible – millions." He shrugged. "Truthfully, Vincent, neither alternative had much chance of success, but thanks to humans we did succeed." He spoke louder to the gathered shadow-Xayans. "Now we *will* reawaken enough Xayans to reach our mental tipping point and achieve what our race must achieve. *Ala'ru* is our destiny."

With yet another abrupt change, he spoke in the cheerful voice of Fernando. "You see how important it is, Vincent. If you joined us, we'd be closer to our goal."

"It's not for me, Fernando. I don't even understand this ... *ala'ru* business." Vincent's dreams had been for a normal life, a fulfilling job, a kind wife, a good home. He had never imagined pushing so far beyond his personal boundaries that he wouldn't even be human anymore.

"I know it's hard to understand the concept of *ala'ru*. It's to accelerate our potential, to evolve right through the glass ceiling of what we are – both human and Xayan." Fernando-Zairic looked ready to explode with yearning to testify about what drove him. His mouth opened and closed, but the right words wouldn't come out; alien sounds and grunts came from his throat, as if he were trying to bend and shape his larynx in ways it could not accommodate.

Fernando's eyes widened, even bulged with the strain, and Vincent was alarmed. The alien noises were unnatural, frightening, and his friend looked like a man with a severe speech impediment trying to call out a fire alarm. His face contorted, but his mouth wouldn't make the right sounds.

Finally, Fernando shook his head in exasperation. "I can't communicate it to you, Vincent. Humans don't have the concepts, the points of reference, the vocabulary. But ... it's the most wonderful thing I've ever had in my head."

As the others murmured their agreement, Vincent felt even more uncomfortable. Yes, he wanted to understand what had so inspired his friend and all these followers, but he didn't feel a need to be anything other than himself. He knew all too well that Fernando had always searched for the pot of gold at the end of the rainbow. Now it was alien gold ... or fool's gold.

That was when Vincent decided to leave Slickwater Springs.

63

As expected, once Turlo and Sunitha Urvancik had been whisked away to their new duties, the stringline center on Sonjeera sent an urgent inquiry about the missing linerunner vessel. General Adolphus innocently responded via message drone, "I'm sorry, but the *HDS Kerris* never arrived on Hallholme. Is it possible they were lost en route?"

The two linerunners were safely out of sight at Ankor, and the *Kerris* had already been installed on the new hub. Soon the pair would begin patrolling the independent DZ network, making sure everything was ready for D-Day.

The General was troubled, though, by a secret warning that one of his remaining loyalists had embedded within the formal transmission: *Diadem Michella sends her personal watchdog on next passenger pod to investigate new religious cult on Hallholme.*

So, Ishop Heer would arrive soon. At least now Adolphus knew to be ready for him.

From previous experience, he knew the Diadem's inspector was hard-edged, brilliant, and humorless; unlike the incompetent Luke Pritikin, Ishop Heer would not be distracted by glittering crystals on a cliff wall. Adolphus would have to show the man something – but not everything. Under no circumstances did he want the Diadem to learn about the Original Xayans or their treasure vault of alien artifacts and technology.

He summoned Cristoph de Carre from his secret investigations in the museum vault. They didn't have much time.

Cristoph arrived at Elba long after dark, accompanied by Encix – a surprise. The alien rode discreetly hidden in the back of the Trakmaster, aware of the need to keep from being seen. When she emerged after Cristoph gave her the all-clear, the female alien stood under the stars. Her skin had a pale, iridescent glow that seemed to reflect that night's turbulent auroras.

Cristoph bowed to the General in a gesture of formality, and Encix imitated him. Adolphus motioned them quickly inside, always worried about unexpected observers, then told them both about Ishop Heer's imminent arrival.

Cristoph immediately grasped the implications. "It's not unexpected, General. Somebody was bound to notice odd things going on at the slickwater pools. I understand there've already been more than a hundred converts from the Crown Jewels. You can't keep that secret."

"None of the outside converts have left Hallholme, but word is spreading." Adolphus pursed his lips. "Even so, Michella can't have much concrete information, just a few strange stories to pique her curiosity. And if any of the rumors tell the true story, she'd never believe it anyway. However, I've met with this Ishop Heer before, and he tends to clamp onto a task." He flashed a hard smile. "It'll be much tougher to fool him. Best if I make sure he stays wary of me."

Encix looked at the two men, not comprehending their tension. "But there is an obvious solution. If this visitor immerses himself in our slickwater pools, he can help us enlist Diadem Michella in our cause. Once we Xayans spread word of our need throughout your Constellation, additional volunteers will come here and awaken more of us. His arrival could be good news."

"You don't understand humans well enough, Encix," Cristoph said sadly.

"That is the reason why I want to keep your existence secret – for your sake and ours." The General was more blunt. "The Diadem is not a person who likes to share. Once she learns about the four Originals, she will seize you and take you to Sonjeera for interrogation and analysis.

She will send her troops to overrun the museum vault and confiscate every one of your artifacts, and she will likely mark the slickwater pools as dangerous and quarantine them."

Cristoph's voice was bitter. "He's not exaggerating, Encix. The Diadem will take everything. It's what she does."

Her soft flesh throbbing, Encix swayed her upper body, and went rigid again as she came to a realization. "Ah ... now I understand. There are factions in the human race."

"We have plenty of them," Cristoph commented.

"Politically, I am required to let Ishop Heer look at Slickwater Springs, but I'll let him draw his own conclusions." Adolphus paced the room with a grim smile. "I will have a word with Fernando-Zairic first. The original Fernando will understand exactly what we should do. If I get a little help from the shadow-Xayans, Mr Heer will have no reason to doubt that this is just some sort of mass delusion."

"All the more reason for him not to see any proof of the Originals," Cristoph cautioned.

"Or any real Xayan artifacts. We need to keep them out of the equation." Adolphus turned to Encix, not sure whether she understood what was at stake.

The female alien said, "We will return to the museum bunker. We four survivors have a task to complete in honor of our lost comrade Allyf. We will continue to remain out of sight."

"I'll seal up the outside station until the Diadem's inspector is gone, sir. Post sentries and guards disguised as mine workers. The records show this is just another exploratory mining operation. Ishop Heer will never know the difference."

"Exactly what I was thinking, Mr de Carre. Once the Diadem's man hears the converts talking about alien memories and lost civilizations, he won't believe a word of it. This planet has seen one crazy cult after another. With a little nudging, he'll conclude that these are nothing more than brainwashed religious converts."

Encix turned her strange face toward him. "Is that how you see our shadow-Xayans, General Adolphus? As brainwashed cult members?"

"I thought they might be misled at first, but not any more. That's why we have to keep you four safe until we understand more about you."

"And we Xayans need to understand more about these quarrelsome factions among humans." Encix bowed fluidly again.

"Keep looking around in the vault, Mr de Carre. See if you can find any artifacts that might prove ... useful."

"Yes, General."

The two departed, and Adolphus sent word out to Ankor to increase security there, too. He shook his head. Why did the Diadem have to turn her attention here *now*, with Destination Day only a month away?

64

As the General's utilitarian staff car arrived at Slickwater Springs after a long journey, Ishop Heer caught his first glimpse of the three circular ponds. He had never been impressed with this filthy and lackluster world, and the sight did not change his opinion. The reservoirs looked like deep mercurial pits with obsidian boulders scattered around them. The Diadem had sent him all the way out here to see *this*?

Seated beside him in the rear of the staff car, Administrator Adolphus acted indifferent to Ishop's presence. The disgraced General's face was a well-disciplined mask, but Ishop knew how to look for subtle signs: facial tics, unconscious gestures, nervous mannerisms. He concluded that Adolphus was less anxious than annoyed.

"Visitors come and go all the time, Mr Heer. I've stifled no reports about the slickwater pools, nor about the numerous religious groups that come to my planet – not now, not at any time over the past decade. It seems everyone is searching for something, and they hope to find it here."

At such close quarters, Ishop could not forget the man's previous threat to cast him out into the static storm. When doing the Diadem's business, Ishop was accustomed to having everyone be afraid of him; they would snap to attention and offer their fullest cooperation. But not Tiber Adolphus. He didn't show any fear of Ishop, or of the Diadem, whatsoever. It was entirely unnerving.

What if Ishop were to discover something vital about these strange pools? Would the General prevent him from reporting back to Sonjeera? He adjusted his facemask, tugged his gloves, and tried not to think about alien germs as the driver halted the vehicle outside the rugged camp. "Diadem Michella expects me to return on the next stringline hauler with my full report."

The General remained gruff. "And I intend to see that you leave with all due haste. I resent having to tolerate these repeated and unnecessary inspections. The Diadem's paranoia gets tiresome."

Ishop snorted. "Sadly, not all of her inspectors are entirely reliable. While this planet was abuzz with news about aliens, you duped Mr Pritikin with images of pretty quartz crystals so that you could carry out your own underhanded schemes."

"Oh? Maybe the man is just that stupid on his own." Adolphus actually smiled. "I informed Mr Pritikin about an interesting anomaly we'd discovered, *as I am required to do*. I can't help that he went chasing after it."

"And so our local inspector was one of the last to know what was going on here." Ishop coughed to cover an unwilling chuckle. In a way, he had to admire how easily Adolphus had manipulated the man. "The Diadem has recalled Pritikin from Hallholme. She will find a more appropriate assignment for him."

The General marveled aloud. "It boggles the mind. A man whose performance is so poor that he's been removed from *Hellhole*! That can't look good on his resume."

The two men emerged from the staff car, and Ishop made a face when he smelled the dusty, alkaline air. And that was only the odor that his facemask did not manage to filter out. Ishop would ask Laderna to find him a better breathing filter if he ever had to come back. This place was even more dirty and rustic than Michella Town.

He tugged his gloves tighter. While Adolphus ignored him, Ishop surveyed the settlement, the boardwalks and fences around the pools, the people standing in separate groups. Using an imager, he documented what he saw; the Diadem would want to know everything. "Tell me what goes on here, Administrator. What are these pools, and what do they do to people? Provide me with a list of individuals I should talk to."

The General shook his head. "Not in the bargain, Mr Heer. I'm required to grant you full access, but not hold your hand and explain every little detail. Feel free to gather your own intelligence. Get your hands dirty."

"My hands are already dirty just from setting foot on this planet." Ishop gritted his teeth, but refused to play the childish game of passive resistance. He drew a deep breath through the mask and changed the subject. "I've heard reports that some of the original aliens are still alive, and you have been seen with them. Apparently they perform parlor tricks for your dinner parties."

Adolphus let out a boisterous laugh. "Aliens at dinner parties? You inspectors will believe any sort of nonsense, Mr Heer! Perhaps I can direct you to those quartz crystals that your colleague Mr Pritikin enjoyed so much? You are welcome to look around for any sign of aliens – keep an eye out for ghosts and goblins, too, while you're at it."

Irritated, Ishop stalked away from the unhelpful General and approached the people working around the site, taking care where he stepped. A gust swirled grainy dirt around his legs. He found this place very unsettling and definitely cultish.

Planet Hallholme had been a haven for nuts and fanatics ever since the Diadem opened up the Deep Zone. What these people accepted in the name of their supposed enlightenment turned his stomach.

Sophie Vence introduced herself to Ishop in a challenging tone, making it plain that she wasn't intimidated by him. "I understand the Diadem has taken a personal interest in our resort. Perhaps she'd like to visit us on her next vacation?" Her antipathy toward Michella was as plain as the General's. "Please let her know that we'd be delighted to let her swim in our therapeutic springs."

Ishop gave her an insincere smile. "I'll pass along your offer." He looked at the visitors gathered around the pools, hesitating on the boardwalks. "Tell me, what do all these people want?"

Sophie spread her hands. "Miracles – at least that's what a lot of them say. They come here to be healed, or to achieve enlightenment. Many claim it works."

"Does it?"

Her brief laughter sounded flat. "It isn't for me to decide whether it works or not. I'm a businesswoman filling a need. They pay, and as long as they're adults, I let them make their own decisions." She added an intentional jab. "We have freedom here on Hellhole."

Trudging around the site, he recorded candid files of a dark-haired young woman who helped new arrivals to their temporary quarters. A young man, identified as the son of Sophie Vence, met the newcomers and answered their questions. When he spoke to Ishop, his attitude seemed friendly enough. "I hope you'll give us a good report, Mr Heer. Do you think you could get the Diadem to write us an endorsement? We're thinking of expanding."

The sarcasm was not lost on Ishop. His response was deadpan. "Perhaps if you disposed of all the dirt first." He swept a meaningful look around at the rugged cabins and tents, the rocks, and dusty boardwalks. It was impossible to imagine this place ever being clean.

A glimmer of humor showed in Devon's eyes. "I'm afraid that dirt is an essential part of the experience at Slickwater Springs. But our satisfied customers say that once you take a soak in our pools, you hardly notice the dirt anymore. I can offer you a discount, if you'd like to dip your toe in . . . ?"

Ishop backed away, shaking his head and moved off to continue his investigation.

One group of people stood apart from the hesitant ones, more like a docile herd than an agitated crowd. Sophie Vence gestured to one of the men, who glided over to Ishop with the grace of a dancer. "This is Fernando," she said, "and also Zairic. He was the first who claimed to take on a Xayan personality. Now he prepares the way for others. He can tell you everything you need to know."

Ishop regarded the man with skepticism. "You won't find me easy to convince, but I'll listen just the same. Wait – I don't forget faces. You were aboard my passenger pod the first time I came to inspect the General's accounts." His impression during that trip had been that this fellow was a fast-talker and maybe even a confidence man.

Fernando-Zairic merely smiled. "That was a different me on the passenger pod, a man at the end of his rope with very little chance of redemption. Let me tell you how I changed, how I came to be completely at peace. You could have the same epiphany."

He spoke in a zealous voice that immediately set Ishop's teeth on edge. The man's tale was preposterous – nonhuman memories stored in a liquid that bubbled up from the ground! His converts jabbered about some imaginary history, pretending to be exotic aliens who had much more glamorous lives than their own. Their opalescent eyes were oddly unfocused, no doubt from drugs. It was like an elaborate, pathetic game of dress-up for hopeless people.

Ishop had seen reincarnation cults before – Constellation records were littered with them – so he wasn't surprised to hear that none of the cultists recalled being ditch-diggers or dishwashers in their previous existence. "My, the Xayans must have been an incredible race indeed, if they had no boring people or mundane tasks whatsoever."

A few curiosity seekers stood on boardwalks; some of the converts swam in the water, beckoning to Ishop. The liquid looked oily and vile. Ishop wondered what kind of disappointment the newcomers would experience when they immersed themselves and no flood of alien memories swept through their minds. Would they be devastated, or would they be too ashamed to expose the lie? Who would want to break the chain of delusion? Or maybe some sort of toxin provoked hallucinations, which they were all eager to believe.

Ishop walked to the edge of the closest unnatural pool, in which he saw cloud patterns that didn't seem to match the ones in the sky. He turned back to the General. "This is obviously some kind of mass hysteria. Drugs in the water?"

Adolphus placed a firm hand on Ishop's shoulder. The contained power within General Tiber Adolphus was unmistakable. "Why not find out for yourself, Mr Heer? It would answer all of your questions. What better way to offer Diadem Michella a complete report?" The grip tightened, and the voice grew stony. "Just a little nudge. Fernando fell in accidentally and, according to him, discovered true enlightenment." Adolphus smiled. "Would you like to be enlightened, Mr Heer?"

Ishop felt an instant of fear. With the slightest shove, the General could indeed knock him in. And Ishop would be powerless against whatever hallucinogenic properties the slickwater contained. Ishop refused to be intimidated by the General, though his own resolve wavered. He could not let himself be manipulated. He was a noble, after all. "As tempting as your offer is, I have a report to file."

Adolphus shrugged. "It would change your life. Maybe you wouldn't want to return to Sonjeera. So far, all the shadow-Xayans have chosen to remain here."

Recognizing how easy it would be for him to succumb to an "accident" now, Ishop scuttled back onto solid ground and retreated toward the staff car with forced nonchalance. "I have seen enough here. Take me back to Michella Town now."

"As the Diadem's representative wishes," Adolphus replied amiably, and he called for Lt Spencer to prepare the car for the return trip.

Ishop decided the trip had been a waste of time: uncomfortable, unsanitary, and unproductive. The newest religious splinter group on Hallholme had beliefs just as oddball as any other, and the Diadem had sent him on a pointless chase.

Ishop was silent on the long drive back to Michella Town. He couldn't wait to leave this awful planet.

65

While the Diadem's inspector snooped around on Hellhole, Cristoph de Carre kept all four Originals hidden deep inside their mountain redoubt. The aliens had been content to make their home here ever since Sophie Vence established her camps out at Slickwater Springs.

Around the tunnel leading to the buried museum bunker, digging machinery had dumped piles of tailings and debris. During the day, Nari and a mining team drove their vehicles in a busy show of moving dirt and rocks. To an outside observer, an exploratory mining operation was under way, and such diggings were plentiful across the continent. Ishop Heer would have no reason to note anything about this particular one – so long as the caterpillarlike Xayans did not show themselves.

Cristoph spent his evenings continuing his work in the eerily lit vault alone with the Originals, while waiting for the General's all-clear signal. He had been through so much turmoil since his family's downfall, his father's suicide; here, in a secret chamber deep inside a mountain, Cristoph finally had a chance to contemplate his changed situation, and what he would do with the remainder of his life.

Though he had grown accustomed to the Xayans by now, the strange creatures still intimidated him. Nevertheless, he was fascinated by the wealth of cultural artifacts, works of art, and historical records. In the midst of this awe and mystery, Cristoph found a sense of peace. But he was aware of the tensions between Hellhole and the Constellation, so he also kept his eyes open for any technology that might be useful for defensive purposes. Weapons. But the Xayans didn't seem to have any.

The vault was filled with cultural items, sculptures, colorful splashes and animated lights that were preserved works of art, subsonic vibrations that – the Originals explained – were the equivalent of symphonies. Sequential, near-microscopic carvings and designs that were Xayan epic poems and recitations of geneaologies. It was what they had chosen to preserve of their civilization.

The most congenial of the four Xayans, Cippiq, rose up in front of the young man, startling him as he pondered. The large creatures could move with remarkable speed and stealth. The alien spoke by vibrating the membrane over his face. "You are quiet for a human. Others speak much more frequently."

His comment interested Cristoph. This Original seemed to have a sense of humor. "It's not just humans," he pointed out. "Zairic seems to talk a lot, too."

The Original said, "Before the impact, Zairic spoke so well and so passionately that he convinced an entire race to follow his desperate idea." He paused. "After the Diadem's inspector departs, you will send more researchers here to study our museum?"

"General Adolphus is very interested to learn more about old Xaya, especially your science and technology. But we have to be conscious of security, at least for now. There are certain concerns."

"Yes, Encix tells us that your race has factions, something we understand from our own experiences. General Tiber Adolphus hopes to find new weapons that incorporate Xayan science – correct?"

Cristoph felt uncomfortable. The alien's assessment was almost certainly accurate. "This planet may face threats from the Constellation. I'm sure the General is anxious to find a way to defend us. I was wondering if your technology could be used to help us keep ourselves safe."

"Weapons."

"Yes ... weapons."

Cippiq lifted his arms, touched soft fingers to the sides of his smooth head. "Our minds are the shapers. Our minds are the tools." His torso swayed back and forth. "Yes ... our minds are the weapons, if we choose to use them as such." He changed the subject abruptly. "Will you turn our vault into a military base, after your enemy spy leaves?"

Cristoph hesitated at the characterization. "I wouldn't say that. Larger research teams will be sent here so we can expand the work. Our trusted experts will study this place, with your assistance, but I don't think I'd call it a military base. And the Diadem's man is just an inspector, not an actual enemy."

"Then why are we hiding from him?"

Cristoph considered. "We are exercising caution. In the meantime, it's a good opportunity for me to inventory this museum and assess what our engineers would need for a . . ." He realized he couldn't think of a better word. "For a base."

The alien, however, did not seem reluctant. "You have been very generous to the Xayans. We are happy to cooperate with General Tiber Adolphus. My comrades and I could use our telemancy to make structural modifications to the vault, should that prove necessary. With suitable expansion, the interior of this mountain could house ten thousand soldiers, where they would be protected from an outside attack. Bring us plans, and we can help you. We are your friends and allies." As Cippiq spoke, sparkling spirals of light surrounded him like spindrift. "In return, we ask only that you encourage your fellow humans to awaken more of our Xayan personalities. We miss our many lost companions."

"That's a very exciting offer." The Original's bluntness surprised Cristoph. But he wondered how the Xayans knew so much about enemies and defenses if they had such a peaceful, unified society.

Hours later, Cristoph dozed in the low light and warm comfort of the underground chamber. The Xayans huddled in meditative silence; they never seemed to need sleep. Up above, it was deep night. Soon enough, he expected to receive word that Ishop Heer had departed from Hellhole.

The young man awoke to unidentifiable noises; he smelled something sharp and pungent, quite unlike the dry, dusty smell to which he was accustomed. He spotted movement by the dormant sarcophagi that had preserved the Xayans for centuries. The four Originals were gathered around the central container that held the body of their dead companion.

In addition to the vault's usual dim illumination, the air felt alive in a different way than before. Spirals and ghostly shapes flitted about on the cavern ceiling, then disappeared to be replaced by other skirling patterns.

Cristoph moved closer, making no sound; he hesitated in uneasy confusion when he saw what the four aliens were doing. The lid had been removed from the malfunctioning coffin container, and the living Xayans extended protoplasmic tentacles from their hands into the corpse, penetrating its outer membrane and *absorbing* it. He heard distinct sucking sounds. A chill coursed down his spine.

Sensing that he was watching, the four aliens turned their large eyes toward him. The eerie wrongness of the scene frightened Cristoph, and he realized how alone he was here in the vault. He took a half-step backwards.

"Do not be alarmed," Encix said. "It is thus that we honor our dead comrade." All four withdrew their finger tentacles from the sarcophagus, leaving the dead Xayan nothing more than a shriveled, twisted lump of dried gelatin and cartilage.

Cristoph suddenly thought of his own father lying in a pool of blood in a Sonjeera prison because he was too weak to face his shame. He continued to back away, imagining what these creatures could do to *his* body.

Cippiq spoke calmly, as if it were the most natural thing in the world, "We assimilate the flesh and memories, preparing the body for eternity."

"Shall we find a more comfortable area for you to sleep, so we do not disturb you?" asked Tryn, the other female and the smallest of the four Originals. "We can decrease the light energy in the air to help you sleep."

"That's all right." Cristoph kept himself apart from them, anxious to be away. "I'm completely awake now."

66

Diadem Michella worked hard to maintain her body and mind in peak physical condition, since she intended to rule for decades more.

Her personal physician watched her from the rooftop patio, monitoring readings of her vital signs. He'd tried to discourage her from strenuous physical activity, which he considered inappropriate for someone her age, but Michella disagreed with his medical opinion. And the Diadem always won her arguments.

Just beyond the south portico of her sprawling palace, her private running track had been built to her specifications only a year before. In a glass-walled gym building beside the track, she kept every form of exercise machine, as well as a staff of trainers. On this cool, foggy morning, she hadn't even broken a sweat as she kept a moderate, steady pace around the red clay track. She made her third lap of the four-hundred meter track and kept running.

Ishop Heer was late for their scheduled meeting.

Finally, after rounding another turn, she saw him hurrying from the main entrance of the gym, dressed in the running clothes she had left out for him. A robust man, Ishop considered himself to be in good shape, but Michella wanted to make him sweat this morning, in more ways than one. As much as she depended on the aide, Ishop had begun to think a bit too highly of himself. He must not be allowed to feel superior; he wasn't, after all, of noble blood.

"Don't dawdle, Ishop," Michella called out as she increased her pace, making him work to keep up. "We have important things to discuss, and my schedule is full."

Her watchdog fell into step beside her, already breathing hard. Perspiration stood out on his bald scalp. "I have a report for you about Hallholme, Eminence. I looked into the alleged religious cult and the rumors of aliens, as you requested."

"Very well, you'd better hurry and tell me before you collapse and need to be carted off." She knew she could outperform him in physical activity.

"Odd things are indeed occurring there, Eminence," he said with a forced chuckle. "The colonists discovered a group of exotic pools, which I believe have psychotropic properties. Anyone who comes in contact with the water becomes delusional, euphoric."

"In a dangerous way? Or are they just intoxicated?"

"They *believe* they are receiving alien memories from the previous inhabitants of the planet. Many converts also believe they have been healed from illness or injury. Their fervor is a bit out of the ordinary, but not alarming compared to the countless other cults that claim exclusive access to a previously unknown source of celestial knowledge."

"What do you know for certain? Did you experience this water yourself?" Michella increased her speed, forcing him to run harder.

Ishop was shocked by the question. "Expose myself to the contamination? No, I took every precaution, Eminence. I wore gloves and a facemask, I washed frequently, and I subjected myself to thorough blood tests as soon as I returned to Sonjeera. However, General Adolphus did imply that he might immerse me in one of the pools. He was trying to intimidate me, but it didn't work."

Though the man panted heavily, he managed to keep up, to Michella's surprise. Perhaps she shouldn't underestimate him. She chuckled. "Ishop, I can't imagine you becoming a member of a deluded cult."

"I would have to be drugged or infected somehow. I certainly would not join by choice." He shuddered visibly. "I have extensive media files of the spa encampment, the converts, the activities around those pools.

We can use the images to warn our citizens of what's really happening there – it won't be hard to make the cult members look ridiculous. We could even make the *General* look ridiculous." He obviously knew she would like that part.

"Good, our media corps can start on that. I'll be sure it's widely distributed. Maybe we can at least stop the gullible from going there. Alien memories? Miraculous healing? Indeed!"

Impatient with the aide's panting and sweating, she turned towards the gym building, where she intended to cool down by swimming twenty lengths of the pool. "What about the rumors of actual, living aliens? Did you see any of them?"

"None, Eminence. The idea is absurd, as you no doubt realize. However, plenty of the converts believe they *are* aliens. They seem genuinely deluded. Before I left Michella Town, Administrator Adolphus had one of the local xenobiologists show me the remains of a large indigenous creature one of their hunters had killed in the wilderness. The first large beast they've encountered on that planet. It appeared to be some kind of herd animal that survived the impact. Maybe that is at the root of the rumors."

Entering the gym building, Michella accepted a towel from an attendant and draped it over her shoulders. Ishop took one for himself and wiped sweat from his face as he kept talking. "In all, I found Adolphus to be vague and elusive. He could be hiding something ... or he might just be intractable."

She headed for the pool, scrubbing her damp hair with the towel. "You are probably correct in both respects, Ishop. Tiber Adolphus hates me as much as I hate him. If there's a way to disgrace, hurt, or embarrass me, he will find it."

Ishop's pale green eyes became calculating, moving to the next item on his mental agenda. "Adolphus is smart, though, Eminence. What if the slickwater is indeed valuable, but he's hiding behind a silly cult to deflect Constellation interest? Hmm, perhaps it was a trick after all?"

She entered the pool room and looked at the enticing smooth water, wondering if Ishop would follow her into the changing area. He was so loyal and intense, he probably wouldn't even notice when he stepped over a boundary. "Interesting thought, and I wouldn't put it past

Adolphus. That planet was supposed to be a dumping ground for all the Constellation's criminals, exiles, and misfits." She squinted. "If there's anything valuable on Hallholme, maybe I want it back."

67

As the number of shadow-Xayans grew at Slickwater Springs, they became a drain on the settlement's resources. The placid converts didn't leave, didn't offer to work for Sophie Vence, didn't go back to their old jobs for the colony. All mundane concerns seemed irrelevant to them.

Finally, like a mother bird chasing her babies out of the nest when they grew too big, Sophie marched out to the large group that sat listening to Zairic's evening sermon, and she laid down the law. "I can't let a bunch of freeloaders stay here indefinitely. Back when this planet was a paradise, maybe you Xayans could sit around and drink milk and eat honey off the ground, but there's a bit more effort involved here on Hellhole. All colonists have to pull their own weight." She pointed her finger at Fernando-Zairic. "You had better figure out what you intend to do, whether it's dredging up something useful from your alien memories, or finding other real employment. Either way, you need to *earn* your food and shelter. No more handouts."

Laughing, Fernando-Zairic applauded and turned to his followers. "Sophie Vence is absolutely right! We have overstayed our welcome, and it is time we established our own city – one that may only be the faintest mirage of what Xaya once was, but we shall see. We have enough telemancers to accomplish this. With our wealth of human and Xayan knowledge, our city may surpass expectations."

Sophie was surprised that convincing them could be so easy. "Well, all right then. I'll loan you enough supplies to get started."

Every resurrected alien life represented a person of significance to the lost race, a leader, a philosopher, a telemancer. Fernando-Zairic had achieved a kind of balance with the bright-humored original human personality coming to the fore at occasional intervals, even though Zairic was in control more often. Other converts, however, rarely showed their human characteristics. Sophie was concerned that the aliens seemed to be dominating the volunteers, and she said so.

"Is that so surprising?" Fernando-Zairic explained. "Of all the lives and memories our race preserved, the first to awaken are the most powerful and important personalities." He shrugged. "Conversely, the first human volunteers are those who were most beaten down and least hopeful, those with nothing to lose. The group is skewed. Strong Xayans and weak humans. As more and more people join us, however, you'll see a change in the balance. Humans and Xayans will be equal partners, I promise."

The next morning at dawn, she watched Fernando-Zairic gather the shadow-Xayans – more than a hundred of them now – and lead them in a prompt and orderly exodus. His actions reminded her of an ancient tale in which the Pied Piper coaxed all of the village children away to their doom. For the Xayans' sake, she hoped their leader was more than a con man . . .

Over the next several days, Fernando-Zairic and his followers established their new city in the nearby bowl-shaped meadow that Vincent had discovered, blanketed with fast-growing red weed. From their Xayan memories, the converts recognized the plant and understood what to do with it. Though their human bodies could not eat the fruit or leaves, they could process the material into a fabric similar to canvas, which they planned to sell in Helltown, with Sophie Vence as their commercial intermediary.

Once the shadow-Xayans moved to their settlement, Vincent Jenet finally moved on to explore more of the wilds of Hellhole. With bittersweet regret, he departed, and Sophie was sad to see him go; he'd been a big help to her, one of those hardworking employees who actually did what he promised and didn't need constant supervision, though she knew the poor man was still hurting inside.

Sophie had seen sad tolls among the converts, too – broken relationships and marriages, people who came together to the slickwater pools but parted when one person accepted alien memories and the other decided against it. General Adolphus had strictly forbidden children from immersing themselves, even though a few parents wanted to take their young sons or daughters with them into the Xayan memories. Adolphus refused to hear the pleas of saddened mothers and fathers. "It's barbaric to burden a child with a complete alien life before he's had a chance to live his own." Nevertheless, families fell apart, no longer able to understand one another. At least in the new settlement, the converts would have their own place.

While the eerie shadow-Xayans rejoiced in what had awakened within them, Vincent understood what the eager-eyed volunteers were *losing*. Sophie felt even worse for him when Fernando-Zairic did not come back to bid his friend farewell . . .

Having lost his partner in the Ankor sinkhole, a grief-stricken Tel Clovis kept to himself at Slickwater Springs, speaking barely a word to the others. For hours, he stood on the boardwalk at the edge of the pond, clutching the flimsy wire barricade. His expression shifted from longing to revulsion or hatred, as if he blamed the slickwater for Renny's death. He had abandoned his administrative position and now lived in a daze.

Tel watched intently while an old woman from Michella Town walked with an elegant stride along the boardwalk. With no fanfare or hesitation, she slipped into the slickwater pool and sank beneath the surface.

Though by now this had become a familiar occurrence, onlookers still regarded each baptism with awed whispers. When the woman emerged from the pool, pulling herself up on the rungs of the ladder, she paused as the last of the fluid drained away from her. She gazed around, inhaled deeply, and walked up to Tel Clovis. She regarded him with her new shimmering eyes. "Renny wants you to stop despairing. Some of his memories are in the pool with us, dissolved in the slickwater. We learned from him."

He gasped, but she continued to stare at him. "Now, will you join us?"

She held out her old wrinkled hand. Crying, Tel took it, and she led him into the pool.

68

Wearing his crisp uniform, Unit Captain Escobar Hallholme fumed as he watched the rotund, outdated FTL ship settle back onto the Lubis Plain landing field not far from where he and his father stood. He didn't want to calm down before he had a chance to reprimand the pilot.

It was the ugliest spacecraft he'd ever seen, with tiny windows on the sides of its bloated body and black streaks scoring the underside of the hull. Used as a troop ship in Adolphus's rebellion, such an old vessel shouldn't still be flying, should never have been powered up without a thorough shakedown and inspection by qualified mechanics. The hulk had been left here with all the others, like an old animal about to die, but the ungainly ship still flew – a tribute to the dedication and skills of the soldiers working at the Lubis Plain yards.

And one of his men had taken it out for a joy ride.

Escobar shook his head in irritation. He still had Diadem Michella's order in his jacket pocket, commanding him to prep the mothballed fleet, to make repairs and run all necessary checks in order to certify the creaking ships as spaceworthy again. She wanted these antique vessels given flight clearance and launched into orbit, where they would be locked to the framework of a large stringline hauler and delivered out to Ridgetop.

Good riddance. Following his orders to the letter, Escobar intended to authorize repairs of only the most critical malfunctions; Territorial Governor Goler could invest the rest of the time and effort.

However, a reckless pilot had launched this vessel for a brief run in the inner Qiorfu solar system, and the ship had barely made it back intact. A death trap. Furious, but trying to control his anger, Escobar stood with his old father at the bottom of the exit ramp, impatient for the test pilot to emerge.

"He landed safely," the retired Commodore mused. "That's what counts."

"Not to me. Captain Ulman had no business taking that ship out until it had passed another full set of ground inspections." As ship after ship was prepped and flown, Escobar knew he was going to lose a pilot sooner or later. He growled in disgust. "This fleet should have been disassembled for components ten years ago."

The old man lowered his voice to calm his son. "The Diadem demands that these vessels be put back into service with all possible speed. In order to follow her orders, some ... shortcuts have to be taken." Percival's sad eyes held a far-away light. "Cut Captain Ulman some slack. Remember, he is an experienced officer, a man who proved himself to me in wartime. He took a direct role in defeating the rebels."

Escobar felt frustrated and hemmed in by his father. "Shortcuts and impulsive actions might have been necessary during wartime, but there was no conceivable need for Ulman to take such a risk for *this*. That ship could have blown up on reentry."

The access hatch opened, and the pilot strode down the ramp, wearing gray flight coveralls and carrying his helmet under one arm. He looked shaken, having been publicly dressed down by the unit captain over the codecall connection. Escobar made sure all the personnel in the shipyards had heard his reprimand.

At the bottom of the ramp, Ulman saluted crisply. "I have successfully identified several systems in need of repair, *sir!*"

The test pilot had been upbraided previously for minor infractions, but a year ago he had taken out another mothballed ship, a small harrier, without clearance. He and his unit captain had argued then as well, with Ulman insisting that the decommissioned vessels be flown regularly (mainly because he wanted to fly them). Escobar had not disagreed in principle – he wanted to fly ships, too – but he could not justify the expense or risk without direct authorization from the Constellation. However, because the lieutenant was a distant relative of Lord Ilvar Crais, his punishment had amounted to little more than a slap on the wrist. No doubt the same would happen now.

"You were insubordinate, Ulman. You misled the base traffic tower into believing this ship was ready for a test flight."

"I thought it was, sir." Lieutenant Ulman avoided Escobar's gaze, but he seemed unsettled by more than just the scolding. "I was wrong. Your insistence on extra inspections for these old ships is . . . quite correct, sir. I apologize for being impetuous."

With a sudden chill, Escobar wondered just how close the test pilot had come to crashing the ship. The man looked completely shaken. Both of them longed to see action, tired of wasting their lives at Lubis Plain, mothballed like the ships.

Before Escobar could lose his temper, he said, "Submit your full report to the repair crew, Captain. You are grounded until further notice." *Until the next ship is ready to be tested.*

Dressed in his tattered old gold-and-black Constellation uniform, Percival patted the cowed officer affectionately on the shoulder, a congenial gesture that horrified Escobar. "Don't take it too hard, Rico. Maybe as punishment you'll be assigned to escort these ships out to the Deep Zone."

Ulman drew a deep breath and straightened. "Sounds better than the brig, sir."

Irritated, Escobar dismissed him. "That will not be necessary, Lieutenant. I intend to deliver the ships to Ridgetop myself." At least he would get some flying time in.

An inspection team entered the troop ship that had barely landed intact. Additional crews were working on other vessels that had been rolled out onto the paved landing field. Looking at all the vessels being refurbished, Escobar shook his head. "I can't understand why anyone would even want these outdated ships."

"Beggars can't be choosers. Governor Goler will use them to monitor suspicious activity."

"The Diadem suspects General Adolphus of trying to escape his exile?"

"She always suspects General Adolphus of something."

Escobar gave a proud sniff. "I'm not worried about him. He could have won the war, but lost his nerve. Even after all the bloodshed he caused, the General did not have the fortitude to see his troops to victory." His voice was filled with scorn.

The old Commodore surprised him. "It was quite noble of him, actually. The Diadem was willing to cross a moral line that Adolphus was not."

"You sound as if you admire the man!" Escobar stared at his father in amazement and dismay. He lowered his voice, though no one stood close enough to hear them. "Keep those comments to yourself, Father. Maybe you retired with a halo of glory, but you had a checkered career before that. Don't jeopardize your legacy, or mine." Percival's careless comments might affect his son's chances for advancement, regardless of Escobar's marriage to a Riomini niece.

The retired Commodore fell silent. Finally Percival cleared his throat. "Time for my first brandy of the day." The aged veteran hobbled away toward a staff car to return to the old manor house that once belonged to Adolphus.

69

The Diadem publicly released the images of her inspector's findings at the slickwater pools, and the Constellation media corps cast the story in a ridiculous light. Government advisers went on record mocking the cult members who claimed to be possessed by aliens.

The tactic backfired, though. Despite the snide media commentators in the news stories, the shadow-Xayan converts were so sincere in describing their wondrous lost civilization that even more curious travelers flooded to Hallholme from the Crown Jewels.

The massive influx of visitors stretched Sophie's abilities to the maximum and overwhelmed her lodging capacity. Money flowed in as well. New converts surrendered most of their possessions to her (which she kept in a separate account), and even the merely curious paid well for their rooms or tents. Her people scrambled to add more housing, even resorting to temporary survival tents, and the sound of construction filled the once-placid air around Slickwater Springs. She feared that an abrupt turn of Hellhole's weather could leave a swath of bodies behind, and Slickwater Springs no longer had shadow-Xayans who could deflect the storms with telemancy . . .

Devon and Antonia ran themselves ragged to keep up with all the arrivals and departures. Four employees from the main Vence operations in Helltown worked full-time just to deliver supplies from her warehouses out to Slickwater Springs. Sophie promoted several lower-level managers as swiftly as she could, and she was constantly on the lookout for new hires as business expanded beyond her wildest dreams. Slickwater Springs was such a success that she didn't have a spare moment to catch her breath and enjoy it.

On Klief, her ex-husband Gregory had probably seen the widespread reports by now. He must be tearing his hair out to see how well she was doing! Despite their scornful tone, the news reports showed Sophie looking proud, healthy, and satisfied next to their son and the lovely Antonia.

She wondered if Gregory regretted what he did to her all those years ago, but it didn't really matter. Now, even if he fumed and sneered and resented her, she wasn't worried that he would hunt her down. Her ex-husband didn't have the stamina to chase her so far, and if he sent his lawyers to Hellhole, they'd be powerless here. Devon was now an adult, and the General certainly wouldn't let Gregory pull any tricks.

Yes, Sophie was set ... if only she could keep up with the madness. Regardless of the number of people who immersed themselves, the level of slickwater remained constant. Apparently, all of the datafluid was connected through aquifers in the planet's crust, constantly flowing and replenishing itself.

A young man, giddy with new Xayan thoughts in his mind, had leaped into the slickwater for a second time, hoping to gain an additional set of alien memories. He succeeded, carrying two separate ancient lives inside his head, so that he exhibited three distinct personas. When other starstruck shadow-Xayans attempted this, though, they emerged from the pools disappointed – only around one in ten seemed capable of hosting multiple Xayan personalities.

At regular intervals, Fernando-Zairic returned to Slickwater Springs to invite the newly baptized shadow-Xayans to join their new city out near the red weed. Every one of them accepted the offer.

Fernando sauntered up to Sophie now, looking beatific as he surveyed the visitors around the pools. "As our numbers grow, our telemancers get stronger, as was our hope. Even those outsiders who choose not to immerse themselves will go home and spread the word. The Constellation knows of our plight now."

"Yes, they do."

She kept waiting for the other shoe to drop, however. Adolphus might have diverted the Diadem's inspectors for the time being, but how long could that last as their numbers grew and news spread? The General was preoccupied, though, with his final stringline preparations, and Destination Day would arrive soon enough. She hoped the Xayans could help them against the Diadem's inevitable harsh response.

As she and Fernando-Zairic watched the pools, a man garbed in clothing much too fine for Hellhole approached them. He spoke in a challenging tone. "You should be ashamed of yourselves!"

Sophie had seen plenty of skeptics or, worse, media reporters eager to expose a conspiracy. "How so?" Somehow, she managed to be polite.

"If these pools are indeed reservoirs of alien knowledge from a lost civilization, then this" – he spread his hands, and his face took on a disgusted expression – "all of this is an *embarrassment*. Wise and noble Xayans turned into a tourist attraction? And humans, dunking themselves into that organic liquid, collecting lives as if they were souvenirs? It's nothing less than sacrilege."

Sophie rolled her eyes. "And when has Diadem Michella refused to exploit anything of value in the Constellation? If this were an iperion quarry, she would have ordered us to dig an open pit half a kilometer wide, and no one would complain."

"This is different," the man insisted. "These are—"

Zairic cut him off. "It is not sacrilege, because we Xayans *wish* for this to happen. This is our future, the only way our civilization can live again. We are real. We are awake. We are being helped, not harmed. And the more people who immerse themselves, the more vibrant our race becomes. That is better than preserving artifacts for a museum."

"And what happens when all these people take Xayan personalities and go back to the Crown Jewels? Your pool is diminished."

Fernando-Zairic responded with a wry smile. "But they don't want to leave. None of them."

Sophie realized he was right. Even those who came from offworld had joined the new shadow-Xayan settlement. Not a single one had left Hellhole. Clearly not satisfied, the skeptic stalked off to speak with the others . . .

70

Although Ishop admired Laderna's tenacity and determination, he needed to be personally involved in solving the upcoming problem, now that he had returned from the dirty pustule of Hallholme. Five noble names remained on his list ... and how was he to deal with the fact that a *Duchenet* name was among them? The only clear and immediate options were Princess Keana and the Diadem herself.

So, killing a Duchenet was going to be difficult, but he was sure he and Laderna could find an eventual solution, though it would require the utmost finesse. A challenge worthy of a true noble. The list was the list, and only a weakling would change the terms just because one item might prove more problematic than the others.

He had an idea, however. Even though months had passed since the death of Louis de Carre, Princess Keana remained obsessed with finding his son Cristoph, much to her mother's dismay. That might provide an opening. Keana thought she was being subtle with her clumsy overtures, but she simply had no skill at keeping secrets or cashing in favors. She continued to make a pest of herself with her probing, ineffective questions, but no one had any reason to help her.

At another time, Ishop might have found it amusing. The Diadem's naïve daughter had never been taught how to function in the delicately structured politics of the Constellation. She remained unskilled and downright oblivious. Poor thing. She wasn't stupid, but utterly out of her league – an accident waiting to happen. He'd known for some time that Keana was the one who would have to die, as soon as he could determine how best to accomplish it.

An idea began to form in his mind, and he asked Laderna to track down all the information she could find on Cristoph de Carre. Just because Keana could not discover his whereabouts did not mean he couldn't be found easily by someone with the right skills.

Apart from the joy of eliminating another name on his list, Ishop felt that the government would benefit from this woman's removal. *For the good of the Constellation.* He very much liked the efficiency of having one task serve two purposes. He smiled to himself as wheels began to turn in his mind.

Using her particular skills, Laderna dug for information with her usual dogged determination. After Cristoph's eviction from the Vielinger estate, the disgraced lordling had simply disappeared. While some gossipers assumed the Riomini overlords had quietly murdered him, Ishop knew that was not the case. Not only would Michella have considered it a waste of time and effort (since the family was ruined anyway), she would have given *Ishop* the job.

It wasn't terribly difficult for Laderna to come up with the answer. Keana might have found it herself, if anyone had been willing to bend rules and put in extra effort for her. Laderna came to Ishop at his new townhouse, beaming, and demanding her reward. As soon as she had sealed the door and covered the windows, she began working at his clothes. "I found Cristoph de Carre."

"So, tell me."

"Not yet." She could be irritating at times.

Though he was anxious to hear the answer, Laderna took her time. Maddening how she was learning to manipulate him! He would have to put a stop to that soon, but for now it was easier to give her what she wanted.

"He went to Hellhole," she finally whispered in his ear, then giggled.

Ishop sat up in bed. It was no surprise that the Riominis would drive the young man away from Vielinger, and the Deep Zone seemed an obvious sanctuary for him. "I was just *on* that awful planet. I saw no sign of him."

"And did you study the entire planet?" She made him realize how absurd his comment had been.

He shook his head. "Of all the places Cristoph de Carre could have picked, why would he go there?" Ishop frowned at the document handed him, skimmed down the neatly organized notes. Yes, the man had gone to Hellhole, no doubt about it.

Laderna snuggled close to him. "Think about it, boss. De Carre must hate the Diadem – and who is the Diadem's greatest enemy in all the universe?"

Ishop hadn't considered that. "You think that disgraced lordling is trying to form an alliance with General Adolphus?"

She couldn't hide her grin. "If *you* were in that situation, that's what I'd advise you to do."

She massaged his shoulders, but he found it distracting. He needed to think. Maybe the man wasn't fleeing from his troubles after all. Despite the numerous accident reports from the Vielinger iperion mines, Cristoph had been a capable administrator, not at all a hedonist like his incompetent father. Maybe the lordling did have plans of his own.

Ishop knew exactly how to undercut them, and take care of another name on his list at the same time. Now the game was getting even more interesting.

The following afternoon, Ishop Heer called upon Keana in her royal apartments. He took care to arrive at a time when Bolton Crais was busy at his offices in the Army's Logistics Department. "Princess, I have good news. I came to you as soon as I found out."

At the doorway, she regarded him with suspicion. "Mr Heer, if you've come on business for my mother, I have no interest in it."

"I'm here on business for *you*, Princess. Your mother knows nothing about my visit. Perhaps we might keep this little exchange between us?" He lowered his voice. "It's about Cristoph de Carre." The name worked like a magic incantation. She quickly invited him in.

Her sitting room had a view of the spaceport and the flurry of passenger-pod shuttles landing and taking off. Perhaps she enjoyed the illusion of being able to run off and leave the planet, though the

Diadem probably kept close tabs on her. Ishop could smell perfumes and cleaning oils, but saw no sign of household staff.

"Princess, I realize you have been in a great deal of pain over the horrific events that took place some months ago. The death of Louis de Carre was a great tragedy." She slumped into a chair, focusing all of her efforts on keeping her emotions under control. "It's plain to everyone that you long to know what happened to his son. My heart goes out to you, so I have taken up your cause. Using my considerable resources, I was able to discover the answer you seek."

Keana caught her breath, half rose out of her chair. "You found Cristoph? Where is he? Is he all right?"

His sincere smile convinced her completely. "Your mother has long known that when something needs to be done, I am the man to accomplish it." He saw that Keana was in no mood for him to draw out the suspense, however, so he quickly continued. "My information is solid, Princess. Cristoph de Carre is on planet Hallholme. Even now, he is in the hands of that monster Adolphus. I don't know how long the young man can survive."

Keana seemed torn between joy and horror. "I was afraid someone might have murdered him, or that he might have killed himself like Louis. But . . . Hallholme? How awful!" She seemed energized. Her dark blue eyes held a determined fire similar to what Ishop had seen in Diadem Michella. "We've got to get him away from there."

"My hands are tied, Princess. I fear what your mother would do to me if she knew I was involved. I have told no one else about what I have found – only you. Please keep this matter between us. I would go myself if I could, but you know how vindictive the Diadem can be."

"It's up to me, then." She began to pace the sitting room with frenetic energy. He didn't even have to voice the suggestion. "I'll go there myself and find him! Can you help me make the travel arrangements, Mr Heer?"

He tried to sound reluctant. He wiped his hands on his clean, trousers. "I'll do what I can. You'd have to travel alone, tell no one, especially the Diadem."

"I don't intend to give my mother the chance to stop me." He could see she had made up her mind. "Yes, I will travel to Hallholme. Cristoph has to see that he's not alone."

"Excellent, Princess. No one else can know." She surprised Ishop by throwing her arms around him in a hug. Awkwardly, he patted her on the back and smiled to himself. The problem was practically taking care of itself.

Naïve, unprepared, unskilled, and unprotected, Keana would not last long on that nightmare planet. Soon, he would be able to cross the Duchenet name off his list.

71

When the alien pools closed down for the night so that Sophie and the workers could have a few hours of quiet time, Slickwater Springs became a peaceful place.

Antonia loved to be outside alone, just absorbing the silence and the stars. Coming to Hellhole, she had given up everything, with no thought of the future beyond getting away. At last she thought she might actually belong here. She could even envision the possibility of becoming happy.

Her small, private cabin was on the other side of the pools, far enough from the more raucous guest facilities; Devon's mother had promised her a more spacious room as soon as the large new guesthouse was finished. Anxious to return to her business concerns in Helltown, Sophie had already suggested that her son could manage the spa resort, with Antonia's help.

When Antonia left the main building, Devon walked her to the door and gave her a longing, puppy-dog look. On impulse she leaned forward and gave him a quick kiss that hinted at more to come. "Good night, Devon." He was startled, then grinned as though she'd just changed his life. She probably had.

Antonia could never forget the old star-struck days – only two years ago – when an incredibly young and naïve girl named Tona Quirrie had believed in romance and everlasting love. She knew much better now.

But Sophie's son was not the same type of man as Jako Rullins. Devon had devoted himself to becoming her friend first, as she had asked, and Antonia found her heart softening towards him.

"Be careful out there," he said to her as she walked off through the resort toward her cabin.

"I'll see you in the morning," she called.

At times, when she felt far enough away from Aeroc, she began to wonder if her terrifying experiences had been real after all, but she could never forget that her parents had been murdered, and she had run as far away from her old life as she could possibly get.

Antonia walked into the night. The yellow light from the open guest-house door continued to shine into the darkness, so she knew Devon was still standing there, watching as she departed. That pleased her.

She and Devon were not lovers. He was so innocent, so old-fashioned that he hadn't made any inappropriate moves whatsoever. She wondered if he even knew how to make a move. Right now, the very thought of sex made her shudder, but if she changed her mind and the moment was right, she realized she would have to be the instigator.

In the guest encampment, many lights remained on, since nearly sixty newcomers had just arrived. All day long, Antonia had worked with the lodge staff to prepare meals for the influx of visitors, while Devon and his mother had greeted them and given tours of the pools. Two of the shadow-Xayans lived at the camp now to serve as docents and talk about Xayan civilization.

One of the new arrivals, a rude man who scoffed at the "gullible dreamers," had jumped into the slickwater just to prove them all wrong. He emerged struggling with himself and trying to disbelieve. "I don't want this, I don't want this!" he'd cried in his human voice. "Take it away – I changed my mind!"

The shadow-Xayans tried to console him. "There is nothing we can do now. We cannot remove the presence once it has become part of you." Angry and fighting the unwanted new identity in his head, the man had been taken away from the others.

Previously, because Hallholme was such a minor stop, stringline haulers had run the route with half of their docking clamps empty. But as word spread throughout the Constellation, thanks to the Diadem's inadvertent publicity, the regular cargo haulers had to be fitted with additional passenger pods just to accommodate the increased demand.

As with all groups, the new arrivals came to Hellhole for varying reasons. Some were curious and needed to share their questions and fears with one another; some were insecure, lonely; some wanted to brood over their decision; some were adventurers, scientists, explorers; and others needed to be healed. Antonia had seen all types.

Now, as she walked the compacted gravel path, a man's shape appeared out of the darkness, standing not far from her cabin. "Excuse me! Can you help, please? There's a young woman in trouble – she hurt herself over by one of the pools."

Antonia couldn't see him well, but something in his voice carried an urgency that made her want to hurry. "I'll call for help."

"No, just you – right away." He switched on a bright light and shone it in her face, blinding her. "I only need you."

The same tone that had made her react instinctively now froze her with fear. She knew that voice.

"*Jako!*"

She tried to dart away, but the dazzling light in her face prevented her from seeing where she was going. He bounded after her, like a horrific figure from her worst nightmare – which he was.

She screamed, but Jako grabbed her shoulder and she felt a stinging in her upper arm. "Well, Tona, I'm glad you remember my name at least."

In his firm grip, she tried to yell again, but her breath had turned cold. She could only wheeze in a weak and pathetic voice. "Help ..."

"I gave you a stun shot. You'll still be able to walk and do a few other things, but it saps your strength. I can't have you collapsing on the ground – you'd be useless to me. I need you to walk out of here under your own power, so we can go back to the way things were."

"No ..." Antonia tried to pull away from him, but her bones had turned rubbery as if she were one of the cartilaginous Original Xayans.

When he dragged her forward, her clumsy feet kicked up dirt and pebbles. "I've been looking for you a long time, Tona." She struggled, tried to pull herself away. She had no weapon, and they were in the shadows, heading toward the outermost pool. She nearly tripped on one of the chunks of obsidian strewn about, but Jako hauled her upright.

She tried to stall. "How did you find me?"

He just snorted. "I taught you how to run and how to hide. I taught you all the tricks that you used against me. And because I'm such a good teacher, I thought I might never find you again ... and then what happens? Your own image gets sent across the Crown Jewels for everyone to see! How stupid was that? Oh, you changed your name and your appearance, but I've seen you in all kinds of disguises. I recognized you right away. Your own parents would have, too ... if they were still alive."

"You killed them." She wanted to shout, but her voice had little strength. Antonia had never confronted him about it, since she ran away as soon as she discovered the truth.

He didn't seem surprised. "I *freed* you from your shackles. Think of those wondrous years we had." Now that her vision had recovered from the dazzling light, she could see his shadowy face – a face she had hoped never to see again. The torch's bright circle of light bobbed around on the ground like one of the skittering spheres of St Elmo's Fire that she had seen atop the greenhouse domes.

"I won't ... go back with you." Even though her muscles still functioned to a degree, Antonia let her body fall limp, refusing to cooperate. He slapped her hard and dragged her, but she resisted. She panted, caught her breath, and tried to scream again, but all that came out was a quiet hooting sound.

"Fine. If you want to be on the ground, then be on your back." Releasing his grip, he pushed her hard onto the crumbly dirt. "We've got unfinished business."

Jako dropped the light beside her so that it illuminated a swath of sand and pebbles like a glowing blanket, as if he had some warped idea of romanticism. Terrified, Antonia tried to get back to her feet, but her muscles would not respond. She felt weak, dizzy.

Always before, Jako had used psychological means to render her helpless so that he could have his way with her. The fact that he would use a debilitating drug showed his cowardly desperation, but it made her essentially powerless at the moment. She tried to raise herself to her elbows, but he shoved her back down, dropped to his knees beside her, and tore her blouse open.

She punched his chest, but without much force. He hit her back, much harder, then stared at her exposed breasts. "Now there's a sight

I've been wanting to see again." He yanked at her pants. She tried to kick out at him, but her rubbery legs flopped up and down. She aimed for his groin but missed.

"Why are you fighting me? I made you what you are, changed you from a pampered vapid little princess into an independent woman. Aren't you grateful I made you strong?"

Summoning a steel core from within herself, Antonia reached up and clawed his face. She scratched the skin of his cheek, trying to gouge out an eye. Though she missed her target, she did draw blood.

"Bitch!" He struck her face so hard that she reeled, fighting for consciousness.

And then he raped her.

He finished quickly, probably more concerned about being caught than about his own pleasure. "It'll be better after this, I promise. There are so many worlds I want to show you. And no one will ever find us."

When Jako stood up, she started to crawl away, using all the strength she could muster. "No . . ." she whispered, only to choke on uncontrollable sobs. She vomited on the ground. Her voice still wasn't strong enough to call for help.

Behind her, she heard a wordless cry of rage and disbelief. She turned to see Devon in the backwash of light, his expression of rage exaggerated by shadows. He rushed forward, his mouth open, his blue eyes blazing with a ferocity that she'd never seen before. He picked up one of the large sharp-edged blocks of obsidian and raised it.

Still refastening his pants, Jako turned, just as Devon smashed him on the side of the head with all of his strength. A splash of crimson sprayed out from where the black volcanic glass struck.

Jako crumpled, raising his hands – as helpless now as Antonia had been a few moments earlier. Devon raised the chunk of obsidian and brought it down on Jako's head again, crushing his skull.

Antonia struggled unsteadily to her feet, trying to block out the dying cries of her assailant. She lurched away into the night, desperate to hide in the darkness, but she didn't think she could ever get away from what had happened to her.

Jako collapsed facedown on the ground, but Devon still wasn't finished. He raised the rock a third time.

72

In the mocking starlight, Antonia staggered to the outermost slick-water pool. The tearing pain between her legs and the ache of the bruises on her face were nothing compared to the anguished horror that rippled through her mind and soul like Hellhole's worst static storm.

She had left her torn clothes behind, but didn't care about her nakedness, couldn't think of it. Her body was wracked with spasms. Her mouth tasted foul from the vomit. She felt filthy in a way that made her want to scrub away her own skin.

Moaning, Antonia grasped the thin wire barrier around the alien pool and stared at its hypnotic surface. She had been foolish to let down her guard, to allow herself a bit of contentment and happiness. That wasn't for her. She would never be free of her memories or of her past.

And now, because of her, Devon had become an animal. She had seen the look on his face and knew what rage had driven him to do. Even though he could justify his actions and had saved her, he would always have blood on his hands. Devon would *always* know what it was like to kill another person. And it was all because of her.

She should have stayed away from him.

Her head spun with images of her slain family, the years of running and living in fear. For so long she had believed Jako's lies about Lord Riomini's hunters pursuing them, and she had been terrified every time she saw a suspicious-looking man or law-enforcement official. Jako had manufactured that terror within her. Now he was dead ... but not before inflicting another unendurable memory on her.

But Antonia had observed the serenity, the absolute acceptance, and gentle calm on the shadow-Xayans. Maybe if she accepted an alien personality, it would smother the voices she could not endure.

Antonia parted the wire fence and climbed through to reach the edge of the shimmering pool. She smelled faint ozone and a rich oily scent from the organic crystalline ooze. The slickwater was waiting for her.

She heard someone running up behind her, breathing hard; in a moment of panic, she thought it was Jako again, coming after her with his skull split open and his brains spilling out, hands extended like claws.

But it wasn't Jako. It was Devon.

"Antonia, he can't hurt you anymore!" The young man came closer. "He can't hurt you! I'm here." He held out his hands, pleading for her to stop, but the fence separated them. His hands were covered in blood.

Without hesitation, she dove into the pool.

The shock of contact became an instant enfolding embrace. She couldn't move or breathe ... but this was entirely different from the stun-drug Jako had used. In a matter of moments, all of her physical pain washed away.

Antonia felt the water swirling in a silver light, like a whirlpool spinning and spinning her. Her mind pleaded for release from her anguish. Her emotional outpouring thrummed like desperate music through the network of information that represented the memories of Xaya.

She observed miracles and fantasies, wondrous cities of curves and colors and crystals, and an unfolding history, the epic saga of a lost race. Now in her mind the Xayans' caterpillar-like forms no longer seemed alien and repulsive, but streamlined, with structures of physical perfection, utility, and beauty.

Antonia understood much more now, but she was still empty, lonely, and yearning for it all to change. Her emotional state acted as a magnet, calling to a strong and sympathetic consciousness in the slickwater pool, a mind that could understand her. She opened herself ... and found exactly the right presence, one that seemed destined for her.

Jhera.

The powerful Xayan consciousness helped her, soothed her ... and became one with her.

On the crumbling shore of the pool, Devon collapsed to his knees, crying out, "Antonia!" He had cut his palms and forearms on the fence wires as he tore his way through in a rush to stop her. But he was too late.

This night had already been so full of horrors. When he remembered what that disgusting man had done to Antonia, Devon wanted to kill him all over again, and yet he hated himself for what he had done. The soft crunch of broken skull had been so easy. The rush of blood, the power he'd felt in taking the man's life ... the feeling sickened him.

His hands were still sticky from the killing. He was appalled that he had meant to reach out and grab Antonia with those hands, to stop her from diving into the slickwater. He shuddered at the thought of getting blood on her skin. Then he collapsed into even greater despair.

She was lost. She had gone into the slickwater. He knew what that meant.

After an interminable interval, Antonia emerged naked, glistening, silvery and beautiful. As she stepped out of the pool, slickwater dripped from her dark hair; her perfect body came toward him like a water angel.

"It's all right, Devon," she said. "My pain is washed way."

His throat was raw and sore from calling out her name. He stared, couldn't find his voice, then finally croaked, "Is it you, Antonia? Is it still you?"

"It is still me ... and also Jhera. This is what I needed, and now I can finally be at peace. I don't have to worry about my past ever again. *We* don't have to worry about it. You and I can still be together."

Devon's heart lurched. For months, he had longed to hear her say those words. When she'd kissed him that night, he had been so hopeful – that one moment, the highest high point in his life had been crushed down to insignificance.

"We can still be together," she repeated, standing in the pool. The water level was shallower than he'd thought, which made no sense, because he had seen her dive in.

"We can't, Antonia." He had seen it before. When couples came to the slickwater and contemplated their future, if one became a shadow-Xayan and the other didn't, a vast gulf appeared, and the relationship was never the same. "We never had a chance."

"But we do now." Antonia smiled. "Jhera is a powerful telemancer, and she is me. She has lost her love, too, in the slickwater pool. Birzh is still dormant in there, and she cannot bear to be separated from him. I love you, Devon – and Jhera loves Birzh. We can be together, both of us . . . all four of us. I can make it happen. If you enter the pool while I am here, Jhera can choose the right one for you . . . for *us*."

Devon stared at the pools, and at her. He felt an impossible longing. He had hoped for so long that he and Antonia could be together, and he wanted her more than anything in the world.

If he entered the slickwater, it would devastate his mother, but everything about this evening was bound to destroy her as soon as she found out. The man he had killed, the attack on Antonia . . .

Devon had never been tempted by the alien baptism before, but if what Antonia said was correct, this might be his only chance to be with her. If he managed to take on the Birzh personality, the lover of Jhera, their future would be doubly cemented together. However, if he hesitated and talked to his mother about it, he knew she would not let him make up his own mind. And, with all the new volunteers that had just arrived, some other convert might receive Birzh's personality. And Devon would lose Antonia forever.

"Devon," she said in a soothing, hypnotic voice, "I'm not afraid any more. You and I belong together . . . and Jhera belongs with her love who is also here in the slickwater pools. She can guide you to him, binding us closer together than you ever imagined."

He didn't want to question it, didn't want to think about it. He knew what they both had been through. Drawing a shuddering breath, Devon extended his hand to her. His fingers were still coated with Jako's blood, but Antonia didn't seem to notice. She took his hand and drew him into the alien water.

73

Though Ishop Heer gave her the necessary information, Keana couldn't rely on anyone but herself to do what needed to be done. No question about it: *she* would have to go to that horrible planet and rescue Cristoph. After so many downturns and missteps, she needed to do something right for once.

With secret assistance from Heer, Keana made arrangements to depart quickly for Hallholme. She disguised her identity, left no record of where she was going, told no one (although she was sure Bolton would be distraught about her disappearance), and packed only the absolute necessities.

Diadem Michella would be furious when she found out what her daughter had done. And that brought a smile to Keana's face.

She just left.

Exiting the passenger pod at the Michella Town spaceport, Keana wore a drab brown dress that she had purchased along with a tattered valise from a serving woman on Sonjeera. Not knowing how much simple clothes were supposed to cost, Keana was sure she had paid far more than the outfit was worth, but the promise of anonymity was worth the extra money. To complete the disguise, she messed up her auburn hair and secured it with a stained band.

The excitement in her eyes could easily be misinterpreted as desperation, and she did look like many of the others who had signed on for a new chance out in the Deep Zone. For Keana, this was a great adventure, unlike anything she had ever done – and it was the *right* thing to do. She was entirely out of her element, and she felt strengthened by it. Louis would have been proud of her.

Tucked into a side compartment of the valise were the only possessions that truly mattered to her – love letters and passionate poems that Louis had written, old-fashioned tokens of his devotion. She had also saved some of her own responses as tangible reminders of those two years of joy. She kept her favorite image of Louis with her at the edge of the Pond of Birds, as well as a picture of Cristoph de Carre, ostensibly so she could show others and ask his whereabouts, but Keana just liked to study the lines of his face and envision his father's features there.

In some imagined happy world, if Fate had been kind instead of cruel, Keana would have found true love with Louis at the proper time, rather than marrying dear, dull Bolton. She and Louis could have been happy, and might have had a son of their own. She could never have that imaginary happy ending now, but at least she could find and help Cristoph . . .

As the other passengers disembarked, she tried to blend in, though she felt dramatically out of place. The rough-looking men and women, probably even some convicted criminals, all seemed self-sufficient, aware of what they had to do, accustomed to being responsible for their own survival. It was a new experience for Keana.

The minute she set foot on the pavement, a blast of dirty air made her cough. She had never smelled anything like it on Sonjeera. A hot wind raised dust devils on the dirt streets. When she arrived in Michella Town, a lean and unshaven vendor tried to sell her a protective hat, but a gust sent his wares spinning away, and he chased them along the composite sidewalk. Something about the man's embarrassment and earnestness softened her suspicions, and she decided to take a chance. She had to ask someone.

Keana set down her battered valise and waited for the vendor to gather his things. She had already concocted a cover story during the stringline passage. "Excuse me, I'm looking for someone. My son signed up for a new life on this planet, and I need to find him. He's a grown man, but still ... a mother worries."

The man's brow furrowed. "You don't talk like the usual down-and-outs who come in on the stringline."

"Our noble family fortunes took a downturn, and we lost all our lands. That's why my son came here for a fresh start, but I think he's made a mistake."

The hat-vendor laughed. "Your fortunes must have fallen a long way if he chose *Hellhole* over the life he had!"

She opened her valise and brought out her small pouch of jewelry. "I can pay for information. His name is Cristoph de Carre. Have you heard of him?"

The man seemed amused by her offer. "I could say anything and take your money, then I'd be gone before you even knew I was lying to you."

"You look like an honest man."

"I haven't heard that one before!" He laughed and ran his gaze over her, not fooled by her rough clothes. "You've got money, or you ran off with some, but I'm not going to take it from you. I used to dupe rich ladies until I was convicted and sent here, but I don't need to take advantage of a defenseless newbie." He pointed down the street to a two-story office building. "Go to Central Records and tell them what you need." He let out a rude snort. "*They'll* be happy to take your bribe."

In the Central Records office she tried to insist on results before paying the clerks. One man referred her to another, then two others, and she had to pay each of them, a gold ring to the first and a set of diamond earrings to the next, then a locket. She had no doubt they were taking advantage of her, but she persisted. She felt she was close to the answer she had wanted for so long.

The third clerk made a great show of sifting through complex databases and even hardcopy ledgers. "Cristoph de Carre ... Looks like he's bounced around. Worked in dust-system maintenance at the spaceport for a few weeks, then ran a mine excavation team before he dropped out of the system. Hmm, that's odd." He looked up. "Ah, now I know where

I've heard the name. General Adolphus transferred him personally."

Keana had to surrender another ring before the clerk gave her the last piece of information. "Go out to Slickwater Springs. Sophie Vence will know."

Keana wasn't entirely convinced of the lead, but at least she had a destination.

74

Adolphus had waited a long time for this day – the completion of the first new stringline route in the Deep Zone. A momentous occasion! Though it sounded like hyperbole, this was indeed the beginning of a new era for the frontier worlds.

At the Ankor launch site, the large sinkhole had been filled in, and vast landing fields were paved. If tests continued to go well, cargo upboxes would soon be lifted to the new stringline hub for distribution to other DZ planets, and downboxes would deliver trade goods from arriving ships.

After today, it would begin. Fueled by the stories of resurrected personalities and the crowds coming to the alien pools, all curious eyes remained distracted by Slickwater Springs and the growing settlement of shadow-Xayans nearby. Nobody paid attention to the Ankor site or the activities there.

He still hoped for a more direct benefit of the converts and the resurrected alien race; their telemancy showed remarkable potential, and he hoped he could add them to his defenses of Hellhole. Sophie Vence had astonished him with her story of how the converts had joined together to deflect a full-force static storm about to devastate Slickwater Springs. But with or without alien telemancy here on Hellhole, he also had to lay down the full strategic plan for the rest of the Deep Zone.

Adolphus knew where his dreams and his destiny lay. Yes, the Xayan race fascinated him, and he imagined its great potential – both for the advancement of his colonists and for the defense of Hallholme – but the independent stringline network was far more important. Once he consolidated the DZ, then he could study the lost race at his leisure.

If anyone survived that long.

Now, in the hours before dawn, bright lights lit up the whole complex. He readied himself a full two hours before the expected arrival, knowing he wouldn't be able to sleep. Though the stringline engineers had calculated and recalculated the travel time from Candela, this was an untried route. Adolphus knew well enough that practice did not always adhere to theory.

Rendo Theris, the man who had taken over Ankor's administrative duties after the grief-stricken Tel Clovis resigned, now paced the interior of the admin shack, full of nervous energy. He had been drinking local coffee to keep himself awake throughout the night. "No message, sir. Let's hope they're on schedule."

Five days ago, a message packet had arrived by FTL ship, announcing that the first trailblazer ship had successfully laid down an iperion path connecting Hellhole and Candela – the first link in the new DZ transportation network. Its significance was akin to the Golden Spike in the transcontinental railroad, an event Adolphus had read about in ancient Earth history. Within weeks, the whole fleet of his carefully coordinated trailblazers would arrive at their destinations throughout the Deep Zone, and all those other planets would soon join the network. But this was the test run.

Rendo looked nervous. "Do you think Candela will just send a volunteer to prove that it can be done? It is an unverified route."

With a faint smile, Adolphus shook his head. "Administrator Hu is going to be on that first stringline ship. She'd fire anyone who tried to suggest otherwise. Our orbiting hub is fully functional?"

"Eight of the twelve nodes are already operational, General, and the rest are approaching completion. A new one powers up and finishes its shakedown every few days. We'll be ready for D-Day, sir. Don't worry."

Even so, Adolphus had plenty to worry about. The provocative situation practically guaranteed war with the Constellation, but he had to cement his victory so swiftly that the Diadem's powerful forces would not be able to react in time – even if he had to destroy the Sonjeera-Deep Zone stringline connections on his end. Tanja Hu, one of his closest allies, would operate the first test route, followed closely by Ian Walfor and then his other nine co-conspirators. They had all discreetly acquired their own ships which would be ready to defend the stringline terminus rings from Sonjeera – a single point of vulnerability, no matter how large a fleet the Army of the Constellation sent against them.

Adolphus had received reports from his sleeper cells on the rest of the DZ planets, and over the past six months they had recruited more locals, increased the grassroots level of dissatisfaction with the Diadem's oppression, even though none of the populations realized that independence might be so close at hand.

He knew he was about to unleash the whirlwind. As closely timed as such incredible distances would allow, trailblazers should arrive at their scattered destinations, unannounced, each installing a terminus ring above a Deep Zone planet. Every eventuality had to be considered and dealt with. With that in mind, secret operatives had been stationed on any DZ world where he and his fellow conspirators felt the planetary administrator might side with the Constellation rather than independence. Those operatives were armed and ready to ensure a swift takeover.

"What about the new connection from here to Buktu? Have we heard from Ian Walfor? He'll be glad to use fast commercial ships for a change instead of his slow FTL clunkers."

Theris checked his records, though he must surely have known the answer off the top of his head. "Administrator Walfor flew the trailblazer himself and should have arrived at Buktu yesterday or the day before. I expect we'll be receiving him on an inaugural return voyage very soon now. If calculations are correct, the Candela hauler will be here within the hour, sir."

Seventy minutes later, just before local dawn, the stringline ship from Candela hurtled into the system – a ten-minute error that puzzled the theoreticians and delighted the pragmatic General. Everything was going precisely according to plan. How he wished he could be up there in orbit, sitting in the hub's command chamber, to receive Tanja Hu directly. But for now he would continue to abide by his promise to the Diadem and remain on the planet; it was a matter of honor.

Except for his handful of allies, the remaining Deep Zone planetary administrators had been kept in the dark about his bold plan. Once the wealth of new opportunities appeared, though, any logical person would see the advantages to the alternative network, even those who still considered themselves patriotic members of the Constellation under Diadem Michella.

However, Adolphus needed to give them something concrete, more than mere words. It was imperative for him to demonstrate the superiority of his vision. It had to *work*.

Rendo Theris touched his earadio and beamed. "Administrator Hu's vessel has safely docked at the stringline terminus!"

On the shack's comm screen, the dark-haired Candela woman leaned into the image area. She looked exceptionally pleased. "Permission to come to the surface, General Adolphus?"

"Most enthusiastically granted."

"Then I'll be right down."

Rendo paced nervously around the landing area while the passenger pod descended from the orbital hub, but Adolphus was confident. "Relax, Mr Theris. If we can establish a whole new stringline network, we should be able to land a passenger pod without too much trouble." He stood under the floodlights. The eastern horizon was suffused with brightening light.

Gazing into the greenish sky, Adolphus tried to catch a glimpse of the descending vehicle. A glint of light was followed by the screech of deceleration engines, and presently the passenger pod landed on one of Ankor's paved landing areas, within five meters of its projected arrival.

With as much decorum as he could summon, given his pride and excitement, Adolphus marched forward in the dawn to greet Tanja Hu. The pod's hatch opened, and the dark-haired woman emerged, blinking in the morning light.

Adolphus brusquely shook her hand. "Welcome to our new Hellhole Spaceport, Administrator."

Tanja looked at the rugged landscape that was still swathed in the shadows of daybreak. "Let me savor this moment, General." She rapped her knuckles quickly on the pod's still-steaming hull; if the hot metal burned her knuckles, she showed no sign of it. "After today, none of us in the Deep Zone needs the Constellation anymore."

75

In her mind – inside Jhera's life – Antonia remembered the last days of Xaya, the vivid terrors and triumphs before the destruction came. At the end, Jhera and Birzh had clung to the hope that Zairic's desperate plan would succeed, although they knew how slim the probabilities were . . .

Antonia embraced Devon in the pool – and Birzh was there with him, a part of him, just as Jhera was part of her. Birzh . . . her lover, her companion! After losing each other in the slickwater, they had waited for centuries, and by the force of their love the two Xayans had come together again. Now, all those memories roared into her mind.

In the final weeks before the world ended, Xayan engineers had dug reservoirs all across the world to be filled with the preserved remnants of an entire generation. As powerful telemancers, Jhera and Birzh encouraged their people to go to the nearest reservoir; they showed their frightened fellows what needed to be done to achieve immortality. Dissolving themselves into the slickwater was the best hope they had. Even the skeptics had no argument. The combined strength of the planet's telemancers was not enough to divert the asteroid, and the impact would kill them all within days.

Ah, but those last days! Each second of life had seemed so desperate, and so fleetingly sweet. The Xayans could not evacuate their planet. Only one faction had the technology to travel among the stars, and they were already gone with some of the most powerful telemancers. Another faction, led by Encix, had squandered their last days digging out and armoring the preservation bunker, in which they placed recordings and artifacts, a sampling of their racial heritage ... a museum. A *crypt*. But even if their plans succeeded, Encix could preserve only five Original Xayans; the rest of the population had no chance of surviving.

But by dissolving their memories in the slickwater, the Xayan race could endure. By the millions, they had surrendered themselves to the slickwater pools, gelatinous bodies sloughing away into the sentience-absorbing liquid that recorded every scrap of information about who they were.

When time grew short at the end, and it became apparent that not everyone could be saved in time, Zairic and the leaders tried to select the best and most important Xayans, the lives and memories that must be preserved.

As the asteroid approached, the crowds grew larger at the slickwater reservoirs. People began to panic, realizing that there was not enough time. Jhera, Birzh, and other powerful telemancers guided by Zairic himself worked up until the last moment, saving as many as possible.

When thunder began to shoot through the sky and the fiery shockwave hammered down upon them, Jhera had extended an appendage, touched Birzh's soft skin. With a shuddering clamor of love that resonated between them, they had used their own powers of telemancy and slumped forward into the slickwater that was already trembling with the impact to come.

That was the last thought Jhera had. She and Birzh had been lost in the pool of lives for centuries. And now they were back.

Zairic's bold vision had proved true, and he had shown them the way to save themselves. Even though their race had lost its chance for *ala'ru*, the racial transformation that was their destiny, the Jhera inside Antonia felt joy to know that they might have another opportunity to change the universe. Zairic had been correct in that, as well.

Rejoicing filled every fiber of her being, and Antonia felt an opening in her mind, *of* her mind, to the powers and possibilities. As all the painful, horrific images of Jako drifted away, she became aware of her own body and realized that she was clasping Devon in the pool. Their touch was completely different from the last one that Jhera and Birzh had shared, yet fundamentally the same.

Holding each other, she and Devon-Birzh levitated out of the pool. Using the telemancy that their alien companions controlled, they continued upward to hover over the settlement of Slickwater Springs. They flew above all that they had been before. Sharing their thoughts as they rose into the sky, the two kissed. They flew higher still.

76

In the middle of the night, Sophie awoke when Devon knocked on the door to her room. He stood, strangely calm, in the dimness, but she knew her son well enough to sense that something had changed. All shreds of sleep vanished. "Devon, what's wrong?"

"I have to tell you all of it, Mother. But first, the terrible part." A chill ran down Sophie's spine, and she sat up in bed. "I killed a man," he said plainly. "He attacked Antonia."

Sophie didn't know which question to ask first. She blurted them all in quick succession. "Is she all right? Are *you* all right? Who was this man?" Sophie got up and put on a pair of shoes without bothering to change out of her loose nightclothes.

"Antonia is outside, and yes, she's all right now. So am I."

Sophie was moving, trying to solve the problem, taking charge of the situation. She hurried to the door, took his arm as she looked for the lights. "Show me the body first. Are you sure he's dead?"

"Yes, he is dead."

It was too much all at once. "We'll contact General Adolphus right away." He was at Ankor for the completion of the new stringline hub, but he would take care of this. She needed to protect Devon. "Your voice sounds strange – you must be in shock." This all seemed so unreal.

"I'm not in shock, Mother. I know exactly what happened."

Speaking very little, Devon led her out of the main house to where Antonia waited in the shadows. Sophie ran forward. "There you are! Devon said you were attacked."

"I was raped." She had pulled her torn clothes back on. In a strangely clinical tone, Antonia explained who Jako Rullins was, what he had done to her family and to her, how he had hunted her down, found her, and nearly destroyed her again.

Sophie reeled. On the barren ground not far from the outermost pool lay the corpse. A small, bright glow spilled across the ground where the man had dropped his torchlight. Sophie did not need to bend closer to see that he was indeed dead. His head was a bloody mess; Devon had not simply struck once, but battered him repeatedly . . .

"Oh, Devon! And you, Antonia!" Sophia reached out and put her arms around them both. "We'll take care of this . . . this garbage. There'll be an investigation, but everything will be all right. It was self-defense. The truth will come out."

She held the two, expecting them to break down and begin sobbing, but felt a rigidity in both of them. They were like statues.

"There's more to tell you, Mother."

Sophie's alarm was invaded by a creeping, dreadful certainty. She picked up the torch on the ground, turned it to their faces. There it was: the odd, but familiar, sheen in their eyes.

They told her the rest, and Sophie nearly collapsed; she kept herself upright only out of sheer habit. She couldn't imagine what these two had been through – and now she couldn't imagine what she would do without Devon. The *real* Devon. "If only you'd come to me first, I could have helped you. And Antonia too!"

But when she raised her head and saw how calm, serene, and centered they were even in the wake of such astonishing events, Sophie was at a loss for words. Finally, she said with forced resignation, "I know you never planned to do this, but there must have been some other way. I don't know this Birzh . . ." Her voice hitched. "But you are still my son, Devon." She held him tightly. "I still love you."

"Without what Jhera has done for me," Antonia said, "I wouldn't have found the strength and peace that I have now. I'd forgotten what it was like to be happy, and now Jhera and I both have what we want."

Devon took Antonia's hand. "So do I."

Sophie knew that no amount of complaining and scolding could undo what they had done. Once exposed to the slickwater, Devon and Antonia could not surrender the alien lives that now resided within them, even if they had been willing to do so – and they certainly didn't seem interested in that.

Sophie forced strength into her voice and hoped she sounded convincing. "It's no secret that I wanted you two to get together. You're a perfect match – but I never expected it to happen this way, this complicated way. I have a thousand things I want to say to you, and a thousand things I wish were different." She heaved a deep breath. "But since I'm running Slickwater Springs and welcoming anyone who comes here to receive an alien consciousness, I can't very well chastise you two for doing exactly what I advertise." Her voice cracked. "But please don't leave me."

"We are still who we are, Mother," Devon said. "Just different. Just *more*. But rest assured, we'll remain here with you."

Before sunrise, Sophie moved with stern determination, her lips pressed together in hard silence as she wrapped up the man's body. Devon and Antonia carried the shapeless package to a storage shed near the main house. Still asleep, none of the newcomers responded to the commotion. She did not want to panic them; they didn't need to know there had been a wolf in the fold.

Throughout the process, Devon and Antonia were entirely unconcerned. In the morning, other people would notice their changed behavior, their odd eyes. Sophie decided she would keep them out of sight for a while. Fernando-Zairic would want to speak with them, and she hoped they wouldn't change their minds about staying at Slickwater Springs. Some part of them was still Devon and Antonia.

For now, Sophie shut off the clamor of other demands in her mind and concentrated on taking care of this nasty piece of business. Jako Rullins had nothing to do with the other visitors. He had not come for the slickwater and had no interest in the alien civilization. He had made his way here only to abduct Antonia Anqui and hurt her. Devon's actions had protected the girl, probably saved her life. No one would argue that.

Hellhole had laws, and General Adolphus strictly enforced them. On a planet with such harsh conditions, so few resources, and so many exiled convicts, lawlessness might well have grown rampant, but he had created a rigid safety net.

The question of a crime committed by someone who was now a shadow-Xayan had never come up. Devon was no longer the person who had killed Antonia's attacker. She steeled herself – that part didn't matter. *Jako* was the criminal, and her son had defended a victim. Considering the uproar this planet was about to experience as soon as he announced the stringline network, she was sure the General would grant some sort of dispensation.

This was the morning the first stringline ship was supposed to arrive from Candela. Sophie knew she would disrupt Adolphus's moment of glory, but she contacted him nevertheless. He needed to know.

Shortly after he and Tanja Hu toasted their triumph, the General received Sophie's distraught message, and he reacted with a slow burn of rage to learn about Antonia's attacker, but Sophie urged him not to leave Ankor, especially now. "I know this needs to be investigated, Tiber – but please keep this as quiet as possible, considering what those two have been through."

From her image on the message screen, he could see how disturbed she was. "I'll send Craig Jordan to look into the matter discreetly," Adolphus said. "But I have to impose the rule of law – it's the basis of civilization. Hellhole already has more than its share of convicts, misfits, and independent colonists. I can't have one justice system for myself and my friends and another system for everyone else."

He pondered as another disturbing thought occurred to him: what if the shadow-Xayans and the settlement Fernando-Zairic had founded did not accept the same laws as the rest of Hellhole? He would have to address that with them – later.

Sophie would never back away from defending Devon. "I'll make a clear enough case, Tiber. We'll get information on Jako Rullins from the

Constellation. Sounds like he's wanted for murder on Aeroc, possibly other crimes, and we know what he did to Antonia." Her nostrils flared. "If I'd been there, I'd have killed him myself."

Adolphus nodded. "And if the facts are as you've described them – which I'm sure they will be – I'll see to it that the body is disposed of in the wastelands. Devon will be cleared. It's an obvious case of self-defense."

Sophie looked satisfied. "Thank you, Tiber. I know you didn't need anything to distract you on this, of all days. Sorry to interrupt you with a personal matter."

"It's more than just a personal matter. It's your son."

She took a moment to find her voice. With a soft smile she said, "Administrator Hu is just the first of many, and I know your hands are full. Now go and show the rest of the Constellation what the future looks like."

77

Out on the clearcut hillsides once covered by goldenwood groves, Territorial Governor Goler found Tasmine on her knees in the dirt. Recent rains had left the sandy soil soft and muddy, but the old woman didn't seem to care. With a swollen sack draped across her shoulder, she knelt where the topsoil had washed away to expose the stumps. Fronds of regrowth already poked up from the root systems.

Tasmine reached into her sack, pulled out seedlings she grew in her garden house, and planted them; her movements were as diligent and purposeful as a prayer. Since the seedlings had such deep meaning for her, she was here after the storm, planting the tiny trees to create another grove. The old woman glanced up at him with a weary and resigned expression. "I have to do this to honor the people who died here. Nobody else remembers them."

Goler looked around. "Does this hillside have special significance?" The secret mass grave of the murdered settlers was in an entirely different valley.

"The loggers think the goldenwood just naturally grows the way it does, but my family planted these trees generations ago. We needed them in order to survive. Goldenwood was a vital resource, back when we couldn't rely on outside supplies."

"Back when Ridgetop didn't have to send off a tribute to Sonjeera."

"We still don't *have* to," Tasmine retorted. "And yet we do it anyway, because it is easier than resisting the Constellation."

"If I don't do as the Diadem commands, she'll just replace me with somebody else." Goler dropped down next to her. "Here, let me help. I don't mind getting my hands a little dirty."

He took one of the seedlings from the sack and copied her motions, scooping out dirt and packing it around the delicate plant. A new grove of fast-growing goldenwood trees would soon reclaim this hillside, only to be harvested once more whenever the Diadem demanded her due.

Tasmine's expression was wistful but troubled as she worked. "It was an old tradition for us – we planted a goldenwood tree in remembrance of our lost loved ones. But I don't have enough seedlings for all the people the Constellation killed here."

No matter how terrible he felt about the "Ridgetop Recovery," Goler could not think of a way to make it right. Yes, he *could* expose the truth of the massacre, cause a scandal ... but that would certainly mean the end of his political career. He was under no illusions about how Michella would respond to the betrayal.

The air was heavy with a rich, loamy fragrance. He and his friend fell into an equable silence as they worked together. She could have spoken names of her lost loved ones aloud as she planted seedlings in their honor, but Tasmine remained silent, keeping that part to herself. He didn't press her.

As the Territorial Governor, Goler was never left undisturbed for long. The codecall receiver buzzed at his side – someone tracking him down, using the high-security frequency. The local deputy administrator was supposed to deal with matters that did not absolutely require Goler's intervention, but now he demanded a response. "A ship has arrived, Governor. The pilot says – he says he flew all the way from *Hallholme!*"

"Hallholme? There's no stringline ship due from Sonjeera for another four days."

"Not via the Sonjeera hub, sir!" The deputy's voice was almost a squawk. "He says he came direct – by a new stringline path! He delivered a new terminus ring in orbit."

The sheer audacity of the idea set off possibilities like fireworks in Goler's mind. "Have security check the man and bring him to my residence." In an abrupt motion he stood, brushing dirt from his hands and trousers. Tasmine regarded him curiously, and he said to her, "Obviously, it can't be true."

"Really?" She bent back to her planting work. "How else could he have gotten here?"

Goler rushed to his residence, where he barely had time to clean up before a gaunt, sickly-looking man was ushered in. Having made such an outrageous claim, the pilot was not at all what Goler had expected. He looked exhausted and obviously unwell; nevertheless, he had taken the time to slick back his hair and put on an impeccable formal suit, as if he meant to attend a grand ball at the Diadem's palace.

The stranger's voice was hoarse and raspy. "Territorial Governor Goler, my name is Ernst Packard – *Captain* Ernst Packard. I've just piloted a trailblazer ship from the new stringline hub above planet Hallholme, and on the way I've laid down an iperion path. Congratulations – your two worlds are now connected by a direct line that bypasses Sonjeera entirely." Pride radiated from him. "What do you have to say about that?"

Goler took the time to draw several quick breaths before he responded. "I say you have my undivided attention. You'd best explain yourself." He crossed his arms over his chest.

"All of the DZ planets are being connected, and there's nothing you can do about it. General Tiber Adolphus launched an entire fleet of trailblazer ships, and within the next week or so, the whole Deep Zone is going to be one big network – a network separate from the Crown Jewels."

"That's ... not possible," Goler said, deadly quiet.

"Now that's a rather rash statement, Governor, since it already exists. I stand before you as proof." Packard remained unfazed and matter-of-fact.

Goler sank heavily into his chair. "Where did you get the iperion? The Vielinger quarries are nearly tapped out. Even black-market supplies could never build such an extensive network."

"You didn't think anybody would find another source of iperion in all the worlds of the Deep Zone?"

"But Diadem Michella—"

"You of all people should understand that the Diadem doesn't know everything."

Brian Herbert and Kevin J. Anderson

Goler wrestled with the seismic implications of this news. Verifying the claim wouldn't be difficult. Either the terminus ring was there, or it wasn't. If Packard's report proved to be true, he was shocked ... but pleased. Only a rebel like Adolphus would attempt to orchestrate something so audacious. Now that he considered it further, it all seemed plausible. The exiled General would rub this in the noses of all the Crown Jewel governments.

Ernst Packard swayed, nearly on the point of collapse. "May I have some water, please, Governor?" He fell into a spasm of coughing, and Goler called for food and drink. Though Tasmine was still out in the groves, other household staff rushed to bring refreshments. Packard looked nearly dead.

Goler was well aware of the ill effects of long-term exposure to iperion. Would the General really send his trailblazer captains on such a mission without adequate protection? Goler had never entirely believed the Diadem's horror stories about the man. "Didn't Administrator Adolphus provide you with shielding on the ship?"

"Oh, don't blame the General, sir. I did this to myself, as a way to treat an unrelated terminal condition. It worked for a while, but gradually it overcame me. I made it to Ridgetop – that's what counts. I even got here early ... I hope that doesn't mess up the General's plans."

Packard sank into a chair he accepted some tea, although he didn't touch the offered food. "Governor, we know you're the Diadem's man out in this sector, but our DZ stringline network is already in place." Packard seemed to dissolve into his seat. He looked done.

Knowing the truth about the Ridgetop Recovery, Goler could guess what Michella would do if she felt her rule threatened. The massacre on this one small colony would pale by comparison.

Packard turned a heavy gaze toward him. "Take my trailblazer ship – it's equipped to run back along the new line. Once you run a full decontamination, it'll be a suitable stringline vessel for you to travel in. Go to Hallholme as fast as you can and make arrangements with General Adolphus. You'll have to choose sides."

"You're assuming what my decision will be," Goler said in a short tone, but he wasn't fooling either of them.

"I'm assuming you're an intelligent man, Governor." Packard began coughing again.

408

Goler considered his situation. For much of his life, he had been a mediocre bureaucrat who never made waves, but in his years as Territorial Governor, at arm's length from the fossilized old ways of Sonjeera, he had begun to blossom. Now, a new future had fallen into his lap, whether he wanted it or not. An independent set of united Deep Zone colonies had much more commercial potential than the antiquated thorn-in-the-side system of tributes demanded by the Constellation.

"Don't forget, Governor," Packard pointed out, "the DZ planets outnumber the old Crown Jewels by almost three to one."

"Not in population, political influence, or military strength."

Packard shrugged, wearing an enigmatic expression. "Just watch what happens."

Goler had been willing to turn a blind eye to the efforts of Ian Walfor and his clunky FTL ships. Those black-market vessels filled a need and demonstrated a small independent streak, a way to blow off steam. But if General Adolphus had truly laid down a new transportation network – a project that dwarfed the Constellation's original plan, with secondary hubs radiating from other key planets as well – Goler knew there could be no going back. Given the untapped wealth of the Deep Zone, not to mention all the colonists who resented paying unreasonable tributes to the Diadem, he could tell which way the wind was blowing.

The sick pilot was right. Carlson Goler was not a stupid man. But Adolphus needed to understand what he was up against. Goler would tell the General the truth about the Ridgetop Recovery.

The governor knew Tasmine would be pleased with him. "Once we refit your ship, I'll travel on the new stringline to Hallholme for a formal meeting with Administrator Adolphus. I'd be honored if you would escort me, sir. You're a brave man."

Packard held his teacup in a hand that trembled so violently that he spilled much of the liquid before he could bring it to his mouth. He shook his head with a wry, fatalistic smile. His skin had gone pale and clammy. "That's not in the cards, Governor. It was all I could do to hold on until I arrived here at Ridgetop and put the terminus in place. I wanted to see the look on your face." He degenerated into another spasm of coughing.

Goler issued orders to give their unexpected guest any medical treatment he might need, then sent teams up to decontaminate the trailblazer ship so it could be used as a diplomatic transport. He could have dispatched a message packet along the line to inform General Adolphus that he was coming, but it would be safer to have no tangible communication between the two of them.

Instead he would go unannounced and deliver his answer in person.

78

Keana was not impressed with her first glimpse of Slickwater Springs, a patchwork camp slapped together out of spare parts: tents of all sizes, prefab shelters, sturdy cabins, a main lodge house and administration building, as well as additional shelters under construction. It was a surprisingly busy place.

As the passengers disembarked from the overland jitney, practically running toward the strange ponds in their excitement to see them, she lugged her valise over to the packed path and waited. After the long trip, Keana felt even dirtier than she had in Michella Town.

During the rough drive, her fellow travelers jabbered constantly about slickwater pools, alien memories, and incomprehensible wonders they thought they were going to find. Keana had seen the mocking reports her mother released and her conclusion that it was all just cultish nonsense.

The tourist attraction held little interest for her, whether or not it was a trick. Finding Cristoph was all that mattered. As she looked around at the bleak Hallholme landscape, she considered how hard his life must be. For the sake of Louis's memory, and to assuage her own guilt, she had to make amends.

Staff members greeted the newcomers and showed them around the site; Keana took a careful look at each person, hoping that Cristoph worked here, but she saw no sign of him. While everyone else hurried to see the slickwater pools, she trudged towards the rustic lodge, looking for the woman named Sophie Vence.

The lodge's lobby was clean and basic, with no wasted artistic flourishes. A young man barely out of his teens looked up at her from the main desk; his eyes had an unsettling sheen. "Welcome. If you would like to be introduced to the slickwater pools, Fernando-Zairic is already there, acting as a guide today. We hope you will want to join us."

"I need to see Sophie Vence. I have business with her." She set her valise on the floor.

The young man's expression changed, as if he had suddenly become a different person. "I'm her son Devon, and I am also Birzh, returned from long ago. May we help you?"

Keana dumped what remained of her pouch of jewelry onto the counter. "I came from Sonjeera to find a man named Cristoph de Carre." Her soiled clothes did not make her feel very regal, but he drew herself up. "I am Princess Keana Duchenet, daughter of Diadem Michella."

The young man took the news in stride. "In that case, my mother will want to see you." He left, moving with a gliding gait. Something about him seemed ... off.

Ten minutes later he returned with a careworn but confident woman, who gave Keana a cool assessment. "You do resemble the Diadem's daughter."

"Because I *am* Keana Duchenet."

"Well, that won't buy you any favors on Hellhole. After what your mother did to General Adolphus, we're not overly fond of the Duchenets here. We get enough harassment from Sonjeera. Did the Diadem send you here?"

Keana stood her ground. "My mother has caused me grief as well. She drove the man I loved to suicide, destroyed his family, and his son was exiled here – Cristoph de Carre. I need to find him."

Sophie's expression remained hard. "And you expect that to change my opinion of you, just like that?" Keana could see that the other woman considered her nothing more than a poor little rich girl. Wasn't it obvious that they had a common complaint?

She nudged the jewels closer to Sophie. "I'm not here on my

mother's behalf, or anything to do with the Constellation. Please, do you know where I might find Cristoph?"

"I can pass along your request."

Keana's heart skipped a beat. "So you do know him?"

Sophie straightened, taking on a stiff businesslike demeanor. "What is the nature of your visit? Why do you want to see him so badly?"

"I have . . . some things of his father's. And I need to make sure he's all right."

"He's doing just fine."

"I still want to see him. Please."

Sophie swept the valuables into her hand and tucked them under the counter. "I'll accept your money, but I can't force a man to see you if he doesn't want to." She sized up Keana. "I hope you don't mind waiting."

Keana squared her shoulders, at last nearing the end of a long and difficult ordeal. "As long as it takes."

Sophie looked down at a ledger screen, then glanced at her son, who stood several steps away. "Devon, do we have any rooms fit for a Sonjeeran princess?"

"We have a small tent outside that was vacated by a customer yesterday. She may need a groundpad to cover the rocks under the sleeping surface."

Sophie smiled sweetly. "For a princess, we can provide *two* groundpads. All the comforts of Hellhole."

Though the woman seemed to be goading her, Keana refused to complain. She made up her mind to endure whatever she had to, even a tent out here in the wilderness. "I shall accept whatever you have for me, so long as you pass my message on to Cristoph."

Sophie turned to her son. "Devon, show our honored guest to her tent. She can wait there until we have further news for her."

In the intervening hours, Keana walked around the camp, looking at the slickwater pools and listening to cult members talk about their alien memories. Her reaction alternated between amusement towards the gullible listeners and a visceral discomfort upon seeing their absolute conviction. Could it be real?

Her tent was cramped, but she convinced herself to endure. Another hour passed, and another. Other visitors moved into tents near hers, and settlement workers found constant busy work nearby; Keana was sure she was being watched closely.

Near nightfall, Sophie Vence finally parted the fabric door and stood framed in the tent opening. "I was tempted to let General Adolphus know that you're here, so he could come deal with you himself."

Keana was surprised. "But I'm not here for him. I only came to find Louis's son. It has nothing to do with politics."

Sophie raised her eyebrows. "You're the Diadem's daughter, so everything you do has political ramifications." She sighed. "The General has more pressing matters anyway, so I took it upon myself to contact Cristoph."

Keana was ready to scramble out of the tent and go anywhere to meet him. "Is he here?"

Sophie groaned, unable to believe the princess's stupidity. "With settlements and facilities all across the continent, did you expect him just to be in the neighborhood? Cristoph has an important job in a high-security area, and he's hours away, but I spoke to him over a military codecall line. I let him know you're here."

Keana prepared herself for disappointment. "When can I see him?"

"He could be here as soon as tomorrow morning, *if* he decides to come."

"Thank you. That's wonderful news!"

Sophie turned to go. "I'm not doing this for you. I'm doing it for Cristoph, on the off chance you can be helpful. But in case you're here for other reasons, Princess, I've got my people keeping an eye on you." With that, she left the tent and walked off into the night.

79

The new stringline network was a symbol of commerce, liberty, financial control, and independence from the repressive government. D-Day would be upon them within a week; some of the trailblazer ships should already be arriving at their destinations. If everything went according to plan, the sudden activation of the new network would deal a crippling blow to the Constellation government. And Diadem Michella Duchenet was not likely to react well.

After successfully testing the new line from Candela, Tanja Hu remained at Ankor for a while to help manage the final preparations. Two days after her arrival, Ian Walfor arrived from Buktu, his ship taking a second position in the orbiting hub. Orbiting construction workers scrambled to complete the last nodes in time, since Adolphus expected a flood of ships soon.

After ten years, the Diadem's watchdogs had grown lax, focusing mainly on the General without caring about the veterans who had served him during the rebellion. At one time, they'd been prepared to give their lives in his cause; now, those loyal men and women were ready to carry out other assignments. Many had already been distributed among the other DZ worlds, ready to move as soon as the stringline network was established. Adolphus had every confidence in them.

When his passenger pod landed at Ankor, Walfor jovially shook the

General's hand and surprised Tanja by sweeping her into a bearlike hug. "I'm going to have to change my business model, General, but I wasn't making much money with those old FTL ships. I prefer stringline travel: it's faster, cheaper, and not nearly so boring."

Tanja asked, "Doesn't a lot of your revenue come from producing and supplying old starship fuel and maintaining the outmoded ships?"

Walfor wasn't worried. "My people will do fine. There'll be plenty of niches open in the new network. We'll need ships and linerunners and maintenance, and I can convert a lot of my old ships into trailblazers to lay down more stringlines using Candela's iperion."

Tanja huffed. "Not so fast. I've spent all my altruism to get this crazy project off the ground. If you're going to haul iperion from my mines, then I demand fair compensation."

"Ah well, we can negotiate. We've always had to be flexible. There's plenty of work to go around, without sacrificing our earnings to keep the Diadem in jewels and expensive perfumes."

Adolphus laughed. "We're all on the same page."

The Ankor production facilities had already been building the frameworks of new stringline haulers and sending them up to orbit. Those vessels would shuttle back and forth along the fresh quantum pathways to demonstrate that the system was indeed a viable, and preferable, alternative to the Constellation monopoly.

Joint trade agreements had already been negotiated among Hallholme, Buktu, and Candela, creating a model for similar treaties with other Deep Zone planets. Inside the lobby of the newly built and virtually empty Ankor Hotel, Tanja outlined her ambitious plans for the secondary expanded network. On her drawings, stringline routes radiated from Candela to other DZ planets. Soon all of the frontier worlds would be connected in an intricate system that was no longer constrained by the bottleneck of one particular leader or planet.

Adolphus swelled with pride. "Your plans are even more ambitious than mine, Tanja – not that I mind. But will we have enough iperion to lay down all these lines?"

"Oh, that won't be a problem. My geologists have done extensive mapping and assessment – the iperion vein we've been mining is just a fraction of Candela's assets. We already found three more huge deposits.

It makes the Vielinger operations look like an appetizer, compared to Candela's feast."

Walfor grinned. "And wouldn't the Diadem love to know about that!"

General Tiber Adolphus liked to plan for the long term, assuming success as a first principle. But before those dreams could reach fruition, he and all of his co-conspirators faced a great obstacle – they had to prevent, or at least *survive*, a war against the immensely powerful Constellation.

80

In her uncomfortable tent, Keana slept little. After months of search-ing, she felt anxious, nervous, even lightheaded at the knowledge that she might see Cristoph in the morning. This would be their first actual meeting, and they could talk about how much they both missed his father.

But Keana also needed to relive the nightmares of finding her beloved Louis dead and how helpless she had felt in the face of over-whelming treachery and politics. From now on, she and Cristoph would be joined by common tragedy. They would take care of each other. Soon, it would be all right.

Outside she heard mysterious whispers and bubbles from the fenced-in slickwater pools. Her mother would be appalled to see her now. The ground felt hard beneath her – not at all like the comfortable and spa-cious bed she had shared with Louis de Carre in those bright, glorious days . . .

Though Keana had failed in countless ways, she *would* rescue Louis's son. One good thing. She would insist that he come back with her to Sonjeera, maybe find a way to restore his good name, or at least make his life more secure. He didn't have to stay here on . . . Hellhole. What an apt name!

Over and over, she practiced conversations in her head, working out how their reunion would go. She was intrigued by Sophie Vence's comment that he held an important job in a high-security area. What responsibilities had Administrator Adolphus given him? Cristoph seemed to be doing well, better than she had expected, so he must be talented, resourceful, and determined. But she could help him do better.

She lay awake in her lonely shelter with a contented smile on her face. Her pillow was so flat that she had to fold it to make it thick enough to support her head. After long, restless hours she dozed fitfully.

At dawn, she heard people rustling, probably curiosity seekers venturing toward the slickwater pools. She had already seen their eager faces, the unreasoning hope, the possibility of a second chance at life. The shadow-Xayans answered questions, encouraged people, and helped potential converts make up their minds. Just after Louis's death, Keana might have been tempted to seek such an escape herself.

A shadow fell across the fabric of her tent. A man's voice spoke. "Keana Duchenet? Are you in there?"

Her pulse sped up, and she scrambled out of the tent. She recognized Cristoph instantly from the pictures she had studied. But he was no longer dressed in the fine noble clothes from his portrait. His brown hair was cut in a short serviceable style; his face was dusty and leaner than his picture. His hard demeanor seemed at odds with the smiling portrait she had memorized.

She sucked in a breath, broke into a smile. She longed to throw her arms around him in an embrace. "Cristoph, I've been searching for you! The Constellation tried to cover up your whereabouts, but I—"

"You have a lot of nerve to come here." His voice was implacable. He stood like a stone pillar, frowning down at her.

Shocked and confused, Keana took a cautious step toward him. "I am so glad to see you're, safe. I've been worried about you. Are you all right?"

He glared. "I lost everything because of you and your political schemes, and how you manipulated my father."

"But . . . I loved your father! Louis was the only real thing in my life. Everything else was just trappings. When I lost him, I lost it all – just as you did. And I'm here to help you. I want to make your life better. Come back with me to Sonjeera. We'll find a way to fix things."

"If you hadn't seduced my father and flaunted your affair, scorning all propriety, he would never have allowed his holdings to fall into such disarray. The Riominis couldn't have made their move." His voice grew in volume as his anger swelled. "Because of you, my father was arrested and charged with countless crimes. *Because of you*, he killed himself, unable to face the shame!"

Tears streamed down her face. "No, that isn't true. We were in love." But her heart told her that she did bear some responsibility.

The young man wasn't finished. "After he met you, he could think of nothing else, and the rest was inevitable. You didn't care what anybody thought, did you? Your mother disapproved of the relationship, the people of Vielinger cried out at the neglect – and what did you do? Nothing! You lived a fantasy life with my father in your Cottage."

Her heart was pounding so hard she could barely breathe. "You can't blame our love for everything."

"No. I'm blaming *you* for everything."

His words beat her like cudgels, hurting her terribly. She didn't want to hear anymore, yet she couldn't turn away. "But I came to help you. I kept searching until I found you here."

"For what? To destroy what little dignity I've managed to rebuild here on Hellhole? You Duchenets certainly are thorough."

Her legs threatened to give way under her. This wasn't what she had visualized; it wasn't how the conversation was supposed to go. She grasped for any way to get closer to Cristoph and make him forgive her. She needed him as a last link, a fragile reminder of his father. "I want to save you. You've suffered great injustice – let me help."

"I've seen your kind of help." He made a disgusted sound.

"It wasn't my fault or your father's. The Riominis used our romance as an excuse to make their political move, but the Black Lord would have found any way to take control from your family. Nothing was going to stop him."

"You're wrong. My father could have prevented it, but he forgot about his people. I ran the business and the mines as well as I could, but *he* had the political connections. You made him powerless." Cristoph held up a blocking hand before she could say another word. "No! Despite the disgrace you brought to my family, I've created a good life for myself here. Go back to Sonjeera – and don't ever try to contact me again." His words burned through her like acid. He strode off, not caring that others in the settlement had gathered around to observe the loud argument.

As she watched him leave, Keana felt more dead than alive, nearly as devastated as when she had found Louis lying in a pool of his own blood.

The man who called himself both Fernando and Zairic looked as if even a monstrous static storm could not disturb him. "Just a brief immersion in the slickwater, and the whole Xayan race will be available to you." He smiled at Keana, confident but applying no pressure. "You will remember wonders you can't even dream of now."

"I don't want any wonders!" She longed to have Louis back, but that was impossible. She had come for Cristoph, imagining that they could at least share their pain, but those hopes were shattered.

Fernando-Zairic seemed to understand her anguish. "You want peace, contentment. You want to fit in, and be important." He stood directly in front of her, uncomfortably close. People watched them as if this were a sideshow at the camp.

"I am the daughter of the Diadem!"

He gave a contemplative nod, and his words cut through the blindfold she had placed over her own eyes. "And still, you need to feel important. You want your life to matter. The slickwater can make that possible."

Through tear-filled eyes, Keana looked at the quicksilver pools in the morning sunlight. A few people gathered on the edge of the boardwalk, pondering their own decisions. The slickwater seemed to beckon her. Yes, she could dive in and never come back out. Light sparkled atop the liquid, but did not penetrate far into it.

"Do you really know who I am?" She realized she was shaking.

Fernando-Zairic's composure didn't change; his words were hypnotic. "You are a human, just as I was ... hurting, searching, or curious. And there is a Xayan life waiting to join with yours, to make you whole."

She gave him no answer, but let him lead her forward.

As they reached the boardwalk, a young blond man with a thin beard climbed out of the slickwater, and his expression was so full of amazement that Keana hesitated. This couldn't just be a trick or a delusion, could it? The young man seemed to have had a *real* experience, something that washed away whatever tragedy or pain that had drawn him to Hallholme. Other shadow-Xayans came forward to welcome him into their community.

Keana edged closer to the pool, trying to escape the pain that burned in her chest like hot metal. Maybe the slickwater did offer peace, escape. Even if it didn't last, even if it wasn't real, there was a chance. And the hollowness in her chest reminded her that she had nothing to lose anyway.

"We would welcome you, daughter of Diadem Michella," Fernando-Zairic said. "None of the Xayans would judge you for anything in your past."

Just then she heard a woman's voice calling from the other side of the pool, back by the lodge. She recognized Sophie Vence waving her arms, shouting with alarm. "Keana Duchenet, don't you dare! Stay away from the slickwater!"

Fernando-Zairic looked naïve and perplexed. He kept his attention on Keana. "Don't listen to her. There is nothing to fear."

Sophie ran toward her, yelling for her own security men. "We can't afford to let this happen!"

In an instant, Keana understood. At Cristoph's behest, Sophie Vence would prevent her from being happy. They wanted to deny her the contentment and peace of the slickwater. How Louis's son must hate her! All her life other people had controlled her, prevented her from doing what she wanted to do, imposed their will upon her.

With a quick step, Keana moved to the edge of the boardwalk and looked down at the compelling, mercurial fluid, the swirling mysteries that glinted in the morning light.

Sophie cried out for her workers. "Carter! Timmons – stop the princess!" The men ran toward her from two different directions. "We'll be in a world of trouble if she—"

Before they could get closer, Keana made her decision. She was sick of who she was, sick of her corrupt family, and sick of the Constellation. Sick of having no one to trust, no true friends ... sick of living without love, sick of her wasted and shallow life.

Ignoring the shouts of protest, she jumped smoothly into the water, as if it wasn't there at all. She heard no splash.

The contact was a shock. Her eyes remained open. Swirling, ghostly shapes appeared from nowhere and dove deeper, pulling her along after them. Keana didn't worry about holding her breath; time seemed to have stopped. The physical limitations of the human body had no relevance in this realm.

The phantom lights drew her much deeper than the pool could possibly be. Ahead, the shapes coalesced into a cloud of bright illumination ... and out of that glow came a nebulous form, shadowy and mysterious. She knew she should feel fear, but she allowed it to cover her completely.

The presence engulfed her, and in its overwhelming power Keana lost her own sense of awareness. Her concerns faded away to be replaced by the sensation of soaring upward ...

81

The Ridgetop medical facilities made Ernst Packard as comfortable as they could in his remaining days. The trailblazer captain lay in a hospital bed, fuzzy with painkillers. Despite giving him large doses of nutritional supplements, the colony's best medical experts were unable to help.

He wheezed in his bed with a full picture-window view of golden-wood groves, his own music played gently in the background. He lifted his hand in what was meant to be a dismissive wave. "When I plotted the story of my life, this wasn't how I foresaw the ending. Even recently, I imagined I'd live just long enough to complete my mission as a trailblazer pilot, then die in full uniform at the helm controls. But here I am as good as dead, barefoot in a hospital gown." His laugh turned into a cough. "I find it quite anticlimactic."

"Your ship is almost ready to go." Goler stood by the bed in a formal business suit. "I'll take you back to Hallholme with me, and we can both let General Adolphus know that you completed your mission."

"You'll have to do most of the talking, Governor." Packard tried to laugh again, but the sound degenerated into convulsive coughing.

Goler ordered his workers to step up the pace in decontaminating the trailblazer ship. The Ridgetop engineers worked around the clock prepping the vessel for a return journey and double-checking the bare-bones stringline terminus that Packard had installed in orbit.

A breathless foreman finally announced that the ship was cleared for departure to Hallholme. Governor Goler thanked him and his crews for their efforts, but Ernst Packard had died five hours before.

Protecting himself politically, out of habit, Goler left a document in his office safe that stated he was traveling to Hallholme "to demand an immediate and thorough explanation from Administrator Tiber Adolphus." It was a plausible enough explanation if the situation should go terribly awry.

He expected to have a very interesting conversation with the General.

Now that the stringline route connected Ridgetop to Hallholme – as well as many other lines, if Packard's information was accurate – the floodgates would open and ships would begin running back and forth. Once the Deep Zone had the option of free trade without the Constellation's tariffs and tribute, there would be no turning back, whether Diadem Michella liked it or not ...

When Goler's refitted trailblazer arrived at the new orbiting hub above the Ankor site, he marveled at the massive complex in space; he couldn't believe Adolphus had performed so much work without the Constellation suspecting. Even *he*, the Territorial Governor, had been aware of nothing. He remembered how outraged Diadem Michella had been to learn of Ian Walfor's amateurish black-market transportation efforts; she would be white-hot with fury when she found out about this problem.

When Goler docked at the new hub, unannounced, the people below scurried about to make preparations. The General set aside all his other duties to meet the territorial governor in person, but he obviously had his suspicions.

Receiving him at the Ankor landing field, Adolphus's expression was controlled, but wary. "Territorial Governor Goler, thank you for being one of the first official representatives to visit our new transportation hub. I am surprised by your prompt arrival."

"You're not the only one who's surprised, Administrator Adolphus." Hallholme was one of the eleven DZ planets under his purview, and Goler had worked with the General many times. This, though, was entirely different.

He cleared his throat, faced Adolphus. "I did not come alone, sir. My cargo pod holds the preserved body of Captain Ernst Packard, who died shortly after arriving at Ridgetop. Considering his dedicated service to you, I thought you'd like to give him a final resting place on Hallholme."

"Captain Packard would appreciate that. I never met a more loyal man."

"He lived long enough to know that his sacrifice was not in vain. He did establish the new stringline to connect our worlds."

The General regarded Goler cautiously, waiting for the other shoe to drop. "And?"

"And, I'm here to inform you that I have decided to throw in my lot with your new enterprise. To use an old cliché, one cannot put the genie back into the bottle."

"As easy as that? After all your years in service to Diadem Michella?"

"Oh, I know the Diadem very well, including some of her dark secrets. That's what helped me make my decision. And it will turn the whole Deep Zone against her." He drew a deep breath. "Let me tell you a story, General ... the truth about the Ridgetop Recovery."

The horrible tale spilled out of him with as much drama, compassion, and horror as if he'd personally witnessed the slaughter of the original colonists who had wanted only to live independently from the Constellation. Tasmine had recounted her nightmarish memories so often he could almost hear the screams, see the smoke and weapons fire, and watch the soldiers' faces as they followed the Diadem's orders with great relish.

The General whitened as he listened, but did not doubt the revelations, especially when Goler played the old video evidence for him and provided his own photographic proof of human bones that had been washed up by rains at one of the burial sites.

Finally, Goler drew a deep breath. "I am tired of the Constellation's version of history, General. I presume they've distorted what really happened during your rebellion as well?"

Adolphus's smile contained no mirth. "In many, many ways. But what you say only makes me fear their reprisals even more."

Goler's eyes glittered. "Ah, but we have more resources and defenses than the Diadem expects. She would never dream that my loyalties might change." He drew out his smile. "You see, a while ago, I requested that the Constellation send me a private military patrol fleet, so that I could keep a better eye on your 'nefarious activities.' The Diadem agreed. As soon as those ships arrive, I'll turn them over to you. No one has any idea that we can now deliver them from Ridgetop to Hallholme by direct stringline."

"Patrol fleet?" Adolphus asked. "How many vessels, and how well armed?"

"General, they're *your* old ships – the fleet you used against the Constellation." Goler bowed slightly in respect. "My gift to you. And this time, you'll win with them."

82

When Sophie Vence told him what Princess Keana had done, Adolphus felt as if another sinkhole had opened up beneath his feet. Not now!

Normally he would have been pleased to see Sophie, but when she arrived at Ankor, she was gray and breathless. He knew her well enough to read the unspoken messages on her face. When she stepped forward, she was all business, without her usual flirtatious smile; even though they had not seen each other for several weeks, she delivered her news as if she were one of his military scouts.

Eldora Fen and Sia Frankov, the planetary administrators from Cles and Theser, had arrived via the new stringlines, looking giddy with the culmination of their ambitious plans. Along with Ian Walfor and Tanja Hu, they all sat together in the admin shack of the launch site, discussing the defenses of their worlds and all of the Deep Zone planets.

Sophie glanced around the group, too preoccupied to respond to their quick greetings and spoke directly to Adolphus. She didn't care if they overheard. "This concerns all of us, Tiber – and it may force us to accelerate our timetable."

"How can we possibly go any faster?" Adolphus had already been operating at the swiftest pace he could orchestrate. "Has something else happened at Slickwater Springs?" He dreaded hearing about another rape or murder.

"Spit it out, if you please!" grumbled Eldora Fen. "Or is this some kind of dance you all enjoy?"

Sophie blurted, "It's Keana Duchenet – she immersed herself in the slickwater."

Tanja Hu already saw the implications. "What the hell was the Diadem's daughter doing on Hellhole?"

"She came to see Cristoph de Carre, but that … didn't go well. I tried to stop her, but she was upset. She dove into the slickwater before anyone could talk her out of it." Sophie drew a long, deep breath and added in a barely audible voice, "Just like Devon did."

Adolphus was so appalled that for a moment he could not find words. "The Diadem's daughter is now a shadow-Xayan? Michella will be … apoplectic!"

Sophie shook her head, sickened. "Worse than that – after Keana immersed herself, she fell into a coma. That's rarely happened – and none of the other victims have woken up. We might lose her for good."

The General's gut turned cold, and he groaned. "Sophie, do you know what this *means?*"

Walfor whistled. "It means the Diadem's head is going to explode."

Sophie lowered her head. "Sorry, Tiber. I screwed up. I should have been watching her every move, keeping the rich little princess from hurting herself, but I thought it might be good for her to sleep on the hard ground for a change. I didn't think she'd do something so stupid." She shook her head, clearly shamed. "She made up her mind and was hell-bent on doing it. Cristoph rejected her, blamed her for the death of his father – and who could say he wasn't right?" Her gaze sharpened at all of them. "It's not his fault."

"You don't have to defend Cristoph, Sophie. The Duchenets don't need any help in mucking up a situation."

"If Keana's in a coma, where is she now?" Tanja asked.

"A hospital in Helltown. Cristoph is with her."

Adolphus clenched his jaw, feeling the consequences ripple through his mind. "This couldn't have happened at a worse time – the final stage of our stringline network! No matter what explanations we make, the Diadem will be convinced this is some plot I concocted as a way to take personal revenge."

"Well," Walfor pointed out, "the old bitch did crush your rebellion and exile you to near-certain death. Sounds like a good enough motive for revenge."

"Oh, I intend to get my revenge against the Diadem, but not using an innocent bystander like Keana. When I choose to strike, I'll hit *primary* targets."

"The moment she learns where her daughter is, the Diadem will demand her return, maybe even send soldiers to seize the Princess by force," Sia Frankov said.

"Unless you hold her hostage." Tanja raised her eyebrows. "We could use her as a bargaining chip."

"I wasn't planning to draw the Diadem's attention *at all*, particularly now. Maybe we should hide Keana, keep this quiet."

"She's in a *medical center*, Tiber," Sophie said. "And she caused something of a stir when she arrived at Slickwater Springs, blundering around in search of Cristoph. The two of them had quite a public quarrel before everyone watched her jump into the pool. That woman's left muddy footprints all over Hellhole, and Michella has enough spies that you can bet a message is already on its way to her."

"We could get rid of her," Tanja Hu said. "Claim she died in an accident. Doctor files, drum up some willing witnesses. It's even believable: Keana Duchenet's past actions."

"Not now!" Adolphus clenched his fists, raised his voice. "Anything like that would cause a firestorm of inquiries, and we simply can't afford to draw so much attention. It's become an all-out race – that's all there is to it. We have to get our hub and all the new stringline ships in operation before the Constellation can do anything about it. Send our ships to guard the terminus rings from Sonjeera, prepare to blow the stringline nodes if we need to. Once our network is set, we can cut them off entirely."

He let out a long sigh, then straightened. "I'll just have to make my announcement sooner than I had hoped."

83

When he received the urgent message from Slickwater Springs, Cristoph turned his vehicle around and retraced his tracks to the alien pools.

He had barely been gone an hour from the settlement, heading out to the museum vault where he worked with the four Originals. He was still furious with Keana, amazed at her gall. After all the harm she had done to his father, and to him, she had expected him to embrace her and forget the past! What a vapid, sheltered, naïve woman. Cristoph didn't regret a single word he had said to her.

Then the fool princess had jumped into a slickwater pool, and she hadn't awakened. Fernando-Zairic and two other shadow-Xayans had fished her out of the pool, where she floated face-down, paralyzed by the contact with the liquid-crystal datafluid.

Everything in Cristoph's rational mind told him to stay away and let the Diadem's daughter die, but now he felt frozen. Chances were that she'd never emerge from her coma. It seemed that neither Keana nor his father had the backbone to face the unpleasant consequences of their own actions ...

At Slickwater Springs, Sophie and her workers had taken the woman into the lodge house and laid her out on a narrow bed. As Cristoph rushed to Keana's side, trying to sort out his feelings, he realized that he did want to see her and needed to do whatever he could, even if that meant just sitting with her and talking without receiving a response. Perhaps somewhere in her subconscious, she could hear his voice. No matter what his father might have done, Cristoph had to take the course of honor.

Even though it was her own damned fault.

"It would have been kinder if I'd just refused to meet with her," he had said as Sophie hovered close. "I could have isolated myself so that she never found me." But such cruelty was not in his nature. In his own despair, he had not recognized hers ...

After the incident, none of the other visitors had dared to enter the slickwater, despite Fernando-Zairic's reassurances that hundreds of shadow-Xayans already lived happily together at the nearby settlement in the jungle-like alien undergrowth.

Sophie appeared greatly disturbed as she regarded the comatose woman. "That could have happened to my Devon," she said in a quiet voice. "Or to Antonia."

She summoned a private flyer to airlift Keana to a hospital in Michella Town, and Cristoph rode along in the aircraft as the tense pilot had to alter course by hundreds of kilometers to avoid a swirling static-storm. Meanwhile, Sophie had gone to Ankor to break the news to General Adolphus ...

When Devon Vence gave him the belongings Keana Duchenet had left in her tent, Cristoph accepted the package, unsure of what he was supposed to do with the items. Why was *he* the one responsible for this foolish woman who had not only ruined his father, but the entire de Carre holdings, and now herself?

He knew his father had been smitten with Keana, but Cristoph always assumed she had tricked him somehow. How could the Diadem's daughter be any less scheming than her mother? Why would she leave Sonjeera and come here to search for *him*? What could she possibly want? He had nothing more for her to take. Of course, Cristoph had made a good enough life here on Hellhole, and General Adolphus gave him worthy responsibilities. Cristoph was thriving – something he had never imagined on that bleak day when he left the Vielenger estate, nearly penniless.

Why had Keana seemed devastated when Cristoph rebuffed her and took away her imagined redemption? He couldn't understand what her game was – unless she was telling the truth, and that didn't make sense either. It defied logic that such a wealthy and powerful woman, entangled in Constellation politics, would pretend to be no more than a romantic heroine in a silly love story.

Yet when Cristoph ransacked her satchel of belongings, he found nothing sinister, no evidence of a hidden agenda. Instead, he found images of his father and Keana, looking happy, glowing with contentment. He found a handsome portrait of Louis de Carre, the familiar picture of Louis's long-dead wife Angelique, as well as several images of Cristoph . . . as if Keana had imagined herself part of the family.

Was that what she had thought? So downtrodden by a corrupt and cynical government that she wanted to cut all ties, give away her wealth and position, and lead a simple life? Cristoph shook his head. How could anyone imagine that day-to-day existence here on Hellhole was simple?

At the bottom of the satchel Cristoph found a packet of letters and poems, handwritten on actual paper. He untied the neat lavender ribbon that bound them together, sorted through the pages. He recognized his father's hand on some of the poems and letters, while others were penned by Keana herself. Cristoph scanned them, trying to absorb what he read.

These were sincere and passionate love letters, romantic poetry that would have been insipid had it not been so heartfelt. He caught his breath, read them again, and wrestled with the conclusion he could not deny: Louis de Carre had been truly and completely in love with Keana Duchenet – and Keana returned his affections with all her heart.

Cristoph held the notes, read the lines again and again. If this oblivious, imprudent woman's seduction wasn't part of a larger scheme, if Keana Duchenet had not been involved in a twisted plan to bring about the downfall of the de Carre line, if she had simply fallen in love with the wrong man at the wrong time – then Cristoph had to reassess everything he had thought about her. Keana's love for his father had made her a pawn.

She had jumped into the slickwater!

Maybe she really did feel guilty. Maybe she was truly hurting and had discarded her old life to reach out to Cristoph because he was the only one who might understand her terrible sense of loss.

And now she was in a coma.

Cristoph remained beside Keana in the medical center for two days. So far, out of hundreds of converts only nine had suffered similar reactions to the slickwater, and they all remained vegetables in a separate ward. None of the Mercifuls or doctors expected Keana to wake up.

While he waited, Cristoph felt no pull of obligation to the job assignment General Adolphus had given him. The Original Xayans could interact with the other investigators in the museum vault. None of those things were important to him anymore. Such duties felt like little more than static buzzing in his head, distracting him from doing what he needed to do.

More than a hundred men were stationed in the mountain vault, working with Encix, Cippiq, Lodo, and Tryn to excavate and retrieve as much ancient information as possible. The General wanted to be briefed on any major new finds, and Cristoph de Carre was supposedly in charge of the operation. Sooner or later, the General would insist that he return to his duties.

The General had accepted Cristoph when he came to Hellhole with nothing, tested his resolve with unpleasant and dirty labor, then placed him in charge of the vault-excavation project.

The more Cristoph got to know General Adolphus, the more he liked and respected him. Despite the man's defeat, dishonor, and exile, Adolphus was a true visionary and an excellent leader who thought of his people and the future, rather than hedonistic distractions and political games. Though it was far too late, Cristoph wished the de Carre family had taken the other side of the rebellion. That might have made the difference between victory and failure.

Or maybe the de Carres would merely have found themselves exiled here a decade sooner. At last, Cristoph knew he was on the right side, the moral side. On this path, he would regain his family honor. Maybe that was what Keana had been trying to do, as well, but he hadn't given her the chance . . .

An attendant checked Keana's monitors and noted the readings.

The woman wore a white uniform and headband, as well as a white ring around her wedding finger, signifying her pledge to help the weak and dying. The Mercifuls were the only group of volunteer nurses who had established a significant presence on Hellhole. She offered Cristoph a polite smile, then left the room.

Alone with Keana, he spoke soothingly to her, repeating her name as well as his father's, pleading with her to come back. As much to remind himself as to trigger a response from her, he reminisced about times he'd spent with his father on Vielinger, roaming the beautiful woods near the manor house, fishing in the streams. Maybe something would shock her out of her coma – a few well-chosen words, an anecdote. Cristoph realized how much he and the Princess had both loved his father, after all.

Here in the quiet hospital room, he could avoid thinking of the uproar that must be taking place outside. When the Diadem learned what Keana had foolishly done, she would almost certainly use it as an excuse to retaliate. He was certain the patient's identity had not remained secret. Too many people at Slickwater Springs had known who she was, had heard them argue and had seen her nearly die after immersion in the pool.

A stringline hauler had departed yesterday. It was only a matter of time.

84

The Diadem felt the vast empire slipping through her fingers, and she blamed much of the chaos on Keana. Some members of the Crais family had whispered openly that if Michella couldn't control her own daughter, how could she control seventy-four widely scattered planets?

A few of the most powerful lords, including her supposed ally Selik Riomini, suggested that she should retire and initiate an election for her successor "in this time of crisis." Their arguments did not sway her; it was always a supposed time of crisis, and someone was always trying to find excuses for what they wanted.

Throughout her reign, Michella had depended upon the private Riomini armies, though she trusted them less and less as the decades passed. Because Lord Selik was growing too powerful, she had been reluctant to let him gain control of Vielinger and the iperion stockpiles there, but Keana's indiscretions with Louis de Carre had given the Riominis the wedge they needed. With his new prominence, the Black Lord climbed higher on the list as her heir-apparent.

For some time now her relationship with the Riominis had gone beyond just business. She had felt a bond of affection with old Gilag Riomini, who helped put her on the Star Throne almost six decades ago. Back then, the Tazaars and Craises had been conspiring to get around the Rule of Succession to have the two families share power and alternate control between them. Gilag Riomini had pegged the young, personable, and ambitious Michella as the solution to break that logjam, and offered the Riominis' burgeoning private military forces to back up his endorsement. It was a devil's bargain. Michella had genuinely liked the old gentleman, but in retrospect she realized how clever he had been in moving his family into position. Politics as usual.

The Craises, Tazaars, Hirdans, and other families had their own sources of revenue and their own economic alliances. During the rebellion fifteen years ago, she had forced a consolidation of all military forces into a unified Army of the Constellation, but without a common enemy that coalition force was already beginning to fragment.

She had hoped her daughter's marriage to Bolton Crais would set wheels in motion so that a Duchenet descendant could again become diadem in the not-too-distant future. But Keana had always refused to put family considerations ahead of her own selfish desires; she was never cut out to be a ruler, anyway.

And now her spies told her that headstrong Keana was gone, disguising herself and slipping away to *Hallholme*, of all places!

Dressed in a monogrammed dressing gown, the aged ruler fumed as she went into an adjacent anteroom where a small dining table had been set up. Her personal chef entered, carrying a large tray of covered plates over his shoulder, and a younger man followed with a silver kiafa service. As they laid out the breakfast, Michella's lady-in-waiting pulled open the drapes to let in sunlight, then hovered close to make certain that the Diadem's needs were met.

When she discovered Keana's recent impetuous disappearance, Michella was greatly flustered, recognizing yet another ill-conceived fool's errand, just as when Keana had run off to Vielinger in search of Cristoph de Carre. She had half a mind to exile the silly girl and seal her away, as she'd done with her own sister, Haveeda.

Trusting no one else to get the answers she needed, Michella had asked Ishop Heer to investigate – she could always rely on the loyal man. Just as she sat down to her breakfast, Ishop arrived, crackling with nervous energy. He was dressed in finer clothes than his usual style. Was he putting on airs?

Pulling up a chair for the guest, the young servant put a napkin on

Ishop's lap, while the chef removed the covers from the food with exaggerated ceremony. Michella smelled the delicate aroma of eggs sonjeer, one of her favorites, but she was too preoccupied to compliment the chef before dismissing him and the servants.

When they were finally alone, Ishop ignored his food and leaned forward across the table. "Eminence, there is bad news from Hallholme."

"Bad news – regarding Keana? Has she been found?" She stifled a groan, already imagining what sort of mess her daughter might have caused. "I want her back home now, with as little public disturbance as possible." She made up her mind to dispatch a well-armed military force immediately to seize Keana and drag her back, with or without her cooperation. "We may have to eliminate Cristoph as well, just to purge Keana of her unhealthy obsession."

When he rubbed his hands nervously and avoided looking at her, Michella's throat went dry. This must be serious after all, not just another clumsy show of rebellion. What if Keana had gotten herself into real danger? "Is she hurt?" She swallowed hard, reluctant to hear the answer.

He hesitated, took a sip of kiafa as he tried to frame the proper words, which made Michella worry even more. Ishop fidgeted with his fingers. "There is more, Eminence. As you might imagine, Hallholme is not a pleasant or safe place. Princess Keana should not have gone there alone and unprepared. So many hazards." He shook his head.

"Tell me, damn you!"

"She joined that silly cult I told you about. She immersed herself in the slickwater and is now drugged, or contaminated, or brainwashed."

Michella lurched to her feet. "My daughter is part of the mass delusion? She now thinks she's ... what? An alien? Ridiculous!" She decided to double the military force she would send there.

"If only she had merely been deluded, Eminence ... but something went terribly wrong with the process and she fell into a coma. The drugs or contamination must be more potent than we ever imagined. Perhaps it was an accident, perhaps an attempt to assassinate her. According to the last report I received, she remains in a vegetative state in a Michella Town hospital. A few other converts have suffered similar reactions. They have never recovered."

The Diadem felt ill. "You underestimated the threat of this cult, Ishop. And now they have my daughter!"

He seemed to have his answer ready. "I underestimated what your daughter would do, Eminence. Perhaps she should have been placed under house arrest here on Sonjeera, where she could not harm herself."

The Diadem knew he was right. Keana had always been flighty and easily swayed, but this was not going to be a simple fix, no matter how many spies or soldiers Michella sent in. She realized she was trembling, and she knew exactly where to direct her anger. It wasn't Ishop's fault.

"General Adolphus is behind this – no question about it. He's getting even with me, and I won't let him have that kind of victory! We must get Keana back, wake her up somehow and deprogram her – then we can lock her up where she'll cause no further harm to herself . . . or to my reputation." She glowered, thinking dark thoughts.

"We have no evidence that the condition is reversible, Eminence. The coma could be caused by some sort of extraterrestrial sickness. We just don't know."

She seethed and said, not for the first time, "I should have executed that bastard Adolphus when I had the chance. I've made up my mind – it's a matter of principle. We'll get Keana back . . . and then quarantine the whole damned planet. I will regain control of every stone, twig, drop of water, and living creature on Hallholme."

85

In the swirl of politics and machinations on Sonjeera, Keana Duchenet had met difficult personalities before – her mother, for one. Her clashes, her grief over Louis, and her hope for change had finally taught her to stand up for herself, and to cling to small personal victories even if she had little power in the government. She had come to Hallholme determined to accomplish something for once.

Such things had prepared her to face the powerful alien presence that engulfed her from within the slickwater. The ancient, exotic personality first sought to dominate her entirely, and then receded into sullen resistance when Keana fought back against his dominion. It was this battle, waged in the confines of her mind, that sent her into a coma.

Though trapped on the dark battlefield of that medical condition, she could still think, still defend herself against the Xayan presence. His name was Uroa, and she knew his entire life, just as he knew hers. They were at an impasse deep within her psyche, struggling for control of her mind and body.

The alien life was desperate to fully reawaken from the pool of stored memories; Uroa made repeated attempts, tried new angles of attack. Even while they struggled, Keana argued and negotiated with that long-lost alien life. "I won't just shrink away and surrender to you. Since the moment I was born, my mother has dictated my life. I did not come all the way to this planet to be taken over by an alien bully! If that is what you intend, then I'll cast you back into your cesspool."

Uroa seemed by turns baffled, amused, and angered by her resistance. "You can make the attempt, Keana Duchenet, but you would lose great wonders."

"You would lose, as well."

Now Uroa said, "I am not accustomed to being countermanded. I was one of the supreme Xayan rulers in our last days."

"And my mother is the supreme ruler of humans. You and I could be stronger if we work together. Or should I let this body wither and die? If that happens, you'll never even return to the slickwater."

The Xayan personality probed her thoughts, studied her life story, her wishes, dreams, and motivations. Keana probed back and finally understood how to achieve an accord with Uroa. The Diadem's daughter realized there were indeed certain advantages . . .

In the stuffy, silent hospital room, Cristoph watched Keana's placid face, wondering if she was submerged in inhuman dreams, living another life behind those closed eyes. Maybe she wanted to shed her human side, as a snake sheds its skin. If she survived this and came back, would there be any remnant of Keana Duchenet's former personality and awareness? Or would she become something else, entirely?

He wanted her to wake up.

Abruptly, Keana jerked and cried out in such a loud voice that nurses rushed into the room. Cristoph tried to let go of her hand, but she clutched him so hard he couldn't pull away. The princess sat straight up in bed, her dark blue eyes open. Her irises were fractured into prismatic spirals even more prominent than he had seen on other shadow-Xayans. She looked stoic, the eyes staring, unmoving.

"Keana! Can you hear me?"

Her voice sounded deep and masculine. The words seemed to come from somewhere far away from Keana's vocal cords. "You may call me Uroa." Then her voice shifted to her own familiar timbre, and her expression became animated. "And Keana is here as well. It took a long time for both of us to find our way back."

As the doctors and medical attendants bustled around her, Keana focused on Cristoph. "Thank you for coming back to me! I heard everything you said to me while I was lost, those wonderful stories about your father, but ... Uroa and I were coming to an arrangement. He's a very strong personality, and we needed to find a balance, or die together. Now we're much stronger ... maybe even strong enough to stand against my mother."

Cristoph knelt over the bed and hugged her awkwardly. The words of the love letters and poems resonated in his mind. Now he was willing to offer at least a little of what she had needed so badly.

"Now I need to see the others," Keana-Uroa said, sounding strong and determined now. "And General Adolphus."

Though the Birzh presence strengthened and comforted him, Devon still felt relief when security chief Craig Jordan concluded his investigation into the killing of Jako Rullins.

Considering everything, including the fact that Jako already had a pending death sentence on Aeroc and had undeniably attacked Antonia Anqui, Jordan formally recommended that no charges be brought against the young man. Under other circumstances, the incident might have been cause for a great uproar, but from his operations at Ankor, General Adolphus declared the case closed and turned his attentions to completing his large-scale plan.

Sophie Vence sent Devon and Antonia back to Helltown to pick up a shipment from one of her warehouses and to inspect the main office operations. Devon knew it wasn't a crucial task, but his mother wanted to reassure herself that he was still the young man she knew, despite his striking change.

When he and Antonia finished their business, they took a side trip out to Elba, asking to see the exotic artifact they had found in the ruined camp of the Children of Amadin. The General still kept his collection on display in his office, but had been too absorbed recently with his stringline plans and his access to the actual aliens to spend much time studying the relics.

Now, Devon-Birzh was curious to see what he recognized among the artifacts. With Antonia beside him, they entered the display area, granted access by the General's household staff. "I've seen these items many times before," Devon said, "but they never meant anything to me." This time, though, he was excited to discover a clue to the lingering mystery of this world.

Through the lens of Birzh's thoughts, Devon easily identified most of the artifacts in the General's collection. Antonia smiled as her Jhera personality also recalled the bits of alien detritus, bittersweet reminders of what had been lost during the impact. "I don't have the words to label it," she said as she looked down at a tangled cluster of shimmering wires that had been fused. "But I remember this was an everyday thing. An appliance."

"And this was a hygiene tool, I think," Devon said. He had the idea it was a completely trivial item in the overall canvas of Xayan society, yet now it seemed very precious. "It's hard to imagine what did or didn't survive."

In his mind, Birzh recalled the objects with the same sad fondness with which their human sides might have regarded mementoes from a lost loved one.

However, the artifact they had found at the devastated camp remained a mystery. The sleek, dark relic called to their Xayan memories with its nested curves, armored casings, and embedded crystals, but even after sifting through their Xayan experiences and knowledge, neither Birzh nor Jhera remembered anything like this. Antonia-Jhera picked up the black object, running her fingers along its edges while imagining other sensory appendages.

Perplexed, she handed the thing to Devon, and he cradled it, probing with his own skills of telemancy. "It's definitely of Xayan design. I recognize the material, but nothing else. It could be . . . anything."

"We should take it out to the shadow-Xayan settlement," Antonia said. "Maybe one of the others will know."

86

Shortly after Goler returned from Hellhole, two heavily loaded stringline haulers arrived at Ridgetop carrying the reconditioned fleet of old ships, exactly as the Diadem had promised. Unit Captain Escobar Hallholme had utilized a pair of joined hauler frameworks from which the dozens of sleek hulls hung like angular metal fruit. The old-style FTL warships had enlarged engines and fuel tanks that looked like engorged sacks.

More than a decade ago, these very ships had terrorized many Constellation systems during Adolphus's rebellion, and now they were being delivered to Territorial Governor Goler so that he could keep the unruly frontier in line. Though distances between DZ planets rendered the FTL ships slow and inefficient, the governor insisted that their mere presence at Ridgetop would help him crack down on suspicious activity in the local systems.

Goler shuttled up to the terminus ring to accept delivery from the son of legendary Commodore Percival Hallholme. When the Ridgetop governor met Escobar inside the small orbiting station, he shook the military man's hand. The younger Hallholme was gruff and formal, giving the impression that Goler should be grateful that he had personally taken an interest in such a minor and irrelevant mission. "I hereby deliver these vessels to you in the name of the Diadem, as ordered, sir."

"And I accept them in the same spirit," Goler replied. "They will be a great help in protecting my planets." Escobar seemed dubious.

There was paperwork to be signed, a thumbprint acknowledgment on a screen, a transfer of control codes for the ships. Once the formalities were completed, Escobar was anxious to reverse the hauler and leave the Deep Zone. He transmitted his order to the hauler's skeleton crew. "Detach the FTL ships from their docking clamps and remote-pilot them a safe distance away. Do not let them block our path for departure. We'll be heading back to the Crown Jewels with due dispatch."

Moments later, twenty-one outdated military vessels dropped away from the expanded hauler frameworks. Goler admired them. "Those ships may be old, Captain, but they still look damned impressive."

Escobar wore a faint grimace, though he seemed relieved to have completed his mission. "Those old wrecks were cluttering up the Lubis Plain shipyards, and my father spends too much time looking at them and reminiscing." He straightened. "They're your responsibility now, Governor. You have the people to crew the ships?"

"I'll manage. There are plenty of qualified veterans out here in the DZ." He gave his best reassuring smile. General Adolphus had recently dispatched nine of his trusted pilots to Ridgetop along the new string-line.

His official business completed, Escobar shook his head just before he prepared to depart. "I admire your optimism, Governor. Keeping a few of these old hulks in orbit won't scare away any criminals – they'll just slip around you. Ridgetop isn't the only place in the Deep Zone where black-marketeers can trade."

"I'm confident these ships will be effective," Goler said amiably. "Such a fleet shows that we mean serious business. Besides, if the black-marketeers are using old FTL ships, best to combat them with the same sort of technology."

"Suit yourself, Governor. I'll be on my way, as soon as you send up your cargo containers with this period's tribute payment."

With a signal to the ground, Goler dispatched seventeen heavy upboxes to fill the haulers' now vacant docking clamps. When the upboxes had settled into the appropriate cradles in the hauler frame-work, Escobar signed and thumbprinted the receipt documents, which identified the inventory as seven hundred tons of processed goldenwood.

Captain Hallholme waited impatiently, eager to get going. "I have important duties for the Constellation, sir. I'll let you manage your disruptive influences out here. Best of luck with that." His arrogance was plain. He seemed to regard Carlson Goler as an object lesson of what might happen to him if he didn't attend to his own career back home.

"Give my regards to the Diadem," Goler said, and the other man left. He liked the fact that the Constellation trusted and underestimated him. The Territorial Governor had been meek and cooperative for so long that no one suspected him of duplicity.

Once the hauler arrived at Sonjeera, however, Captain Hallholme would probably be in substantial trouble – when all the tribute upboxes were found to be full of rocks, covered by a thin layer of goldenwood planks . . .

With the stringline hauler safely gone, Goler summoned General Adolphus's veteran pilots to prepare the new ships for further transport. The twenty-one refitted warships were moved to orbit the secret terminus ring that anchored the new line to Hellhole. While the veteran pilots prepped the vessels, Goler sent a personal message via one of the stringline mail drones originally designed for sending important governmental dispatches to Sonjeera. This time, he sent the drone to planet Hallholme: "General, your ships are here."

As the sun set on Ridgetop, Goler relaxed in a chair, looking through the transparent panes at the hillsides, the lush trees, and the ever-shifting colors that streamed through the air. To welcome him into their conspiracy, Sophie Vence had sent one of her bottles of wine from Hellhole, and now the Territorial Governor held a glass in his hand, swirling the garnet liquid and staring out at the landscape. He poured a second glass of wine for Tasmine, but the old servant claimed she had too many household duties.

Goler stopped her. "I insist. Take a moment to celebrate, Tasmine. Everyone on Ridgetop will soon be wealthy, because we won't have to surrender so much of our hard earnings to the Constellation."

The old woman stopped, took a dutiful sip of wine, and puckered. "Enjoy it while you can, sir, because the bitch and her Constellation soldiers aren't going to let you get away with it. We'll be in trouble soon enough." Tasmine set the still-full glass back on the table with a hard, impatient click. "The rest of the Deezees aren't prepared for what she'll do."

"Then we'll have to tell them just what Michella is capable of. Don't you think it's about time that the whole Constellation knew the truth?" Goler smiled at her startled expression. "General Adolphus once said you can't join a revolution by degrees. You have to commit." He finished his wine with a gulp, stood from his chair, and extended a hand to her. "I've already recorded the basics about the Ridgetop Recovery, along with the corroborating evidence we obtained from the burial sites, but you can add a lot of authenticity."

Tasmine quailed. "I've kept my mouth shut for so long. You can't just ask this now!"

"I can, and I am. We need you. *You* are the only person who was there when it happened. No one else can tell this story the way you can. Expose what the Diadem is really like." He drew her toward his study, where he had left the imagers in place. "Come, you've thought about it long enough. Now get it off your chest."

Tasmine scowled at the equipment. "You'll send the message to all the planets?"

"As many as will receive it. Even Sonjeera. You'll deal a greater blow to the Diadem's authority than all those ships we just received."

The old servant's expression darkened as anger and nightmares bubbled in her memory. "Yes, it'll be good to expose what the bitch did." She sat down heavily in the chair – his chair – and turned her bird-bright eyes directly toward the imager. "I loathe how she smiles and pretends to be a sweet grandmother to the Constellation. She's really just a viper."

Goler played the grainy old recording that Tasmine had shown him earlier, and while images of the massacre ran in the background, he recorded her commentary. Like a flood unleashed from a crumbling dam, Tasmine spilled out the full story of the massacre, adding details that even Carlson Goler had never heard. He shuddered as Tasmine talked on and on … and on.

She held nothing back.

87

As he escorted Keana-Uroa to the deep mountain vault filled with Xayan marvels, Cristoph de Carre felt awkward. His own feelings had whiplashed into sympathy for this woman, despite the damage she had caused to his family. He felt some hope that she claimed to dislike Diadem Michella as much as he did, if not more. Joined with a once formidable Xayan leader, she might hold a solution for their current dilemma. A defense, perhaps?

Cristoph halted the Trakmaster at the shaft entrance on the side of the rugged mountain. Machinery, piles of rubble, and mineral-processing beds made the area look like any other mining operation. "By coming to Hallholme and joining the shadow-Xayans, you've really thrown a wrench into the General's plans."

She gave him a distant smile. "Once we talk with Encix and the other Originals, perhaps I can offer help as well. This colony needs to be strong, needs to be ready to face my mother's anger. The shadow-Xayans and I might be able to offer defenses you can't afford to ignore. Don't underestimate telemancy."

"We'll see."

Cristoph had spent the past several months in the mountain vault with the team of investigators as well as the four Originals. Their very strangeness made them frightening, though they claimed to be allies. He found them fascinating, but did not understand them. Not as well as Keana did – now.

In her deeper Uroa voice, she said, "I look forward to being reunited with Encix, Lodo, Tryn, and Cippiq. I will also grieve for Allyf ... although so many Xayans have perished, it makes no sense to mourn just one. Still, he represents all who were lost."

"If you were the supreme leader of their race, then they'll be glad to see you as well," Cristoph said.

"My role was not quite as straightforward as that," Uroa said. "We each led our factions."

Nothing's ever straightforward, Cristoph thought. "General Adolphus will meet us here." He saw no sign of the General or his staff, who were coming here directly from Ankor.

Keana emerged from the Trakmaster without waiting for him and marched ahead by herself, drawn toward the tunnel that led to the buried museum vault. She was no longer as delicate and spoiled as he had expected. He led her to the shaft crawler that whisked them deep into the mountain, where numerous engineers and scientists were studying the library of Xayan artifacts.

As they reached the vault, the four pale-skinned alien creatures stood on a platform facing them, their large eyes gleaming in low illumination that oozed from the walls.

"We have waited for you, Uroa," said Encix.

After several days of sharing her human body, Keana and Uroa had developed a cooperative routine. Now, as they faced the four Original Xayans, Keana felt a joined presence wrap around her – akin to the way Uroa had swept up on her in the slickwater pool, but these shared thoughts did not try to dominate her; they merely wanted to make a connection. She felt a sense of supreme calm and exhilaration, as if all the old pains in her body and heart were gone and would never return.

Light spiraled and sparkled over their heads. Keana stared in awe as the chamber's walls and ceiling lit up in a parade of three-dimensional images that showed large populations of Xayans in the midst of ever-changing, animated structures. Music that her human ears could not hear vibrated against her sensitive skin, but the mental presence of Uroa allowed her to remember … and enjoy it.

"That was our ancient capital city, now contained in the memories of these four," Uroa explained to her. "They do this to honor both of us."

As Keana watched the changing images on the walls, Uroa was her guide. The sky over the remembered city glowed in a borealis display that bathed the buildings in shifting hues and shadows. Everything was alive, nothing static.

Now all of it was dead, obliterated by the asteroid impact.

When the display faded, Encix spoke aloud in a voice that sounded distant, but ironically closer than Uroa's. "You are royalty, Keana Duchenet, so it is fitting that you are partnered with our leader. Though Uroa was anxious to awaken, he waited for the proper person – you." The alien eyes spiraled faster. "Why would you resist him?"

Keana wrinkled her brow, trying to absorb the rapid inflow of information. "He and I have worked out an arrangement."

With a pang, she recalled that she and Bolton Crais also had an "arrangement," but everything had crumbled because of pressures and interference from others …

Encix bowed her flexible body. "Long ago, Uroa and I worked closely together. Each of us had great responsibilities."

"To be more precise," Uroa said inside her mind, though all of the Originals could hear him, "Encix and I were rivals, but we need not be in the future. We will set aside ancient differences for the good of our race, for our return and ascension. The only goal must be *ala'ru*."

"I share that desire," Encix said.

"We may have more pressing problems if the Constellation declares war on us first," Cristoph pointed out.

"Then we will have to deal with that as well." Uroa did not seem perturbed. "We cannot let human factions divert us from *ala'ru*."

While Keana moved through the vault and the innumerable storage alcoves for cultural items Encix and her survivors had considered worth saving, General Adolphus arrived, escorted in by his security chief. He stood next to Cristoph de Carre, regarding Keana and the four Originals. "I can't say I'm pleased to have you here, Princess Keana. You have created an unexpected crisis at a very inconvenient time, and this is a highly secure area."

"She's not just Keana anymore, General," Cristoph said.

Keana gave Adolphus a courteous nod. "You may be my mother's nemesis, General Tiber Adolphus, but I came to this planet of my own accord." She looked at Cristoph. "And I am now much different from the person I was. I am more than Keana Duchenet."

"You can say that all you want, but I doubt the Diadem will see it that way." The General was obviously still suspicious. "We are at a critical point in the history of the Deep Zone colonies. For your personal safety as well as the safety of my people I need to keep you . . . sequestered. I'm sure you understand."

"I understand your desire to keep me hidden – or hold me hostage, if that is your intent – but I can be of greater assistance in other ways. I was constrained by my mother, forced to follow her orders, to meekly accept whatever she commanded. Because of her, I lost much. I'm tired of being a pawn, and now I have a purpose. I can be worth a great deal to you, General." She threw him off balance when she said, "I know about your new stringline network and your operations at Ankor."

Astonished, Adolphus turned accusingly to Cristoph, who held up his hands. "I didn't reveal anything to her, sir."

Keana explained, "I know all about it because Uroa has picked up memories from the slickwater reservoirs throughout the planet, General. A man named Renny Clovis fell into the pool, and Tel Clovis has also joined the shadow-Xayans. Those two men knew about your plan to establish an independent transportation network. Uroa and I both understand the implications. I must say, your scheme is ingenious."

The General and Cristoph looked at each other. Unspoken thoughts flashed between them. "And how do you propose to help us?" Adolphus asked. "From the beginning, I gambled on letting my people take on Xayan lives at the slickwater pools. I hope it pays off – I have other tricks up my sleeve, but I could certainly use some other defenses."

"The Xayans are your allies. We understand your situation. Helping you is in our interests as well, because that makes it possible for us to move toward our racial goal again." Her voice alternated between her own and her alien partner's, but now Uroa's speech pattern became dominant and clear.

Encix added, "And thanks to the memories of Keana Duchenet, we now fully understand that Diadem Michella and the Constellation nobles would not be our preferred allies. The Xayans side with you, General Tiber Maximilian Adolphus."

"Thank you. Your abilities may be critical to our survival." The General frowned deeply. "By now, though, the Diadem has likely learned of your presence here on Hallholme, Princess. She probably also knows of your ... accident."

"It was not an accident," Keana and Uroa said in odd harmony.

"I considered embargoing all outbound stringline haulers to prevent word from leaking out, but that would have alarmed the Constellation even more. It would have drawn all their attention beyond just one woman lost on a foolish misadventure. Understand, I needed just another week or so to lock down my new network. All hell is about to break loose." Adolphus let out a long sigh. "Since you know the Diadem so well, Princess, how do you think she'll react when she learns about your conversion ... and the stringline network?"

Keana paused to consider what Michella would do. "My mother feels a need to be in control at all times. If she believes she has been slighted or tricked, she becomes vengeful. She will summon the Army of the Constellation to take possession of this planet and everything on it – including the Xayans. And the stringline network. And me."

The General's face darkened in the uncertain light of the museum vault. The four Originals stood close, also listening to the discussion with grave concern. They seemed to understand their danger.

"General," Encix said, "our race is reawakening. All of the resurrected Xayans must confer to decide how we can help to defend this planet. We cannot allow our plans to be hindered now."

"Nor I, mine." Adolphus straightened. "It is time to put everything on the table. I've been waiting years for this."

88

Destination Day.

On the General's timeline this was a neat, precise date when all the threads of his plan were pulled tight in a single knot. The culmination of his plans had been years in the making – a lifetime, in fact, because everything that had shaped Tiber Adolphus had also led to this triumph.

Very few people understood the old Earth historical reference to "D-Day" any more, but the idea raised a visceral reaction within him: the end of a massive, super-secret plan that would fundamentally change the course of humanity.

It was done. By now all fifty-three trailblazer ships had arrived at their destinations, throughout the vast wilderness of the Deep Zone. Adolphus had received completed-circuit pingbacks from each of the lonely captains who had spent months or years crawling along and reeling out a path of processed iperion. Upon their unannounced arrival, each captain had detached his vessel's aft section, which became the new terminus ring. The new stringline route was ready for business, just like that.

Destination Day.

The surprise appearance of the trailblazer ships caused an uproar on each frontier planet, and the rebel cell members established there over the past few years acted in a coordinated fashion. Bewildered planetary administrators were caught completely unprepared. Adolphus's secret supporters took over spaceport operations and embargoed outbound communications, then provided a loud and confident rallying cry for the rest of the populace, whose dissatisfaction with the oppressive Constellation had been carefully cultivated. The General received regular progress reports via stringline mail drones.

The initial eleven planetary administrators involved in the conspiracy assisted him as well. Tanja Hu had recruited several additional DZ leaders to their cause in the last two months, spreading and strengthening their cause. Though Adolphus was concerned about the potential for betrayal, or at least a leak, the Candela administrator was a good judge of character.

And the momentum continued to build, enough to make Adolphus feel even more confident. The Deezees had long resented being treated as second-class citizens, whose taxes and tariffs were increased regularly, while their needs were given little attention by the Diadem.

His unexpected ally Carlson Goler had forwarded his fleet of FTL patrol ships from Ridgetop; a dozen were now stationed at the main Hallholme hub, and the rest had been dispatched to guard the newly installed terminus rings at other vulnerable DZ worlds.

Once he issued his declaration, Adolphus knew he might have to destroy the old Sonjeera lines and cut off Hallholme from the old Crown Jewels network – as a last resort. Many people weren't going to like that. He didn't want to deal with a civil war among the disaffected old guard in the DZ at the same time as he worried about a full-scale strike from Sonjeera. This required finesse and meticulous planning; fortunately, that was what General Adolphus did well.

Now, with all the components in place, it was time for him to speak.

As usual, Sophie was his sounding board. Given all the tensions and uncertainties, Adolphus needed her now more than ever. He needed her advice, her common sense, her support, and her love.

"Time to stand up to the inevitable and laugh in its face," she said. "Whether the Constellation likes it or not, your stringline network exists." She had spent the night out at Elba, and as the two washed and dressed for the morning, she helped him prepare.

By becoming a part of him, Sophie had given him a solid foundation, a strength and sureness that he had lacked before. And with so many of his followers who had accompanied him into exile, as well as colonists who depended on him for survival, the General had a secret weapon Diadem Michella Duchenet could never possess: loyalty and love. Their future existence – individually, as a colony, and as a new union of human-settled planets – depended upon it.

"I have been ready to give this speech for ten years, Sophie. I bit my tongue and abided by my agreements. I followed the terms of my exile to the letter, and it ate a hole inside of me. Oh, yes, I am ready to speak out." He turned to face her. "I've decided to wear my uniform today, to remind everyone of what I tried to do more than a decade ago. The uniform is a way to make people think of what we almost had – and what we can have now."

Sophie brushed off his shoulders after he donned his uniform shirt and jacket. "And what if, instead, they remember that you're the General who was defeated?"

Adolphus tugged at his cuffs and applied the colorful rank insignia to his collar. "If they remember that, then they'll also remember *why* I was defeated – because I refused to achieve victory over the bodies of innocents."

"Fortune favors the bold," Sophie reminded him. She accompanied him to his staff car, then leaned over to whisper, "You do look dashing."

Even though the weathersats tracked a brewing static storm 300 kilometers away, a large crowd still gathered in Michella Town. For some time now, the colonists had suspected something was afoot, despite the General's efforts at security.

Given the turmoil across the DZ caused by the sudden arrival of the trailblazers, he was sure that some frantic messages had already leaked out to the Constellation, but that was impossible to prevent. Even now, Michella couldn't possibly have more than a vague idea of what he had actually done to her. Whenever possible, his own well-placed troublemakers would dispatch conflicting reports to foster confusion. The Diadem would receive such wildly unreliable information that she would probably disbelieve what she heard . . .

Sophie had arranged for a podium and loudspeakers at the center of town near her main warehouse. The General's speech would be transmitted to the small independent settlements, mining and industrial complexes, and even the wandering topographical prospectors. Although turbulence and electrical discharges often hampered long-range transmissions, everyone would know sooner or later, anyway.

Sophie followed him to the stage, whispering encouragement. Before Adolphus could ascend the steps, she kissed him on the lips, long and hard. He did not break away, didn't want to, though his ears were burning when he heard wolf-whistles from the crowd. Struggling to keep his dignity, he stepped up to the podium.

The people fell silent, anxious to listen. "When I was exiled to Hallholme, I made certain promises to Diadem Michella and the Constellation. I have lived my life as an honorable man. I keep my vows. But when the foundation of those promises falls apart, then how valid are those vows? Listen to the truth about Diadem Michella's 'honor.'" The last word was spoken like an insult.

He reminded them how Commodore Hallholme had achieved victory over the militarily and morally superior rebellion fleet by using dishonorable tactics. He cited all the reasons why the Deep Zone no longer needed to depend on the Constellation government. And then he played the recording that Governor Goler had sent, exposing the truth of the Ridgetop Recovery.

As the crowd listened to the revelations in stunned silence, he added, "Sonjeera and the Crown Jewels are a useless appendage. As of today, we have a complete stringline network that links the fifty-four worlds – *independent* Deep Zone worlds. And with open trade and self-determination, our colonies can supply all of their own material needs. Without the Constellation to bleed us dry, we shall profit and prosper."

He drew a breath. This was it. "Today, we cut ourselves off from the Constellation until such time as they come to terms with us and choose to treat the Deep Zone Union as equal partners rather than underlings." Adolphus added another archaic reference, hoping that at some point in the future, historians would make the connection. "Let this be a shot heard 'round the galaxy.'"

Planning ahead, he had prepared diplomatic mail drones, each of which contained a copy of his speech. Now he dispatched them to the other DZ planetary capitals. Just to make it official, he sent a courtesy copy to Diadem Michella on Sonjeera.

89

Within an hour after Adolphus's declaration arrived at Sonjeera, the Council of Lords assembled for an emergency session. Trying to maintain her regal composure, Diadem Michella raced to the central government building, accompanied by a troupe of guards and advisers, including Ishop Heer. Crowded with her into the motor carriage, they offered conflicting counsel, and her head clamored with frantic thoughts. She was thunderstruck by what the General had done. Damn him!

Though she hadn't yet decided what she would say from the Star Throne, she did not dare delay. Any Council member who happened to be on Sonjeera would attend the debate; others could join the discussion later. The Diadem refused to postpone the meeting by even an hour so that Enva Tazaar, daughter and heir of the murdered Azio Tazaar, could arrive on the next stringline vessel.

As far as Michella was concerned, all stringline travel was now suspect. The bloodthirsty Adolphus might well have sabotaged all of the operations. Oh, how he would love it if powerful nobles were killed in tragic transportation accidents! The depth of the man's plan was only now becoming apparent.

The recent deaths of so many important noblemen had raised eyebrows throughout the Crown Jewels. Other than the Paternos-Tazaar feud, there seemed no rhyme or reason, no connection among the various victims, weak and powerful families alike, talented schemers or innocuous rulers who could barely hold a continent together. It made no sense, but they couldn't all be accidents. The Diadem began to wonder now if every one of those deaths could be blamed on General Adolphus as part of a plot to overthrow the rightful Constellation government.

She wanted to kill him herself.

An hour earlier, Ishop Heer had come running into her palace chambers, his face pale and his pale green eyes wide, to tell her about the message drone. "I should have known, Eminence!" Perspiring heavily, he described everything he knew about the illegal stringline network that now branched out from Hallholme to every other Deep Zone planet. "Such a plan must have been a long time in development. The General is a monster."

Michella had understood that all along. She should have ignored popular opinion and executed the traitor a decade ago. That one act of compassion might be coming back to destroy her and the whole Constellation, as well. She should never have listened to Selik Riomini's suggestion. Now she and her military leaders would have to deal with staggering logistical problems in securing fifty-four intransigent planets at the same time. Presumably, all of the DZ worlds were weak, but it would be a challenge and annoyance to determine where to focus her assets. And now all of those worlds were *connected*. It defied belief.

The General's trailblazer ships had arrived on all of the frontier worlds without any forewarning. Planetary administrators throughout the DZ suddenly had an extensive transportation and commerce network that didn't depend on the Constellation at all. Yes, Michella could issue a proclamation threatening harsh reprisals against anyone who used the illegal system, but the frontier colonies would not be eager to let go of such a remarkable boon.

Damn him!

When her carriage stopped in Heart Square, she rushed toward the huge Council headquarters as her entourage hurried to keep up. Today there were no well-placed crowds of adoring citizens to cheer her arrival, but she couldn't concern herself about that. Right now, she had to deal with this debacle.

Ishop Heer remained at her side, wisely keeping his silence. How could her trusted aide have been so easily fooled? During his two recent trips to planet Hallholme, he'd noticed no evidence of such a gigantic operation. Ishop was not prone to letting her down, but she did not like to be disappointed ... did not like it at all.

Storming up the marblene steps, she was so intent on imagining painful deaths to inflict on General Tiber Adolphus that she didn't see Lord Bolton Crais standing at the doorway until he came right up to her. "Eminence! This is a horrible crisis. I just heard."

"We've all just heard, Bolton."

He appeared befuddled, wringing his hands. "We must do something. I'll offer whatever help I can to rescue Keana. We have to break her free from the clutches of that horrible religious cult and get her off of Hallholme."

Michella paused in her step. "That's yesterday's crisis, Bolton. I have far more important concerns right now than the actions of my foolish daughter."

He looked so earnest and so powerless – a soft-hearted, soft-headed fool, without an ambitious bone in his body. In the past, she had found his mannerisms endearing, but now he just seemed to be in her way. In all the years Michella had known him, Bolton Crais had been a sexless, unromantic man, more interested in hobbies such as bird-watching than in satisfying his own wife. She could understand why Keana had looked elsewhere for passion and romance. If only her idiot daughter had shown more common sense and discretion – and if only she'd chosen a lover whose holdings had not included a planet that the Riominis wanted ...

Still, Michella's alliance with the Crais family was key to maintaining her influence as to who her successor would be. Politically, she couldn't simply get rid of the man. Now, however, it looked as if Keana had gotten rid of herself, and in the middle of a revolt, no one could guarantee her daughter's safety.

"But, Diadem – she's my wife. We can't just give up on her. You must care about your daughter?" Bolton Crais looked as foolish and naïve as Keana did.

Trying to soften her voice, Michella said, "We will save her if we can, but by the time I get through with Hallholme, the planet may be worse off than it was after the asteroid impact." She brushed past, seeing his dismayed expression out of the corner of her eye, but her mind had already moved on to other things.

"Eminence, it will take us some time to gather the Army of the Constellation and send it to Hallholme for a proper response," Ishop said in a quiet voice. "All the nobles would have to pitch in."

"I know that full well. We haven't been on a wartime footing for years, and most of my troops couldn't pass a *real* service physical. The majority of our ships have been on stand-down in parking orbits. It was just too damned expensive to send them out to the Deep Zone for practice maneuvers." She paused. "Ah, there may be a bright spot after all! I just sent Territorial Governor Goler all those decommissioned warships. Maybe he can use them to crack down on the General."

Ishop cleared his throat as he held one of the ornate doors open for the Diadem. "Yes, uh, Eminence ... about Governor Goler."

She paused before moving inside. "Yes? What about him?"

"There was another surprise in the message packet that Adolphus sent. A testament recorded by Governor Goler, in which he revealed the full story of the atrocities committed during the Ridgetop Recovery."

"Atrocities?" She tried to remember the matter, then frowned. "Why would Goler say that? And how did he find out about it in the first place? I thought we had cleaned up the whole mess before he took his assignment on Ridgetop."

As they marched down the corridor, guards and bureaucrats snapped to attention, startled by her swift passage. "Apparently one of the original colonists survived, and Governor Goler learned the truth from her." He twitched as he walked. "Hasn't Escobar Hallholme's report reached you?"

"What report?"

"The last tribute shipment from Ridgetop contained only worthless rocks instead of goldenwood. The governor is thumbing his nose at us."

Michella froze. "Are you saying Goler has *sided* with Adolphus? After all I've done for his career? Blast the man to hell! It seems another Ridgetop Recovery may soon be in order. What would he have to gain by revealing this?"

"There are certain ramifications, Eminence." Ishop swallowed. "By revealing the massacre on Ridgetop, Governor Goler has no doubt touched off a fire across the Deep Zone. Any DZ populations who may have been wavering about General Adolphus now see how bloodthirsty and inhuman your troops were to a defenseless squatter colony."

"Bloodthirsty and inhuman! It was necessary, a simple administrative matter. Let's not blow this out of proportion."

Ishop walked briskly beside her. "The colonies will see it differently, Eminence. The Ridgetop survivor was quite graphic and extensive in her descriptions, and Governor Goler offered incontrovertible evidence."

The Diadem would have found it amusing if she weren't so furious. "Evidence can be fabricated. I will issue an immediate statement that this is a false report. Censure Governor Goler."

"I'm sorry, Eminence, but nobody will believe it. And ..." He hesitated.

She barely kept her fury in check. "And ... *what?* What else could you possibly have to tell me, Ishop?"

"And along with this revelation, Eminence, is the accusation that your official story of General Adolphus and his rebellion has been similarly distorted and sanitized. Adolphus still has plenty of sympathizers even in the core of the Constellation. This raises uncomfortable questions even among the Crown Jewel planets."

"Then quash those questions! It shouldn't be difficult ... or do I need a new special aide?"

A disturbing and frightening flash of anger crossed his face before he quickly quelled it. "I will do my best, Eminence."

The Council members had their own spies, and the shocking news spread rapidly throughout the city. The cavernous chamber was abuzz with agitated conversation.

Because the information was fresh and unconfirmed, hearsay reigned. Michella herself had not listened to the entire contents of Adolphus's speech. Over the next few days, her analysts could study every line in great detail – but not now. She'd heard enough, and she had made up her mind about Tiber Adolphus long ago.

Though Michella kept her gaze straight ahead, her vision encompassed all the people scrambling to take their seats, anxious to hear what she had to say. They wanted real leadership. As she glanced from side to side and saw all of the empty seats, Michella feared that she might not have a quorum, but she would not allow the Council members to bicker and vote and delay the necessary immediate action. She had made her decision for the good of the Constellation, and they would all have to abide by it.

She walked up the steps to the dais, spun about, and dropped onto the ornate throne with a stiff violence that revealed only a fraction of her anger.

A hush fell throughout the chamber. At no other time in her entire reign had Michella held their attention so completely. "Ladies and gentlemen, members of the Council. From this moment forward, the Constellation is at war."

90

It was time for Keana to join the other shadow-Xayans like herself. In her psyche, Uroa was eager to be among the reawakened personalities in the new alien city they had built. Using his telemancy, Uroa flew her there.

To Keana, it felt like riding the crest of a wave across the barren landscape of Hellhole toward the burgeoning settlement. Uroa carried her across the skies and away from the mountains. The sensation of flying was both thrilling and terrifying, while inside her head Uroa tried to calm her, "You must trust and submit completely. Your panic causes me difficulties."

Though she and Uroa shared control of her body, at times the Xayan leader overstepped his bounds and Keana had to push back. But not now, while they were high above the landscape. She let him revel in his new-found freedom.

They could easily have taken an overland vehicle to the red-forested valley near Slickwater Springs, but Uroa had insisted on flying, if only to demonstrate how exhilarating the synthesis with a Xayan personality could be. For the first time in her life, Keana truly felt *powerful* and completely liberated from her mother's control.

But as her body raced along, Keana couldn't seem to take a breath, didn't feel as if she even had a pulse. By submitting to him for a time, she became a mere passenger inside while Uroa used his alien abilities. Still, the potential of his telekinesis thrilled her, so long as she and Uroa could be partners, and strong together . . .

After General Adolphus departed from the mountain vault to prepare for his bombshell declaration, Keana-Uroa had spent time with the four Originals in the deep chamber, studying and *remembering* all those preserved artifacts. She and her unseen alien partner had absorbed their new understanding of each other.

Now, to foster the reawakened Xayan people, she would travel out to the settlement where all the converts, with their shared experiences, congregated to bond. Keana remembered how she and Louis had liked to retreat to her private, luxurious Cottage on the Pond of Birds . . .

Eavesdropping on her reminiscences, Uroa spoke inside her head. "Your lover is dead, and you and I need a new beginning. Long ago, when Zairic offered his plan to save our race with slickwater, none of us knew how we would be awakened after the impact. Now that humans have revived us, we shadow-Xayans must re-learn how to achieve *ala'ru*."

Keana understood that no person could remain unaffected by the experience. Adopting another full life amazed and nearly overwhelmed her. The symbiotic alliance with Uroa had made her realize the parochial insignificance of the entire Constellation, and how petty her mother's politics truly were. How could human power squabbles compare with the possibility of Xayan ascension?

Although she could feel and understand Uroa's exuberance, Keana also understood the *human* crisis that Xaya – Hallholme – now faced. This planet, the slickwater reservoirs, and the whole population must be protected. "After what General Adolphus has just done, we might soon face severe reprisals. It's an immediate problem we'll have to confront."

"Together," Uroa said.

"Together."

In a valley filled with wild and tangled Xayan growth, nearly a thousand shadow-Xayans had established their colony, a pale mirror of the ethereal, animated cities that had once covered this world. Though the inhabitants appeared human, the buildings themselves were unusual and freeform, morphing in subtle ways from one shape into another.

Keana felt the excitement inside Uroa's personality, a sense of memory akin to her wonder. As they landed gently in the center of the settlement, Keana caught the afterglow of his memories, gliding along in lush groves of the scarlet fronds, letting the fleshy plants stroke his sensitive, moist skin. Through his outer membrane, Uroa remembered flavors, the smells and sounds of the crimson forests, and the whispering of Xaya's lushness.

"My world is awakening," he said, his voice quiet inside of her.

And the shadow-Xayan city was even more magnificent. On the streets between the translucent, changing buildings, some people walked, while others levitated. Several converts leaped from atop tall structures, practicing their telemancy; some of them streaked away awkwardly, barely in control of their abilities.

A narrow-faced man with long brown hair approached Keana-Uroa. She recognized Fernando-Zairic, the man who had convinced Keana to jump into the slickwater after Cristoph rejected her. They shook hands in a human greeting, while the two Xayan personalities linked for a brief telepathic exchange.

Fernando-Zairic led them along the street, where Keana was astonished by the sights, smells, and concepts around her. As they walked together through the settlement, Uroa explained many of the things he saw, even though she did not have the vocabulary to describe it. However, Keana realized that if her mother observed this through the more limited filter of human experience, she would command that everything be seized, or destroyed, "for the good of the Constellation."

This thought made her uneasy, and she refused to let Uroa forget the imminent threat from the Constellation. "My mother could ruin Xayan hopes as surely as the asteroid impact did."

Uroa accepted her concerns. "We may be able to help General Adolphus in ways the Diadem will never expect. Look around you."

Fernando-Zairic understood as well. "That is why you see so many shadow-Xayans practicing their skills. They must learn to set aside human impediments and coordinate their new abilities. We are much more powerful together, as partners, than the original telemancers were. It is a step towards the evolutionary shift." He seemed happy rather than concerned. "When a few small difficulties are worked out, our two races will stand on each other's shoulders."

In a clearing where the dense and thriving alien weed had been harvested, hundreds of shadow-Xayans stood in a spiral arrangement, their prismatic eyes focused far away. Above their heads, peculiar shapes sparkled and flashed in an ever-changing parade of coils and geometric forms. Nearby, the tall alien weed seemed to sway in time to unheard music.

Wondrous living buildings surrounded the central spiral, leaning and expanding, changing colors, shapes, and textures by the moment. Window and door arrangements came and went; elevated walkways appeared beside structural extrusions, extensions, and moldings. The buildings themselves were telemantically generated, shaped and altered by the powers of the alien minds.

"Shadow-Xayan telemancers are imagining these new buildings into existence," Uroa explained to her. Keana sensed a restless energy, as if the creators remained dissatisfied with their creations.

Fernando-Zairic watched their attempts. "Even with the slickwater, there are memory gaps, holes in recollection. But we keep trying. It is a relentless collective effort."

Keana did not feel afraid even when the towering, unstable structures leaned toward her and hovered overhead. Inside, she sensed that Uroa's own telemancy could easily deflect any danger. Finally the group of telemancers reached consensus, causing the shape of the building to hold and solidify.

When the wind blew around and through the structures, it created sounds that Keana found inexplicably comforting. Though she wasn't aware of having moved, she discovered that she had joined the others in the spiral, and Uroa was guiding their thoughts, pressing gently, coaxing her to help him – and to learn.

Her human mind could not be entirely at ease, because she knew what her mother would do in response to the General's announcement. But she still held out hope of preventing bloodshed. Perhaps with the Xayan ideas of Uroa and Zairic, along with a bold move she had in mind, they might find a way to avert a second catastrophe on this world.

91

With the new DZ stringline network in place, Adolphus received rapid reports from all the other planets via emergency mail drones.

On Destination Day, only one of the other territorial governors had been out in the Deep Zone rather than back at her offices on Sonjeera. Unfortunately, the governor chose to stand with the Constellation government, issuing orders to destroy the unwanted terminus rings and sever the new stringlines linking her planet with Hellhole. Adolphus's secret operatives staged a coup and imprisoned the intractable governor, then took steps to secure all the planets in her territory. With astonishing speed and zeal, the deputy planetary administrator rallied the people against the territorial governor and put the woman under house arrest for "acting against the common good."

Adolphus saw to it that the old Constellation terminus rings above DZ worlds were rigged with scuttling charges that could be detonated on a moment's notice – if he was forced to do so. For now, the lines would be left open for communication purposes, and as a bargaining chip, although Adolphus held little expectation that war might be avoided.

Now, he could only wait.

Two aliens in human bodies arrived at Elba shortly before dawn. When Adolphus met them in his parlor, he recognized Fernando and Keana. Fernando-Zairic spoke without formalities. "General Adolphus, we have come to offer a possible solution to the current crisis with the Constellation." He looked over at his companion.

Keana-Uroa said, "I understand the turmoil I inadvertently caused when I entered the slickwater. I did not mean to place you in such a difficult position."

"Your joining the shadow-Xayans is only part of the problem, Princess, but I'll be happy to hear suggestions for a way to avoid bloodshed."

Keana said, "Allow me to go to Sonjeera as an ambassador – I am in a position to represent both you and the Xayans. This is a critical time. No shots have been fired yet, no violence unleashed, so we may still salvage this. Remember who I am – both Keana Duchenet and the Xayan leader Uroa. I can negotiate an end to these tensions if you let me play both roles. The Diadem will at least listen to me."

"We must make the attempt to avoid killing," Fernando-Zairic said, nodding in agreement. "A prolonged and destructive war does not serve your interests, the Diadem's, or the Xayans'. We must prevent that at all costs."

Keana-Uroa continued, as if they had planned and choreographed their speech to the last detail. "This is a watershed moment in many ways, General. Much hinges on how the Constellation reacts. Diadem Michella needs to understand exactly what has happened here. She needs to hear it from *us*, rather than through her spies."

Adolphus shook his head. "Absolutely not. I cannot allow you to go back to Sonjeera, Princess Keana. That should be self-evident."

"So am I a hostage after all?"

"Not in so many words. I didn't want you here in the first place, and I certainly didn't want you to take on a Xayan personality, but you're here now, and there's no way around it. Much as I hate to admit it, you are our best bargaining chip, because your mother may not launch an open attack on Hallholme as long as you are in the line of fire."

Keana seemed amused. "So now you are using me as a human shield, just as Commodore Hallholme used innocent hostages at the end of your rebellion?"

Adolphus didn't like the comparison. "The tactic was effective, wasn't it?"

"Effective against you, but you are a man of honor and compassion. My mother is quite different."

"I'm sorry, but I can't just hand you over to the Diadem."

Fernando-Zairic remained silent, deep in thought. When he finally spoke, he drew upon both his alien and human oratory skills. "Then *I* should be the one to go to Sonjeera. The Xayan race regarded Zairic highly. I was their visionary, their prophet, and their general. My words inspired our people to dream of our race's *ala'ru*, and I helped preserve them before the asteroid struck. I drew together many factions, unified most of the Xayans."

"And how does that help us?"

The other man grinned as the old Fernando personality came to the fore. "I'll go back to Sonjeera, along with several other shadow-Xayans. *We'll* tell the Diadem the news, explain the wondrous thing that has happened to us and to Princess Keana. Seeing us, Michella will have to believe. And, let's face it, General, as a human, I mean nothing to the Diadem."

"You're both being naïve. It won't be that simple – we already fooled the Diadem's inspector, convincing him that your group was just another deluded cult here on Hellhole. Why should Michella believe you now? And what if she doesn't care?"

"Then one of the Originals must go along," Keana said. "How else to show her the sheer import of what's happening here? What better way to dispel skepticism? Show her something she can't deny. Once she sees a genuine Xayan, she will know this is not just some mass delusion. And if Zairic can get through to her, if he can make her listen and give her a demonstration of relevancy, then the whole playing field will change."

Zairic's soft yet compelling voice was insistent. "This goes well beyond mere political or economic disagreements, General Adolphus. You have seen the powers we Xayans demonstrate. Our overarching goal is to revive the Xayan race, and for that we will need the help of your people. It benefits us all if we insist on peace."

"Easier said than done." Adolphus thought the two were being obtuse, but he continued to ponder. After revealing his stringline network and making his announcement, he had impounded the

Constellation hauler in orbit and prevented it from leaving. He had also taken the Diadem's known representatives into custody, just to prevent them from causing trouble.

At this point, he was waiting for the other side to make their move. And what did he really have to lose?

Adolphus made his decision. "For obvious reasons, I can't accompany you myself, any more than I can let Keana go back to Sonjeera. I've got to maintain any advantage I have." He scratched his cheek, considering. Maybe he could surprise the Diadem enough, make her hesitate . . . Zairic and his emissaries might be able to accomplish that, putting the old tyrant off balance. "One way or another, we'll have to open the communication channels." The General let out a long breath. "I don't want to minimize the risk. If you go, bear in mind that I will do whatever is necessary to protect this planet and the new stringline hub and all fifty-four Deep Zone planets. I may find it necessary to close down the Michella Town spaceport, perhaps even terminate all stringline travel back to the Crown Jewel worlds. If things go badly, you might not be able to get back here. Or the Diadem could just execute you. Are you still willing to go?"

"If we succeed, such desperate measures will not be necessary," Zairic said. "I believe there are always solutions. Even in the face of our race's imminent extinction, I found a solution."

The General reached out to shake his hand. Fernando-Zairic's grip was limp now, as if he still hadn't become accustomed to the rigidity of bones. "Go ahead, then. Maybe you can pull off a miracle and make the Diadem see reason." In his heart, though, he thought it was a fool's errand.

After taking his leave of Slickwater Springs and returning to his job as a topographical prospector, Vincent Jenet spent most of his time alone in the wilderness, mapping blank grid squares from his Trakmaster. He remained blissfully unaware of news and politics from the rest of the Constellation. The open landscape was his comfort, and he enjoyed being alone. He found it fulfilling.

Returning to Michella Town from a weeks-long expedition, he learned from the agitated people on the streets what had happened. So much had changed in only a month! Hellhole and all of the Deep Zone had broken away from the Crown Jewels, and soon enough they might actually be at war. And he had thought Hellhole was so far from the heart of politics that no one would care about it one way or another.

In town, when he heard about the eleventh-hour peace mission Fernando intended to undertake, Vincent thought it sounded entirely unlike anything his fast-talking friend would do. It also sounded like a very bad idea.

Since the party of shadow-Xayan peacemakers had not yet departed on their hare-brained mission, Vincent hurried to the spaceport to locate them; he probably wouldn't be able to talk Fernando out of going, but at least he hoped for a chance to say goodbye.

At the spaceport, he met crowds of annoyed and terrified offworlders who desperately wanted to get away from Hellhole, but all travel had been restricted. An impounded stringline hauler remained docked at the old terminus, its female captain taken captive and placed in detention on the planet's surface. No one else was allowed to leave. The passenger pod containing Fernando and his emissaries would be the only vessel allowed to depart Hellhole for the time being.

Vincent finally spotted Fernando-Zairic and three placid human converts wearing comfortable clothes made from the red weed. While their features were human, their demeanor was strikingly different from the others in the crowd. Moving ponderously but with a liquid grace, the Original alien Cippiq had come to the spaceport, showing himself openly now that the secret was out. He was an object of awe among the spectators. Cippiq had volunteered to accompany the group to Sonjeera, to show the whole Constellation that the Xayans were real.

Vincent ran up to his old friend. "Fernando! I'm glad I got here in time to say goodbye – and maybe talk some sense into you. What do you think you're doing? Can't someone else go?" The whole idea of this expedition to Sonjeera gave him a sense of foreboding.

Fernando brightened upon seeing him. "You worry too much, as always! But you don't have to say goodbye." He raised his chin and spoke impulsively. "I want you to go with me. Come on! You and I were a great team. We have plenty of room on the passenger pod, and you can help me."

Vincent was taken aback by the comment. "Help you? How?"

"We have other shadow-Xayans and one of the Originals, but we need an objective human representative as well, to give unbiased perspectives. You can speak to the Sonjeerans as someone who's seen the slickwater pools and knows us. And because you aren't a convert, the Diadem can't accuse you of being brainwashed."

Vincent's pulse raced. He didn't like this at all. "I'm sure the General could find a more qualified person among all these people clamoring to get off the planet."

"But you have my recommendation, and that trumps everything else. What did you have planned for the next several days?"

"I was going to map another grid square . . ."

"It'll still be there when we get back." Fernando took his arm, talking him into the plan, as he had talked Vincent into so many other ill-advised decisions.

"I'm still not sure it's a good idea." Vincent had never expected to leave Hellhole again, but he realized that he did want to accompany his old friend, to help Fernando remain in touch with his human side, if nothing else. "You really think I can help you?"

"Maybe. And you know me – I'll probably get in trouble without you. This is another big adventure, and I'd rather have you there. Just go along for the ride if you want. Do it out of friendship."

Because it was obvious that it was truly Fernando twisting his arm, not the aloof Xayan leader, Vincent made up his mind. "I can do that."

"Besides," Fernando said with a wink, "I'm not convinced Zairic is prepared for meeting with Diadem Michella." Abruptly his voice changed, and Vincent saw a glimmer of the debate going on inside the other man's head. "I will not be easily fooled or out-debated. Once I explain the significance of *ala'ru*, the people of the Constellation will put aside their war and join us. We all stand to benefit."

Vincent shook his head, now fully convinced that he *had* to go along. This group reminded him of starry-eyed missionaries heading into hostile territory with more faith than common sense. Maybe he could add a more compelling perspective to their position, a human perspective. Or at least he could keep them safe.

"Yes, I'd like to go with you," he said. "If the General gives his approval."

"The human goes with us," Cippiq said, ending the discussion.

92

While responses and plans hurtled back and forth along the new stringline connections, Ian Walfor remained at Hellhole's new, independent spaceport. His own people could do without him for the time being. They were probably the safest in the whole Deep Zone; since Michella herself had abandoned the stringline to Buktu and couldn't send her military there even if she wanted to.

General Adolphus had made his announcement, and without a doubt, the shit was going to hit the fan. It was imperative that the DZ stringline network succeed. Right now, test ships were returning from the last of the new routes, demonstrating the viability of the entire network.

Administrator Rendo Theris was doing his best to manage operations at Ankor, but the responsibilities had begun to overwhelm him. Walfor, though, was perfectly comfortable with the operations, and he decided to assist the man. Theris didn't seem to mind him looking over his shoulder as a double-check.

In the afternoon, the two men inspected the mechanism for launching upboxes and passenger pods to the orbiting hub. An engineer by training, rather than an administrator, Theris had a knack for troubleshooting. Based on a slight drop in the efficiency of the fuel cubes, he sniffed out a hidden reaction-chamber crack. Teams of workers promptly made repairs.

Though relieved that they had caught the problem before a disaster could happen, Walfor studied the error with razor-sharp suspicion. If a passenger pod or upbox exploded and damaged the orbiting hub, the General's plan would be severely compromised – just the sort of sabotage a Constellation operative might plan. However, after studying the matter carefully, they concluded that the flaw was exactly what it seemed.

Just to be sure, he and Theris conducted a thorough ground inspection of the launch and receiving facilities, alert for additional problems. Everything seemed to be fine. Back inside the admin tower, Walfor took a seat at his borrowed desk to read the reports trickling in from the other DZ worlds: linerunners checking substations, new vessels arriving at Hellhole from all across the Deep Zone. Back on Buktu, Walfor's crew was adapting their FTL ships for interplanetary commerce as well as defense of the independent frontier worlds. The scope was breathtaking.

Theris interrupted his thoughts with a loud yelp. "What the hell is that?"

Around the tower room, scanscreens from the numerous orbiting surveillance satellites showed a flurry of blips that indicated large objects converging in the sky over Ankor. The blips flew in an odd, squared-off formation and at remarkable speed.

Racing to the perimeter scan panels, Walfor shouldered one of the techs aside and enhanced the images. He zoomed in on the undersides of the strange craft to display hulls of textured, coppery metal with several segments that glowed red. Static flurried across the screens. Long-distance analytical equipment in the tower blanked out. Sparks sprayed out of one console, while workers cursed at their stations.

"That's a damned powerful scan!" Theris shouted.

"I don't recognize those craft," Walfor said. He and his engineers had stripped and rebuilt just about every kind of vessel that had ever been used out here. "Are they Constellation vessels? How did they get here? Any activity on the old Sonjeera stringline?"

"None, sir!" one of the techs called out. "I don't know where they came from."

Without consulting the administrator, Walfor activated the defenses the General had installed to protect both the launch site and the orbiting hub. The weaponry had been designed to thwart spies or unexpected visitors, not to repel a full-fledged military assault. Though the strange ships had not yet opened fire, he triggered the automated systems. His weapons sprayed wide arcs of color across the sky. Supersonic projectiles screamed toward the intruders.

As urgent alarms went off at the Ankor site, the grouping of odd ships tilted for an instant, moving like a linked flock of birds. They neatly dodged every one of the incoming projectiles, not even breaking formation, before the blips streaked away to vanish in a blur.

"What were those ships and what did they want?" Theris asked. "Walfor, have you ever seen anything like that? They were off – stringline!"

It didn't make sense to him either, but Walfor understood well enough what he had seen. "They were gathering details on this space-port. I think we just witnessed the Constellation's first move."

93

"All those old warships gone from Lubis Plain," the retired Commodore said with a sigh, as if he had been disappointed to see them go. For the past several years, the old man had often stood on the edge of the field just to look at all the hulls glinting in the sunlight, lost in his memories. Now that he and his son had traveled to the Black Lord's world of Aeroc, he was still obsessed with the antique warships. "You did a very creditable job of getting them spaceworthy again and shipping them out to the Deep Zone, Escobar. You've proved yourself, son."

"And good riddance to them," Escobar said. "Though Governor Goler has apparently sided with the General, according to that Ridgetop Recovery confession he transmitted. He already cheated on his tribute – the shipment *I* delivered to Sonjeera." The younger officer ground his teeth together. "What if Goler turns those ships against the Constellation? Then the error could reflect on me."

Percival just shrugged. "That's none of your concern. The rightful territorial governor certified the shipment. You will not be held responsible because another man lied. You had your orders, son, and you followed them impeccably. Most impressive."

Escobar took heart, but he remained guarded. "Do you think my work was good enough for Lord Riomini to notice, sir? He's going to need a point man in his operations against the Deep Zone . . . unless he wants to take command himself." Escobar was reluctant to have his wife send a cheery note to her grand-uncle, along with a subtle hint about her husband, but he was considering it. With the General causing trouble again, Escobar might never have another chance like this.

Dressed in his trim modern uniform, he stood with his father at a tram station on the Riomini homeworld of Aeroc, overlooking a vast trampled prairie where the largest divisions of the Constellation strike force were being assembled and readied for combat, as the Diadem had ordered. Percival Hallholme wore his customary old uniform; though he had not seen active duty for years, he did not feel comfortable in casual civilian clothes.

"Oh, the Black Lord won't want to get his hands dirty, son. He may eventually take the credit if the operation is successful, but I wouldn't be surprised if he selected you for the front lines." The retired Commodore made a tsk-tsk sound. "You've always wanted to go into battle, haven't you?"

Escobar flinched, wary of encouraging another one of the old man's stories. "I had a brief taste when I led the Vielinger occupation. Some of the locals were quite incensed, and there could have been violent resistance. I ensured that the people remained calm – and the iperion mines didn't miss a day of production during the changeover. Lord Riomini noticed that, I'm sure."

"Ah," said Percival. He had a way of annoying his son even when he said nothing or very little.

The Black Lord had just promoted Escobar to the rank of Red Commodore, or Redcom, putting him on track toward ultimately becoming a full Commodore. Escobar felt pleased to be called to the Aeroc training grounds to assist in the preparations against General Adolphus. If he ever hoped to match (or exceed) the old man's illustrious war record, this was his chance to prove himself . . . or it would forever be said that he could not measure up. When he departed from the old Adolphus estate to assist the Army of the Constellation, with his father tagging along, Escobar had kissed his wife and given his sons a formal farewell. Then the old officer had swept the boys up in a big hug. The display of affection was somewhat embarrassing, and certainly not the way Percival Hallholme had raised *him*.

After Adolphus's provocative revelation, and the Diadem's unequivocal declaration of war, Lord Selik Riomini had wasted no time preparing the Army of the Constellation for combat. Michella announced her intention to tighten her grip on the Deep Zone worlds, insisting on absolute compliance from her subjects ... but so far, the frontier administrators had failed to respond. Escobar privately decided that the planetary leaders feared General Adolphus more than they feared the Army of the Constellation. That would have to change.

In the distance he saw skirmish aircraft flying in practice formations and heard the drone of heavy machinery all around as cargo ships were loaded with the necessities of war to be uplifted onto huge military stringline haulers that could transport an entire fleet at a time. The Army of the Constellation would hurtle down on General Adolphus and his nest of traitors like a brand new asteroid impact.

Soon enough, Escobar realized with some amusement, the Deep Zone was going to need a lot of new planetary administrators.

The old Commodore interrupted his thoughts. "When you go into battle, son, remember that you carry our family name and honor on your shoulders. You won't know who you really are until you face a genuine war." He paused, looking troubled. "I learned things about myself in that process, you know ..."

When the old man's voice trailed off, Escobar broke in, not wanting to hear more. "I passed my school exams near the top of my class and received excellent combat training. I am fully prepared to distinguish myself in the assault force against Adolphus. It will be a short little war, Father. Just wait for the news, and watch for my name."

The old man's gray eyes were moist and rheumy as he wallowed in another round of reminiscing. "I just want you to keep things in perspective, son. Don't place too much importance on your limited experience."

Escobar let out a laugh that wasn't really a laugh. "That would be impossible around you."

They traveled to Lord Riomini's Aeroc estate for a strategy session that included officers and nobles of the Hirdan and Tazaar families, along with a lackluster minor cousin who claimed to be in charge of coordinating official military documents. Old Percival referred to the man privately as a "desk general" – a nobleman who was proficient at office work but not to be trusted with making combat decisions.

Logistics Officer Bolton Crais was also there representing his family, but he was primarily interested in ensuring Keana's safety. The men sat at a large conference table by a window that looked out on the gardens of the Aeroc estate. "We can send our ships to form a blockade around planet Hallholme and destroy the new stringline hub," Crais said. "But we don't dare launch outright military strikes against the cities on the ground! There are civilians and ... and Princess Keana is there. We have to ensure her safety."

Escobar said coldly, "That might not be in alignment with the overall military objective."

Dressed in black, as always, Lord Riomini prevented Keana's cuckolded husband from pressing the point. He spoke from the head of the long table, his voice laced with acid. "You should have kept your foolish wife under better control, Bolton. She's gotten herself into the thick of things, and we cannot risk the security of the whole Constellation for her sake."

"But she's the Diadem's daughter!" Crais seemed genuinely distraught, which Escobar found surprising. Everyone knew they had a loveless marriage.

With an annoyed sigh, the Black Lord unfurled a document that bore Michella's prominent stamp. "These are the Diadem's instructions explicitly sanctioning 'all necessary militarily actions, without regard to the safety of any particular individual.' She knew exactly what I was asking her to sign. This discussion is ended."

Crais slumped back in his chair, and did not speak for the rest of the meeting. Escobar did not feel that his lack of input was much of a loss. Military decisions should be based on military considerations. Even though Escobar's own wife was a Riomini, he would never have suggested changing tactics simply to keep her safe. There were too many other considerations.

"One more thing," Riomini said, with a wink in the direction of old Percival. "I've completed my review of recommendations concerning who should lead the assault force against Adolphus. I'll remain in overall command of our forces, but for this job I have another name in mind, one whose family has distinguished itself in past service to the Constellation."

He looked down the table from side to side at the various officers (many of whom came from military families), and let his gaze rest on Escobar, who found himself short of breath, waiting for the next words. The Black Lord fiddled with his collar, then said, "Escobar Hallholme, you are hereby assigned to command the initial assault force." He smiled. "If you accept, of course."

"Sir, with all of my heart!" In his excitement Escobar stood up, and in the dazed moments that followed he was surrounded by other officers who congratulated him and patted him on the back. This did not include his father, who stood off to one side, watching somberly.

When the strategy session ended, he and his father boarded a tram bound for an officers' compound where they would be staying. The officers spoke of a celebration that evening as a send-off to war, insisting that the Hallholmes attend. Escobar knew what that meant: fresh-faced soldiers gathering around the legendary Commodore, listening with rapt attention as the old man talked and talked and talked until dawn. Escobar politely begged off. In his own quarters, at least, he would have a bit of peace.

The two of them were closer now, but Escobar had a lot of planning to do. He didn't want to make mistakes; he needed to select a cadre of officers who would assist him closely, and on whom he could depend. Some of those names were already obvious, due to seniority and past performance, but some were not.

As the tramcar accelerated along its aerial track, his father cleared his throat. "You think I am too hard on you, son. You think I expect too much."

"I am proud of my own record, sir, no matter what you believe. And I have managed to steer clear of all the black marks that blotted your early career. When you were my age, you had very little to brag about."

"Ah, yes." The old man paused a moment, as if mulling over some of those misadventures before returning his thoughts to the present. "Whenever I give an example about military matters, it is intended as an object lesson for you. That's why you should pay close attention. You may have been hampered by a peacetime career, but you were also weaned on the service. With your family name, as my son, you have advanced ahead of many others."

"I intend to make my own name, and now I have that opportunity.

Two military careers made by facing the same man: Tiber Maximilian Adolphus. Isn't it ironic that both of us would defeat the same opponent?"

"You'll have to succeed to make it ironic. Don't get ahead of yourself."

Ignoring his father's comment, Escobar mused, "I wish this had the potential to be a larger war. Adolphus will be tougher than the de Carres, certainly, but he's only leading a ragtag bunch of Deezees operating tired old equipment. A couple of weeks and it'll be over."

"Don't forget that our Army of the Constellation is a bloated military force led by too many political favorites. Yes, we have some talented commanders, but there are weaknesses, and the enemy is clever enough to exploit them. I urge you not to underestimate Tiber Adolphus – or he'll bury you."

Escobar didn't believe it for a moment, of course. His father was a doddering old man who had spent years exaggerating his own achievements. The upstart Adolphus wouldn't last long.

94

During the stringline trip to Sonjeera, Vincent had plenty of room aboard the passenger pod. The hauler had no other cargo upboxes or additional passenger pods; isolated up in her rig, the captain was happy to be released to the Crown Jewels, terrified to be caught up in the whirlwind of a brewing conflict.

Aboard the pod, Vincent's only companions were Fernando-Zairic, three shadow-Xayans, and Cippiq. The others accepted Vincent's presence politely enough, yet he felt like the odd man out; he wasn't like them. He stuck it out anyway.

Fortunately, because human mouths could not make the resonating thrums required by the natural Xayan language, everyone spoke Constellation standard, even the Original alien. Vincent could understand their words, but more often than not he didn't comprehend what they were talking about.

As the nearly empty stringline hauler hurtled along, Zairic spoke of his bright hopes that the people of the Constellation would join them and help resurrect the Xayan race. While the rapt followers listened, Vincent interjected, "First you'll have to convince Diadem Michella that we're no threat. She'll be furious with General Adolphus. I expect she will want to deal with Deep Zone independence before she worries about your alien dreams."

Zairic dismissed the idea. "With the possibility of *ala'ru* for our race, such parochial concerns are irrelevant and minor."

"The Diadem won't see it that way."

A hint of cockiness in his friend's expression suggested that the real Fernando had come to the fore again, if only for a moment. "Don't worry, Vincent. I'll just have to be persuasive."

The stringline ship arrived at the bustling Sonjeera hub, a huge orbiting wheel with twenty-seven active stations at which haulers docked, disengaged their boxes and passenger pods, and hooked up outgoing containers, before heading out again.

The hauler captain, relieved to be back in civilization, sent a codecall message explaining the odd set of passengers she had brought from Hellhole. She used a confidential emergency frequency to request procedural clarifications.

While Fernando-Zairic, Vincent, and the others waited in the passenger pod for clearance to land at the spaceport, cargo downboxes were detached from adjacent haulers and passed over to orbital handling facilities. Because not all of the containers were destined for the capital world, shipments would be realigned and cross-loaded onto haulers bound for other planets.

For more than an hour they heard no word from any official representatives, so Fernando-Zairic used the passenger pod's codecall system to send his own message over a broad range of common frequencies. "Attention, people of Sonjeera! I am Zairic, emissary from the Xayan race. We have come to meet with you and tell our exciting story to your people. We request a personal meeting with Diadem Michella Duchenet. As proof of who we are, we brought one of the survivors of our original people." For shocking emphasis, Zairic brought Cippiq into the transmission frame. It was the first time anyone from the Crown Jewels had ever seen an Original Xayan.

Cippiq bowed his supple neck, and his large eyes never blinked. His mouth membrane thrummed as he spoke. "Diadem Michella, leader of the Constellation, we look forward to telling you of our history and our hopes. We wish to explain how you can all share the lives of our lost race."

Before Zairic could speak again, a high-pitched sound exploded from the codecall speakers, followed by a burst of feedback. Vincent wasn't surprised. "They're jamming us, Fernando. I don't know how much of your message got through to the general public before you were cut off. Someone must be monitoring the pod frequency. They shut us down."

Zairic did not seem disturbed. "We have been patient for centuries. We can be patient now. Sooner or later, Diadem Michella will let us deliver our message to the Constellation."

Vincent drew a deep, frustrated breath. "Zairic, *please* listen to me! This isn't going to be as simple or straightforward as you imagine. The Diadem won't *want* to hear what you have to say. After what General Adolphus just did, she'll be suspicious of anything that comes from Hellhole."

"Then we must allay her suspicions." Zairic turned away from the now-useless codecall panel, and Vincent felt as if he had been dismissed.

Without explanation or warning, the passenger pod disengaged from its docking clamp, dropped away from the hauler framework, and began to fall, guided remotely to the city-studded surface. Sonjeera was a mosaic of lights and urban grids, along with geometric, multilayered agricultural plots for maximum productivity, rivers that no longer misbehaved but flowed in straight lines, and sapphire oceans that had been well tamed.

Vincent peered through the windowport, remembering the only other time he had seen the capital world, when he was transferred out to Hellhole. Despite the optimism Fernando-Zairic now exuded, Vincent was not convinced this trip would be any better than when he had been sent to the Deep Zone. Nevertheless, he would do his best to offer assistance, no matter how much anxiety gnawed at his stomach.

As the pod plowed through the atmosphere, Vincent got a good view of Sonjeera's primary spaceport. Cippiq and the shadow-Xayans seemed completely placid, accepting wherever they might be taken; the group remained in their seats, not bothering to look through the windowports.

The main landing area was a targeting zone littered with upboxes to be shot into orbit and downboxes that had already been received. Heavy machinery moved cargo to supply stations, while rail delivery systems sent passenger pods to waiting areas and terminals.

Vincent was the first to realize that their pod was being redirected to a military area with a red-demarcated landing zone. A rough male voice crackled out of the reactivated codecall speakers. "Attention, unauthorized passengers from Hallholme – you are being placed in quarantine."

"There is no need for that," Fernando-Zairic replied. "We merely wish to speak with the Diadem."

"You exhibit signs of mass delusional behavior, and the alien creature you brought aboard the passenger pod could be a host for extraterrestrial disease organisms. Our precautions are necessary."

"We agree to abide by your conditions," Zairic said, "but the truth is no mass delusion. We have proof of what we say."

"Tell it to the Diadem. Once you're safely sealed and under guard in the warehouse, she will meet with you."

"We look forward to it." Zairic smiled, but not convincingly. He still hadn't practiced his facial expressions enough, Vincent thought.

The moment they landed (none too gently) in the target zone, armored vehicles surrounded the passenger pod, as if they expected an invasion force to surge out. A heavy loader picked up the pod and crawled forward on wide treads, rumbling over the fused surface of the landing zone. Peering through the windowport, Vincent saw that they were heading toward a large, ominous-looking hangar.

Sensing his uneasiness, Zairic said, "You have nothing to fear, Vincent Jenet. As soon as I explain everything to Diadem Michella, we will be set free."

Vincent shook his head. "Fernando, if you're still in there, you'd better caution your friend about human political matters."

"Fernando Neron has relegated this matter to me."

Vincent sighed. Fernando would just tell him he worried too much anyway.

Once the pod entered the hangar and the large metal doors rolled shut, intense lights blazed down upon them, bathing the entire vessel. Vincent assumed they were being deep-scanned, but the Constellation military inspectors would find nothing other than the passengers. Even that, however, might be considered dangerous from the Diadem's point of view.

The codecall panel remained silent. No one gave them any updates. The shadow-Xayans were content to wait until the Diadem or her representative arrived. Vincent struggled to control his panic.

As another hour crawled by, he watched through the windowport until he saw a diplomatic vehicle arrive. When an old woman emerged, Vincent recognized the familiar figure he had seen all his life, the dowager leader of the Constellation. She was accompanied by a large, bald man. Vincent recognized him as the Constellation inspector who had been aboard his passenger pod during the journey out to Hellhole: the Diadem's watchdog and special aide. So, she had come well prepared.

Michella stood in the brightly lit hangar, gazing at the passenger pod while keeping her distance. If she noticed Vincent's face at the windowport, she gave no indication. After regarding them for some time, she walked out of sight.

When the codecall screen glowed to life, Michella's face filled the pane. "Have you brought my daughter with you? I demand that she be returned unharmed." Thus far, Cippiq and the others remained outside of the imager's field of view.

"She is not harmed," Zairic said pleasantly, "but she cannot come. Not yet. We decided you would hear our message more clearly if an objective person explained it to you."

"You kidnapped and brainwashed her!"

"Do not jump to conclusions, Diadem Michella. We have much to discuss. Please free us from this quarantine so that you and I may speak face-to-face, as fellow leaders."

"I don't recognize you as a leader at all."

"But in centuries past I guided the entire Xayan race, preserved them in slickwater before the destruction of our world, and helped usher them through their awakening. While I am merged into a human, my companion Cippiq is one of only four survivors of our original race. You can see what a majestic people we were. He also wishes to meet you, if you will unseal this passenger pod."

"We will speak via codecall for the time being," Michella said. "You're staying right there."

Zairic bowed in resignation, and his opalescent eyes shone. "I have so much to tell you. All of your people should hear our marvelous news."

In an impassioned speech, he described the Xayan quest for *ala'ru* and how the human race could make that goal possible again. He issued his call for volunteers to help revive the Xayan memories. He droned on and on, caught up in his own dreams. Around him, the shadow-Xayans seemed engrossed in his words.

All the while, Vincent watched Michella's expression and demeanor carefully. He could see she hadn't been swayed. Finally she said in a calculating voice, "I am much more interested in what you can reveal about the plans of General Tiber Adolphus. You'd earn a great deal of goodwill by providing me with vital information. What is his true reason for sending you here? Are you spies?"

"He did not send us, Diadem. We offered to come." Zairic gestured to Cippiq, who now moved into the projected field of view. "Our races have strikingly different physical appearances, but we are much the same. Hear me, Diadem. To our great sorrow, even the Xayans suffered from dissent. A major rift in our people nearly destroyed us, and therefore I understand the rift among humans. You must heal the breach before it causes further damage."

Vincent saw unconcealed alarm in Michella's expression. "What sort of monster is that with you?"

"He's not a monster. This is Cippiq, an Original Xayan who surfaced on Hallholme."

A mumbled male voice came from off screen. The Diadem muted and blanked the screen abruptly for privacy.

Vincent leaned toward Zairic, speaking in a hushed voice. "What great rift are you talking about among the Xayan people? Do you mean how you and Encix disagreed about the way to save the Xayans from the impact?"

"No, this was much more serious, a breach of our entire race and destiny. Unfortunately in that instance, I failed utterly."

"Are you going to do a demonstration of telemancy to impress the Diadem?" Vincent asked. Zairic shook his head, having adopted a human gesture. "Not yet. Cippiq does not want to upset her further, or frighten her."

Before Vincent could raise further questions, Michella reappeared, speaking like a politician again. "You have given me much to think about, and now I ask you to be patient while I contemplate these revelations and decide how to respond. Your arrival opens up possibilities that the human race has never before considered. Just wait here, and this will all be taken care of. Please be patient."

Then she offered them her warm and sincere grandmotherly smile – a smile that Vincent had seen in so many of her public appearances over the years. The expression seemed artificial to him now, and he sensed that they needed to get out of there, *fast*.

95

Even quarantined in their passenger pod, the brainwashed human converts were so sincere and earnest that they made Ishop Heer's skin crawl – even more so than the bizarre caterpillar-like creature did.

Seeing the slimy thing, Ishop couldn't convince his mind to accept the fact: the damned aliens were real! Worse, he had failed to discover the truth. Adolphus had tricked him, making him appear to be an incompetent fool before the Diadem and the whole Constellation. If he were to proudly reveal his noble lineage now, he'd be a laughingstock!

The aliens had been real all along – and the General had access to them, as well as whatever powers they might possess.

Did Xayan minds take possession of human bodies and impose their memories upon them? Potentially, this revelation had even more frightening consequences than the rebel stringline network. How much more had Adolphus concealed from the Constellation?

Standing next to him, isolated in the hangar, Michella said in a low voice, "I don't like this, Ishop – not at all."

"Nor do I, Eminence."

"These aliens and their delusions pose a terrible danger to us. It's contamination."

With a shudder, he hoped that the Diadem didn't think *he* had been infected during his visit to Hallholme. He hadn't fallen into one of those pools, or been shoved into one, and yet . . . Ishop watched her for any sign of suspicion directed toward him, but saw none. Yet.

He swallowed. "I absolutely agree, Eminence. You cannot take any chances. We must not allow anyone on Sonjeera to be exposed to the contamination carried by these converts and that slug-alien – whether it's a debilitating micro-organism, an inhuman psychic force . . . or just dangerous ideas."

While the man who called himself Zairic preached over the code-call link about the Xayan race and their plans for some strange evolutionary and spiritual ascension, the Diadem walked with Ishop out into the hangar, careful to avoid the pod's windowports. The travelers quarantined inside had only a limited view, so it was easy to remain unseen. Bodyguards and soldiers ringed the hangar door and staffed the observation stations, but left Michella alone as she regarded the ovoid vessel. Like any other passenger pod, it was entirely sealed for passage in space and reentry into the atmosphere. No sound – no germ – could get out.

The dowager leader pursed her wrinkled lips. "In order to stand against the rest of humanity and its rightful government, General Adolphus has allied himself with an alien race. This situation is a bomb that could explode on us at any moment." She turned to the pod. "Just listen to that man talk."

"Zairic's words *are* dangerous, Eminence," Ishop agreed. "Seditious! I saw the growing cult on Hallholme – the people surrender everything and pretend to be aliens." His gaze sharpened. "We don't dare let that mass hysteria spread here on Sonjeera. Or the disease, or psychic pollution . . . whatever it is." He heard the alarm building in his own voice.

"This man, this *creature* wants to infect us in some way, certainly with the General's blessing," she said. "It's got to be part of a greater scheme. Zairic thinks we should welcome him, that people will flock from across the Crown Jewels, give up their lives so they can imagine themselves to be . . ." She waved a hand, as if trying to remember a word she had considered unimportant, though Ishop knew Michella would never forget such a detail. ". . . Xayans."

Ishop's expression soured. "I'm sure many people would surrender their mundane lives in the belief that they could become princes or philosophers from a vanished race. Look at that living alien as proof!

Every person wants to feel part of something grand and important." He fidgeted, wanting to wipe his hands somewhere.

Michella scowled at him. "My people are already part of something grand! They're part of my Constellation."

"If they become Xayans, they will no longer be part of your Constellation, Eminence."

The Diadem was growing angrier by the moment. "This is exactly the sort of unorthodox tactic Adolphus would use to get under my skin. I know what he must intend. While this spreading alien cult throws our government into turmoil, the General will be building his rebel empire out in the Deep Zone. It's insidious!" Michella paced the hangar's cold, hard floor. Breezes from outside rattled the sheet alloy walls, making odd echoing sounds in the chamber. "How am I supposed to respond, Ishop? Zairic wants to meet me face to face! What if he touches me and transmits some of that . . . slickwater, so that I become contaminated, too?"

"You must not allow that to happen, Diadem! And you cannot allow him to address and hypnotize the people of Sonjeera." He struggled to prove himself to her, yet again. This was a perilous time, a perilous moment. "Think of second- and third-order consequences. Not only would this shadow-Xayan infestation demonstrate that you have lost control of Hallholme, delusions would run rampant throughout the Crown Jewels. Those converts are *not well.*"

"And my own daughter is one of them! This just gets worse and worse the more I think about it. The General must be planning to use Keana in some devious manner, unless I can prevent it. How do I get her back?"

She had to see the reality. "We may never get her back, Majesty." The Diadem rounded on him with a murderous gaze. He had hoped Keana would blunder into some fatal situation on the hellish planet so he could remove the Duchenet name from his list, but he had never expected this. Nevertheless, he had to make the most of it. "Princess Keana has switched sides and joined the enemy. That just demonstrates how effective and dangerous this alien influence is. Your daughter is lost to us . . . and we will lose much more if you allow her to become a bargaining chip for the General and these aliens."

Michella groaned, then glared at the passenger pod as if her gaze could burn through the thick armored hull. She was taken aback by her own abrupt realization. "Yes, Ishop – if my own daughter can be swayed by such nonsense, just imagine how many other weak-willed people would also succumb!" She snorted. "Of course, Keana was always somewhat vapid. She certainly didn't take after me."

. "Shall we send the passenger pod back to Hallholme and deny these people any sort of platform here on Sonjeera? It's plain that Zairic can be very persuasive, very disruptive."

For a long moment Michella fell silent, then said, "I have no intention of letting quasi-religious fanatics overrun my Constellation. I thought we got rid of all those types by shipping them off to the Deep Zone in the first place."

Ishop considered, and his voice hardened. "Then just sending them away will not be good enough. Zairic is their leader, their spokesman. How much harm could he do if he continues to spread his message?"

Diadem Michella gave him the sweet maternal smile that worked so well on the populace, but he knew it was often the harbinger of furious reprisal. "You're right as usual, dear Ishop. It's best for the Constellation, and for all of humanity, if no one else hears those seductive words – if no one comes into contact with any aspect of these inhuman things."

Her own scientists would want to take cell scrapings and other biological samples, run diagnostics, even vivisect that slug-like creature. They would want to run brain scans and complete chemical tests on the duped human converts. Every single step posed the hazard that something, any tiny speck of contamination, could escape. Ishop didn't dare let her open that dangerous door.

Fortunately, Diadem Michella thought the same way. She looked at him, and her eyes gleamed with deadly purpose. "Eliminate the entire delegation, Ishop. Cleanly, with absolutely no risk of contaminating anyone outside the pod. This is war after all."

96

The longer they remained inside the passenger pod in isolated silence, the more worried Vincent grew. He rose for the hundredth time and looked out the windowport, but saw nothing. "This has gone on for much too long."

No one else seemed to be concerned. "We have given them much to contemplate, and that takes time." Zairic was obviously confident that his Xayan recruitment speech was convincing, that he had answered all questions and dispensed with any fears or reservations.

"The Diadem has already sent her inspector, and probably other spies, to Slickwater Springs," Vincent said. "She already knows about the shadow-Xayans. Most of what you said wasn't news to her."

Zairic closed his eyes gently, let out a low sigh. "But hearing the words from us *directly*, Vincent, is far different from a mere report. And now that she has seen Cippiq with her own eyes, she can have no further doubts. She knows our claims are real, not just delusions."

"Precisely! And that proof won't help us. Cippiq alone is unsettling enough. What if you terrify her, push her over the edge? After what General Adolphus has done, she's already reeling. She'll want to take firm and definitive action."

"A wise ruler does not make precipitous decisions. After listening to us, she will be pondering how to frame her positive response." Fernando-Zairic just smiled.

Cippiq looked on in silence, but Vincent presumed he was in telepathic contact with the shadow-Xayans.

Vincent felt panic rising within him. His companions were too passive and complacent, too trusting. "This isn't right – and I'm *not* worrying too much. This is a real problem." He regarded the shadow-Xayans, trying to imagine how they must look to Diadem Michella. They really did seem like a religious cult who sat in a circle singing oblivious hymns.

As an idea occurred to him, Vincent leaned forward and spoke in an urgent voice. "We need to convince the Diadem in some other way. We need to fascinate her, tantalize her, show her what the Xayan race has to offer. She needs to see the amazing *potential*, not just the threat."

"We have already done that, Vincent." Zairic was maddeningly emotionless. "We are no threat."

"You don't understand! Please listen to me. Let *Fernando* talk with her just for a little while. I've seen him in action – he can dance circles around anyone in conversation. He can be damned convincing."

"Fernando and I are both aware of his history and reputation among humans. Yes, he may be persuasive, but my voice – as the spokesperson for the Xayan race – has more gravity with the Diadem of the Constellation."

Vincent turned on Zairic as panic and frustration rose within him. "Then let *me* talk with Fernando – directly. I want to hear my friend. I want to see him. He's always been there before!" Vincent was beginning to wonder whether Fernando's personality had been eclipsed by the dominating Xayan presence. He also knew that his friend would understand the reason for suspicion and urgency. Vincent could sense that the Diadem was holding something back, and Fernando was an even better judge of veracity and sincerity.

The sounds of machinery came from outside the passenger pod. Hurrying to the windowport again, Vincent saw a slow-moving engine rig rolling forward until it came to rest against the quarantined vessel. A large red drum sat on the flat body above flexible treads. An automated, versatile explorer vehicle: Vincent had seen such equipment in the repair shop on Orsini.

With a resounding *thunk*, a heavy suction plate pressed against the pod's hull. The machine raised a backward-articulated arm, at the end of which buzzed a spinning carbide cutter. "That's a lamprey drill. What is it doing?"

"The Diadem will explain," Zairic said.

The automated rover sprayed something on the outer hull plate, scoured with an abrasive, and finally, after carefully aligning the cutting area, applied the spinning lamprey saw.

"They're drilling in." Vincent ran to the hatch, worked the controls, but found them frozen. "We're sealed inside here. Why don't they just open the access hatch if they want contact with us?"

"Perhaps the Diadem is exercising extreme caution."

A soft plastic sheath that looked like an embryonic sac extended from the cutting arm, folding around the saw blade to seal the metal being cut. Vincent heard the teeth-grinding vibration as the cutter gnawed through the reinforced hull.

Vincent ran to the codecall screen. "Diadem, please explain what's happening out there."

Michella's face reappeared, still wearing her sincere smile. "You may relax, gentlemen. We're simply obtaining in-situ samples of the air within the pod. We will run tests to verify there's no contamination. We can't be too careful about letting an extraterrestrial disease organism loose on Sonjeera. I'm sure it will be fine. We'll take care of all this – I promise." She sounded so warm and friendly.

Vincent's skin crawled. If the explanation was so innocuous, then why not tell them beforehand? Since regular travel and commerce from Hellhole had continued for months following the discovery of the slick-water pools, any contamination should have been obvious by now.

Dread uncoiled within him. "Zairic, listen to Fernando inside you. Ask him – isn't he at all suspicious?" Vincent jerked his head to one side as, with a shrill whine of distressed metal, the cutter bit through the inner wall. Rotating jagged teeth slashed a raw wound into the pod's interior.

The emotion radiating from Vincent alarmed Cippiq more than the others. The Original glided forward on his long, soft body and spoke in an incomprehensible burst of sound, and Zairic nodded. "Very well then, Vincent Jenet. Fernando would like to talk with you also."

The voice changed, became more animated. It was Fernando Neron again. "Taking a sample of the air for quarantine testing? Hmm, it sounds reasonable, but it's complete bullshit. We may indeed have something to worry about, my friend."

Vincent swallowed hard. "Our companions are very trusting, Fernando – too trusting."

The lamprey drill retracted now to be replaced by a dark, large-diameter tube that sealed around the inner hole.

Fernando nudged Vincent aside and activated the codecall. He flashed a grin, then replaced it with a grave expression. "Diadem Michella, there are a few things I neglected to tell you." He paused, but got no response. "Eminence, are you there? You do need to hear this."

Instead of drawing atmospheric samples from the chamber, the tube began to exhaust *into* the pod, blowing air, followed by a spray of puffy white balls that flew like a blizzard of tree pollen. They drifted and floated about, to the amazement of the shadow-Xayans. Several of the fluffy white spheres clung like lint to Cippiq's soft, moist skin.

"That's no air analysis sample!" Vincent cried. "The Diadem's got to listen to you, Fernando. Talk to her!"

His friend spoke into the codecall again, an anxious, calculating look on his face. "Diadem, there is something important you should know about your daughter. We can tell you about the General's plans. It's vital information."

Now Michella's face appeared on the screen, her expression urgent. "What is it? Tell me quickly."

"Only face-to-face, Diadem. You must let us out of here or you'll never know the answer."

Obviously alarmed, the Diadem barked orders. The fluffy white globules now filled the air inside the pod. Vincent waved them away from his face and automatically covered his nose and mouth with his shirt.

The puffballs began to spangle and spark, bursting in tiny flashes of light.

"Stop it – Ishop, stop it!" the Diadem shrieked. She was yelling to someone outside the range of the codecall screen, then turned back to the pane, wildly. "Zairic, tell me now! What about my daughter? What does the General intend to do?"

Fernando waggled his finger at her image. "Ah-ah, I told you the rules, Eminence. Get us out of here, and I'll tell you every juicy detail."

The Diadem was livid.

As the white balls continued to flash and vaporize, a filmy smoke oozed through the air. The shadow-Xayans began to cough and retch. On the screen, Michella yelled again to someone out of view.

Cippiq lurched forward, and rippling convulsions ran along his translucent skin. Though Fernando's personality was dominant in his own body, the other shadow-Xayans linked together, finally feeling the desperation. As the poison swirled in the air, their telemancy throbbed. Cippiq added his own mental force, and the walls of the sealed passenger pod bowed outward, bending, ready to burst.

Michella shouted into the codecall panel, demanding answers, but Fernando blanked the screen.

"What were you going to tell her?" Vincent asked

His friend managed a weak shrug. "Nothing that would matter now. I was going to make something up."

The air pressed against Vincent's head, and he felt the ripples of telemancy build. The shadow-Xayans had decided to fight back at last . . . but too late.

The thick transparent pane of the nearest windowport cracked, then blasted outward. Some of the faint white vapor trailed out. The bulkhead bent, twisted; the hatch buckled and cracked.

Outside in the hangar, alarms shrieked. People fled from the breach. Vehicles rolled out, and Vincent knew the Diadem must be evacuating.

He couldn't breathe. Cippiq had slumped down, his small caterpillar legs twitching, his soft body thrashing one way and another. The press of telemancy faltered; two of the shadow-Xayans collapsed. The passenger pod had cracked open, but the small amount of ventilation was not enough, and Cippiq's motions were slowing. They couldn't escape. The toxin was already inside them.

Vincent fell to the floor, feeling the poison eat away at him. He looked fatalistically over at Fernando who was also reeling. "We didn't act in time, did we?"

"I don't think so. Zairic should have listened to you. I'm sorry." Fernando seemed resigned, perhaps tranquilized by the alien presence within.

Vincent closed his eyes, cursing his own foolishness. His next breath felt as if he'd inhaled caustic vapors. He had hoped that the drifting gas inside the chamber would merely render them unconscious, but that was as naïve and optimistic as Zairic's misunderstanding of the Diadem's true nature.

"She's afraid of what we are." Fernando's voice was hoarse now. "She can't help us, you know. If she could, she wouldn't be so panicked. I suppose I can take some comfort in having a last little joke on her, for what she's done to us." He looked over at Vincent, his face filled with sadness and compassion. He could barely speak now. "Even so, I wish you had joined me in the slickwater. That way you would finally have understood what I was talking about."

Vincent retorted with the last of his strength. "How can you say that? Wasn't I a good enough friend to you as I am? The slickwater did this – to *all* of us! It's what made the Constellation so afraid ... and now it's killed us."

"Oh no, I did most of this to myself, every step of the way," Fernando said with a beatific smile. "But I'm glad to have known you, Vincent Jenet. You were a good friend." He sounded like a perfectly meshed combination of himself and the alien Zairic, totally at ease with what he had become – and his fate. "It has been an adventure."

Vincent was despairing and afraid, but Fernando clasped his hand. Vincent felt cold inside and out now. He tried to speak, but only a strange noise came from his throat. His muscles seized up.

Many of the shadow-Xayans had already collapsed to the deck, and stopped coughing. Cippiq writhed and thrashed, and his translucent skin seemed to be boiling away from his cartilaginous frame. The cracks in the pod's hull let only wisps of fresh air inside.

Fernando held on just a moment longer, speaking through the memories of Zairic. "This reminds me of just before the asteroid impact. It is a shame we don't have the slickwater this time ..." He slumped to the deck.

Vincent sprawled immobile beside him. He managed to draw a few more ragged breaths: his mind filled with whiteness, followed by gray, and then nothing but black.

97

The invisible blow hit Keana with a percussive force that came out of nowhere. She felt as if the synapses and neurons of her brain had detonated from a series of hidden landmines. She could barely see as wave after wave of shock and despair flooded into her mind. Inextricably joined with Uroa, she cried out in agony and fell to the ground.

All around her in the exotic settlement, other shadow-Xayans writhed in pain, screaming words that sounded like no language at all. The telemancers in the central spiral collapsed as if their joints and bones had turned to jelly.

The living structures thrashed in response, twisting and shuddering. One fanciful tower bent sharply downward, contorting, cracking and falling. No longer sustained by telemancy, it thundered to the ground, sending dust and debris into the air. Other structures tumbled in an escalating, deafening roar; wobbly alien prototypes disintegrated and collapsed.

Several shadow-Xayan telemancers who had been flying high overhead fell to the ground and were crushed by the impact. These deaths only added to the dark resonance. Even the forest of red alien weed convulsed in a sympathetic reaction.

After interminable, confusing moments, the shuddering pain finally passed, leaving Keana incapable of thinking in her native language. Only Uroa's alien tongue flooded her consciousness, attempting to convey the horror and disbelief of the awakened members of the Xayan race.

In a rush of nightmarish alien history, she relived the last moments before the asteroid impact, after most of the people had been dissolved into the slickwater reservoirs – but not all could be saved. Some were doomed, and she heard their ancient cries reverberating, their collective fear mounting to a crescendo that she couldn't bear. Tears poured from her eyes like blood from a grievous wound.

But Keana realized that this new aftershock had nothing to do with the long-ago asteroid impact. It was because of something that had just occurred. This was different ... sickening. In the entire shadow-Xayan village, half of the buildings had collapsed.

Separated from the acolyte telemancers who had been concentrating in their spiral, Keana saw Encix standing with three of the most powerful shadow-Xayans. The Original alien had come from the mountain vault to visit the new city built by the converts, and now this disaster had struck. As Encix concentrated, phantom swirls of light, glowing chains, and showers of sparks crackled in the air and shored up some of the freeform edifices, reinforcing their integrity and preventing further destruction. Encix's alien face thrummed with agony and grief. Her facial membrane contorted and the motions of her arms and hands were graceless. Although the other two Originals, Lodo and Tryn, remained inside the mountain vault, Keana was sure they had received the same painful shock.

Keana struggled to her knees and looked around, gasping; inside her, the presence of Uroa was stunned with disbelief. "They're dead," Uroa said inside her head. "Cippiq is murdered. Zairic is murdered. The entire delegation. The Diadem killed them all!"

Keana knew that her mother was indeed capable of such treachery, cruelty, and ruthlessness. She found herself shaking uncontrollably and saw others reeling with the knowledge of what the Constellation had done.

"This time their lives are not stored in a slickwater pool," Uroa said. "They are truly gone."

98

Michella had no regrets.

Standing outside the secure hangar, breathing hard after her very close escape, the Diadem looked back at the heavy metal doors that had been hauled into place. She and a panicked Ishop, along with the guards who could run swiftly enough, had evacuated when the monstrous aliens tried to bash their way out of their confinement. Her fears had been correct.

As soon as she raced outside into the bright sunlight, holding her breath to avoid inhaling any of the released poisons or insidious alien toxins, she made frantic gestures – which Ishop correctly translated. He cried out to the guards. "Seal the hangar completely, before any contamination escapes!"

He helped slam the big door shut, yelling at the soldiers who hesitated because their comrades were inside. Anyone still inside must be sacrificed, for the good of Sonjeera, for the good of the Constellation. Michella drew in a deep gasp when she could hold her breath no longer. "Seal it . . . seal it all! Don't let anything out!"

In a blindingly fast action, the standby security personnel encircled the building and sprayed the doors, windows, and even the smallest cracks with thick epoxy sealant, slathering it over to prevent any possible leaks.

In a matter of minutes, the whole hangar was encased in a heavy, impenetrable cocoon.

Ishop ran back to her, his bald pate oily with perspiration, his skin flushed. "Eminence, I've tuned this to the codecall channel inside the pod." He handed her a portable screen.

Now that the contamination was safely locked down, she could concentrate on the images of the victims on the floor of the pod. Though the hull was twisted and the windowports shattered, their escape attempt had completely failed, and now they lay still. The dead slug alien looked disgusting, dissolving into a puddle of ooze on the deck that seeped up against the contorted human bodies.

Dangerous ... very dangerous. "And they almost got loose," she gasped.

The slickwater converts did not merely suffer from mass hysteria – they were all truly under an irreversible, dangerous alien influence.

After hearing the Xayan guru's frightening nonsense, Michella was convinced that his message – his disease – must not spread throughout the Constellation. And seeing the actual hideous alien that General Adolphus had dug up on his exile world gave her further justification for her actions. The bizarre cult had already run amok on Hallholme, and she could not allow it to spread here to Sonjeera. She had to stop it for the stability of her reign ... and she could use the situation to her political advantage.

By squashing these so-called emissaries, Michella would hinder General Adolphus in his plans to destroy the legitimate government. Maybe he had been deluded or brainwashed as well ... but she didn't need excuses to explain his treacherous behavior.

"You were right not to let them speak further with you, or anyone else, Eminence," said Ishop Heer. He looked queasy. "Why expose yourself to such risk?"

"It was an alien plot against all of humanity." She thought again of the sturdy hull that had been bent and twisted by the sheer force of their minds. "Did you see the damage they caused, the destructive power? They almost escaped, Ishop!" She firmed up her voice, already imagining how it would sound when she addressed the nobles of the Crown Jewels. "And General Adolphus has formed an unholy alliance with those disgusting creatures *to destroy humanity*. This goes far beyond even his crimes during the rebellion."

Ishop smiled, as he saw what she was doing. "Yes, Eminence, your harsh response was perfectly justified."

"Yes, it was. Everyone will agree."

Contemplating the situation, she considered cracking through the protective barrier, and sending in probes to take samples for analysis – cell scrapings and fluids, as her experts would demand. Constellation scientists would still want to dissect the remains and study the residue from the dissolved alien creature, but she didn't intend to let them. The risk of contamination, of accidents, of human error was too great.

In fact, she would insist that Ishop Heer undergo a thorough evaluation. He had been there at the slickwater pools ... what if he'd been contaminated somehow? She narrowed her eyes. The aliens could have planted him here as an insidious covert operative ... What if he'd already passed on the infection to her?

No, she decided. Not him. She had never known anyone so loyal.

"See that the entire hangar is sterilized and encased in plexite, Ishop. Fill the interior with resin, wall up the outside." She paused. "This is a quarantine zone. Post round-the-clock guards and install self-destruct incineration charges all around the building. I want to discourage anyone from tampering with it."

"As you wish, Eminence. But even if you contain this danger zone, it doesn't eradicate the contamination on Hallholme."

She steadied herself. "We will take care of the General in our own way. The Army of the Constellation launches soon." Straightening her gown and adjusting her coif, she drew a deep breath. "And now that this ordeal is over, I think I'll have lunch."

Michella took a last glance at her screen to see the interior of the pod, where the bodies lay sprawled. As she watched, even the human figures began to soften and slump into goo, dissolving just as the hideous alien had. She shuddered; yes, indeed, they were all contaminated. Before long, the corpses were unrecognizable grisly bits of flesh and bone in a viscous stew mixed with the slime exuded by the dying slug creature.

She felt a twinge in her stomach and a reflex that made her gag. Michella vowed to eat a fine lunch anyway, if for no other reason than to prove to herself how strong she could be, and how much she deserved to rule the Constellation.

On her way to her waiting vehicle, she paused and turned back to Ishop. "Compose a story about how the delegation from Hallholme died in an unfortunate accident. Let me sign off on the content before you disseminate it. I may want to improve on your words."

When Ishop looked hurt, she winked at him, an afterthought that was her form of apology. Though she had treated him badly before, he was genuinely her most loyal aide. Ishop was too useful, and she wanted no gulf between them. As she walked away, the Diadem's step was brisk, not like an old woman but like a vibrant, determined leader.

99

After years as a linerunner maintaining the Constellation string-lines, Turlo Urvancik found it refreshing to work for someone who knew what he was doing – someone he and his wife could believe in.

Following his declaration of independence, General Adolphus had pulled him and Sunitha from the new DZ network and moved the *Kerris* back to the original terminus point from the Sonjeera line. They would be heading out on their old route.

"We have time, but not much," the General said. "For good or ill, the Diadem will feel compelled to respond with extreme force, and we have to be ready for her when she does."

"We'll do everything we can, sir," Turlo promised. "Just give us the order."

Since switching sides, he had noticed that his wife looked harder and more determined, more fiery than Turlo had ever seen her. Sunitha said, "It's the least we can do for our son's memory. We always considered ourselves good citizens. We never doubted the Diadem – *believed* her smiles – and now, the very thought of her disgusts me."

"Yes, General," Turlo said. "She deceived us all, and countless families like ours. How many other parents have private memorials for their fallen sons and daughters? How many other families believed the propaganda, and suffered for it?"

General Adolphus gave them his solemn promise. "If it is within my power, no more of them will."

Leaving Hellhole for what might be the most important run of their careers, Turlo and Sunitha flew along the Sonjeera stringline, following the iperion path they had so lovingly maintained as their duty for the Constellation. They both had the sense that they were taking significant action, that they would be a fundamental part in the long-overdue changes, rather than just being swept along by events . . .

Two days out from Hellhole, they arrived at the large power-generating substation and the iperion collimator. Turlo decelerated the *Kerris*, disengaged the vessel from the stringline, and powered down. To wait.

"I never set out to be a hero, you know," he said aloud. "All of our lives, we've trained for just the opposite."

Sunitha's expression softened, and her eyes glittered with moisture. "Anyone who sets out with a life plan to become a hero is on a fool's mission. But if you're a good person, a strong person, you could become a hero when circumstances demand it." She smiled stiffly. "Like now."

"Up until today, it hasn't seemed particularly worthwhile to put my neck on the line. It's a new feeling, a satisfying one." He began to understand the fervor and optimism Kerris had felt when he signed up for service – though their son had lost that dedication and drive before his shameful, unnecessary death.

Turlo anchored the linerunner in place so that Sunitha could suit up – her turn this time – and go outside to install the explosive charges. Should the need arise, at a single command from the General, they could cut the long-established stringline and maroon any ships that were en route from Sonjeera.

After all the years they had spent maintaining this line, Turlo hoped it wouldn't come to that. But he had long since surrendered his naïve belief that the Constellation government would respond rationally.

100

Ishop and Laderna Nell hovered close to a security door, from which they could discreetly watch the lords and ladies take their seats to hear the Diadem's speech. Ishop was sure this revelation would shake them even more than her recent declaration of war.

He knew exactly what she was going to say, having offered her a carefully crafted statement that described how a "tragic accident" had taken the lives of the Hallholme delegation and the alien creature. She'd barely scanned the words, however, before tearing the paper in half and handing him the pieces.

"I won't need this, Ishop." He hadn't expected her to. "I've decided that we will not mince words. Cover ups are for cowards. We carried out a necessary action to eliminate a threat to the Constellation and the human race." She gave him her warmest grandmotherly smile. "I want everyone to understand my righteous indignation. After this speech today, no one will doubt the justness of my cause or the deadliness of my purpose. We shall stand against potentially violent fanatics, mind-controlling alien creatures, and the greatest enemy humanity has ever had – General Tiber Maximilian Adolphus."

"And so, Eminence . . . Princess Keana is forfeit?" He could barely keep the smile from his face.

"Everyone on Hallholme is forfeit."

He hung his head. "I am sorry to hear it." *Another name to be crossed off the list.* After Keana, that would leave four . . .

Now, as the audience gathered to hear her and media imagers recorded every moment, he waited with building joy. He scanned the nobles gathered in their seats, unnerved by the crisis that threatened to shake their stagnant lives. Soon enough, Ishop would join those respected noble representatives in the Council chamber as one of them – but not until he finished his little business of revenge. And since Princess Keana would pay the necessary price for the Duchenet family, he could continue to make himself indispensible to the Diadem. There was no conflict of interest. Everything fitted so neatly together. He wondered which seat would be his . . .

Laderna leaned close. "If the Diadem does launch a war against the Deep Zone, the members of many noble families will enlist simply to make a name for themselves. We'll have ample opportunities to cause an accident here and there, maybe a lethal radiation exposure or a bit of friendly fire. By the time this conflict is over, boss, the landscape of noble bloodlines will look quite different. You'll have plenty of room to maneuver."

He kissed her on the cheek, which made her flush with pleasure. "I admire your methodical mind, Laderna, but I'll be glad to have the list finished, so we can move on to more ambitious things." He shushed her before she could say more. Michella had entered through the main door and made her way to the dais and the Star Throne.

Without notes or a holographic word-prompter, the old woman glowered around the chamber, as if searching for details that displeased her. The entire Council fell into a hush. These lords, ladies, and officials knew something of her moods, as Ishop did.

She spoke in a firm voice, her words filled with great tragedy and compassion. "The Constellation finds itself confronted with some of the worst crises in our history, and all at the same time." She raised her ring-studded hands. "General Adolphus's unlawful declaration of independence, the revelation of his clandestine stringline network that would ruin the Constellation's economy . . . and a resurrected alien race on Hallholme that has subverted human minds and is planning an expansion that threatens us all."

Thick sadness deepened in her voice, even as the audience muttered and gasped. "My daughter Keana has herself been possessed by one of these aliens. The enemy has co-opted her, no doubt to use her against us. She is lost."

Michella took several moments to compose herself – in a calculated fashion, Ishop thought – before she continued. "Recently, a group of alien-possessed converts came to spread their infection across Sonjeera. Once corrupted by Xayan slickwater, such people break all loyalties with the government and their own race. I shudder to think what would have happened if they'd been able to run loose among the Crown Jewels, but I intercepted them in time to stop this terrible threat against humanity. I saved us all – for now."

She had already released images of the hideous slug-alien, much to the horror of the populace. "However, back in the Deep Zone those aliens are still allied with General Adolphus, and no doubt continue to draw their plans against us." She paused for the rush of angry muttering, which came exactly as anticipated.

"In direct violation of the terms of his exile, General Tiber Adolphus has refused to cooperate with Constellation representatives and has intentionally engaged in a campaign of misinformation. As the revelation of his new stringline network proves, as well as taking charge of all fifty-four Deep Zone worlds, he has become more of a rogue than ever. Even some of the DZ planetary administrators have joined his movement, and one of our loyal territorial governors has been overthrown and imprisoned."

Ishop saw that her face was red with a rage that did not seem feigned. She took a moment to compose herself. "The General is building a large military force to stand against us. His alien allies are probably spreading their contamination throughout the Deep Zone as we speak. Adolphus and his followers leave us no choice. The sooner the Constellation moves against him, the better."

Michella spoke faster and with great sincerity. "Lords and Ladies of the realm, justice is clearly on our side. When Adolphus diverts revenues from us, he robs the Constellation of funds that we use to support our standard of living and strengthen our worlds. Because of his treachery, schools will close and innocents will starve." She shook her head. "In my benevolence a decade ago, I gave that man a second chance, allowed him to live. But now it's obvious that we should have executed the General at the end of his rebellion in order to protect the Constellation."

"Kill the traitors!" a man shouted from the audience. An angry din arose in the chamber. "Kill the aliens! Kill them all!"

The Diadem had to raise her voice to be heard over the noise as she dropped her last bombshell. "And, judging by Adolphus's irrational and suicidal actions, I believe he is himself possessed by an alien and intends to strike against the Constellation on behalf of the Xayans!"

Ishop was impressed by the way she managed to outrage the audience. The population of the Crown Jewel planets would be putty in her hands; they'd rush in droves to climb aboard military stringline ships to crush Hallholme. He had learned a great deal from her on his own path to power.

As the uproar slowly died down, Michella raised her fist. "Lord Selik Riomini has prepared the Army of the Constellation, and now we are ready. We intend to strike planet Hallholme with the full force of our military."

In a great upward motion like a storm-swelled tide, the dignitaries surged to their feet, cheering. They wanted blood.

101

Back at Elba, clinging to a last normal evening, the General tried not to let Sophie see his tension.

Now that he had dropped all pretenses and declared his independence from the Constellation, he no longer considered himself bound by the terms of his surrender vows and his exile agreement. He would go where he wanted to go and do what needed to be done. But, oddly enough, he felt no desire to leave Hellhole, not yet. Not until this was over.

He had plenty of experience coping with battlefield jitters. Sophie was nervous enough for both of them, and she didn't fool him when she feigned nonchalance with lighthearted comments. "So what do you think of our chances, Tiber? The pieces have come together the way we expected – for the most part."

Nevertheless, Adolphus was very glad to have her company. He leaned back in his chair, and in a thoughtful tone said, "Battlefield commanders must not allow themselves to feel anything but optimism, faith, and fervor before an engagement, even in private. And to be honest, at any point along the way, the Diadem could have discovered what we were up to, sent in her troops, and seized all of us. We actually made it to the endgame."

"A dangerous game," she noted.

The General let out a sigh. "Because of logistical challenges, the Constellation would never go to war with fifty-four planets at the same time. We need to exploit that to the extent we can, make them think we have more forces than we do. This will involve some guerrilla attacks on our part, but we also have to defend the stringline termini at a number of key Deep Zone worlds. If all else fails, I'll cut the lines."

Sophie's gray eyes opened wide. "You'd actually sever the stringlines to Sonjeera? If you do, there'll be no going back."

He waited a long moment before answering. "The new network makes us all independent from the Crown Jewels. A good commander considers every option."

"You are a *great* commander, but I'm still worried. The old bitch's wrath is nothing to be taken lightly."

"The Army of the Constellation is bloated and unwieldy, unprac- ticed, possibly even incompetent. Some of their commanders are less than top-notch, promoted because of family connections, not skills. But the Diadem does have plenty of ships, no disputing that. And if we do cut the stringlines, they'll still lumber toward us, even if it takes months or years."

"But we'll have months or years to get ready for them," Sophie said. "And so long as you know where they're heading, we'll have all the time in the world to use our *fast* stringlines to gather Deep Zone defenses, including your old fleet. We'll be ready and waiting for them."

He smiled at her. "I wish all of my own commanders saw the picture as clearly as you do, Sophie."

Adolphus regarded the wall chart showing all the DZ planets strung together with a web of scarlet pathways that radiated from Hallholme. The bright red made him think of bloodlines, vital connections that ensured survival. A second web of old connections, marked in blue, emanated from Sonjeera. For an energetic economy and civilization, he would have preferred to keep both networks online while building sev- eral new hubs. But Michella would never allow that, not without a fight.

Sophie interrupted his thoughts. "But they still have some formid- able leaders and thousands of battleships to throw against us. Do you think the Army of the Constellation will dust off Percival Hallholme and send him after you again?"

Adolphus slowly shook his head. "Oh no, not him. Commodore

Hallholme broke his own personal code to achieve that final victory, even though he did it under direct orders. *He* was defeated in a more fundamental way than we were. Even though they painted him as a great hero, he was morally humiliated." The General remained silent for a long moment. "That doesn't mean Michella won't find some other unprincipled lackey to do her dirty work, though."

The unknown factor in all their plans was the Xayans. With their powers of telemancy and their mysterious racial goal of *ala'ru,* no one could say what they might do, what role they could play. But they had promised to help. And Keana Duchenet had become one of them.

Yesterday, Rendo Theris had sent him an urgent message from the Ankor hub, along with blurry images of the unexpected vessels that had appeared around the orbital complex, scanning the structures before flying away. The probe ships had taken no overt action against Ankor, sent no signal from the Constellation, and neatly avoided all of the facility's defenses. They had merely appeared for a few moments, observed, and departed.

The General had already assigned his engineers to study the images, but the unusual, fast-moving ships fitted no known configuration. Even Ian Walfor had no idea what they might be.

He hadn't imagined the stodgy Constellation would ever develop such innovative spaceflight technology. The old government had long been content to milk the existing system, and Adolphus was disquieted to see these hints of bold imagination. He wondered what the Diadem was up to. It was a reminder that he could not anticipate every scenario, and that he needed to be alert, prepared for anything.

Though it was late at night, a flustered Craig Jordan hurried into the General's private drawing room. Ordinarily, the security chief would have been hesitant to interrupt his quiet time with Sophie. "Sir, we have a security situation, and I – I don't know what to do about it. There are visitors outside asking to see you."

"Visitors?"

"A lot of them, sir."

Setting aside his wine glass, Adolphus left the quiet sanctuary, realizing that his last peaceful moment might already have ended. He hadn't even managed to relish it. He and Sophie stepped out onto the wooden porch, astonished by what they saw.

A crowd had gathered there in eerie silence. Hundreds and hundreds of people had arrived without fanfare and surrounded the residence house. When he saw Peter Herald, Tel Clovis, and dozens of other familiar converts among them, he realized they were all shadow-Xayans.

Sophie was running the numbers in her head. "Tiber ... this might be *all* of the converts."

Up front, as their speaker, stood Keana-Uroa. "Yes, we have all come because our message is so important. A grave thing has occurred." Behind her stood Devon-Birzh and Antonia-Jhera, holding hands.

Adolphus had received plenty of disheartening battle reports in his day. It was better to know the truth and be prepared than to remain blissfully ignorant. "Tell me."

"Diadem Michella has murdered Zairic, Cippiq, and all of the other shadow-Xayans we sent as emissaries to Sonjeera. The whole delegation was executed. We sensed it through telemancy."

Sophie gasped. "That's appalling! They were our spokesmen. Oh, poor Vincent! And Fernando – how could she just kill them?"

Adolphus said, "I'm not surprised at all."

Keana's voice loosened and became her own natural voice. "I agree with you, General. Knowing my mother, I should have prepared them better, but Zairic was so confident. Long ago he unified the Xayan race, and I thought the Diadem would listen to him."

"This means she's no longer hesitating." The General turned to Sophie. "There isn't as much time as I'd hoped. The Army of the Constellation will be on its way. We had better expect the worst."

Keana-Uroa stepped forward, and when she spoke her voice was clear and sharp, but with an added reverberation as every one of the shadow-Xayans echoed the same words, the same intonation. "We are ready to help, General Adolphus."

A chill breeze passed through the air. Keana's lips quirked in a secret smile and she spoke in her own voice. "My mother will be in for quite a surprise when she sees what we can do."

102

On Aeroc, the broad and vacant prairie had become an improvised military camp, hastily erected. Under the fresh but stern command of Red Commodore Escobar Hallholme, the officers set up new divisions and prepared for a coordinated attack against planet Hallholme and the other unruly DZ planets. Out of the 182 noble families, major and minor, every one of them contributed to the new war effort.

From the patio balcony of Supreme Commander Riomini's palatial home, Michella Duchenet could not see the limit of the gathered forces as they stretched across the prairie. Munitions, soldiers, and supplies would all be loaded into military upboxes, and troop transports to be carried up to the stringline terminus above Aeroc. From there, the Constellation's largest military ships would travel to the Sonjeera hub, and from there transfer out to the Deep Zone.

Lord Riomini, Bolton Crais, and Escobar Hallholme stood beside her at the balustrade of the wide stone balcony. Fifty other officers were gathered outside on the balcony, most of them men. Since dawn, they had been going over tactical decisions in the Black Lord's ballroom, which had been converted into a war room. Now, they would all share a sendoff toast in the cool late afternoon.

The ships would strike Hallholme first and destroy the illegal stringline hub. That would cut off General Adolphus from any help he might expect from his fellow Deezee traitors. Then they would proceed to dismantle the illegal operations, execute the General, burn the shadow-Xayan camps, and pave over the slickwater pools.

Afterward, her forces would proceed to the other Deep Zone planets and strike them one by one. Those fools didn't have a chance. Michella allowed herself a small smile of anticipation.

Two servants moved among the officers on the patio balcony, distributing glasses of sparkling Qiorfu wine. It seemed appropriate to drink a vintage made from grapes that the Adolphus family had once cultivated. Michella accepted her own glass but didn't sip yet. She waited for the others to be served.

"This is the largest task force ever assembled in Constellation history," Lord Riomini said. "More than enough to annihilate the rebel bastards."

"I think it's excessive," mumbled Bolton Crais, who had been giving logistical advice to his superior officers.

Escobar glared in his direction. "Not excessive, Crais. Reassuring. We do have to make our point. It's good to give the military a real purpose again."

Bolton flushed. "Why does no one give a thought to rescuing my wife?"

"We would rescue her if we could," Michella said, "but you are forgetting, dear boy, that she has defected to the other side. She is now an enemy combatant."

Her son-in-law stalked away.

The Diadem nodded to Escobar Hallholme. Though he had only been following her instructions, the Redcom remained incensed for having been deceived into delivering the old FTL vessels to Ridgetop – another trick of the General's. Adolphus had somehow blackmailed or otherwise coerced Territorial Governor Goler into switching his loyalty.

Michella had personally approved the action of Lord Riomini in promoting the younger Hallholme, giving him command of the assault force against Adolphus. She expected great things from him. And it wasn't an unwarranted promotion, because Escobar had succeeded at every assignment he'd been given, and he came from an illustrious military family. She knew how eager he was to prove himself in action.

"Death to the rebel bastards!" Escobar said, raising his glass in a toast.

"Take no prisoners," said Lord Riomini, sounding almost disinterested.

Michella nodded but suddenly felt unsettled. Despite her comment to Bolton, she remained disturbed that she could not save Keana and save face at the same time. As Diadem, she could not play favorites. All who allied themselves with Adolphus this time would die, noble blood or not. It was a necessary house cleaning that would cover the whole Deep Zone.

All the officers on the patio held their glasses, and the Diadem saw that it was time for their formal toast. At her signal, the men and women gathered in the traditional circle, facing inward and holding their drinks high in the air, as if launching the warships with their cheers.

"Brave officers, you know your assignments. You fight for the Constellation and for the eternal honor of your families."

"To the stars!" The officers gave the traditional response in unison.

Michella quaffed the wine. Everyone followed her example, and then all shattered their glasses by hurling them onto the rocks beneath the patio.

Lord Riomini looked over the railing at all the broken crystal. "Just like *that*, Adolphus's support will shatter."

"No doubt," Michella replied. "With this war, we will make his planet a true hellhole."

APPENDIX A

THE CROWN JEWEL WORLDS

Aedl
Aeroc
Barassa
Cherby
Fleer
Indos
Jonn
Kappas
Klief
Machi
Marubi
Noab
Ogg
Orsini
Patel
Qiorfu
Sandusky
Sonjeera
Tanine
Vielinger

APPENDIX B

DEEP ZONE PLANETS

Aimerej
Ankheny
Argyth
Astervillius
Atab Abas
Balkast
Bija'dom
Blythe System
Boj
Brevor
Brezane
Buchad
Buktu
Candela
Casagan
Cles
Cobalt
Darenthia
Ehemi
El Kuara
Enesi

Erebusal
Eviticu
Haiasi
Hallholme/Hellhole
Hossetea
Karadakk
Karum and Kanes
Kirsi
Moloch
Nephilim
Nicles
Nielad
Nomolos
Ondor's Gambit
Oshu
Osian
Qolme
Qotem
Ridgetop
Rinthi
Ronom

Salm

Setsai

Signik

Tehila

Teron

Theser

Thiop

Triol

Ueter

Umber

Vytr

Xodu

APPENDIX C

THE STRINGLINE NETWORK

During the Constellation's early millennia, space travel among the main twenty worlds (the "Crown Jewels") was accomplished through workhorse, faster-than-light spacecraft. The Crown Jewel star systems were close enough together to make this both a feasible and an efficient system, with travel times ranging between days and weeks.

More than a century before the reign of Diadem Michella Duchenet, a much faster stardrive was developed. Using the innovative new stardrive, vessels could achieve speeds a hundred to a thousand times faster than were possible with old FTL drives. However, because the ships were faster than any sensor systems or navigation controls could react, pilots were flying blind at superluminal speeds, unable to see where they were going or when to stop.

Such a system was not greeted with much enthusiasm.

A second, unrelated discovery, however, made travel with the faster engines practical at last. Ever since the first demonstration of the new system, physicists across the Constellation had sought a way to keep the superfast starvessels on track. They had to mark a clear path, a discrete route that constrained the ships from flying helter-skelter at unimaginable velocities.

A scientist from Vielinger, Elwar Cori, discovered that when a rare mineral, iperion, was processed and activated into a higher-quantum state, it could be used to create a line of crucial markers, a path of what was jokingly called "quantum breadcrumbs." After a trailblazer ship had marked the path, or "paved the roadway," high-speed starvessels could follow it and fly up to 1,100 times faster than was previously achievable.

Thus, transportation companies created stringline routes, a defined path from point A to point B. With substations and collimation units placed along the way, the stringline markings allowed the new hyperluminal ships to fly without fear of getting lost or crashing into unforeseen obstacles.

In the century before the reign of Diadem Michella Duchenet, lines were laid from Sonjeera to each of the Crown Jewel planets, each route ending at a terminus ring in orbit above the destination. Sonjeera was the main and only hub from which ships launched (a strict requirement imposed by the Diadem, because it was her treasury that had paid for creation of all the stringlines in the first place). Once the twenty Crown Jewels were connected with lines regularly maintained, citizens could travel amongst the planets within hours or, at most, days.

THE DEEP ZONE

Over the centuries, fifty-four habitable planets beyond the Crown Jewels had been catalogued in the galactic wilderness called the Deep Zone, a region that was peripherally mapped by probes and intrepid explorers. The planets offered tantalizing opportunities, but most Constellation citizens saw them as much too far away to bother with. Some were closer than others and some more worthwhile than others, but all were considered too much trouble for anyone but the hardiest and most desperate. Few people had the wherewithal, or the interest, to mount hugely expensive years-long expeditions just to see what was out there.

Still, over the years a few groups did trickle out, leaving the Constellation forever and setting up their own colonies on the nearer and more hospitable worlds: Ridgetop, Candela, Nielad, Umber, and Hossetea. Anyone who decided to colonize these planets knew it would be a one-way trip. No starship could go back and forth across such vast distances; the vessels didn't have enough fuel, and there were no facilities on the other end. Upon arrival, the colonists abandoned or dismantled their ships, then set up their new lives.

But the expanded stringline network from Sonjeera out to the Deep Zone changed all that. By dispatching her trailblazer vessels to lay down new routes to the frontier, Diadem Michella opened up fifty-four new worlds to a land rush of disaffected people from the Constellation.

Naturally, the handful of people already on the planets, the ones who had consciously emigrated from the Constellation, were incensed about this. They had been surviving just fine without any help or interference from the old system, and they certainly didn't want to pay huge new taxes. Several uprisings occurred, but the Diadem dispatched her military to squash them, particularly on Ridgetop, where the military eradicated the original settlement and re-established a Constellation colony.

Each of the Deep Zone worlds was run by a planetary administrator chosen (or at least approved) by the Constellation government. Five territorial governors oversaw ten to eleven planets each, administering the worlds from main offices on Sonjeera; their primary responsibility was to ensure that the colony worlds paid the required tribute to the Diadem whether they liked it or not.

Glossary

ADKINS, DUFF – retired sergeant in Army of the Constellation, served under Commodore Percival Hallholme during General Adolphus's rebellion.

ADOLPHUS, GENERAL TIBER MAXIMILIAN – leader of a failed rebellion against the Constellation, now the exiled leader on the planet Hallholme. Commonly called the General.

ADOLPHUS, JACOB – father of Tiber Adolphus, patriarch of Adolphus family on Qiorfu.

ADOLPHUS, STEFANO – brother of Tiber Adolphus.

AEROC – one of the Crown Jewels, ruled by Lord Selik Riomini, the Black Cord; original home of Antonia Anqui.

ALA'RU – Xayan evolutionary and spiritual ascension. In translation, the Constellation word "soar" comes closest to the Xayan "ala'ru," a word not easily expressable in other languages. Depending upon how *ala'ru* is pronounced (and to whom, and by whom), the word can mean various degrees of sacredness in the actions of the Xayan individual as he progresses toward a state of perfection and merges his psyche with those of his fellows. In its ultimate form, *ala'ru* refers to the ascension of the entire Xayan race, a word that is uttered with a great exhalation of passion, from the deepest portion of the alien soul.

ALLYF – one of the five preserved Xayans in the museum vault; he did not survive the long sleep.

ANKOR – isolated, high-security industrial outpost on Hellhole, Adolphus's secret launch site.

ANQUI, ANTONIA – young woman on the run, originally from Aeroc, who chooses to settle on Hellhole. Her real name is Tona Quirrie.

ARMY OF THE CONSTELLATION – space navy and ground-based military that was consolidated during Adolphus's rebellion, commanded by Lord Selik Riomini.

BARASSA – Crown Jewel planet, original home of the Children of Amadin.

BIRZH – Xayan memory, lover of Jhera.

BLACK LORD – nickname for Lord Selik Riomini, based on his penchant for wearing black.

BOJ – Deep Zone planet.

BUKTU – isolated Deep Zone planet, administered by Ian Walfor; cold and frozen, recently cut off from the Constellation stringline network.

CANDELA – Deep Zone planet administered by Tanja Hu.

CAREY, LUJAH – leader of the Children of Amadin group on Hellhole.

CARTER, ANDREW – one of Sophie Vence's line managers.

CELANO GEESE – waterfowl native to Sonjeera.

CHERBY – Crown Jewel planet, original home of Franck Tello.

CHILDREN OF AMADIN – isolationist religious group from Barassa that has come to settle on Hellhole.

CIPPIQ – male Xayan, one of the four Originals.

CLES – Deep Zone planet.

CLOVIS, RENNY – one of the two site administrators at Ankor, partner of Tel.

CLOVIS, TEL – one of the two site administrators at Ankor, partner of Renny.

CODECALL SYSTEM – encrypted communications system used throughout the Constellation. When set up properly and operated by trained communications officers, it is said to be impenetrable – but some experts say this way of thinking is a fallacy, because there is no such thing as an ultimate form of any technology.

CONSTELLATION – stellar empire of seventy-four planets, twenty core worlds called the Crown Jewels and fifty-four frontier worlds in the Deep Zone. Capital is Sonjeera, ruled by the Diadem.

CONSTELLATION CHARTER – primary binding document that defines the government of the Constellation.

CORI, ELWAR – Vielinger physicist who discovered how to use processed iperion to mark a path in space, defining a constrained route that the new stardrives could use.

COTTAGE – private residence at the Pond of Birds used as a discreet retreat on the grounds of the Diadem's palace on Sonjeera.

COUNCIL CITY – government center on Sonjeera.

CRAIS, ALBO – elder member of Crais family whose political ambitions were thwarted by Michella.

CRAIS, BOLTON – husband of Keana Duchenet, logistics officer in the Army of the Constellation.

CRAIS, ILVAR – current head of the Crais noble family.

CRAIS, NOK II – former Diadem, Bolton's great-great-grandfather; the Council City Spaceport building was constructed during his reign.

CROWN JEWELS – twenty core planets in the Constellation, the most closely packed worlds and most civilized.

DE CARRE, CRISTOPH – son of Louis de Carre and manager of iperion mines on Vielinger.

DE CARRE, LORD LOUIS – planetary leader of Vielinger, lover of Keana Duchenet.

DEEP ZONE – the fifty-four frontier worlds in the Constellation, recently opened to settlement.

DEEZEE – derogatory term for a Deep Zone settler.

DESTINATION DAY – the scheduled completion date of Adolphus's new stringline transportation network; commonly referred to on D-Day.

DIADEM – the leader of the Constellation government.

DOWNBOX – cargo boxes dropped from a stringline hauler down to the surface of a destination planet.

DOZER – large construction machine.

DUCHENET, DIADEM MICHELLA – current leader of the Constellation.

DUCHENET, HAVEEDA – Michella's younger sister, rumored to be a witness to the murder of their brother, Jamos, as a child; she has not been seen in public for many years.

DUCHENET, JAMOS – Michella's older brother, murdered when he was young (Michella is rumored to be responsible).

DUCHENET, KEANA – only daughter of Diadem Michella.

DZ – Deep Zone.

EDWOND HOUSE – building where Edwond the First, the Warrior Diadem, held war-cabinet meetings. Ishop Heer's new residence.

EDWOND THE FIRST – former Diadem of the Constellation, also called the Warrior Diadem.

ELBA – Adolphus's estate outside of Michella Town.

ELBERT, WILL – one of Sophie Vence's line managers.

ENCIX – female Xayan, leader of the four Originals.

ENGERMANN, OLV – owner of a machine-repair shop on Orsini, former boss of Vincent Jenet.

FEN, ELDORA – planetary administrator of Cles.

FLEER – Crown Jewel planet where Tel and Renny Clovis served a prison term, homeworld of the Duchenets.

FRANKOV, SIA – planetary administrator of Theser.

GAXEN – draft animals native to Sonjeera.

GAVO – one of Tanja Hu's cousins.

GOLDENWOOD – valuable trees native to Ridgetop.

GOLER, TERRITORIAL GOVERNOR CARLSON – admininistrator of Ridgetop and territorial governor of eleven planets, including Hallholme and Candela.

GROWLER – colloquial term for a static storm on Hallholme.

HALLHOLME – hellish frontier world, considered the most inhospitable of the Deep Zone worlds, also colloquially called Hellhole.

HALLHOLME, CAPTAIN ESCOBAR – son of Commodore Percival Hallholme, current administrator of the Lubis Plain shipyards on Qiorfu.

HALLHOLME, COMMODORE PERCIVAL – retired leader of the Army of the Constellation; he defeated General Adolphus and quashed his rebellion.

HEART SQUARE – central square in Sonjeera's Council City.

HEER, ISHOP – Diadem Michella's confidential aide, spy, and hatchet man.

HELLHOLE – colloquial name for planet Hallholme.

HELLTOWN – colloquial name for Michella Town on Hellhole.

HERALD, PETER – former lieutenant in General Adolphus's rebellion.

HIRDAN – noble family, rivals of the Tello family.

HORP – Sonjeeran racing animal.

HU, QUINN – Tanja Hu's uncle, supervisor of large mining projects on Candela.

HU, TANJA – administrator of Candela, secretly in alliance with General Adolphus on Hallholme.

IMPERIAL MUSEUM – hall of documents on Sonjeera.

IPERION – rare mineral that, when processed, is used to lay down stringline paths across space. The Constellation's primary source of iperion is found on the planet Vielinger. Additional deposits have also been discovered on Candela (but not reported to the Diadem).

JENET, DREW – Vincent's terminally ill father.

JENET, VINCENT – new Hellhole colonist, sentenced to live there as punishment after he was convicted of a crime.

JHERA – Xayan memory, lover of Birzh.

JONN – Crown Jewel planet, ruled by the Hirdan family.

JORDAN, CRAIG – Adolphus's chief of security.

KAPPAS – Crown Jewel planet, ruled by the Paternos family.

KERRIS, HDS – linerunner ship operated by Turlo and Sunitha Urvancik, named after their dead son.

KIAFA – popular, heavily sweetened hot beverage.

KLIEF – Crown Jewel planet, former home of Sophie and Devon Vence.

KOMUN, GEORGE – planetary administrator of Umber.

KOUVET, CAPTAIN – security officer at Council City Spaceport.

LINERUNNER – maintenance ship that travels along the stringline paths to check iperion integrity.

LODO – male Xayan, one of the four Originals.

LUBIS PLAIN – large military shipyard on Qiorfu.

LUMINOUS GARDEN – one of the spectacular gardens on the grounds of the Diadem's palace.

MACHI – Crown Jewel planet.

MAGEROS, LADY OPRA – noblewoman, descendant of one of the families that brought about the downfall of the Osheers.

MAIL DRONE – small automated packet that travels along the stringlines.

MARUBI – Crown Jewel planet.

MCLUHAN, EVA – a linerunner who committed suicide in deep space between destinations.

MERCIFULS – secular order of nurses.

MICHELLA TOWN – main colony town on Hallholme; referred to colloquially as Helltown.

MORAE, ELWYN – first administrator of Candela.

NARI – drilling supervisor on Hellhole.

NAX, BEBE – Tanja Hu's administrative assitant on Candela.

NELL, LADERNA – assistant to Ishop Heer.

NERON, FERNANDO – new Hellhole colonist, a fast talker, a man searching for new opportunities; linked to the Xayan personality Zairic.

NICLES – Deep Zone planet.

NOMOLOS – Deep Zone planet.

OBERON, LANNY – supervisor in iperion mines on Vielinger.

OGG – Crown Jewel world where Osheer family was exiled.

ONGENET, ARIA – beautiful wife of historical Diadem Philippe the Whisperer, known for her numerous lovers, which she often entertained at her Cottage on the Pond of Birds.

ORIGINAL – name for the four resurrected Xayans that were preserved in the museum vault.

ORSINI – one of the Crown Jewels, ruled by Lord Azio Tazaar; original home of Vincent Jenet.

OSHEER – centuries-old variation of Ishop Heer's family name.

OSHU – Deep Zone planet.

PACKARD, ERNST – one of Adolphus's trailblazer captains.

PASSENGER POD – cargo container with life support and amenities, used for transporting people along stringline network.

PATERNOS, LADY JENINE – ruler of Crown Jewel planet Kappas, sworn enemy of Lord Azio Tazaar.

PENCE, TORII – trade representative of the Hirdan family from Jonn.

PHILIPPE THE WHISPERER – historical diadem, husband of Aria Ongenet.

POND OF BIRDS – small body of water on the grounds of the Diadem's palace, site of the romantic, luxurious Cottage.

PRINIFLOWER – medicinal plant native to Ridgetop.

PRITIKIN, LUKE – one of the Diadem's inspectors on Hellhole.

PUHAU – isolated mining village on Candela.

QIORFU – Crown Jewel planet, primarily agricultural, site of the Lubis Plain shipyards and original home of the Adolphus family.

QUIRRIE, TONA – real name of Antonia Anqui.

RAPANA – iperion processing center on Vielinger, site of an industrial fire.

RIDGETOP – forested Deep Zone planet best known for its valuable goldenwood groves, administered by Carlson Goler.

RIDGETOP RECOVERY – massacre that occurred when Constellation forces razed an existing colony on Ridgetop to clear the way for new settlement; the truth was covered up by the Diadem.

RIOMINI – powerful noble family headquartered on Aeroc, rivals of the Tazaars.

RIOMINI, GILAG – former Riomini lord who helped Michella establish her power base.

RIOMINI, LORD SELIK – head of the Riomini family, also in charge of the Army of the Constellation; he is also called the Black Lord.

ROLLER – small all-terrain vehicle.

RONOM – Deep Zone planet.

ROYAL RETREAT – one of the Diadem's seven official residences.

RUE DE LA MUSIQUE – the Street of Music, rundown section of Council City where Ishop Heer has his secret office.

RULLINS, JAKO – abusive man, former lover of Antonia Anqui.

SANDUSKY – one of the Crown Jewel planets, known for biological research.

SAPORO – harbor city on Candela.

SETSAI – Deep Zone planet.

SHADOW-XAYANS – humans who have accepted a Xayan personality from the slickwater pools.

SLICKWATER – Xayan liquid database of lives.

SLICKWATER SPRINGS – settlement out at the three original slickwater pools.

SMOKE STORM – meteorological event on Hallholme.

SPENCER, LIEUTENANT JOHAD – former weapons officer during Adolphus's rebellion, now his staff driver.

STAR THRONE – the Diadem's throne on Sonjeera.

STATIC STORM – dangerous electrical-discharge storm that occurs on Hallholme; colloquially called a "growler."

STRINGLINE – ultra-fast interstellar transportation system that follows quantum lines laid down across space.

STRINGLINE HAULER – large framework ship that is loaded with cargo containers and passenger pods; travels back and forth from Sonjeera to a designated stringline terminus.

STRINGLINE HUB – central point from which all the transportation lines radiate; the Constellation's only hub is on Sonjeera.

STRINGLINE TERMINUS – end point of a stringline, a station in orbit over a destination planet.

SUZUKI, RANDOLPH – chocolatier, member of a fallen noble family.

SVC-1185 – blue, giant star, site of a stringline power substation on the route to Ridgetop.

TANINE – Crown Jewel planet, site of a brief uprising.

TASMINE – Governor Goler's old household servant, only survivor of the Ridgetop Recovery.

TAZAAR – powerful noble family headquartered on Orsini, rivals of the Riominis.

TAZAAR, LORD AZIO – head of the Tazaar family.

TAZAAR, ENVA – daughter of Lord Azio Tazaar, an aspiring artist known for creating exotic aerogel sculptures. She is responsible for Vincent Jenet's exile.

TEHILA – Deep Zone planet, home of semi-intelligent herd animals.

TELEMANCY – Xayan telekinetic power.

TELLO, FRANCK – second-in-command of General Adolphus's rebellion.

THERIS, RENDO – replacement administrator at the Ankor complex.

THESER – Deep Zone planet.

TIER, DOM CELLAN – planetary administrator of Oshu.

TILLMAN, ARMAND – cattle rancher on Hellhole.

TRAILBLAZER – a ship that lays down a path of processed iperion to create a new stringline route.

TRAKMASTER – heavy-duty overland vehicle used on Hellhole.

TROMBIE, BUXTON – Duchenet family attorney.

TRYN – female Xayan, one of the four surviving Originals.

ULMAN, RICO, LIEUTENANT – daredevil test pilot at the Lubis Plain shipyards.

UMBER – Deep Zone planet.

UPBOX – cargo container launched into orbit, where it is picked up by a stringline hauler.

UROA – Xayan leader.

URVANCIK, SUNITHA – stringline runner, married to Turlo.

URVANCIK, KERRIS – son of Turlo and Sunitha, killed in military service shortly after the end of Adolphus's rebellion.

URVANCIK, TURLO – stringline runner, married to Sunitha.

VENCE, DEVON – son of Sophie Vence.

VENCE, GREGORY – former husband of Sophie Vence, father of Devon.

VENCE, SOPHIE – powerful merchant in Michella Town, in a relationship with General Adolphus.

VIELINGER – Crown Jewel planet, source of iperion, ruled by the de Carre family.

VOJA TREE – a type of willow common on Vielinger, whose bark is said to have medicinal (and some say spiritual) qualities.

WALFOR, IAN – administrator of Deep Zone planet Buktu, who also runs substantial black-market commerce that does not depend on the stringline network.

WARRIOR DIADEM – Edwond the First.

WEILIN, EVELYN – socialite woman from a noble family fallen on hard times; descendant of one of the twelve nobles who caused the disgrace of the Osheer family.

XAYAN – original race of inhabitants on Hellhole, nearly exterminated by asteroid impact five centuries ago.

YARICK – Constellation noble family.

ZAIRIC – Xayan leader who proposed the slickwater preservation plan.